DAFFODILS

Chasing DAFFODILS

A NOVEL

EMILY SAM

DIMPLES
PUBLISHING

Published by
Dimples Publishing

ISBN: 978-1-7370264-0-2 (paperback edition)
ISBN: 978-1-7370264-1-9 (eBook edition)

Contributing Edit by: Sarah Vy Nguyen
Book Cover Design by: Olga Vynnychenko
Interior formatting: Mark Thomas

Library of Congress Cataloging-in-Publication Data

I dedicate this novel to my Mom, Dad, Brother and all the people I met that inspired me.

SUMMER

CHAPTER 1

The man seems to be in his early forties; his long frame resembles a tall building as he stands with excellent posture. I like to watch him when I'm on my lunch break, sitting on a bench across the street. To some, that might sound strange, but to me, this activity has begun to feel quite normal. During my magnificent thirty-minute lunch break, I watch this man pick the best bouquet—the same exact flowers every time. He runs his big, strong hand through his brown, pushed-back gelled hair, studying each perfectly wrapped bouquet in front of him. His face is stern yet relaxed at the same time. He buys them on the corner of Elms Street from an elderly Korean lady. Her flower stand seems to have every type of flower imaginable. It's set up next to a quaint cart filled with an array of beautiful farm-fresh fruits and vegetables. This street is the heart of Brooklyn. People come from different boroughs to buy apples for their pies and rosemary for their soups.

Every day, as I shove two slices of cheese pizza in my mouth, I like to imagine where he goes after he buys the flowers. It's a different scenario every time. Who's the lucky woman receiving them? Is she waiting for him by a pond, hoping to see him one last time before he leaves to go on a safari exhibition? Just when she is about to lose hope, he suddenly appears and brings her the flowers of her dreams. Then, he sweeps her off her feet and plants a big kiss on her lips. I imagine him whispering sweet things like, "I'll always love you," and "Never forget me." What can I say? I'm a twenty-four-year-old hopeless romantic in need of a cheesy love story. I watch this man, also known as *flower guy*, finally pick his favorite bouquet of white flowers. He raises them to his perfect nose. He closes his eyes as he takes a quick sniff, then he walks away, disappearing into the packed crowd.

I wipe the crumbs off my puke-green apron as I lift myself off the wooden bench. I sigh, fixing my hat as well. When I reach the tall glass door that reads Coffee Bean Express, I open it for the woman behind me. She gives me a small, kind smile but suddenly lowers her head as she makes her way to the end of the long line.

"Always fucking late, Jade," Wanda barks at me, arms crossed against her short, stubby body. She taps her foot impatiently as she waits for me to respond.

I give her an obnoxious smile. "Very classy, Wanda. I'm here, aren't I?"

She rolls her eyes and walks past me.

"It wouldn't hurt to show some love to your favorite employee," I mock.

She shakes her head and disappears into the back.

I stand by the register, lazily tapping my fingers on the counter. A group of girls with high ponytails giggle as they reach the front of the line.

"Do you sell pumpkin spice lattes?" one of the girls asks, her blue eyes staring into mine.

I blink a couple of times and sigh. "No, we don't sell pumpkin spice lattes this time of year."

She starts playing with her ponytail as she stares at our menu on the wall, giving her friend a funny look as I gaze at her youthful face covered in too much makeup.

"What's the least fattening thing you sell?" she asks as she chews her gum obnoxiously.

"Water," I say. Her friend laughs, and I spot Wanda out of the corner of my eye. I stand up a little straighter and give them a smile, hoping they understood my little joke.

"Um, well, our macchiatos are very good," I tell her, hoping I didn't piss them off with my sarcastic humor. I wish I didn't need this job. My audition the other day for a cereal commercial didn't go so well, and I don't feel like finding another job. And besides, the last show I performed in, I totally bombed. I guess space aliens and dinosaurs don't mix very well. But the five people at the show seemed to really like it.

"Okay, I guess I'll have a large caramel with double espresso shots."

The young girl hands me a card, and I stare at it in disbelief. "I'm sorry, but this is a Starbucks card..."

She looks up from her phone. "Yeah, so?"

"This isn't Starbucks. We don't accept gift cards from there. This is Coffee Bean Express," I tell her.

She crosses her arms. "I don't see why you can't use it."

Before I can say anything, Wanda pushes me aside. I apologize to her and the customer, then I leave to wipe down the empty tables. I clear away abandoned plates with crumbs and a mug with red lipstick on the rim.

After refilling the milk cartons and organizing the sugar packets, I can finally leave. It's getting dark, and I can't wait to lay in my bed. All this hard labor makes me sleepy. Luckily, my apartment is only a block away, and I don't mind the walk since it's the only "exercise" I'm willing to do.

An hour later, I walk up the dirty staircase, passing old man Mr. Kens as he is smoking a cigarette. This building must have been built in the early 1900s since sadly, there aren't any elevators.

My parents bought my apartment as an investment twenty years ago. Before he moved to the United States, my father was told to invest in real estate, and that's exactly what he did. It worked out for our family because it became our secondary source of income. The first being the income from our restaurant. I've always adored this apartment building. I find its vintage brick-built structure so intriguing. And it helps that it's literally a block from Coney Island Beach and a close walk to the subway. When I graduated high school, I begged my mother to rent out the apartment to me and my best friend, Reese. It took a lot of persuading, but eventually, she caved because our tenant had moved out and the apartment was vacant. So technically, my mother is my landlord.

I was so happy that Natasha, my older sister, didn't want the apartment. It's always the older sibling who has the first choice in everything. After she graduated—three years before me—she chose a completely different path from me. She attended a college in Ohio and has been there ever since. She graduated with a marketing degree then decided to live there permanently. My sister has never been into the hustle and bustle of New York like I am, so when she got the chance to move to Ohio, she gladly took it. Since then, I've been working as hard as I can to afford my portion of the rent. I take as many shifts as I can as a barista to pursue my love for acting.

After high school, I ended up going to a local community college in Brooklyn. I got my two-year degree, but I'm now taking some time off school to really focus on my acting career.

By the time I get to my front door, I'm out of breath. I take off my ugly Coffee Bean hat and let out a deep breath, feeling so relieved to be home.

"Honey, I'm home," I say, dropping my bag by the front door.

"How was your day, my love?"

I give my best friend a smile and plop down next to her on the couch. "Long."

She lowers the volume on the television a bit and takes a sip of her wine. "I'm having a five-minute wine break then going back to studying," she tells me.

"No, you're not, Nurse Reese. It's Sunday."

"Jade, I'm not a nurse yet, unfortunately." She laughs nervously. "I still have a bunch of classes ahead of me." She turns so she is facing me and sighs.

"But you do know what time it is, right?"

Reese looks up with a smile, closing her laptop excitedly. She grabs the remote from the coffee table and flips through the channels until she spots our favorite show.

Love Match is a show about a bunch of weirdos making love connections. It sounds sort of lame when I describe it that way, but a bottle of rosé and a big bowl of popcorn always does the trick. It's something Reese and I have done ever since we became roommates.

"Okay, fine! You pop the popcorn."

I clap my hands excitedly before getting up. "Sure! But first, I have to change. This uniform is a disgrace to all humankind. I don't think I want my actual clothes to see me wearing this," I say as I point to my ugly black polo shirt.

Reese rolls her eyes and pours more wine into her glass. "Always so dramatic."

I walk into my bedroom and quickly take off my uniform. Then, I throw it into my hamper. I miss, of course, and groan. They deserve to stay on the floor anyway. I take my outfits very seriously; most people would say I have peculiar taste in clothes. To me, I believe I have a unique point of view. I'm not afraid to mix different patterns and colors together. My mother tells me it just adds more to my already quirky personality. So, when I'm stuck wearing my ugly uniform, I feel like I'm shaming the fashion gods or Molly Ringwald in *Pretty in Pink*.

I put my brown hair in a high bun, clip my bangs away from my forehead, and throw on a long, comfy T-shirt. Then, I walk outside and into the living room. Reese is in the kitchen, already microwaving the popcorn. I guess she couldn't wait for me.

"Is that the extra cheesy flavor?" I ask.

"No, I'm making the Cinnamon Toast Crunch flavor I bought last week," she calls out, even though the kitchen is steps from the living room.

"It's starting; hurry up!" I yell.

Reese jumps up and down, and the sound of the microwave beeping is so damn soothing. I pour myself some wine and throw my sea lion blanket over my legs. Reese plops next to me, hands me the big bowl. I grab a bunch of popcorn and shove the kernels in my tiny mouth like a cavewoman.

"What do you think?" she asks while munching on the popcorn.

"They're all right. I still like the cheesy movie popcorn better."

She nods. "I agree."

As Richard Right, the host of *Love Match*, appears on the screen, Reese and I look at each other knowingly. I have no idea why Reese and I get so excited about this show, but we've been watching it for three great years and we are still not bored of it.

"Turn it up louder!" Reese orders, shoving her shoulder against mine.

I reach for the remote on the coffee table. "I love Richard," I say.

Reese laughs and throws a popcorn kernel at me. "Yuck, gross. He's like fifty."

"He's fifty and thriving." I laugh.

Reese shakes her head with disgust. "I think the guy with the glasses is going to pick the girl who plays tennis."

I nod. "Yeah, I agree. I think they were the most compatible."

"Yeah, compared to the southern girl. What was her name again?"

"Tammy, I think." I take a sip of my wine. "Or maybe it was Savanna."

"Oh right, Tammy," Reese says, looking at her phone. An air freshener commercial comes on, and I let out a laugh.

"What's so funny?" Reese says as she continues to stare at her phone.

"I just thought of something."

Reese doesn't say anything. She's probably texting her boyfriend, Wesley, or as Reese calls him, her soulmate.

They locked eyes in some low-level math class during her freshman year of college, and they've been dating ever since. They are the perfect couple. I can't deny that—Reese being her beautiful self with her pin-straight blonde hair and her light brown eyes. Then, there's Wes, with his brown eyes and dark complexion. They will make beautiful babies.

"About what?" she eventually asks.

"What if I went on *Love Match*?" I say casually.

She looks up from her phone and opens her mouth. She wants to say something but clearly, she can't find the right words. "*Haha*, very funny," she finally says, grabbing a handful of popcorn.

I stare at her for a couple of seconds. "I'm actually serious."

"And why exactly would you want to be on *Love Match*?" She raises a brow.

I sigh. "Well, ya know, I've been single for quite a while, and it would be nice to meet someone."

She laughs. "Yeah, but not on this show. We always make fun of the contestants, Jade. And besides, they never end up together anyway."

"I'm just sick of all the guys in New York," I groan. "They're all douches, Reese."

"You haven't met every single one, and Wes isn't a douche," she teases.

"Wes is from California; so technically, he doesn't count."

She leans her head on one of our throw pillows, then puts her legs on my lap. "He's out there, Jade. I promise you," she says before letting out a yawn.

"I haven't slept with anyone since Noah. And if you remember, we broke up two years ago."

"Yeah, you're missing out." She smiles.

I roll my eyes, hitting her with a pillow.

Reese laughs and covers her face. "Stop!" she yells between laughs, and I can't help but giggle too.

~

The following day, I decided to get out of the house early to go on a little stroll. And by little stroll, I mean a walk to my favorite thrift shop a couple of blocks away.

It's a beautiful day, and there isn't a single cloud in the sky. I sip on my sugary iced coffee while people rush past me, trying to get to work on time. When I get to the thrift store, I throw away the last of my coffee and head inside. This thrift store is located in a vacant shopping center, squeezed between a pet shop and a dry cleaner.

I came across it many years ago when I was with Reese. After school, Reese and I did what normal sixteen-year-olds would do— eat black and white cookies, sing, and dance down each street of Brooklyn. It was love at first sight for me. Reese, of course, was bothered by this place. She's not a fan of thrift stores and didn't even want to go inside, not even to look. Instead, she waited patiently outside while I looked through racks and racks of pre-owned clothing. I ended up buying a whole rack of clothes and completely redesigned them when I got home. They still fit me now. I'm not sure if that's a good thing, though. That means my boobs and butt haven't grown since high school….

Lee is standing behind the counter when I walk in, and he gives me a small smile when he sees me. Lee has owned this shop for twenty years, but I have no idea how it is still in business because every time I come in, it is empty.

"How are you, Jade?"

"Never been better." I give him a smile as I walk over to the jean rack in the corner. This place is small and sort of smells like curry, but man oh man, I can really find a good bargain here. I've been begging Reese to just take a look, but she refuses to come with me. She's always had a little bit of a distaste for wearing used clothing. While I, on the other hand, believe it adds to the uniqueness of an outfit.

"Are you looking for anything in particular?" he asks, leaning his skinny elbows against the glass counter.

I look over to him and shake my head. "Nope, just browsing."

"We got some new shipments in yesterday." He points to a nearby rack, rubbing his balding head.

I walk over to the rack and carefully look for something that will catch my eye.

"Any auditions lately?" Lee asks.

"Yeah, a commercial about tampons." I laugh.

He nods then gives me a smile. "Hey, work is work."

"So true." I ended up picking out a long plaid skirt and a matching halter top. "I think I'll get this," I say as I walk over to the counter and lay the skirt and top down.

"Good choice, Jade." Lee smiles. "You always have an eye for spotting my best items." He reaches for something under the counter and hands it to me. "Here, I think these sunglasses will go great with that skirt and top, however you choose to style them. I have faith in you."

"How much are they?" I ask him, examining the circle-shaped lenses in my hands.

"Zero. It's on me."

I shake my head. "Please, Lee, let me pay."

"Put them on," he orders.

I smile, sliding the sunglasses on my face.

Lee snaps his fingers and nods. "This amount of beauty shouldn't cost a thing."

My morning goes by too fast. Before I know it, I'm back at the café for another shift. After making what feels like the one-hundredth macchiato, I'm ready for my lunch break.

I walk outside and notice that the streets are very crowded this afternoon, which means my favorite bench is most likely taken. I start to rush past people, even though I fear that I am rushing in vain. I almost reach the bench, preparing myself for disappointment when I spot Reese sitting on my bench with two sandwiches in her hand. I let out a big smile as I walk over to her.

"You're a lifesaver, Reese McKeely," I say before taking a bite of my chicken sandwich.

"So, where's this romantic man I've been hearing about?"

I grin. "Right over there, actually. The good-looking guy in the white button-down."

"So, he does this every day?" Reese raises her eyebrow as she takes a sip of her iced tea.

"I assume so. Always at one-thirty in the afternoon."

"Does he ever buy any other flowers? Like roses or sunflowers?" she asks.

I shake my head. "It's the same white flowers, and it always takes him a while to pick out the right bouquet." I smile, biting my lip gently.

"Wow, I wonder who she is."

"Me too, Reese… Me too," I sigh.

Reese finishes the last of her sandwich then crumples the wrapper in her hands. She then takes a quick sip of her drink and starts moving the ice around with her straw. Suddenly, she turns to me. "So, remember what we were talking about last night?"

I tilt my head to the side and wait for her to finish.

"About how every guy in New York is a douche?"

"Ah, yes." I nod. "I still believe that. It's a fact."

"Well, Wes' good friend from Pasadena just moved to the city a year ago, and—"

"Nope," I say, shaking my head.

"Why not? You literally said you wanted to go on *Love Match* or whatever last night and that you haven't been with a guy since Noah."

"I was drunk."

Reese leans back on the hard bench and crosses her arms. "You're so full of shit, Jade. Just come out with us Friday night and have a drink. If you don't like him, then fine."

I let out a sigh of resignation. "All right. I'll be there."

~

Later that same day, I walk down the crowded streets with a soft pretzel in one hand and an iced coffee in the other hand. One perk of working at a coffee shop is being able to grab a cup of coffee after my shift ends.

"I'd do anything for a piece of that," my red-headed friend says as soon as I approach her. She's leaning against an old brick building with a disgusting-looking green smoothie in her hand. I offer her some of my soft pretzel, but she quickly declines. "You know I'm not eating any carbs. I need my body in tip-top shape."

I turn my head and watch as she runs her long skinny fingers through layers of hair.

Meet Suzanna Lodge, formally known as Suzy Boozy (let's just say the girl can't handle her liquor). I've known Suzy my whole life, from lemonade stands on the streets of Brooklyn to riding the subway with no destination. This girl has been through puberty with me, and that says a lot. I met her the first day of elementary school, and we've been best friends ever since. Sadly, she ended up living with her dad after her parents separated and had to go to some stuffy private high school in the city. However, I was still able to see Suzy on the weekends. She'd sometimes hang with Reese and me, but she mostly stayed in Manhattan. Even through all of that, we still remained very close.

Oh, and did I forget to mention that she's also marrying my ex-boyfriend? I'm not joking either. I didn't see it coming at all. Suzy never, and I mean never, made a play for Noah when I was dating him. And I dated Noah for four years—all through high school.

Even Reese knew that Suzy had been there through it all, and I never suspected a thing. I laughed when she first told me, but my laughter quickly dissipated when I realized she was telling the truth. She was spewing all this bullshit to me about how he gets her or whatever, and at the time, I was still mad at him, so it was hard for me to believe her. We were broken up for about five months then, and I was sort of still grieving. But eventually, I wasn't mad anymore, and I actually supported them. I was able to be friends with them both in my own way. To put it simply, I just didn't care anymore.

I nod, and we continue down the street.

"I've been obsessed with this one magazine. What I like most about it is that it tells you where and how to purchase the dress you like."

"*Ah,* so this is why you've dragged me out so damn early," I say, raising my brow.

"Okay, you got me! But Jade, I need to see if I like this dress. It could possibly be *the one.*"

I take a big bite of my pretzel as we look for the store. It's on the corner of 13th Street. I've passed by this area before, but I never even noticed this place.

We walk inside, and I take it all in—hundreds of white dresses, all in different styles surround me.

A lady with a boyish haircut approaches us with her hands folded in front of her. She gives us both a kind smile. "So, who is the lucky bride to be?"

Suzy raises her hand and lets out a little squeal.

As they begin their boring conversation, I decide to look around. I've never been in a place like this. So many dresses. So white and so fluffy.

Ten minutes later, I'm sitting on a comfortable cushioned couch with a glass of white wine in hand. "Does it fit?" I call out.

"Gimme one more second."

I take a sip of my wine and casually look through the wedding magazines beside me. All these women look so happy. Their eyes glisten, and their teeth are so straight and white.

"What do you think?"

I look up from a picture of a bride wearing a big feather in her hair, and my eyes go completely wide. "Wow, Suzy, that dress is—"

Before I can think of a word to even describe what I see, she says, "I know, it's perfect."

The lady walks over to us and smiles. "That dress looks so wonderful on you, sweetheart, just wonderful. It's a trumpet style. Stark white." She pauses, looking pleased with her inventory. "Would you like to see a different style of dress? Perhaps a different color? There's natural white, ivory, and champagne."

Suzy twirls in front of the three diagonal mirrors then rests her hands on her chest. "Well, I think I'm most likely going to take this dress, but sure, I'd love to see some more."

～

Three long hours later, Suzy and I finally leave the dress shop. I'm completely exhausted, and I wasn't even the one trying on the dresses.

"The first one was the best, right? I can't wait to show my mom and sister."

"They're both going to love it." I smile at her as we walk down the busy sidewalk. "Are you hungry? Do you want to get some food?" I ask her.

"Well, I have plans with Noah for dinner." She pauses. "Would you like to join us?"

I laugh. "I'd rather not barge in on your date night. Have fun with your fiancé."

She gives me a half-smile and a hug. "Thanks, Jade." She gives me one last wave before blending in with the large crowd of people crossing the busy intersection.

I let out a deep breath and continue down the sidewalk, eventually finding the one and only Burrito Wonderland. I order a bean burrito and a Corona, then I find a seat facing the window. I people-watch on the street as I eat my crappy dinner.

~

On Friday night, as Reese and I are heading to dinner, I ask, "So, what's his name?"

We're meeting her boyfriend, Wes, and my "soon-to-be-boyfriend." I'm not sure if I am getting ahead of myself here.... Anyway, we're meeting them at this pub down on 45th Street known for its gigantic pretzels and cheap beer. We're sort of late though because Reese was putting a lot of pressure on me to find the best outfit. She didn't like anything I showed her. By the third outfit, I said screw it, and I wore what I wanted. But I'm already regretting wearing my red platform boots because my feet are sweating from the humid summer air. Or maybe it's because Reese and I practically ran all the way to the bar.

"Colin," she tells me. "He's Wes' childhood friend, and he's really hot," she squeals.

I laugh. "You've met him?"

She nods. "A few times."

"So why are you only setting us up now?"

"Because you said you were tired of dating guys from here."

I shake my head. "I have to think twice before saying anything to you from now on."

"I think you'll like him. He's in a band."

"Is that supposed to impress me?"

"Well, he's a musician, and you're an actress. So you guys will have that artsy stuff in common."

"Oh, he's a classical musician?" I ask with a smirk.

"No," she answers breathlessly.

"Great, you lost me."

"When in the world have you ever listened to classical music?" She glares at me.

I shut my mouth. She got me there. Before I can come up with a remark, she turns to me. "Just go with the flow, Jade. I know that's hard for you, but just try. Okay? For me?"

I nod. When we get there, I open the door and follow Reese inside. The pub is full of drunk people, and they're all dancing to folk music. I look towards the stage and see that the band is made up of a bunch of guys with long grey beards.

We soon approach Wes and a couple of people I've never met before. Reese and Wes begin their *we-love-each-other-so-much* PDA. And me, well, I stand awkwardly next to them, taking off my pink denim jacket.

"There's an empty table over there," Wes says, giving me a hug as he drapes his arm around Reese.

We follow him to the table that is literally in the middle of the room, and we all sit down.

"I'll get you two something to drink. Beer?" he asks us, and we nod.

"So, where's my Prince Charming?" I ask, giving Reese a wide grin.

"I'm not sure," she says. I don't think she caught onto my sarcastic remark.

Wes comes back seconds later with an unfamiliar face behind him. The guy is a bit taller than Wes. Wes hands us our beers and sits down beside Reese, putting his arm around her waist.

"Jade, this is my buddy, Colin. Colin, this is Reese's roommate, Jade. The one I've been telling you about."

I give Reese and Wes a funny look as I take a sip of my cold beer. Wes nods in my direction, motioning for me to turn my head to meet his friend. He then gives me a smirky smile.

Colin and I make eye contact. Then I watch as he pulls out the chair across from me and plops down, leaning his elbows on the table.

I look at the guy across from me and wonder why the heck Reese would set us up. I mean, he's nothing like the guys I usually go for. But maybe that's the reason I should be here. After all, every guy I meet is usually a letdown. Colin is tall, and from what I can see under his black t-shirt, he definitely has those muscles girls go wild for. And that jaw... It's all chiseled and whatever. And the hair? Dirty blonde and perfect. I mean, if you're into that sort of thing. It's sort of funny, really; if someone were to look at me and then Colin, who doesn't look like he has a problem in the dating department, that person might wonder why in the world we are on this date. Well, if you can even call it a date.

Reese stands up, grabs Wes's hand, and announces, "Let's dance!"

I watch them practically shimmy to the dance area.

"So, I heard you're in a band," I say, loud enough for him to hear.

Colin takes a sip of his beer and turns in my direction. "Yeah." He nods.

"What do you play?" I ask him, staring into his piercing blue eyes. "Guitar."

I'm loving these one-word answers.... I get it if the guy doesn't find me attractive. I'm not everyone's type, but he doesn't have to be such a dick. Sigh, just my luck.

Seconds pass, and I decide to try one last time. "How are you liking New York? I grew up here, so I'm used to all the busyness," I say with a half-smile.

Colin looks at me hard-nosed. There is not a drop of emotion on his perfect, symmetrical face. His eyes bleed into mine then he lets out a little chuckle and runs his hand through his hair, exposing an outlined tattoo on the back of his arm. He finishes the last of his beer and says something under his breath. I tilt my head to the side as I watch him stand to his feet. He gives me one last glance before he walks away, not even bothering to say goodbye.

I let out a cough—the level of jerk Colin is on completely takes my breath away.

I grab my jacket and find Reese and Wes by the bar. They are standing close to one another, laughing and whispering as I approach them.

"I think I'm gonna head out," I say, giving them both a hug before they can force me to stay.

"Why?" Reese looks at me skeptically. "We just got here."

I see Colin out of the corner of my eye, putting his hand up as he orders another drink. He leans half his body against the bar as he listens to our conversation.

"I totally forgot to feed my bird," I say with a sigh.

Reese crosses her arms and leans on the bar. "You don't have a bird."

"Yeah, well, I'm going to leave, buy one, and then feed him. I'll see you tomorrow," I say, giving Reese another hug.

"Okay, whatever," she says, turning away. I know she's pissed, but I just don't want to be here. This isn't my scene.

I glance over at Colin, and all I see is a mischievous smirk plastered on his face. Thankfully, I'll never have to see him again.

CHAPTER 2

U nfortunately, I was wrong. After that god-awful night, it's like Reese wasn't done torturing me. Colin is always around now, whether it be birthday parties, our last month of summer barbecues, or just a friendly game night at Wes'. You name it, and Colin was there. And he never ceased to remind me of how much of a cocky, womanizing musician he was.

"I think we should play charades," Reese says lazily.

I glance up from my phone. I am sprawled on Wes' couch, super tired.

"I think we should go to the bar," Colin says as he takes one final big sip of his beer, crushing the can in seconds.

Reese rolls her eyes and nudges her shoulder with mine. "Jade?"

I look up and sigh. "Uh, I don't care."

Reese gets up and walks into Wes' room, and I'm left alone with Colin.

I sit up and grab my beer from the coffee table. Wes and Reese come out, laughing about something.

"I think I wanna stay home tonight," Wes says, looking at a very pleased Reese.

Colin groans. "All right, fine. I just texted this girl I met the other night, and she's coming over."

I let out a little laugh, then I take a sip of my beer.

"What?" he asks.

I turn to him. "Oh, nothing."

I find it amusing that in the short amount of time that I've known Colin, he treats every woman he meets like she is easily replaceable.

Reese plops down next to me, grabbing the bowl of pretzels. "So, Charades? Or Uno?"

Wes turns on the television and automatically switches the channel to a sports game. As Colin and Wes turn their attention to the television, Reese and I are left twiddling our thumbs.

"Should I order pizza?" Reese asks.

"Yes!" we all say in unison.

Reese says something under her breath that I can't make out, so when she stands up and walks into the kitchen, I follow her.

"I guess I'll just order a plain pie," she says, since she knows we all prefer no toppings. I nod, watching her dial the number to a local place.

A couple of shouts can be heard from the other room, but I still give Reese my full attention. I know she has something on her mind. I wait patiently as she opens Wes' fridge and grabs the sangria we brought over.

"I just thought we'd have some fun and play a game tonight," Reese says, her voice tinged with disappointment as she pours a glass for each of us. We casually tap our glasses and stand in silence as we lean against the kitchen counter.

I move my hair away from my face and give her a small smile.

"Colin's new lady friend is coming over, so when she gets here, maybe we can all play something."

"Yeah, not gonna happen." She exhales.

"Why not?"

"Because it's like this every night, Jade. Colin texts one of his girls from his *very, very* long list, and all they do is have sex on the couch…or in the bathroom, if Wes and I are out in the living room."

I laugh. "Every night?"

"Well, the nights I stay over." She groans, turning towards me. "It's so annoying. I hate that he crashes here."

"So, what you're saying is he's having too much sex for your liking?"

There's a silence between us, and I watch as she tries to come up with the best response to my silly question. Reese pushes a stubborn strand of hair behind her ear and gives me a funny look. "Yes," she says, holding back a laugh.

Suddenly, we hear a loud bang on the front door, followed by laughter and a stranger's voice. I take a big sip of my sangria and follow Reese back into the living room. We are immediately greeted by a slim blonde wearing short shorts and a tight V-neck. She smiles from cheek to cheek as she reaches in for a hug. "Hiya, girls!"

Reese and I glance at each other as the tall blonde lets out a squeal. The next thing we know, she is straddling Colin's lap on the leather couch. She immediately introduces herself, going into a story about how she was named—her eyes open wide, hands moving in all directions. The four of us just nod, waiting for her to finish.

"So that's why my name is Krista," she concludes, draping her arm around Colin's neck.

"Krista is a great name," I say, finishing the last of my drink, "and that was a very, um, interesting story." A story that was utterly nonessential.

I hear Colin chuckle under his breath as we continue to listen to Krista randomly babble. Reese leans into Wes, and he nods as the sound of Krista's high-pitched words fills the whole apartment.

"I'll be right back," Wes says nonchalantly, leaning in and giving Reese a peck before grabbing his jacket.

"So, Krista, how do you feel about pizza?" Reese asks, kindly interrupting her story about her recent trip to the chiropractor.

"I actually gave up pizza a year ago. Funny story, actually—"

FALL

CHAPTER 3

The pearly white invitation has officially arrived. I trace my finger across the elaborate olive-green vines printed on the sides. Then, I look at the soon-to-be bride and groom's name printed in large, cursive print. As I stand in silence in the apartment's foyer, the tiny space by the mailboxes seems to get smaller and smaller by the second. The sound of keys jingling beside me takes me out of my hypnotic state of mind, and I give the old lady that lives above me a tiny wave. Then, I practically run upstairs, hoping Reese is home.

I swing open the front door and breathe heavily as I slam it shut. My eyes are still glued to the elegant rectangle that feels heavier than a boulder.

I don't know how long I was standing in front of the door for, but it felt like years until I'm able to walk my way over to the couch. Reese gives me a strange look. She automatically pauses the television, already sensing how dramatic I will be in several seconds.

"Have you opened it yet?"

I look up, shaking my head. "I don't know if I can."

Reese lets out a laugh, grabbing the invitation out of my sweaty hands. "They went all out," she says, nodding with approval.

"I knew it was happening, but I didn't know it would be this soon." I sigh, slouching down on the couch and placing my palm against my forehead.

"You're a bridesmaid, shouldn't you have known the date and everything? You even went dress shopping with her."

"Yeah, I'm a bridesmaid, but that doesn't mean I'm a good one."

Reese sighs and softly throws the invitation on the coffee table. "It's a year from now, Jade. That means you'll have plenty of time to get ready for it." She pauses. "Ya know, like mentally?"

I let out a nervous laugh and sigh. "Yeah, well, I'm going to have a little bit of trouble finding a date." I lean my elbows on both of my thighs and let out a deep breath, blowing my frizzy bangs away from my face.

"Does it matter if you do?" she asks.

I turn to face her, and I can see she already regrets asking me that question. "Of course it does, Reese! I'm going to my ex-boyfriend's wedding." I throw my hands up in the air. "You don't attend your ex's wedding, and you especially don't attend it alone. I mean, that's like ex-boyfriend 101."

"But you have to."

I rub the back of my neck and nod. "Well, that does it. I-I have over a year. I have over a year to meet Mr. Right and bring him to the wedding."

Reese laughs.

"What's so funny?"

"Oh, nothing," she says.

I get up and pace around the room. "Do you think that's enough time? I don't want to bring someone I just met. I want it to be a real relationship."

"I don't know, Jade. You did say, and I quote, 'All guys in New York are douches.'"

I nod and cross my arms. "Yes, but I can't show up to their wedding without a date. How's that going to make me look?" I don't let her answer. "I'm going to tell Suzy that I'm bringing a date. I'm just not going to tell her who."

"It's not too late to back out," Reese says.

"Oh, please. I have to go. If I don't, then people, especially Noah, will think I still have feelings for him, and I clearly don't."

"*Hmm*," is all Reese manages to say.

"What?" I walk over to her and plop on the couch.

"Are you one hundred percent over Noah?"

My eyes widen. "Of course I am! I wouldn't have agreed to be a bridesmaid in the first place if I wasn't. Noah and I are in a good place. We're friends, and I completely support this wedding."

"Okay, I was just making sure, ya know? Because Noah is your first love and all…"

"Thank you for reminding me, but in all honesty, I am happy for them."

Reese puts her hands up and watches me with great determination as I check the "I'm bringing a date" box. I nod, almost as if I'm trying to convince myself that this is a good idea.

It's a good idea. It's a good idea.

Deep, deep, deep down inside, somewhere so far down that I'll never admit to Reese, I want Noah to see that I've completely moved on. Is that so horrible?

~

Later that night, after eating a whole bag of peanut butter and chocolate dipped pretzels and practically binging an entire season of *Sex and the City*, I decided to look at the invitation again—without

Reese this time. I stare at it for a few minutes. I can't help but envision myself at the wedding—the wedding that seems so far away, but it also feels like a thumbtack pushed on the forefront of my mind.

I carefully study the card, reading each cursive word slowly.

"Always & Forever," is written in large print followed by "together with their family and friends" in smaller print.

I read it a couple of times in my head, then I read it out loud.

Suzanna Lodge & Noah Jadeson.
May 15th, 2018, 5:00 PM.
3501 Fall River Road.
Colts Neck, New Jersey.

The wedding of Suzy's dreams will be presented in her grandparents' backyard. This gives the whole bridal party, including me, a place to stay for the weekend. I'm suddenly flooded with many memories of the three-story house. I think back to the summers we'd spent there—catching fireflies and playing hide and go seek on every floor. Always practicing for Suzy's wedding day, in the same backyard where her wedding will soon take place. I trace her name with my finger and smile before closing my eyes.

Five months ago...

"Hi, I'm meeting a friend here; the reservation is under the name Suzanna."

The hostess gives me a tight smile. "Please follow me."

The hostess leads me to the outdoor portion of the restaurant. Outside, the patio is filled with young couples drinking mimosas. I spot Suzy, and she gives me a small wave. She stands up as soon as

I approach the table and gives me a soft kiss and a hug. The hostess hands me a menu then walks away.

"This place is—"

But before I can finish, Suzy says, "Marvelous, right?"

I nod and quickly scan the menu.

"Jade?"

I look up, and Suzy has a mischievous look on her face. She looks different—a good different. The lighting out here must be perfect because her green eyes seem to sparkle a little extra, and her skin is so clear, it's practically glowing.

"What's going on?" I ask slowly.

"Well…" She smiles, scratching the side of her nose. And there it was.

My eyes open wide, and I drop my menu, making a loud noise. Suzy looks around. She's embarrassed, but I can also tell she wants to scream with excitement.

"Is that what I think it is?"

She nods her head up and down and holds her hand out so I can see the ring more clearly.

"He-he asked me yesterday—during our picnic in Central Park. I was so surprised, Jade. I really was. He got down on one knee and everything. It was so romantic," she squeals.

I stare at the rock in front of me and swallow hard.

Silence fills our table as she waits for me to respond, but all I can do is stare at the pear-shaped diamond in front of me. I look up, and I can see worry forming on her face. So I push my feelings aside and give her a wide smile.

"I'm so happy for you, Suzy! Congratulations." I get up then, giving her a hug.

"You scared me there a little." She laughs nervously, taking a sip of her mimosa. "There's just one more thing." She drags out each word, and I sigh, already guessing what she's going to ask me.

"I've known you for so long." She pauses. "Jade, you're like a sister to me. So, I'm asking if you would like to be one of my bridesmaids?"

I fiddle my fingers on my lap and let out a deep breath as she waits patiently for me to answer.

"I understand if you say no. Since ya know, Noah is your ex and all, but it won't be the same if you're not up there with me." She sighs. "I even spoke about it with Noah."

"And what did he say?" I ask her.

"Well, he said he'd love for you to be a part of our wedding," she says with a smile.

I tilt my head to the side and stare at Suzy. She looks happy, thrilled. "Okay, count me in," I say.

Suzy gets up and puts her arms around me, giving me a gentle squeeze. "Oh, Jade, you're the best."

~

My cell phone vibrates from the coffee table, making my body jolt as I gasp out loud. I groan from my sudden mini-heart attack and reach for my phone.

My screen reads "Wesley," and I get a ping of nervousness as I answer.

"Hello?"

"Hey! It's Reese. I'm using Wes' phone." My heart rate suddenly steadies when I hear her voice. "My phone sort of broke." She laughs.

"What happened?"

"Long story, but I'm not coming home tonight. I'm gonna sleep at Wes', so don't wait up."

"Okay, sounds good. Night, Reese."

I can hear a couple of other voices that don't sound familiar on the other line. She mumbles something else and then hangs up. I let out a deep breath, bringing my Hello Kitty sweatpants to my chest as I lean my chin on my knees.

"I need to get out more," I say out loud, staring at my phone screen. It reads: Saturday, 10:30 p.m.

CHAPTER 4

Lisa Cara, a friend from high school, throws a Friendsgiving every year in her penthouse apartment in the city. She was raised a Brooklyn girl, but eventually, after high school, she met a man who came from old money. When I say man, I mean a forty-something-year-old attorney who was thrilled to have someone like Lisa even look at him.

Reese and I usually pass every year, but Reese has been getting tons of pressure to come. She has this way of being too nice sometimes and apparently, she "needed" to say yes when she got cornered one day over lunch. The fact that she even takes time out of her life to have a friendly lunch with Lisa says a lot.

The only reason I'm currently standing in the middle of Lisa's luxury apartment is because Reese is too chicken to attend Friendsgiving by herself. And besides, I can never say no to Reese when she gives me one of her famous begs. Free alcohol and food help a little as well.

There's something about Lisa and her posse that just doesn't sit well with me. All of them are blonde, and they know exactly how beautiful they are. They all wear the most in-style designer clothes, and they love bragging about how they used to roam the hallways with their football players of the week. For some reason, Reese has managed to stay close to Lisa and her crew all these years. I guess she's able to blend with them since she fits their "look." And then there's me...

"All right, I'll get us some wine, and you grab some of those bacon-wrapped shrimp. I'm starving," I order Reese and she nods. Then, we separate from each other. I make my way to the long bar in the corner. As I reach for two glasses of red wine, I hear a familiar voice approaching on my left.

"Oh my gosh! If it isn't Jade Everly!"

I turn my head and allow a very tall blonde named Kelly Ann to give me a side hug, her fake boobs pressing into my arm.

"How are you doing?" she asks. "I haven't seen you since high school!"

I open my mouth to respond but suddenly get interrupted as Lisa Cara appears beside Kelly Ann. She has her hands folded in front of her.

"I'm so happy you and Reese finally made it out! It's been too long." She flashes a fake smile at me. "You definitely haven't changed." She laughs. "I've always loved your style."

Lisa glances at my black and white polka dot ruffled sweater, and I smile back. I take a sip of my wine from my left hand and a sip of Reese's from my right.

"It's so great that you and Reese are still so close. Reese is the best." Lisa smiles.

"She's okay." I grin.

"You have to invite me over sometime. I'd love to see your

apartment before Reese moves out."

I tilt my head to the side and stare at Lisa with a strange expression.

"Oh, did I hear wrong? Is she not moving out anymore?" Lisa asks, looking at Kelly Ann then back at me.

"Well, Lisa, that's news to me." I smile as I watch Reese walking towards us, two plates filled with shrimp in her hands.

"Here you go," she says, handing me a plate and taking a glass from my right hand.

"Excuse me." I smile and walk away as fast as I can in my heels. I head over to the buffet table and let out a deep breath, eyes glued to the bowl of spiked apple cider.

"Hey, are you okay?"

I glance at Reese and sigh.

"When were you going to tell me that you're moving out?"

Reese looks down and moves her hair away from her face. "Soon. I'm assuming Lisa told you?"

"Honestly, that's what I hate the most." I shake my head with disgust. "That I heard it first from Lisa Cara. When did you decide you wanted to move out?"

"A month ago," she tells me. Her face turns to a frown as she watches my eyes widen.

"A month ago? Why are you moving out?"

"Wes and I decided that it was time we lived together. We think…" She pauses. "We *know* it's time."

I nod. "Well, I'm glad Lisa said something because God knows when you would have actually told me," I say gruffly as I put my plate down and walk away.

"Where are you going?" she calls out as I look for the nearest exit.

"I have to go find a roommate!"

～

I make it back to my place hours before Reese gets home. The front door opens and closes, and I pause the television because I already know Reese will have something to say.

"You're so dramatic."

Yep, I was right.

"How was the party?" I ask curtly.

"A lot of fun. Too bad you left." She sighs, opening the fridge. My back is still facing her, but I can hear her shoving leftovers inside the fridge. I shake my head then unpause the television.

"How's the roommate search going?"

"Amazing," I respond sarcastically.

Reese takes off her black high heels and walks over to the couch. She gives me a look and plops down on the couch. "Jade, I'm sorry. Okay? I didn't want this to happen. I didn't know Lisa was going to say anything. *I* wanted to be the one to tell you."

"What's been taking you so long then?"

She runs her fingers through her silky hair and shrugs. "It began with Wes and I sort of fantasizing about the idea of living together. Then we started to really talk about it, and we're sick of taking turns staying over at each other's place…."

I study Reese's face for a moment as her words begin to sink in. I'm not mad about her news. She and Wes moving in together *does* seem like the next logical move.

"I understand."

She looks at me strangely. "Did someone hit you on the head or something?"

I roll my eyes. "Really, Reese?"

She laughs. "I'm sorry, okay? I won't keep things from you, *and* I especially won't tell Lisa anything anymore."

"So, when do you think you'll be moving?" I ask.

Reese exhales. "When Wes and I actually find somewhere we like. It's hard because I'm still in school, so the only source of income is coming from Wes. But he told me not to worry because he already talked to his family, and they said they'd help us out."

"Are you guys staying in Brooklyn?"

She nods. "Oh, of course. I would never want to be so much as a train ride away from you."

I nod with a smile as I turn my attention back to the television. "I just want you to be happy, Reese," I say.

She gives me a big smile before leaning her head on my shoulder.

CHAPTER 5

I have to say, finding a roommate isn't as easy as it looks in the movies. In the movies, the main character posts some sort of ad, and all these weird-looking people come. Then scene after scene, the audience watches all these god-awful people saying crazy things until *BAM*—the perfect person walks in. Well, here I am, getting nothing, *zilch*. And I even posted my ad on Craigslist! That's how desperate I am for a good movie scene.

"Struggling actress in need of a clean, quiet person who won't steal her shit."

Maybe I should have come up with a better ad….

At one point, Reese and Wes sit me down. It reminds me of when I used to live with my parents. They'd sit me down to give me some sort of life lesson, even though my parents didn't have any idea what was going on in my life. When I was twelve years old, I'd travel by myself all the way to Manhattan from Brooklyn for an audition. My mother only cared about the family restaurant and whether or not I applied enough sunscreen at the beach.

"Wes, I know about Reese moving out. And that's why I've been trying to find a roommate."

Reese sighs and sits next to me. "We know. How's the search going?" Before I can answer, Reese adds, "We know you hate every second of this, and I just want you to know that I will continue to pay my portion of the rent until you find someone you are comfortable living with."

"Reese, that's not necessary." I wave off her offer.

"It's the least I could do," Reese says, and I know she feels bad. "I know you are super stressed out."

I nod. It's true. This process stresses me out a lot, mainly because I haven't exactly told my mother that Reese is moving out yet. And I'm not planning on doing so until I know for sure who my next roommate will be. If my mother gets involved, she'll do the searching herself, and who knows who'd she'd find? Maybe someone religious from our church or one of her friends from her Russian club. I don't even want to know. And Reese knows exactly how my mother can be.

"I am, but I am not going to take your money. If you guys have any other solutions to help me, I'm all ears."

Reese looks over at Wes, and he nods. "We came up with a great solution for you, Jade," Wes says, then he looks over at Reese.

"I'm moving out in a couple of days into Wes' place while we search for an apartment."

I nod and wait for her to continue.

Reese grabs my hand. "Wes' friend, you know, Colin? He got kicked out of his apartment and has been crashing on Wes' couch for a while, so we thought he could move in here! Problem solved for both of you."

"*No.*"

"Oh, c'mon, Jade. Why not? It's him or someone your mother finds."

"Because I dislike him very much. That's final. No."

Colin checks out the place.

Colin moves in.

I hated that I had to succumb to this, but I was desperate.

⁓

It's the day of the big move, and there are boxes everywhere. Wes and Colin are walking in and out with all of Colin's stuff. I had a long dreadful talk with my mother about Reese moving out and Colin moving in. I was actually surprised by how well she took the news. All she cared about was that he knew how much the rent would be every month and that I was one hundred percent sure he wasn't some serial killer. After that was all cleared up, I left my room to see what was going on out there.

Reese is sitting at the kitchen table with a cup of what I assume is hot chocolate in her hands. Colin and Wes are moving this gigantic brown Lazy Boy into the living room. My eyes go wide, and I think I may pass out. They sit the chair down, facing the television, right beside my beautiful white and blue striped couch. He's ruining the look of this living room with that disgusting piece of furniture.

"You can't be serious…." I say, crossing my arms.

They both look at me. "Can't be serious about what?" Colin asks.

"That ugly chair!" I say, pointing at it for emphasis.

"Yeah, well, too bad. This place is mine too. Fifty-fifty, roomie. Get used to it."

It irks me how the word "roomie" falls off his tongue so quickly.

"Colin, don't you see how it ruins the whole feel of the living room?"

They continue to move his stuff, completely ignoring me. I'm getting madder and madder by the second. I can't believe this caveman is moving into my space. Colin walks past us and drops a large cooler beside his chair. I stare at it for a second before making my way over to it. I open the lid to find stacks of ice and beer.

"Um, what's this?" I ask.

Colin moves my hand away and plops on his chair, grabbing a couple of beers out of the cooler. He throws one to Wes and opens his in one quick motion. He takes a big sip and lets out an "*ahh.*" He finally glances at me and rolls his eyes. "My cooler. Can't you see?"

I'm still kneeling next to it. "Yes, I can see that, but what's it doing here?"

"So, I can always have a cold one when I watch TV," he says calmly.

"But there's the fridge like four steps from the couch."

"I've been living here for like five minutes, and you're already up my ass."

I get up and disregard the last thing he said. Reese is leaning against the counter in the kitchen, putting out some of the cookies she brought over earlier. Reese has always been thoughtful, and she always knows how to ease my stress level. I pull the kitchen chair out and sit, watching Reese put the plate of cookies in front of me.

"Don't worry, Jade. Everything will work out. I promise." Reese gives me a smile.

I glance at the brown chair, then at his cooler, and finally at Colin. I let out a deep breath. We'll see.

~

That night, we all decided to grab some drinks at this bar that opened in Greenwich Village. I wanted to stay in Brooklyn, but I got outnumbered. But hey, I'm desperate to hang out with my best friend before she embraces a new life living with her boyfriend.

This bar is the definition of hip, and I'm actually sort of happy we came here, even though I'll never admit it. It's just the type of person I am. But the face Reese gives me as we walk in shows that she already knows I am digging this place. People all over the place are playing Uno or Connect Four, and they're all drinking fabulous-looking cocktails. And the music... amazing. 80s classic rock. Just what I like. It's like everyone who looks like me is here, and my friends and Colin are the outcasts.

Everyone sort of separates due to the large crowds surrounding the place, and somehow, I'm left alone. I look around the area, eyeing a group of people taking shots and an older man singing along to the live band. I smile to myself as I spot Colin. He's leaning against the tall table, and a couple of girls with long, blonde hair approach him. I head over to the bar to find Reese and Wes. If they aren't dancing, then they are most likely getting a drink at the crowded bar. I stand on my tippy toes, trying my hardest to capture Reese's yellow hair. I let out a sigh. Now all I want is a drink.

"Why does it look like you're about to cry?" says a voice beside me, and I cringe when I see who it is—my soon-to-be roommate.

I shake my head and decide to ignore him.

"You can't hate me forever. Soon, we're going to be sharing the same bathroom," he jokes.

"And to think this whole time, I figured you'd go outside like a dog." I dramatically bat my eyelashes at him.

Colin shakes his head and takes a sip of his drink as he obnoxiously taunts me with it. "You can have a sip if you want, roomie."

I laugh. "A sip from that? No, thank you."

He gives me a cheeky smile that exposes his deep dimples. Gosh, he really gets on my nerves.

"How'd you get that anyway?" I say as loudly as I can over the blasting music.

"I have my ways," he says casually. "My—"

I cut him off, laughing. "Isn't it supposed to be the other way around? You buy the girl a drink?"

"Not when you're this good-looking." He grins, which turns into a laugh seconds later.

"You're so full of yourself."

Colin places his hand by his ear. "Huh? I can't hear ya, roomie. What did you say?" he asks, walking away from me before I can even respond.

A space by the bar opens up, and I squeeze in as quickly as possible, ordering an espresso martini. I lazily tap my fingers to the beat of the music, bobbing my head as I wait patiently for my drink to be made. A tall man with long, curly brown hair walks up to the bar and stands next to me. He's wearing a loosely fitted button-down and a pair of Levis. I bite my lip gently, glancing at this beautiful stranger beside me. The bartender hands me my drink, and I take my first sip, hoping this man will talk to me before I'm forced to leave. We finally make eye contact as he checks out my drink before ordering his. He gives me a smile but quickly turns away as a short brunette appears next to him, putting her arms around his muscular bicep. I groan inwardly as I leave the bar area. Why are all the cute ones always taken?

"Jade!" I hear my name being called over the music. I turn around and spot Wes, Reese, and Colin in the corner of the bar, by the large window. They're all sitting at a high top.

"Took me forever to get a drink." I laugh, pulling out a wooden stool to sit.

"We were wondering where you went. One of the guys in Colin's band works here and gave us free drinks!" Reese squeals, taking a sip of her beer.

I glance at Colin, who is laughing at something Wes said across the table.

"How come Colin didn't tell me that?" I say in Reese's ear.

She shrugs. "He said he tried to tell you, but you didn't want to hear it."

I laugh. "Sounds about right."

~

Later that night, Wes drops Colin and me off in front of our apartment building. It's kind of weird saying *our* since I can't imagine Colin and me having anything in common. We head upstairs in complete silence, mainly because it's one a.m. but also because I'm a tad intoxicated.

"Night, roomie," Colin says quietly before he walks into his room, shutting the door behind him. I stand still for a second, staring at the closed door that used to be Reese's.

"Goodnight," I whisper.

~

The fridge is completely stocked with food—some mine but mostly Colin's. I haven't gotten a chance to go grocery shopping, and now I'm regretting my laziness. I stand in the kitchen for a while, trying to decide if I want leftover Pizza Hut or slightly stale waffles.

"Oh, hi. Um, Colin said I could make a peanut butter sandwich."

I turn around and see a very tall brunette with tannish skin in front of me. I close the refrigerator door and move to the side so she's able to grab the bread. I examine her from the back—she's wearing Colin's boxers and one of his shirts.

"You must be his roommate?" she asks.

I sit down at the table and nod, sipping on my black coffee. "Yes, and you are?" I ask.

"I'm Monique. I met Colin last night at that bar, Dawns."

"It's nice to meet you." I give her a fake smile.

I didn't have to deal with this type of stuff when I lived with Reese. This "type of stuff" as in I didn't have to make small talk with some stranger at eight o'clock in the morning. But from what I'm seeing of Colin, this may be a regular thing, so I'll just have to get used to it.

"Have a great day," she says as she grabs her sandwiches and walks back into Colin's room.

At least she was nice.

CHAPTER 6

T hanksgiving.

November 22nd, the day where people reunite with their families and fill their bellies with turkey, stuffing, and cranberry sauce. For me, well, I prefer to stay home, order takeout, and read *To Kill a Mockingbird* for the hundredth time. Even though my parents weren't born in America, they always embraced Thanksgiving as one of the holidays to celebrate. It gave my mother an excuse to cook a giant meal for all of us.

Usually, my mom has a gathering at the house where she makes her famous turkey stew, and we eat and listen to my grandpa's stories about his chess games. My older sister Nat even comes home for the weekend. But this year and the year before that, I made my own tradition—stay home, eat excellent Chinese food, and read. There were times in high school where Reese knew I hated celebrating Thanksgiving with my family, so she'd beg me to come to her house. I can't lie and say I didn't have fun. Reese's mom made everything enjoyable, primarily due to her cheerful personality. She'd make food for an army, and we'd have leftovers for days. Reese's little brother, Tyler, would follow us around like a little lost puppy, and her older cousin would tell us stories. She'd go on and on about all the cute boys at her preppy school on Long Island. She and her friends would sneak out in the middle of the night and spy on the cute boys that wore university ties and sweater vests. She was intriguing, to say the least.

One year, I actually went to Noah's house for Thanksgiving. I didn't have as much fun as I did at Reese's house because Noah's whole family is exceptionally uptight, and I never felt like I could be myself. At least there was always wine. His parents never cared when we would sneak a bottle that was lying around. We'd climb into his treehouse, drink, and just make out for hours until his twin sister, Brooke, would catch us.

This year, I'm staying home.

Colin grabs a beer from his cooler and plops on his Lazy Boy. He opens the beer can in one quick motion, downing half of it in seconds. I look up from my fashion magazine and watch as he surfs through the channels.

"Shouldn't you be packing?" I ask him. "And leaving for California?"

"Why would I do that?" he says, eyes still glued on the television.

I glance at my phone, just to be one hundred percent sure that it's Thanksgiving tomorrow. I have definitely been out of it lately.

"Oh, ya know because of the national holiday where people all over the country stuff their faces with turkey?"

Colin looks over to me and rolls his eyes. "Oh, yeah… that. Yeah, no, I'm not going home this year."

"And why's that?" I ask him.

"Same reason you're not going home."

"How do you know I'm not?" I raise an eyebrow.

"I overheard you and Reese talking about it," he says as he grabs another beer.

"Well, I prefer to just stay home this year. Besides, my family is great but can be a lot sometimes. I also need to prepare for an upcoming audition."

"What a bummer," he says unenthusiastically.

"So, what exactly are you doing for Thanksgiving?" I ask.

"Exactly this, roomie," he says, throwing his hands in the air and burping like a caveman.

My eyes widen, and I sit up, losing my page. "Oh no you're not! Colin, Thanksgiving is a time where I have the apartment to myself."

"Well, too bad, roomie. This is my apartment too, remember?"

"I know Reese invited all of us to her house! Just go there."

"That's a hard pass." He burps again.

I shake my head with disgust and stand up, crossing my arms. "This is going to be a problem, Colin."

He looks up at me and shrugs. "There is nothing you can do to kick me out, Jade. I fucking hate Thanksgiving, and I really hate my family."

"What a bummer," I mock, walking away from him.

I open the fridge and take out the pitcher of lemonade I made last week. I'm too lazy to find a clean cup, so I grab the straw that has been lying on the counter. I ordered sushi the other day, and they gave me an extra straw with my drink. I was too lazy to toss it out, but now it is coming in handy.

I sit down, making sure my back is to Colin. At least this way I won't have to see the person who is ruining my favorite holiday.

Colin shuts the television off then walks into his room, closing the door behind him. A couple of minutes later, he comes out dressed in his workout clothes, music blasting in his ears. He walks by me and grabs a Gatorade from the fridge. He burps again. Honestly, I could strangle him, and we haven't even lived together that long. How am I going to make it through his lease?

～

Later in the day, I decided to call Reese and meet her at our favorite sushi restaurant a few blocks from her place. Some fresh air to clear my head and the best salmon rolls are exactly what I need.

"You should come to my house for Thanksgiving," Reese says, putting some ginger on her sushi roll.

I shrug. "I like to be alone on this holiday."

"So, you never liked coming to my house?"

Is she seriously getting offended right now? It's not always about Reese and her feelings. "Are you really going there right now?" I raise an eyebrow.

Reese sighs and takes a sip of her beer. "It'll be fun! You haven't been to my house in years. Everyone would love to see you again."

"I'm sorry, Reese. I love your family, and I especially love you, but it's a very, very hard no."

Reese shoves the whole roll in her mouth. "So, what are you gonna do then?" she asks in between bites.

I shrug. "I'm going to try to convince him to go with Wes or have him go to your house."

"Yeah, good luck with that." She laughs.

"I'll tell him about your slutty cousin! Maybe that will entice him. Do you think she'll sleep with him if I pay her?"

"Jade! My cousin isn't some prostitute."

"It was just an idea," I say, putting my hands up in surrender.

"Besides, I'm pretty sure she has a boyfriend. He's a marine." Reese's eyes widen as she says this. I'm not sure if Reese is surprised that her cousin is dating a marine or that she's actually dating someone.

I lean back on my chair and throw my dirty napkin onto my finished plate. "Boyfriend? Well, that's a first for her."

"Yeah, I know. My mother told me last week! She thinks they'll get engaged."

"Well, fuck that then. I guess she won't sleep with Colin." I sulk.

Reese rolls her eyes. "I guess she won't."

I shake my head and cross my arms. "Life isn't fair sometimes."

"My door is always open if you decide to come," Reese says, finishing the last of her beer.

～

The next morning, I decided to sleep in. Sleep in, meaning sleep till nine. I haven't been able to do that in a while, so it feels nice to catch up on some much-needed slumber.

I hear some movement in the kitchen, and I get out of bed. I grab my sweater and see Colin making some eggs. His back is to me. I watch as he scoops the scrambled eggs onto a glass plate. He whistles a soft tune as I remain silent, walking into the kitchen.

"Morning." I plop on the kitchen chair, still sort of pissed about the whole Thanksgiving situation.

"Good morning, my roomie," Colin says.

I roll my eyes, only because he's a morning person and I'm the complete opposite.

I hear a knock at the door. Groaning, I get up and open the door. Reese is standing in front of me with a huge grin plastered on her face. She's wearing a long, fuzzy maroon sweater and leggings. Her smile is still wide as she adorably points to the turkey hat sitting on top of her head.

"Quick question, did you travel all the way here wearing that?"

Reese walks past me and goes straight over to Colin's chair. She doesn't answer me until she sits down. "Yes. Yes, I did, Jade."

I stand still and blink a couple times. "Oh, okay. I'm not judging."

"She totally is," Colin says behind me.

Reese rolls her eyes and gets on her feet. She takes off the turkey hat and walks over to me, playing with it in her hands. I grab two mugs in the cabinet and pour some coffee for us. I hand Reese her mug as she hands me the hat.

I let out a chuckle. "One would assume I'd wear this, but you're so wrong."

Reese takes a small sip of her coffee then puts it down on the kitchen table where Colin is shoveling his eggs. She opens the fridge, grabbing Colin's almond milk.

"You guys need to get into the Thanksgiving spirit!" she chides, pouring some milk into her black coffee.

"It's too early." I yawn, taking a seat across from Colin.

Reese crosses her arms. "Oh, c'mon! You guys are so lame, I swear."

"How am I lame? I'm wearing a freakin' turkey hat, for crying out loud." I laugh, putting the hat on my head.

"And I just want to eat my eggs," Colin adds.

"I thought you'd be traveling to your parents' house by now," I say, looking down at my steaming cup of coffee.

"Well, I'm going to head over there as soon as I leave here, but I'm taking both of you with me," she says.

Colin and I both look at her. I place my cup down as I turn to face her. Colin remains still, holding a half-eaten piece of toast in one hand and his fork in the other.

"Reese, I already told you no," I whine.

"I'm not taking no for an answer from either of you. Thanksgiving is like Christmas—you can't leave the people you love alone."

"But we're not alone. I have my Thai food and my book," I say.

"Pathetic," Colin says under his breath.

"Oh please, Colin," I say, crossing my arms. "What exactly will you be doing? Oh wait, I know! Watch sports and masturbate?"

"That sounds like a fucking good time." He winks at me.

I groan with disgust and turn back to Reese.

She lets out a tiny laugh and shakes her head. "You guys are both pathetic."

"All right, fine! I'll go," I say. I'm not sure why I'm agreeing to this; it probably has to do with the happy look Reese has on her face. And mostly because I know exactly what she'd do if I said no to her again. She'd most likely call my mother and tell her I'm not going to her house for Thanksgiving, which is where she thinks I'm going, and she'll let her know what I've been doing for the last couple of years.

Reese claps her hands and smiles. "'Bout time."

"Fucking finally, you two have fun."

"Oh no, you're coming too!" Reese yells.

"Says who?"

"Me," Reese responds.

"Reese has a slutty cousin!" I shout.

Reese playfully smacks my shoulder. "Jade!"

"Please leave me out of whatever you just said." Colin rolls his eyes, still recovering from his frustration about going to Reese's house in a couple of hours.

～

Colin and I both pack lightly. I don't know how Reese did it, but she managed to get both of us to squeeze into Wes' shitty Honda Civic. Soon, we were on the way to her parent's house on Long Island. I thought it had to do with Reese's cousin, but Colin said he wasn't interested. According to Reese, I'm not allowed to talk about her cousin and her slutty days anymore.

"How much longer?" Colin groans from the backseat.

"Ten more minutes," I say, glancing at the GPS.

"Can you please move your seat up?" Colin says, banging into the seat with his shoulder.

"I don't have any more room," I say, turning my head to see him squished in the backseat. Part of me finds it a bit funny.

"I seriously hate Wes' car and the fact that I'm the biggest and stuck in the back!" Colin sighs.

"Stop being a baby." I laugh at him.

Before Colin can even respond, Reese opens her mouth. "Can you both stop? We're almost there," Reese says, taking a sip from her iced coffee.

"I can't believe I agreed to come," Colin says.

"Yeah, me too."

Reese turns into her neighborhood, and the memories start flooding back.

"Wow, nothing's changed," I say, looking out my window in awe.

Reese turns down the music before turning onto another street, passing familiar houses. Reese's parents moved into this house when Reese graduated high school. They were tired of the apartment life in Brooklyn and wanted to settle down in a home on Long Island. They've been living in this house for about six years.

"Home sweet home." Reese smiles, pulling onto the gravel driveway.

"Fucking finally," Colin groans, banging into my seat one more time.

We all get out and grab our bags from the trunk. Colin follows Reese and me up the concrete pathway leading up to a brick-paved porch with a white two-seater swing and some pots filled with blue and yellow flowers. Reese unlocks the red-painted front door without knocking, and the smell of food cooking in the kitchen immediately fills our nostrils.

"Mom! We're home."

We leave our bags in the foyer and follow Reese into a long hallway, leading into the kitchen.

"Hey, Mom," Reese says excitedly as soon as we enter the small kitchen.

It takes a second for Reese's mother to hear us. She's humming to herself as she mixes what looks like dough with her hands. She's wearing an apron, and her short wavy red hair is in a tight bun. She turns her head and lets out a yelp, making eye contact with all of us, one after the other. Reese's mother grabs a rag that's lying next to the sink, wiping the excess dough off her hands.

"My baby is finally home!" she cries as she places her hands onto her pale chest.

She gives Reese a long tight hug then she moves over to me. "My sweet, sweet Jade! How is my fashionista doin'?"

"Good." I smile, pulling my rainbow-striped shirt down.

Lastly, she eyes Colin up and down, giving him a hug then grabbing my hand. "So, this must be Colin." She grins at all of us.

"Mom, yes, this is Colin. Wes' childhood friend, and Jade's roommate."

"It's a pleasure to meet you, Mrs. McKinley," Colin says, giving her one of his famous smiles.

"Oh please, call me Lauren." She laughs to herself.

"May I say, Lauren, you have a beautiful home. Reese never told me how beautiful her mom is."

Lauren covers her face, and I can see she's hiding her blush.

"Seriously, Colin?" I say.

"What? My eyes are liking what they see," he says nonchalantly.

"And Reese never told me how sweet you are!" She grins.

"Both of you, get a room," Reese says, letting out a laugh.

Lauren turns away in embarrassment and walks back to her dough that's sitting in a bowl.

"Your father and uncle are in the living room," she tells Reese. "And your brother is outside playing with one of the neighbor boys." Lauren gives us a smile then continues to knead her dough.

We follow Reese down a long hallway, and I can't help but look at the pictures hanging on the beige walls—from pictures of Reese and her brother hiking to cute wedding photos of Lauren and Alvin. And there it was, the embarrassing graduation picture of Reese and me. I must have been on something that day; I went full out on the hair and makeup. I stop in my tracks and stare at my purple lipstick and the Princess Leia balls on the top of my head—not one person told me it wouldn't be the best idea to wear that on graduation day.

I hear Colin laugh behind me, but I'm too focused on how I can grab this picture, run away, and never look back.

"So, tell me, roomie, what were you going for? Space alien meets 80s slut?" Colin asks with a hint of mockery.

Reese puts her arm around me and smiles. "It's just one of Jade's unique put-together."

I glance at her and sigh. "I have to speak to Lauren about taking this down." I walk past both of them and enter the smoky living room.

"Jade! It's a really nice picture. It was either that or the one with Noah," Reese says as I walk away.

I completely ignore her and approach Reese's dad and uncle, who are intensely watching the game on television. Reese's Uncle Richard glances at us then lowers the volume on the television. Afterwards, he gives Alvin a massive knock on the shoulder.

Alvin stands to his feet and rubs the chip crumbs off his beer belly in one quick motion.

"Reese, Jade!" He smiles, giving us both a big squeeze.

"This must be Jade's boyfriend," Richard says while giving Reese a hug.

I cough. "Oh gosh, no. Richard, this is my roommate."

Alvin and Richard both give Colin a handshake. "Sorry about that, Jade, I just figured."

"Daddy, Colin is Wes' childhood friend."

"And where might Wes be?" Alvin asks with his arms wrapped around Reese.

"I told you! He went back home to California."

"You watch sports?" Richard asks, putting his hand on Colin's shoulder.

"Yes, sir."

"And who's your team?" Alvin asks like it's a big deal or something.

"Of course, it'd have to be the 49ers."

I grab Reese's hand, pulling her away from all the sports talk in the living room. We open the back door and walk onto her deck. It is completely covered in red and orange leaves. We quickly spot Tyler and his friend playing baseball in the yard.

"I think my parents like Colin," Reese says as we walk down the steps of her deck.

"Everyone always likes Colin." I pause, looking at her. "I don't get it."

Reese lets out a little laugh. In the middle of her yard, there is a giant swing set. Reese plops on one of the swings, and I sit down next to her. We then watch her brother and his neighbor play. A few minutes later, Tyler drops his baseball mitt and runs over to us. He gives us both a tiny hug then he wipes away the sweat that's dripping off his face.

"My mom told me you brought your boyfriend," Tyler says, looking at me.

"He's not my boyfriend!" I say loudly.

"Gosh, sorry, moody pants."

Reese and I both look at each other and let out a laugh. Reese gives me a nod, and we both jump off the swing simultaneously to tackle Tyler. Just like old times. Tyler is a lot taller, so it's challenging to do, but with both of us combined, we manage.

Soon, we hear Lauren on the deck, calling for us to come inside.

Tyler says bye to his friend, and we all race to the door. Of course, Tyler wins. We walk inside, breathless and laughing.

I walk into the living room to see Colin, Richard, and Alvin watching the game.

"Everyone, I put appetizers on the table! Go sit, please," Lauren orders, turning the television off. If she doesn't do it now, that television would stay on all night.

I hear Tyler and Colin talking behind me as we enter the dining room. We all take a seat, and of course, Colin is next to me. I don't hate Colin; I've just been annoyed with him. I never know what's going to shoot out of his mouth, and I like to be ready when that happens.

Everyone fills their plates with some finger foods while Reese's mother and grandma finish cooking in the kitchen. Reese's grandfather walks down the stairs and enters the dining room. He looks tired. By his messy hair, I assume he had just woken up from a nap. He gives Reese and me a kiss then sits down at the head of the table.

"Grandpa, do you want some food?" Reese asks, and he nods.

She grabs some of the mini-quiches and pigs-in-a-blanket for him to eat. Grandpa Lenny gives her a pleased smile as he shoves the finger food into his mouth. Everyone begins their conversation about school, work, and, of course, sports, as Lauren does the last-minute preparations.

The rest of Reese's family come just in time. Her aunt and uncle are flustered, apologizing for being late. Her cousin Jenna automatically grabs food from the table. Reese and I then get up to help Lauren. We bring all the food to the table, trying to time everything perfectly so the dishes wouldn't get cold. We make sure Lauren doesn't get overwhelmed like she usually does on Thanksgiving.

I spoon some cranberry sauce onto my already filled plate and listen to the familiar chatter that doesn't seem to change no matter how many years go by. I glance at Colin who is having an in-depth conversation about history and politics with Reese's dad. This is a serious and knowledgeable side of Colin, one I've never seen before. Reese's dad is a political science teacher at a local high school and seems to be impressed by Colin's opinions. Reese and I catch eyes as we eavesdrop on their friendly conversation. She gives me a grin as she fills her mouth with a big helping of stuffing.

WINTER

CHAPTER 7

"I know I've been sort of procrastinating finding a new apartment," Reese sighs before taking a bite of her wrap.

I nod. "I know you were excited about it a couple months ago. So, what happened?"

"Oh, I still am, but I've been really stressed out about my classes. Wes has been focused on his job, so I guess we've both been putting it off," she tells me. "But Wes told me last night that his lease is ending soon, and we really need to start finding somewhere to live."

"What's wrong with the place you have now? It doesn't seem so bad there," I say.

She takes a sip of her water before answering. "I don't know. I guess we just want to start fresh somewhere together, you know?"

I smile. "Of course."

Reese dips a couple of fries into her ketchup then tilts her head to the side. "What are you doing after this?"

"Probably nothing, why?" I ask her.

"Wes made an appointment for us with this realtor he found

online. However, he's going to be stuck at work all day. Can you please come with me to take a look at a couple of apartments?"

I exhale and nod. "When do I ever say no to you?"

~

Later in the day, as we are getting out of a cab, I ask Reese, "So, who's the realtor?"

"His name is Jason." She pauses. "Jason, um, well, I can't remember his last name."

I follow her into the small lobby of one of the apartment buildings we're supposed to see. We walk past mailboxes that line both sides of each wall. The smell of fresh paint fills the air as I quickly scan the lobby, eying the large mirror on the wall and the tall plant in the corner.

A man with short brown hair and a big pointy nose enters the lobby a couple of minutes after us. He's wearing a light grey suit and a huge smile. He's definitely on the shorter side, but the look of confidence on his face makes him seem a lot taller.

"You must be Reese," he says, reaching out and shaking her hand. They exchange a couple of words, then he turns his gaze to me. "You don't look like a Wesley," he says, following up his joke with a laugh.

Reese smiles and pats my shoulder. "Oh, this is my friend Jade. Wesley's my boyfriend. He's the one who made the appointment, but he couldn't make it today."

"Oh, that's too bad. He sounded like a very nice guy on the phone," Jason says to Reese. To me, he asks, "So, you're just here for some moral support?"

I nod with a smile.

"Okay, sounds great. So, before we go on and check out the amazing apartment," he says. "I just want to tell you a little about myself."

Reese and I nod, waiting for him to continue.

"My name is Jason Heeren. I was born and raised in Vermont. I've been a realtor in New York for about six years, and I am very good at my job. My happiness revolves around my clients finding the right place to call home. So, are you ready to do the damn thing?" he says, with too much enthusiasm. I raise a brow and glance at Reese, but all I see is a gigantic smile plastered on her face. Did she really just fall for that crap?

We follow Jason into the elevator, and he begins to tell us all about the building's history. However, all I can focus on is the smell of his strong cologne and his cheerful personality.

"So, this is it," Jason says, opening the front door for us. "Wesley was very clear about your budget and the certain things you like."

Reese nods and grabs my hand, dragging me immediately into the master bedroom.

"So, this apartment does come furnished," Jason says, leaning on the doorway to the master bedroom. "One bedroom, one bath. Reasonably sized kitchen. The living room is very open," he says.

Reese follows him, walking around slowly.

"These two windows right over there bring in a lot of light." He points towards them. "And there is a nice sized storage room on the bottom floor."

I linger by the kitchen, examining the brown countertops and cabinets.

"It looks kinda old, right?" Reese whispers to me, tapping the countertops.

"It doesn't look terrible," I say to her.

"So, what do you think? I know it's small and a little run down, but it could look cute if you put some effort into it," she says.

"Does this building allow pets?" I ask Jason.

He looks away from the window and nods. "It certainly does. Sorry, I forgot to mention that your boyfriend Wesley informed me about your pet situation, and I will only show apartments that allow pets."

"I definitely think this apartment is a hard maybe," I say, eyeing the space and its yellowish-colored walls.

~

After looking at two more potential apartments, we say our goodbyes to Jason and head over to our favorite donut shop to discuss the three apartments.

"So, which one was your favorite of the three?" Reese asks, biting into her glazed donut.

I rip a piece of my strawberry-glazed donut and let out a breath. "Um, I liked them all, to be honest, but the first one seemed the most reasonable."

She nods. "Yeah, I agree. The layout on the third one was kind of odd, doncha think?"

"Yeah, and the second one is right above a pizza place. It might be loud at night."

"That is true… and dangerous." She laughs. Her phone starts to buzz, and she grabs it from her back pocket. "Hold on, it's Wes."

She gets up and leaves the shop. I finish the last of my donut, and I'm deciding if I want another, even though there's a line that's practically out the door.

Reese returns seconds later, thank goodness. She just saved me from another sugary donut.

"I'm meeting Wes at home, and I'm going to show him the few videos we took."

I nod. "All right. I'm gonna stay here for a couple more minutes."

Reese gives me a wave goodbye and leaves the shop. I turn my head and watch someone from another table practically stuff a whole donut in her mouth.

"Oh, fuck it," I say under my breath as I walk towards the end of the line.

~

The next morning, I linger by the mailboxes on the bottom floor of my apartment building. I look through the glass door and sigh as I hear a big gust of wind outside. I pull down on my winter jacket so it'll cover more of my butt, then I fix my hat so my ears won't feel like they are going to fall off in the cold winter air.

As soon as I drag myself outside, I'm cursing every step to work. Some might ask, "*Jade, why walk in negative two-degree weather? Just hop in a cab. Problem solved.*" But no, I'd rather freeze my skinny ass off than pay for an expensive cab ride. Around this time of year, with the snow and brutally cold winds, cab companies tend to make their rides a bit more expensive. Most people are not as stupid as me, so they would not want to walk in this level of cold.

I walk past a couple of Santa Claus carolers singing for donations and notice many people buying Christmas presents. It seems as if they are all in a hurry. I haven't even begun to buy any gifts yet. I'm not like some people who, as soon as Thanksgiving ends, are already out buying presents. I step into work and exhale, finally able to feel my face.

"You're late," Wanda says behind me. I take off my jacket and completely ignore her. I'm not in the mood. I walk past a young couple sitting at a nearby table. They look warm in their turtlenecks and Ugg boots.

"Cold enough for ya?" my coworker jokes.

I put my apron on and smile. "I miss autumn."

We chat for a bit as he finishes the last of his bagel, then we both leave the kitchen.

Our menu has completely changed from pumpkin spice everything to peppermint mocha winter wonderland. "Frosty the Snowman" plays from the speakers, and I can't help but sing along.

"Someone's getting into the jolly Christmas mood," my boss says, raising a brow.

"Yeah, well, someone has to," I respond.

Or maybe I'm in a good mood because of that Christmas bonus you promised.

During my lunch break, I decided to stay in the cafe where there's heat. My usual bench isn't practical around this time of year. Besides, there's a table by the large window in the front with a perfect view of the flower guy in his winter coat. I scan the whole cafe, but there are no empty tables. I let out a groan. Just as I am about to grab my winter jacket from the kitchen, a little old lady in a blue sweater a couple feet away says, "Hello, darling."

I look over and smile. "Hello, ma'am. Would you like anything?"

"Oh no, not at all. I saw you were looking around for a table, and my table has an empty seat." She points. "Come sit, eat that scone of yours."

I smile and sit down. "Thank you so much, ma'am."

"Oh, please stop with the ma'am calling. Makes me sound so…" She pauses and looks around the cafe. "Old."

I take a sip of my coffee and smile. "Sorry about that."

"I'm Claire, and you are?"

"Jade."

"So, tell me, Jade, how long have you been working at this cafe?"

"Well, I'd say a year and a half. Maybe more."

"I enjoy a hot cup of coffee and a chocolate chip cookie every day," she tells me. "For ten years, before this cafe was even a mention, my husband…" She touches her chest and stares into my eyes. "… may he rest in peace, would sit with me, and we'd talk and eat and drink our coffees."

I smile. "That sounds great."

"I'm still carrying on our little tradition, but it gets very lonesome all by yourself." Claire scratches the side of her nose, exposing her long red painted nails. "I was born and raised in this very borough."

"So was I," I tell her.

"And your parents?"

"Russia, actually. My mother is from Russia, but my father was born and raised in Ireland. They met when they were in their twenties. She and her friends took a vacation to Ireland, and the rest is history."

She smiles. "How lovely, do you have any siblings?"

I nod. "Yes, an older sister, Natasha."

"So, they decided to give Natasha the Russian name and you the American name," she says with a grin.

"Well, when my mother was eighteen, she was a model—a pretty well-known model in Russia, from one photoshoot she did." I smile. "She's wearing this beautiful cotton white dress. Her hair was braided with these big green flowers, and she wore a jade necklace."

Claire nods with a smile on her face.

"My mother told me that when I was born, she stared into my gigantic green eyes and decided to name me after her famous photograph, 'The Jade.' She told me it was meant to be, and she knew I'd be a star someday."

"And what are you, Jade? Are you a star?"

"Well…" I pause. "Not yet. I'm an actress. A struggling actress, to be more exact."

Claire smiles and gives my hand a gentle squeeze. "That was such a beautiful story, Jade. Thank you for sharing."

I glance out the window, taking a sip of my latte as I watch the flower guy leave with his usual bouquet of white flowers.

"Expecting someone?" Claire asks from across the table.

I peel my eyes away from the flower guy and give her a smile. "No, just observing."

～

Later that day, I'm standing outside on Franksville Avenue. I'm waiting in front of one of the apartment buildings I agreed to check out with Reese.

"Reese, where are you?" I ask through the phone.

"So, here's the thing." She pauses. "I, um, can't meet you."

I exhale, watching the cloud of air forming in front of my face.

Before I can say anything, she explains, "I was about to leave early, but my professor announced that if you stay after, she'll allow you to do some extra credit. And I need the extra points."

"You should have texted me earlier, then I wouldn't have come, and I wouldn't be freezing my ass off waiting for you."

"I'm sorry! But I was wondering if you could just meet with Jason and take a look at the apartment for me?"

Before I can even make a run for it and say *hell no* to her, I spot Jason walking towards me. "All right, fine. You owe me big time, Reese," I say and then hang up.

"Jade! What a pleasure to see you again. Are we waiting for Reese?" he asks. Before I could answer, Jason opens the door for me, and we walk inside the warm lobby.

"Well, Reese won't be able to meet us, so it's just me today."

"Okay, sounds good. But wow, may I say, you're a great friend."

"Tell me about it," I say under my breath.

"So, this place does not have an elevator," he tells me as we drag our bodies up two flights of stairs.

"Reese is used to the whole 'no elevator' thing. She was my roommate," I tell him. "My building doesn't have an elevator either."

"Ah, okay. Where do you live, if you don't mind me asking?" He smiles. "Sorry, it's just something realtors find interesting."

"I don't mind at all. It's the old-looking brown brick building on Brighton 3rd Street."

"Oh, okay, I know exactly where you're talking about. I had actually sold an apartment in that building a few months ago." He unlocks the front door with two keys and allows me to walk inside first.

"One bed, one bath," he tells me. I take my phone out and snap some pictures of the living room and kitchen.

"So, what are you planning on doing this weekend?" he asks me.

"I'm not sure yet. Probably nothing." I give him a half-smile.

"Yeah, me too." He sighs. "I don't have too many friends here."

I don't know how to respond to that, so I just nod. I then walk over to the bathroom and inspect the size of the tub—reasonable, I guess.

"Well, if you aren't doing anything this weekend," he says slowly, "I'd love to take you out Saturday night."

I turn around and stare into his eyes, giving him a smile. I'm used to the upbeat Jason, not this shy, sort of sweaty Jason. "Are you asking me out on a date?" *Wait, what is going on right now?*

"Yes, yes I am."

"I didn't think realtors dated their clients." I grin.

"Well, they don't." He smiles, exposing his pearly white teeth. "But technically, you aren't my client."

I lean half my body on one hip and study the man in front of me.

His eyes are on the floor, waiting patiently for me to respond. "Okay, sure."

Jason finally meets my eyes, giving me a broad smile. "So, what do you say? Want to check out another place?"

~

The next night, I am sliding into my long black and white striped sweater, and my black denim jeans. After I am dressed, I grab my long black boots and make my way over to the couch, plopping down beside Wes. Reese sits up from the couch and gives me a look as I slide my boots on. Without looking at Reese, I glance over to Colin, who is also dressed up. He's wearing a white long-sleeved button down and some grey slacks. Despite how nicely he is dressed, he is still sitting casually on his chair, drinking a beer.

"You look cute. Where are you going?" Reese asks me, setting her empty bowl of ice cream on the coffee table. I stand up, grab the bowl, walk to the kitchen, and put the bowl in the sink. As if that thirty seconds would give me enough courage to tell my friends I'm about to go on a date with their realtor.

"I have a date," I say.

Wes pauses the television and turns towards me. "With whom?"

I walk back to the couch and sit back down. I mess with my bangs a bit, hoping they don't look too messy. "Oh, you know... a guy," I say quietly.

Colin mumbles something under his breath, and I glare at him.

Reese looks at me strangely. She then reaches over Wes to give my shoulder a light push. "Why are you acting weird? Who is he?"

"His name is uh—" I pause for a second. "Jason."

Reese's mouth falls open and she whispers something in Wes' ear. He lets out a laugh.

"What's so funny?" Colin asks, finishing the last of his beer.

"You have a date with our realtor?" Wes asks.

Colin laughs as well, and I turn to Reese and Wes. "Yeah, what's so bad about that?"

"Oh, nothing, Jade. It's just, he's um… a bit much."

"That's why I didn't want to tell you guys." I cross my arms.

"How did it happen?" Wes asks.

"Well, when Reese bailed on me Friday, he showed me that one apartment. Afterwards, he asked me out," I say nonchalantly.

"What time is he picking you up?" Reese asks.

"Any minute now, actually," I say as I check my invisible watch. I feel awkward as they stare at me.

"Well, I hope you have a fun time with him." Reese smiles.

My phone starts to buzz, and Jason's name appears. "Hello?"

"Hi, Jade! It's Jason. I'm downstairs. Did you want me to come up?" Jason asks.

"It's okay! I'll just come down."

"Oh, okay," Jason says. "I'll see you soon then."

"Okay, I'll be right down. Bye." I hang up the phone and look up to see Colin smiling.

"No, have him come up. I want to meet him, roomie," Colin says to me.

"Yeah, not gonna happen."

And with that, I grab my jacket and leave my nosey friends. I walk down the steps of my building and immediately catch eyes with Jason.

"Wow, you look amazing, Jade." Jason smiles, giving me a hug.

"Thank you." I grin.

Jason opens the car door for me, which is such a gentlemanly thing to do. He jumps in seconds later and automatically turns on the heater. "Gosh, it's like an icebox out there." He laughs, driving down the icy roads. "So, I made a reservation for this Italian restaurant. Is that okay? I wasn't sure if you liked Italian food."

"I love Italian food," I say with a grin.

～

The waiter comes by our small round table, adorned with a red and white tablecloth. He pours us each a glass of red wine from the bottle that Jason ordered for the table.

"This place is so cute," I say before taking a tiny sip of my wine.

Jason smiles. "I've eaten here a few times. They have good food."

"Okay good because I only like to eat at restaurants that serve good food." I grin.

Jason rips a piece of bread from the basket and laughs. He pours some oil on his little side plate.

"So, Jade, tell me, what do you do besides look at apartments with your friend's amazing realtor?"

I smile. "Well, I'm actually an actress, but I work part-time at this coffee shop in Brighton beach."

Jason looks surprised by that. "Wow, I'm on a date with an actress! What have you been in?"

The waiter interrupts us then and hands us both our menus.

I wait until he leaves before answering. "Not very much, actually. I've been acting since I was six—three commercials, tons of theater, but the dream is to be on a real stage." I sigh.

"That's impressive. Like Broadway?"

I look up from my menu and smile. "Yeah, or even off-Broadway is fine."

"What coffee shop do you work at? I'm a huge coffee drinker."

"Coffee Bean Express. It's on the corner of 3rd Avenue."

"Oh, no way! Love that place."

I raise a brow. "Really? Or are you just trying to be nice?"

He laughs. "Don't worry about it."

I give him a tiny smile, even though I'm not too sure what he means by that.

Jason looks down at his menu and sighs. "Okay, so I usually get the chicken parm, but I'm thinking of changing things up tonight."

"You're such a daredevil." I swallow a piece of bread.

Jason takes a sip of his wine. "Oh, I don't know about that."

"I'm actually an eggplant parm type of gal, but maybe I'll be a daredevil like you and order something else too."

Jason grins and leans his body into the table. "How about this? You order for me, and I'll order for you, but it can't be chicken or eggplant parm."

I tilt my head to the side. "Oh, I don't know. You might order snail parm for me," I joke.

"I promise, no snail parm." He laughs. Jason then calls the waiter over. "So, I think we're ready to order."

The waiter takes out his pad and turns to me.

"Okay, so I'll have the Chicken Francese with penne pasta." I glance at Jason.

He gives me a wink and leans his hand under his clean, shaved chin. "And I'll have the spinach and cream gnocchi," he says. Jason then orders a couple of other things for the table.

"Spinach?" I ask him.

He laughs. "Don't knock it until ya try it."

I play with the long breadstick in my hand and smile. This little game we're playing makes me feel less nervous. After a while, I'm finally able to relax. There is something so soothing about Jason. I think it might be his calm demeanor and sweet smile that makes him easy to be around.

"So, you've been living in New York for six years?" I ask.

He nods. "Yeah, I have a small apartment in Brooklyn, and I still have my old place in Vermont."

"Oh really? Why is that?"

"Well, I go back to Vermont a lot. All my family and friends live there, so it just made sense to keep my place."

"So, the real estate in Vermont isn't as good as New York?" I raise my eyebrow.

"Well." He pauses, trying to find the right word to say. "Yes." He laughs. "My whole life, I've always been into a lot of movement and excitement, and I wasn't getting that in Vermont."

"New York has a lot of movement."

"Exactly." He smiles. "I was actually doing great in Vermont, but I found myself always—" He pauses. "Bored."

I nod, understanding that mindset completely.

"So, I decided to pack my bags and try things out here. But I kid you not, I still get calls from people in Vermont, so that's why I go back and forth so much."

The waiter comes by our table and sets our food in front of us. I inspect the circular noodle in front of me, saturated in a greenish cream sauce. My first reaction is to push anything green away, but the steam that arises from the dish makes my mouth water instantly.

"Trust me, Jade. I have a feeling you'll like it." He winks, cutting into his chicken.

I poke my fork into one of the noodles and eat it in one bite. I smile. "Okay, Jason, you're right."

"Told ya so," he teases.

～

"I would suggest we take a walk, but it's a little too cold for that," he says, opening the car door for me.

"A little?" I chuckle.

As soon as Jason turns the car on, he turns on the heater, which I appreciate. We sit in silence, trying to get as warm as possible.

Jason turns to me and says, "I don't want this night to end, Jade."

"Well, I'm pretty sure my friends are at this bar called Zayns. Do you want to go?" I suggest.

He nods and before I know it, he turns up the soulful music and drives us down the crowded streets.

～

By the time Jason and I arrive at Zayns, it's packed. The bouncer, of course, asks for my ID.

"This happens to me all the time. I blame my gigantic eyes," I say in his ear. Jason laughs and grabs my hand, giving it a gentle squeeze. I don't spot my friends right away, and I'm sort of relieved. I do not want them to make faces at me as soon as Jason looks away, especially Colin. Jason and I make our way over to the bar, and he orders us both a rum and coke.

"I usually don't drink," he tells me.

I sip on the thin straw and nod. "Oh yeah, same." There is nothing wrong with a little fibbing here and there, right?

We find a bench by the window and decide to enjoy our drinks before making a fool in front of each other on the dance floor. Jason tells me all about his college years as I nonchalantly sip on my drink. I nod and smile as he speaks, but I do find it weird that he is talking so intently about his college years.

He leans his back against the old chipped painted wall, occasionally touching my leg with his cold hand. "Sorry, I feel like I'm hogging this conversation." He laughs nervously.

I shake my head. "Oh, gosh, no. I'm just surprised to hear that you were in a fraternity."

Jason smiles. "Well, it's not the type of fraternity you're probably picturing," he tells me.

"Oh really?" Now, I'm intrigued.

"I was a part of a business fraternity." He sounds a bit bashful as he admits this. "We wore suits and went to business conventions, but there were girls in it too."

Jason is right. I was not imagining a business fraternity. In the movies, fraternities are filled with good-looking guys who love to party and get at every girl.

Jason rests his hand on my knee. "I should have just let you believe I was in one of those partying frats." He laughs, finishing the last of his drink.

"No! I'm relieved you weren't," I say. "I've never been interested in those types of guys."

Jason looks a bit relieved by my comment. "So, are you saying that you're interested in me?"

I part my lips, trying to think of what to say, but Jason chimes in before I could say anything. "Ya know, the nerdy business guy? Clearly."

I laugh. "Yes, clearly."

"College seems like such a distant memory." He shakes his head. "But if I could, I would definitely go back. Would you?"

I consider this before answering. "Uh, I would probably say no to your question."

Jason smiles but doesn't say anything to my comment.

"My college life—if you can even call it that—was pretty much the same as my life is now. The only difference is that I was younger and had to study for stupid classes."

Jason raises his plastic cup towards me, an attempt to cheer, but accidentally spills some of the liquid on my purse. Luckily, he had already finished his drink so the liquid was from the ice that had melted.

"Sorry." He laughs as I wipe the water that spilled on my purse. "Cheers to that," he shouts, moving the cup around in his hand. "For, of course, opening my eyes about taking pointless classes and being younger."

"Cheers, I guess," I say with a laugh, tapping my cup to his.

Jason nudges his shoulder with mine, and it seems like he wants to say something.

"Hey, guys."

I look up and see Reese standing in front of us, holding a glass of white wine.

"Hey! Reese!" I stand and give her a hug.

"When did you guys get to Zayns?" she asks me, giving Jason a kind smile.

"Just a few minutes ago," I say. "It's so crowded in here, so we figured we'd just bump into you guys eventually."

"Hi, Reese," Jason says nervously, giving her a kind wave.

I know Reese would have preferred that I texted her when we got to the bar, but she should understand that I'm technically still on my date.

"We're all by the bar if you guys want to join," Reese tells us.

"Uh, sure, but I think Jason and I are good here. Thanks, Reese."

She gives me a wink only I can see, then she turns towards the bar.

"I'm having a great time with you, Jade," he says to me.

I move a piece of my bangs away from my eye and smile. "I am too."

"I was actually really nervous to ask you out. I don't know if you could tell," he whispers. I don't know why he is whispering since it's so loud in here.

"I did," I say. "But you're lucky I thought it was cute."

"Well, I think you're cute too, so we both win." He winks, finally showing the coquet side of himself. I didn't peg myself for someone who could be intimidating, but I'd like to think I can be. I like that he is opening up more and that he seems less nervous.

Jason looks into my eyes, and I realize I hadn't noticed the green spots in his hazel eyes. I like how his long, dark brown eyelashes move gracefully each time he blinks. I was always so focused on his extended yet pointy nose to ever notice how attractive he really is.

His face moves closer to mine, and it's as if we're the only two people at this bar in Red Hook. I don't mind though. The anticipation of feeling Jason's lips against mine is killing me, but I am staying strong. I want him to take the lead.

Suddenly, Jason tilts his head and moves his parted lips closer to mine, and I follow his lead. I close my eyes, but all I get are tiny pecks. Jason's lips are soft; it's like kissing a cushioned pillow. When we release from whatever kiss that might have been, I immediately bring my recyclable straw to my mouth and finish the last of my drink.

Jason and I decide to navigate through the crowded bar and meet up with my friends. It was luckily not as awkward as I imagined it would be. Relief floods through me, and I'm able to enjoy my night with everyone.

Colin eventually ends up meeting us at the bar as well. He has his arm wrapped around this tall blonde wearing a sweater dress and knee-high leather boots. He seems too consumed with his next conquest to even acknowledge or possibly tease me about my date with Jason the realtor.

∽

"So, what happened next?" Reese asks Jason. She giggles loudly as we all drunkenly leave the bar. I watch Wes order an Uber and cringe at Reese, who is very intoxicated. When Reese is drunk, she gets obnoxious. Reese hangs onto me while Jason tells her a story about when he went to Nashville for the weekend.

Colin and his date come out seconds later. He has his arm wrapped around her tiny waist.

"I got me and Reese an Uber." Wes turns to us. "I can order one for you guys if—"

"No, thank you, man. I can drive," Jason says, pointing to the lot his car is parked in a couple streets down.

"Are you sure?" I ask, watching my breath form in front of me. It's so cold out.

"Yeah, I only had one drink, remember?"

I nod and we both smile at one another.

"Aren't you a responsible adult, Jason-uh-something?" Reese laughs loudly. "I must have forgotten your last name. How silly of me."

Wes lightly pulls her from me and says something in her ear.

The Uber pulls up, and Reese automatically gets in without saying goodbye. I glance at Jason, giving him an awkward smile. "She's not the best at handling her alcohol."

Jason rubs the back of his neck. "I think we can all relate to that."

We stand in silence, watching Wes and Reese get in the car. The cold has made my bones stiff. I turn towards Jason and give him a small smile.

"Do you want me to get my car and come pick you up? I would hate for you to have to suffer in the cold. It's quite a walk," he offers, ever the gentleman.

I glance at Colin and his date and sigh. "I'll walk. I don't mind."

"Hey, roomie," Colin says, walking towards Jason and me.

"Yes, Colin?" I cross my arms.

"It's pretty brutal out here, and I'm thinking we should put our heads together and discuss a transportation service that will take us home. Ya know, somewhere warm? I don't know about you guys, but Yalissa is already getting into survival mode." Colin leans in closer, as if he's telling us a secret. His face is mere inches from mine. "I told her that you may look frail, but you sure can put up a good fight for that heavy jacket of yours."

I roll my eyes as I hear Yalissa laugh behind us. "You're so obnoxious."

"Hey man, I don't mind driving you guys," Jason says nonchalantly, and I want to facepalm myself.

"Well, would you look at that," Colin sneers at me.

⌒

Jason and I walk in silence, occasionally sharing sweet glances with one another. It's hard to keep a conversation going when all I can think about is Jason's insulated car. Oh, and it's also hard to ignore the sound of Colin flirting, and his date's constant giggling.

By the time we get to Jason's Toyota, I am freezing. When he unlocks his car, the sound is like music to my ears. Apparently everyone feels the same way because the second his car unlocks, we all jump in simultaneously. I have never seen anyone's hand move as fast as Jason's as he turns on the heater.

⌒

Jason pulls over to the side of our street and puts the car in park. I remove my hands from under my butt and place them on my lap. I hear Colin and Yalissa laughing as they unbuckle their seatbelts.

"Thanks for the ride, realtor Jacob," Colin says from the backseat, lightly tapping Jason's shoulder.

"Uh, it's Jason, and yeah, no problem." He coughs.

Yalissa opens her door, but Colin doesn't seem to want to leave. Yalissa looks puzzled, and we are too.

"So, tell me, Jason, what are your intentions with my roomie?"

Silence fills the car, and I want to smack Colin for even asking a question like that. He doesn't care about Jason's intentions, all Colin cares about is embarrassing me and making me want to crawl out of my skin in shame.

Jason turns so he's fully facing Colin. I do the same, watching him give Colin a mischievous grin. "I would like to date her."

And with that, Colin and his date finally leave, and I find my lips exactly where they want to be.

CHAPTER 8

"I swear, I'm getting so tired of all this Christmas music," I groan, watching the wavy hair above my eyes fall to the side.

Mandy, my coworker, gives me an amen, and I laugh, watching a guy with a heavy winter jacket approach the counter. I've been happy. *Really* happy, actually. I've been going on tons of auditions, and I even got one call back. I'm taking a relationship slowly for the first time in a long time. I now see the appeal of dating an older man. I know Jason would love to take our casual relationship up a level, but he doesn't push it because he respects me. I'm really trying to enjoy this month-in relationship without sex.

He already met my family, well, my mother, one afternoon for tea. He made her laugh, and we sat for a few hours talking about life and all the recipes my mother loves to create. Reese and Wes like him as well. He sort of fits into our little group—if you can even call it that. I believe the main reason they adore him so much is because he found them a great apartment in Brooklyn. It is reasonably sized and located in a nice area.

Colin hasn't said much about Jason since that night we all hung out at Zayns. I'm thinking that may be a good thing, but I've come to learn that with Colin, you never know what really goes on in that head of his.

The man approaches the counter, and I ask him what he wants to order. I make sure to bring forth the holly jolly Christmas spirit that my boss insists on. I always remind myself that Christmas time is the worst time to get fired. Plus, I'm lazy—being a barista may just be my calling in life. He shakes his head no, and I stand still there confused, wondering why he's holding up the line.

"Then how can I help you?" I ask him.

He reaches into his pocket and hands me a piece of paper that's folded in two. As soon as I take the paper from his gloved hands, he gives me a smile and walks away. I stand there for a while, staring at the paper in my hands.

"Hey, Liza, do you mind taking over the register for a little?"

I hold the paper tightly between my fingers and head to the back of the cafe. I sit down at one of the tables and unfold it slowly.

As soon as I open the small, folded paper in my hand, my heart skips a beat.

> *You look beautiful, so beautiful in that uniform. Dinner.*
> *Tonight. My place. See you then, gorgeous.*
> *— Jason.*

∼

"Did you hire that guy?" I ask before taking a sip of my wine. I haven't stopped smiling since I read his note. I set my glass down on Jason's coffee table and lean back on his soft red leather couch. Jason lets out a tiny laugh from the kitchen. I can hear him chopping, and from the smell of it, I'm assuming it's onions. I get up from the couch and make my way towards him. Once I get in the kitchen, I take a seat on the barstool, sipping my wine.

"Are you sure you don't need any help?" I ask.

He shakes his head and begins to chop some red and green peppers. "No, I'm making you dinner, missy. And to answer your first question, no, Barren is a friend from work."

"Ah, another fellow realtor. Good to know if I ever need one." I grin, leaning my chin on the back of my hand.

"Ha-ha, very funny." Jason stirs something in the pot, then he checks on the chicken that's baking in the oven.

"So, Chef Jason, what's on the menu for tonight?"

He looks up and smiles, showing me his white teeth. "All right, Miss Jade. On tonight's menu we are having oven baked chicken, potatoes with goat cheese, and rice with onions and peppers. And to top it off, some Pinot Noir."

"That sounds amazing, Chef. But I'm sorry, I can't take you seriously when you're wearing that funny apron."

He tugs on the fabric and lets out a tiny laugh. "Don't hate on my Grandma Gege's apron."

"Oh, I'm not hating."

"I think this apron goes great with my eyes," he says as he stirs the rice in the pot.

"Yeah, don't say that." I laugh. I get up and walk over to where he's standing and open the oven door.

"Hey! What did I say? Go back to your seat!" Jason teases.

"It just smells so good in here. I have to see what's cooking," I whine.

"Well, too bad." He crosses his arms, looking down at me.

I grab the bottle of wine that's sitting on the kitchen table and take a big swig of it.

"Classy." Jason shakes his head, but he's smiling.

"Always."

~

Jason cuts me a piece of the roasted chicken and plops it on my plate. I thank him while simultaneously serving myself some potatoes and rice.

"I hope you like it," he says as he pours us some more wine.

"From the smell of it, I know I will," I say.

Jason gives me a pleased smile and begins cutting into his chicken.

"So, what made you get into cooking?" I ask him while taking a bite of potato.

Jason takes a sip of his wine, washing down his bite of chicken. "Well, more like who," he says. "My grandma was actually the one who got me into cooking."

"Is this the famous Grandma Gege?" I ask, giving him a smile.

Jason nods. "The one and only."

"She sounds so sweet from the stories you've told me."

"Oh, she was," he says. "She had this way of cooking that was simple, fun, and amusing." He smiles. "I swear, her kitchen was her own little stage."

I laugh. "That's adorable. So, she taught you the joy of cooking?"

He nods. "One summer, I was probably about sixteen, all the neighborhood kids were outside playing sports, and I was inside, learning how to cook. She taught me so much. Ever since then, I've always taken a liking to it."

"Well, I'd love to do this more often." I smile. "And by the way, Jason, the food is amazing."

"Thank you, Jade," he says, leaning in and giving me a peck on the lips.

After that, we eat in silence. The only sounds being the scraping of forks and knives against glass plates. Minutes go by without a single word being spoken. Usually, I'd try to find something to talk about, even if it's awkward chit-chat, but the silence between us isn't as bad as I thought it would be. Maybe in the past it was, but with Jason, silence isn't uncomfortable. It's just silence.

Jason looks up from his food and places his hand over mine. I finish the last of my wine, and before I can even pour some more for myself, Jason does it for me.

"You know what I just thought of?" he asks.

I shake my head no.

"That I never technically asked you to be my girlfriend."

I look up and stare into his eyes. "Oh, right, I guess you never did."

"It just kind of happened, and we both assumed that we were in a relationship together," he says, and I nod.

Abruptly, Jason stands up, and my mouth slightly parts, wondering what he's about to do. He looks around his tiny apartment, and it's like I could see an invisible light bulb turn on in his mind. He walks over to the vase sitting by the living room window, and he grabs one long blue flower. Jason then walks over to me and kneels on his knees. He finally looks up at me, giving me the cutest puppy dog grin I've ever seen.

"These past couple of months have been amazing with you. I wouldn't want to freeze my butt off and walk around small, tiny apartments with anyone else but you, Jade Everly."

I laugh, resting both my hands on his broad shoulders. He twirls the flower in his hand before handing it to me. I smell the flower and realize it's fake. Jason lets out a loud laugh, and so do I.

"Jade, will you please be my girlfriend?"

I tilt my head to the side and grin. "Of course."

Jason stands up and claps, then he pulls me in for a long, passionate kiss.

"Sorry I didn't do that earlier," he says after releasing me from our kiss.

"That's okay, you made up for it." I bite my bottom lip.

⌇

After cleaning up the kitchen, Jason and I decided to drink hot cocoa and watch a movie. Jason talks me into watching *Goodfellas*, and I don't mind. I'm just happy sipping on my cocoa, packed with tiny marshmallows, while Jason gently moves his fingers up and down my legs.

⌇

The movie credits roll, and I yawn, definitely feeling the three glasses of wine I drank. I follow Jason into his room, and he gives me one of his t-shirts and comfy sweats to wear. I sniff the fabric as I put my head through the hole, and I can't help but smile.

"What?" he asks. He is now taking out his contact lenses.

"I'm just happy." I grin.

The corners of Jason's mouth turn up as he jumps into his bed, moving his face closer to mine until we are nose to nose. He gives me a small kiss on the lips and begins to play with the collar of his old t-shirt.

"What are your plans for tomorrow?" he asks.

"Nothing," I say lazily. My eyes are starting to feel heavy.

"Can I see you tomorrow, or are you gonna disappear in the morning?"

"Yeah, that's—" Suddenly, I remembered. My sister will be in town tomorrow, and I promised that I'd spend some quality time with her.

"I can't," I sigh. "My sister, Natasha, is coming in tomorrow and will be here until Christmas."

"Is that bad?" he asks.

"No. I just haven't seen my sister in a while. She lives in Ohio. She's just, ah…" I pause. "She's a lot."

"Ah, I see. If you need an excuse to escape, I got you," he jokes.

I might take you up on that offer, Jason….

~

The next morning, I spot Natasha sitting by the fireplace in a small cafe in Bay Ridge. Her hair is a lot shorter since the last time I saw her, which must have been last Christmas. Her face has matured, and her strong cheekbones remind me of our dad. She's wearing a loose red turtleneck sweater, jeans, and from the look of it, a pair of expensive boots that she probably had the last time I saw her. Nat has always been into name brands. She doesn't mind spending a small fortune on one article of clothing.

I walk past a couple of tables, watching people chat as they eat their food and sip on their hot beverages. I am assuming my sister has ordered a cup of tea since she doesn't like coffee. She's also on the phone, probably having a deep conversation with her boyfriend, Sean. I don't think my sister has ever had a fun, joyful conversation. She's either annoyed or on the verge of being annoyed.

Once she spots me, she doesn't even smile. "Jade just got here. I'll call you later," she says through the phone.

As soon as I approach her table, she stands up and gives me a cold hug. "Jade. Hi."

"Hey, Nat." I take off my coat before sitting down and giving her a smile.

"I wasn't sure if you still drink coffee, so I ordered you a cup of tea," she says.

"I do, but thank you." I smile, taking a sip of my tea. I then open the lid and pour some milk into my cup.

"This cafe is nice, right?" I like all the uniquely shaped mirrors on the walls. Plus the fireplace gives us all this extra warmth which is needed since it's been so cold.

Natasha shrugs, and my smile drops.

"Yeah, it's nice. But it's just too busy for my liking. I find that the cafes in Ohio are just as nice or even nicer," she says nonchalantly.

"Well, according to you, everything is nicer in Ohio," I say sarcastically.

"Yeah, I guess so." She laughs.

I force myself to take a sip of tea. I don't want to say anything snarky to her. After all, we haven't seen each other in a while. "How was the flight?"

"Extremely bumpy. I had to complain. That's what I get for not flying first class."

"Nat, it would have been bumpy either way," I say.

Natasha eyes my outfit, and I'm already expecting her to have a comment about my plaid high-waisted pants and my matching long-sleeved sweater.

But instead, she says, "So Mommy informed me you're living with some guy she never met."

I nod.

"That's it? Just a nod?"

"What do you want me to say, Nat?"

"More than a nod, sis."

"His name is Colin."

"What happened to your friend, Reese?" she asks, completely disregarding what I just told her.

"She moved in with her boyfriend," I say. "Colin is her boyfriend's best friend."

"I don't get why you didn't just have Mommy choose your

housemate. It's her and Daddy's apartment, remember?"

"Yes, I know, but I'd rather have Colin living with me than a religious fifty-year-old Russian," I say in the most monotone voice I can muster.

Nat shrugs then takes a sip of her tea.

Did I pass the interrogation? Or is she going to keep grilling me?

"Personally, I just wouldn't feel comfortable sleeping while some guy I've never met is in the apartment."

I look away from the fireplace then back at my sister. "What did you just say?"

"Mommy said I should just stay at the apartment with you until Christmas."

"And why would she say that?" I ask, moving my chair a little further away from the fire. This conversation is starting to get me hot.

"Because Grandma and Grandpa are living at home right now, so there isn't much room for me. I mean, you're cool with it, right?"

I stare at my sister's face. The face that I don't recognize anymore. The features on her face are so different from mine. Sometimes, I can't believe we're related. She resembles my father, with her thin lips and brown eyes. Her short hair is lighter than mine, too and her frame is short and curvy.

I nod, knowing that if I take on this battle, I'll never win. "Where's all your stuff?" I ask.

"It's already at your place. I used the spare key. I was there pretty early, so I didn't meet your roommate, but I did knock on your door. However, you didn't answer, so I went inside, and you weren't in your bed. Where were you at six a.m.?"

"I was at my boyfriend's," I say quickly.

"You have a boyfriend?" she asks.

I nod, not wanting to share any more information with her.

"Do Mommy and Daddy know about him?"

"Yeah, Mom met Jason." I recall how Jason made Mom laugh, and it makes me smile.

"Oh, that's nice. You're seeing someone and everyone knows but me."

"Nat, we weren't purposely keeping it from you. It just didn't come up."

"Is it serious?" she asks, ignoring my explanation.

I give her question some thought before answering. "Well, I've only been dating him for a month or so."

She nods, moving her tiny curls away from her frowny face. "Well, I'd like to meet him at least once while I'm here."

"Yeah, definitely," I say.

～

Saks Fifth Avenue's entrance door is long and heavy. This is the first thought that pops into my mind as I open it for my sister. Once she walks in, I follow behind. The store is filled with beautiful Christmas decorations, and I can feel the excitement around me. I look through racks of clothes while Natasha is arguing with someone on the phone. I roll my eyes and try to block it out. I find a cute pair of denim jeans with pretty flower stitching and a matching off the shoulder sweater for Reese.

Natasha walks over to me in a huff, and I try my hardest to pretend I don't notice.

"My team is idiotic," she spits.

Here we go...

"What now?" I ask as I continue to look through the racks of clothes.

"They want me to work on software that I don't know anything about."

"Maybe you should at least look at it first."

"Why are you on their side?" She glares at me.

Is she serious right now?

"Nat, don't go there," I say, walking past her.

She says something under her breath and walks down a completely different aisle. I notice that she pulls out her phone, probably calling her boyfriend. She calls her boyfriend about literally everything. I look through the shoe department, but I don't see anything I like, so I decide to head over to the makeup section. I casually scan the blushes and smell the perfumes until it hits me—Jason and I never really discussed if we're buying each other anything for Christmas.

So, I do precisely what my sister did—I call for advice. I call Reese.

"You should get him something," she says after I talk her ear off.

"Do you think he's gonna get me something? Because I don't want him to feel awkward if I get him something and he doesn't get me anything," I sigh. Why is this so complicated?

I hear Reese taking a deep breath. "Jade, you've been dating him long enough for both of you to get each other something for Christmas. Why don't you get him something small?"

"Yeah, okay. You're right." I pick up a cologne, sniffing it.

"Where are you?"

"Saks," I say. "I'm waiting for Nat to finish up whatever she's doing."

"How's it going with her?"

"Reese, she's already driving me nuts, and I've only been with her for a couple of hours," I say, looking around the store to ensure she isn't around me.

"She's still the same?" She laughs.

"Yes, and the worst part is, she's staying at my place until Christmas," I cry, switching my phone to my other ear as I try to drown out the Christmas music playing through the store.

"Oh gosh. Why did you agree to that?"

"I didn't," I whisper. "She told me today. Apparently, my mom and Nat decided without informing me."

"Well, you better get the okay from Colin."

"That's the least of my problems right now," I sigh. "I just hope I don't try to jump off my terrace or check into an insane asylum by the end of the week."

Reese laughs. "Just try to stay away from her as best as you can."

I spot Natasha walking towards me. "I'll talk to you later. Satan's approaching."

"Who were you just talking to?" she asks, picking up a lipstick.

"Reese," I tell her.

"Oh, *her*." I can tell by her tone that she isn't a fan of Reese.

I look at my sister. "What's wrong with Reese?"

"Nothing's wrong with her. I just thought she was a little weird. That's all."

"There's nothing weird about Reese, Nat."

"All right! Calm down." She glares at me as if I am the one insulting her.

I walk away from my sister and pay for the jeans and sweater. There's no use talking to her when she's like this.

We hit a couple more stores, and I was able to get the majority of my shopping done. I ended up finding the perfect gift for my parents as well as something cute for Wes and Reese's apartment. I even bought Colin something funny, but for Jason, nothing was perfect enough. I wanted to ask my sister for her opinion, but I held my tongue.

We split a cab back to my place after shopping. Nat insists we stop by the corner market by my apartment.

"If I'm going to be living in that apartment for a week, I'll need to stock the fridge with food I like," she says as she continues to throw more items in the cart.

I keep my mouth shut and continue to follow her.

By the time we get back home, I'm exhausted. I put all of Nat's groceries away, and I watch her check out the place like she's never seen it before, even though she was literally here ten hours ago.

"What's this?" She points to Colin's cooler.

"Don't get me started with that." I laugh.

She makes a disgusted face and opens the cooler. "Is that beer?"

"It's not mine, Nat. The chair and the cooler are both Colin's."

I walk into my room and grab an extra pillow and blanket. I throw it on the couch, and my sister leans on one hip, arms crossed.

"What's wrong?" I ask her.

"Why can't I just sleep in the bed with you?"

"Because my bed isn't big enough for both of us," I tell her.

"You seemed to manage with all your boyfriends." She rolls her eyes.

"Well, you're not my boyfriend!" I shoot back.

"Jade, I don't want to sleep on that uncomfortable couch for a week."

"Then sleep at Mom's."

She disregards what I say and plops down on Colin's chair.

"Where's this roommate of yours?"

"How would I know?" I snap. I'm already tired and done for today.

"Jeez, Miss Grumpy." She shakes her head. Nat's phone starts to buzz, and she walks out onto the terrace, slamming the door behind her.

I let out a sigh of frustration as I plop down on the couch.

The front door opens and closes, and I hear Colin humming.

"Hey, roomie," I hear him say as he opens the fridge.

"*Hmm*," I say, feeling my eyes grow heavy as I stare blankly at the nearest wall.

"What's with you?" he asks, walking over to me.

I cover my eyes with my forearm and point to my sister.

"Who's that?" he asks.

"My sister, Natasha," I groan.

Colin grabs a beer from his cooler. "Oh shit, there's another one of you."

"Not funny," I whine.

He picks up my feet and moves them so he could sit down on the couch. "What's so bad about her?" he asks.

"Everything," I sigh.

Natasha opens the glass door and walks over to us. "Jade?"

"Yes?"

"Aren't you going to introduce us?"

Colin gets up and holds his hand out. "You must be Natasha. I'm Colin."

"Hi," my sister says shyly. My sister can be awkward when it comes to meeting new people. She really needs to get comfortable around someone before she lets her obnoxious side shine.

"How long are you in town for?" he asks her.

"Uh, for a couple weeks. Thanks for letting me crash on the couch."

Colin glances at me, and I nervously hide my face behind the pillow. "It's my pleasure," he says through his teeth.

Natasha's phone starts to buzz again. She rolls her eyes but heads back to the terrace.

"Thanks for informing me that we are having a guest live with us," Colin says.

"I'm sorry, but I didn't have a choice." I get up and walk over to the kitchen. "On the bright side, my sister bought a lot of food."

Colin walks over to me and pours himself some water. "Honestly, your sister doesn't seem so bad."

"Oh, she is." I chuckle. "She's exactly your type, Colin. She's bitchy."

He puts his hands up and shakes his head. "Not gonna happen."

"Sorry, that was Sean," my sister says, closing the glass door behind her.

Colin gives her a smile. Then, he gives me a look before walking into his room.

"So, what are you doing tonight?" Nat asks.

"I'm going out with Reese and Wes," I tell her.

"To a bar?"

I nod.

"Oh, nice."

Silence fills the air. Everything in me wants to just leave it there and walk away, but I can't do that. "Would you like to join us?"

"Sure, I guess," she says before walking away.

I smack my forehead and let out a deep sigh.

This will be fun.

CHAPTER 9

"One whiskey sour and—" I turn to Nat. "Do you want anything to drink?"

She shakes her head.

"That's it," I say to the bartender, leaning my hands against the smooth mahogany bar.

"Not drinking tonight?" I ask my sister as she stands uncomfortably behind me, ignoring all the people all around her.

"I don't drink anymore."

Reese comes from behind and pokes my shoulder. I grin and give her the tightest hug. "Thank goodness you're here!" I say in her ear.

Reese and Wes order a couple of drinks. I casually sip on mine as I wait for their drinks to be made.

Nat gives Reese a small hug, and I introduce her to Wes, who probably already got the scoop about Nat on the cab ride over from Reese.

"Where's Colin?" I ask them.

"He's working tonight," Wes tells me.

"He got a job?" I ask over the music.

"He didn't tell you? He's a bartender at Cave on 85th Street," Reese says. I didn't peg Colin for a bartender. I thought he had a day job because he's hardly home during the day.

We get our drinks and head over to a less busy area. Jason arrives ten minutes later, and I finally introduce him to my sister. She eyes him up and down but doesn't say much to him. Jason excuses himself to get a drink, and I follow.

"So, that's Natasha," he says before giving me a kiss on the cheek. I lean on the bar, letting out a tiny groan.

"What's wrong?" he asks, rubbing his hand on my lower back.

"I'm surprised you heard my tired groan over the music."

"I've got amazing ears," he says, handing the bartender his credit card.

I wrap my arms around him and give him a small kiss on his temple. "I wish you were staying in New York for Christmas and New Year's."

I feel Jason's arm wrap around my hips. "Me too, but I promised my family I'd be in Vermont for the holidays."

"When do you leave again?"

"What?" he asks. "I can't hear you."

"I thought you said you have amazing ears," I yell over the music. "I said, when are you leaving?"

"This Wednesday," he tells me.

I frown. "I'm going to miss you so much."

"I'll miss you more. Trust me," he says, squeezing my left hip.

"You better talk to me while you're there. I might need you." I smile, glancing at my sister.

"I'll try, Jade. My, um, parents are weird about using technology."

Nat walks over to us then and pulls on my arm. "What's taking so long?"

I point to Jason who is now grabbing his Corona.

"Where's Reese and Wes?" I ask, looking around the bar.

"How should I know?" she asks, already sounding annoyed.

I take a big sip of my drink, then I finally spot my friends on the dance floor. Jason, Nat, and I decide to hang by the bar, and I'm already in need of another drink.

"Are you sure you don't want a drink, Nat?" I say in my sister's ear. She nods. "Sean and I decided to give up alcohol. I think you should do the same," she says judgmentally, eyeing my second drink.

"Yeah, I'm good," I say loudly, already feeling the buzz that I love so much. Reese runs over to us and grabs my hand. "Jadeeeee, come dance with me. Pleeeease."

I laugh. "Let's go!"

I leave Jason and Natasha alone. Jason is old enough to handle my sister's questions. He's lucky though. The music is blaringly loud, so he might not hear them at all.

I glance over at them, and they seem to be getting along okay from the looks of it. If Jason can get along with my stuck-up sister, then he can definitely get along with everyone at Suzy and Noah's wedding. I smile to myself and continue to dance with Reese.

～

The next morning, I stare at my reflection through my bathroom mirror and let out a tiny sigh. I fix my Coffee Bean hat and apply some more red lipstick. Just as I am closing the tube, I hear a knock on the door.

"Yes?"

"I need to use the bathroom," Nat says.

I look at myself one last time, doing one of those three-sixty spins. I then open the bathroom door to find my sister wearing a thick red flannel robe.

"What were you doing in there?"

"Using the bathroom," I say unenthusiastically.

She mutters something under her breath that I pretend I didn't hear. I'm trying to block out my sister as much as possible. Dealing with her rigid ways has been exhausting. She complains all the time, and it reminds me of when we were both living with our parents. I'm trying to get into a joyful Christmas spirit despite my sister's attitude. I give her the fakest smile I can muster and head over to the kitchen to finish off the last of my coffee and peanut butter on toast. Before I leave, I grab my coat and open the front door.

"Natasha, I'm going to work."

I leave without waiting for a response.

~

The walk to work was brutal—cold and unbearable—but I was able to manage. I wave to Claire on my way in then head to the back.

When I walk in, I see that my boss and a couple of the other employees are having a conversation. We exchange our good mornings, and I make my way to the counter. The morning rush suddenly appears. Usually, I'm less than thrilled about having to deal with impatient and caffeine-addicted people. This morning though, I don't seem to mind. I guess I'd rather be in this warm cafe with the customers than in my cold apartment with my uptight sister.

After the rush fizzles down, I hand the register over to the new guy and decide to wipe down the tables.

"Jade, darling, how is your morning so far?" Claire asks me before swallowing a piece of her cookie.

"I've been looking forward to going back to sleep since the moment I woke up today." I give her an over-enthusiastic smile.

She lets out a laugh and shakes her head. "You kill me, Jade."

I fix my hat and pull out the chair across from her.

"What's wrong? You seem so down."

The last few weeks have been sorta funny. After my little exchange with Claire, we became friends. I guess she likes to listen to my problems the same way I like looking at the guy buying flowers across the street. It's a friendship that I'm really enjoying.

"My sister is in town."

"I'd assume that'd be a good thing, no?"

I nod, but my nod suddenly becomes a shaking *no*. "My sister is a lot to handle, and she's staying at my place."

"Ah, I see." Claire nods, and I wait for her to say more, but it looks like that's all she's got.

"Yeah, so I've just been a little stressed, and Jason won't be here for Christmas and New Year's," I sulk, glancing out the window. I watch the flower guy walk away with his bouquet of flowers and picture him handing them over to the woman of his dreams.

"Where will he be?"

"In Vermont, with his family," I tell her.

"From what you have told me about your family situation, why don't you just squeeze yourself with Jason and his family?"

I nod. "I would have, if he had invited me."

"There must be a reason why he didn't." Claire always sees the good in people, and that's one reason I like her so much.

"It's just going to be a long Christmas." I laugh nervously.

"Well, you can always come to my house for Christmas, my dear. I'd love for you to meet my grandson. He's an artist in the city and—"

But before Claire can tell me about her grandson, Wanda gives me a death glare, and I know my little therapy session with Claire has come to an end.

～

After work, I decided to walk to Jason's place. I know he's home because last night he told me he's not showing any of his clients any properties. He's leaving in a couple of days, so I want to see him as much as I can. I was able to snatch some of yesterday's bagels and an old butter container, which hopefully hasn't expired. I knock softly on his front door while holding the bagels, already attempting to take off my scarf. Jason opens the door, but I can see he's on the phone. He gives me a little peck, and I walk past him, putting the bagels down and taking off my heavy winter jacket.

"Yes, yes, yes, I know. And I will. Okay, okay." Jason mouths, *"I'm sorry,"* and I give him the okay with a simple smile. "You know what, Mom? I can't talk right now. My client just arrived, and I'm busy. See you soon. Okay. Love you too. Bye-bye."

I tilt my head to the side, somewhat confused. Jason comes over to where I'm sitting on his barstool and gives me a kiss on the cheek. "You brought over bagels!" he says happily.

"Jason?"

"Yes, Jade?" He smiles, grabbing a sesame bagel from the bag.

"Why did you refer to me as your client?" I cross my arms.

"When?"

"Just now."

Does he suffer from short-term memory or something?

"Does your mom not know about me?" I ask him.

"Oh, of course, she does," he stutters a little.

I squint my eyes. "So why did you tell her I was your client if she knew about me?"

"Because it was an easy way to get off the phone. If I told her that you stopped by, she'd want to talk to you too and we'd be on the phone forever."

I nod and watch as he grabs a butter knife from a drawer. I still think that the whole situation is a little sketchy, but I decided to let it go.

"Are you excited for Christmas?" I ask.

"Uh, yeah, I guess so. It's just so busy for my family and me," he tells me. "Trust me, I'd rather be there with you all Christmas." He smiles, pointing to his couch.

"Then why can't we? I hate Christmas too. We can hate all the busyness together." I smile.

Jason swallows and lets out a deep breath. "I wish I could, but I can't."

"Why not? You're an adult, right? You've celebrated thirty-four years with your family."

"Jade, please," he says, giving me a kiss on my forehead. "You know it would kill my mom. She's been dealing with... you know."

"Cancer?"

He nods, looking really sad.

"I'm sorry," I say, rubbing one of his shoulders. "You should be with your family."

"Thank you." He smiles.

I get up and walk over to the refrigerator. "So, Reese wants to go to that rooftop New Year's party at Kai's."

"That sounds fun," Jason says, taking a big bite of his bagel.

I shrug. "Yeah, I guess. Too bad I don't have anyone to kiss at midnight."

Jason looks up from his lap, and his eyes meet mine. "I hope you know that I feel terrible about not spending Christmas with you and—"

I cut him off. "Don't be!"

He laughs. "Let me finish. I feel bad, so I'm going to try my hardest to come home early so I can kiss those beautiful lips of yours on New Year's Eve."

My eyes open wide, and I practically run over to him. "Aww, really?" I say, wrapping my arms around his neck.

He laughs. "I said I'll try! Okay?"

"Okay." I smile, giving him a kiss on the lips. "So, she knows we're dating?" I ask him again, and he nods. It looks like he wants to end this conversation. Jason appears to be afraid of confrontation, so I drop it.

"But I want to give you something because I know we're not going to be seeing each other on Christmas." Jason smiles before getting up and walking into his room. I follow him and plop on his bed. I start to bite my nails. The anticipation and the fact that I haven't gotten him anything is killing me. This gift will say it all… How much does he really dig me?

"Jason, I feel terrible. I haven't exactly gotten you anything." I pause. "Yet!"

I move my bangs away from my eyes, watching him grab a box in his closet. Oh gosh, is he proposing? I then realize how crazy that would be and try not to laugh. I'm being ridiculous.

"It's no big deal," he says with a smile.

Jason then kneels down in front of me and looks into my eyes.

"Jason, are you proposing?" I laugh at my own joke, trying to lighten the mood.

But he doesn't laugh. He blinks a couple times then disregards my question. I guess he doesn't like to joke about marriage. Good to know.

He hands me the box, and I smile, pulling the silky ribbon apart. I open the box and see a simple sterling silver bracelet. I look up and smile. "Wow, Jason. It's gorgeous!"

"Really? I was nervous that you wouldn't like it." Jason then picks up the bracelet and attaches it to my wrist.

"Why wouldn't I?" I say, still admiring the piece of jewelry.

"Oh, well, you always wear brighter and more intricate things. This is just simple and—"

I cut him off by wrapping my arms around his neck. "And perfect."

He looks relieved, giving me a big toothy smile as he leans in for a kiss.

CHAPTER 10

"Jade! Can you please stop using my towels and then leaving them wet on the bathroom floor?" Colin growls, throwing the wet towel at me.

"Hey! I didn't do that." I walk over to the bathroom, pick up the towel, then hang it over the shower curtain.

"Okay, then can you please tell your annoying sister to stop using my shit?"

I ignore him but decide to follow him into the kitchen. "Why are you in such a shitty mood?" I ask.

Colin sits down at the kitchen table, and I do the same. We both simultaneously glance at my sister, who is having a heated conversation on the terrace.

"It's all this holiday shit," he says, letting out a long sigh.

"Tell me about it. I hate it too."

Colin runs his hand through his hair, and I can't help but stare at his perfect frown.

"When are you and princess leaving?" he asks.

"Tomorrow," I say. "Are you leaving with Wes in a couple days?"

He shakes his head no. I wait for a response, but I get none.

"So where will you be then?"

"Don't worry about it."

"Colin, I know we have our differences, but you can't be alone on Christmas."

"So, what are you saying? Are you inviting me home with you?"

I stare into his eyes then I glance at my sister. "I guess I am."

Colin lets out a laugh. "I'm gonna have to decline, but thanks, roomie."

"Will you at least be with us on New Year's?"

He nods. "I could never miss a rooftop party."

I get up and grab a Christmas cookie from the container on the kitchen counter. As I take a bite, he asks, "Will the forty-year-old realtor be there too?"

I look up from my cookie and roll my eyes. "He's thirty-four, and yeah. Well, I hope so. He's going to try."

"What do you mean *try*?"

"Well, he's going home for Christmas, but he said he'll try to come back to kiss me at midnight." I grin.

Colin laughs, leaning back against the chair.

"What's so funny?"

"Oh, nothing," he says calmly. He's still leaning back against the chair as he plays with the water bottle on the table.

"Colin. Spill."

"The guy just seems sketchy. That's all. Don't mark my words if you find something out."

I sit back down. "Wait, why do you think he's sketchy?"

"These walls are thin, roomie. I hear what you tell Reese, and I've met him too. He's just a little odd but don't let me sway you."

"Oh, trust me, you're not," I say as I nervously bite my lower lip.

Colin shrugs and gets up. He grabs the cookie out of my hand and shoves the whole thing in his mouth. I don't want to admit that he could be right, that the weird vibes I'm getting from Jason might be a bigger issue than I want to believe at this point in our relationship.

～

Later that day, on my lunch break, Reese squeals, "Two more days!"

I can't help but groan to myself as I glance from Reese back to the flower guy. I hear Claire say something to Reese, but I'm too focused on the flower guy's determination.

As soon as I introduced Reese to Claire, Reese has been joining us between her classes. They both partake in watching flower guy with me, coming up with different scenarios. Of course, in the midst of our therapy sessions, we make it a little game.

"Jade, why do you look so down?" Reese asks.

I take a sip of my latte. "I just have a lot of things on my mind. That's all."

"Like what?"

"More like who…"

"What now?" she sighs.

"He's just been acting weird."

"Has he left yet?" she asks.

I nod. "Yesterday."

"You can't be sad that he's choosing his family over you."

"Yeah, I know. Don't get me wrong, I love that he's a dedicated son and that he loves his family. But for a guy who loves his family that much, why can't he talk about them? Whenever I ask him about his family or his trip, he just stutters and gets really weird. I have a feeling he hasn't even told them about me, and he's lying that he has."

"He probably has a crazy family," Claire comments, breaking a piece of her cookie and plopping it in her mouth.

"Yeah, that's what I'm thinking. I know his mother was recently diagnosed with cancer."

"Oh, that's terrible." Reese frowns.

"I tried talking about it with him, but he can't wait to change the subject. It's just upsetting that he doesn't want to let me in more," I sigh.

"It sounds like you're really falling for this guy," Reese says, giving me a tiny smile.

I tilt my head to look at her. "Yeah, I guess so. He's just so sweet to me," I say, glancing at the bracelet he got me. "But do you think it's too soon in the relationship to already be falling?"

"Of course not, dear. I only dated my husband for three weeks before he proposed, and we were married for sixty years," Claire says proudly.

"Hey! I have an idea. Why don't you go to Vermont and surprise him?" Reese says abruptly.

I laugh. "That's funny. *You're* funny."

"I wasn't trying to be. Jade, you're really into this guy, right?"

I nod.

"So, go see for yourself if he has this crazy family."

"You can't be serious. I can't do that. I'm not going somewhere I'm not invited."

I look at Claire. "She's talking crazy, right?"

Claire looks at us and sighs. "That would be very bold of you."

"Ha, see!" Reese shouts.

"But very dumb, too," Claire says.

I give Reese an I-told-you-so look, and she sulks in her chair.

"I'm not going. I can't. I won't."

And with that, the conversation about Jason ends.

~

On Christmas Eve, Nat and I load up a cab full of unwanted things like candles, socks, and mugs. I couldn't forget those deep cleansing Bath and Body Works soaps that we all love to give as gifts either. Luckily, Reese and I already exchanged gifts, so I don't have to add those to the pile. But on the way to my parent's place, I couldn't help but think about how badly I messed up by not getting Jason anything. He shrugged it off like it was no big deal, but it is a big deal. It's his fault, actually; if he wasn't so weird and secretive, then I wouldn't have had such a difficult time picking out a gift for him. It's hard to know what to get him when I realize I don't know much about him.

"Hey, Nat?"

"Yeah?"

"How long into your relationship with Sean did you guys exchange Christmas gifts?"

Natasha looks up from her phone and looks at me. "Um, the first Christmas we were together. Why?"

"No reason," I say, ending the conversation. I look out the window and play with the zipper on my winter jacket.

I messed up.

～

Mom and Dad are waiting downstairs for us. I can already see the excitement plastered on my mother's face as the cab pulls over by the curb. They help us carry all the gifts and our bags. We take the elevator up to the twentieth floor and enter the place where I grew up. The familiar smell of pot roast and rosemary enter my nostrils, and I know I'm home. The apartment is small but very cozy. Everyone's inside, taking off several layers of clothing.

"Cold. Very cold outside," my mother says in her thick Russian accent. She gives me a kiss on my cheek, and I can hear the rest of the family in the kitchen.

One by one, my family gives Nat and me warm, welcoming hugs. After all the hellos, we all finally settled in the living room. I sit down by the fire, sipping on the hot chocolate my dad makes every year.

Eventually, we all take our places at the dining room table. My father and grandfather, of course, sit at the heads of the table. The others fill in around the table, including a few of my cousins from Ireland, my babushka (which is "grandmother" in Russian), my Aunt Taya (my mom's sister) and her husband, Uncle Ben. Nat and my grandma sit on either side of me. My babushka gives my hand a squeeze, and I smile. Then, we all say grace. Even though we're not religious at all, Uncle Ben is, so we say grace as a way of honoring him and my Aunt Taya.

Everyone begins making their plates. We pile our plates with pot roast, turkey, cooked potatoes, and my grandma's homemade cabbage casserole. Glasses of wine are also being poured. I'm usually a fast drinker when it comes to wine, so I have to keep reminding myself that I have a bunch of judgmental eyes on me. Everyone begins talking and laughing, but I remain silent. I'm just enjoying a home-cooked meal and the Christmas music playing in the background. I hear Natasha going off about Sean in one ear. In the other, I hear my babushka talk about how exactly she came up with this amazing casserole. *It is good, Babushka. It really is.*

"Well, his plane got delayed due to the storm," Nat tells everyone. "He really wanted to spend Christmas with all of us. Especially you, Babu," Nat says, looking at grandma. My babushka smiles and says how sweet Sean is in Russian.

I pour myself some more wine, and I can see my mother's eyes on me.

"Jade always loved her wine," my mother says.

And so it begins.

"Well, it's the Irish in her, Nadia," my father says, giving me a wink. I smile, taking another sip of wine.

Everyone helps my mother clear off the table except for my father and grandpa, who prefer to get served. My mother puts out homemade Christmas cookies and Russian tea cakes, which look like snowballs, and Vzvar, a ritual drink we have every Christmas Eve. And that's what my dad is pounding down as we speak. My father isn't really into desserts. His idea of fun is vodka and more vodka. By the end of the night, my dad is slurring on the sofa. Nat and I used to draw a white beard on him whenever he would finally pass out. That way, it looked like Santa Clause was at our house. Most people might find that cute, but we did that to mask the pain we felt—that our dad was just some drunk. Nat and I glance at each other then back at Dad, who laughs obnoxiously with one of my cousins. I know she remembers too.

My grandpa talks about the first time he met my grandma. This story has become a new Christmas Eve ritual. He tells this story because they met on Christmas Eve. He goes on about how desperately he wanted her attention which was why he ran for miles, chasing after the bus she was on. My grandpa was bold. He was brave because he took a chance at love. He ran all that way for a possible rejection. Luckily, she liked him back because if she didn't, then we all wouldn't be here right now. I glance at the bracelet Jason got me, and I can't help but think about the conversation I had with Reese and Claire. Shouldn't I also be as bold as my grandpa? Should I pay Jason a visit in Vermont? Maybe I should run to Vermont the same way my grandpa ran after that bus....

"Jade?" my mother says. I look up, and everyone is staring at me. "How's that boy you're seeing? Jason, is it?"

"Yes, and fine." I swallow, looking down at my bracelet again.

"I didn't know Jade was seeing someone," my babushka says.

I nod and smile at her. "Yes, I am."

"Oh, how nice! I'd love to meet him. Your sister told us she got to meet him as well."

"Yeah, we all went out for some drinks. It was fun, right, Nat?" I ask her.

Nat takes a bite of her tea cake and nods but doesn't say anything.

I get up and take my plate to the kitchen, dumping it in the sink. I stand there for a second, letting out a deep breath.

I grab my mom's Christmas sweater that she left on the back of one of the chairs, and I put it on before opening the sliding door to the terrace. The cold and brisk winter air enters my lungs. It's so cold that I can see the white smoke in front of me. I look around the familiar buildings around me and spot many Christmas trees through the windows. The sliding door opens, and I turn to find my Aunt Taya behind me.

"Mind if I join you out here?" she asks.

I shake my head no, and she smiles, standing next to me.

"Gotta appreciate the cold air when it's so stuffy inside," she says.

"Yes, exactly." I nod.

"It looked like you wanted to hide under that table when your mom mentioned the guy you're seeing."

I half-smile. "Was it that obvious?"

"You're a lot like me, Jade. That's exactly how I would have felt at your age."

"I've always been very open when it comes to relationships. Especially to my friends, but when it comes to my mother and sister asking, I just want to escape."

She nods. "I agree."

I look at her. "You do?"

"Why do you think I've been living with host families in America almost all my life? I always felt like an outcast, and when I had a chance to leave Russia and start my life in America with Ben, I did."

"I guess that's how I feel. My parents, grandparents, and especially Natasha, are so different from me, and they don't get it. I don't fit in here."

"You feel like you have to create your own family with friends or even boyfriends, right?"

My mouth drops open. She gets it. "Yes! How did you know?"

"Because that was me, Jade."

I laugh. "We have more in common than I thought."

Taya moves my frizzy hair away from my face and smiles. "More than you think."

Taya and I stay outside for a few more minutes until we can't bear the cold any longer. Everyone is in the living room, talking and dancing to the music.

I decide to leave the party and head to my room. It hasn't changed. My Marilyn Monroe poster is still here along with my precious autograph from Marc Jacobs, who I bumped into when I was in the city. I still freak out about that, by the way. I sit down on my twin-sized bed and glance at a funny picture of Reese and me in Coney Island. We waited in line for an hour to ride the Cyclone one summer. Reese was already sick from eating two caramel apples and the bumps and sharp turns of the rollercoaster that we were on turned out to be too much. We ended up leaving the amusement park to smoke her mother's cigarettes on her terrace. Good times.

I get up from my bed and grab a cute picture of Noah and me at Seabreeze Park one afternoon. He paid his sister to take really corny pictures of us. The photo stuck to my mirror is one where we are both behind a tree, but all you can see is our heads on each side. I have no idea what we were thinking. After Noah and I broke up a few weeks later, Reese and I moved into my apartment, so I didn't have time to redecorate my room. I shove the picture in my drawer, the place it should have been all these years, and I decide to go and enjoy my time with my family. I tried calling Jason before heading back to the living room, but, of course, he didn't answer. It goes straight to voicemail.

"Jade! Your sister was telling us about this new roommate of yours! I heard he's a real hunk. That's what the kids say now, right?" Aunt Taya smiles.

I let out a laugh and shake my head. "Oh yeah, he's cool. I guess."

"You guess?" My mother raises a brow from the couch.

"No, he's great, Mom. Perfect roommate," I say. I picture Colin's stupid grin as if he's overhearing this conversation. I sit down on the floor next to my cousin and put my hands out in front of me, feeling the heat from the fire.

My father is probably on his fifth drink by now, and nobody tries to stop him because nobody wants to fight on Christmas. I think about Claire and her offer, and I wonder how spending the holidays with her and her family would have been. I probably would have the best time. Aunt Taya hands me a glass of wine and gives me a wink. I thank her and take a big sip. My sister then puts on our traditional Christmas movie, *Frosty the Snowman*.

After the movie ends, everyone leaves except for my grandparents. There isn't enough room for all of us in this three-bedroom apartment, so I have to sleep in the living room. My grandparents get my sister's room because she has a queen-sized bed, and Nat gets my room because she has a bad back and can't sleep on the pull-out mattress. My mom makes the bed for me, then everyone leaves to go into their rooms. I'm left alone in the living room, but at least I have the fireplace near me. I call Jason one last time but still no answer. This time, I decided to leave a voicemail.

"Hey Jace, it's me. I just wanted to check in to see how your Christmas Eve is going, but you're probably so busy with your family." I breathe heavily into the phone. "Okay, well, when you get this message, call me back. Okay? Okay. Well, goodnight. Sweet dreams, babe."

I end the call and pull the covers over my head. This is going to be a long night.

CHAPTER 11

*C*hristmas Day.

I get up early, way earlier than I would have liked. My mother didn't pick the best curtains since they don't block out any sunlight. I let out a yawn, and I can already hear my mother in the kitchen making breakfast. I get up and stretch my body, feeling every bone in my back crack like a glow stick.

"Good morning, Jadey," my mother chirps.

"Good morning," I say quietly. I'm not a morning person, even when it's Christmas. I need coffee. I see that my mother has already brewed some coffee, so I walk over and pour myself a cup. I then glance over at the stove—bacon and eggs.

"Jade, can you grab me the bread from the fridge?"

I nod and do what I'm told. "How's Dad?"

Mom sighs. "Still sleeping. He was up a few times last night."

"I would be too if I drank that much."

"How did you sleep?" she asks, changing the subject.

"Fine. Better if I slept in my actual bed."

"You know your sister has a bad back."

"So she says," I say under my breath, but luckily my mother didn't hear.

My grandparents wake up soon after, and so does my sister. I guess they can smell breakfast being made. We all eat in silence, all of us glancing at the empty chair designated for my father.

"Maybe we should have waited," my babushka says.

"Mama, no, it's fine. I'll bring him his breakfast."

I finish the last of my coffee and food, then I get up and clear everyone's plates. I watch as my mother makes a plate for my father before disappearing into their room. Seconds later, she comes back with the plate still in her hands.

"He wasn't hungry," she announces. She then pours a glass of water and fetches some Tylenol from the cabinet. My phone starts to buzz, and I smile when I see Reese's name on my screen.

"Hey!" I say, walking on the terrace.

"Merry Christmas, Jade!" she squeals.

"You too, Reese!"

"Did you and your family open presents yet?" she asks.

"No, not yet. We aren't exactly in the Christmas spirit right now," I sigh.

"Your dad again?"

"Yup. I don't want to bring your Christmas down one bit, though." I laugh. "So, how has your Christmas been so far?"

"Great! We've already opened all our presents." She laughs through the phone. "Tyler woke us up literally at the crack of dawn."

"Did you get anything spectacular?" I ask.

"Just the usual stuff everyone gets." She laughs. "Have you heard from Jason?"

"Nope!" I say with fake enthusiasm.

"Oh," is all she responds with.

"I left a voicemail last night, so hopefully, he'll call to wish me a Merry Christmas."

"I bet he will. From the look of it, he seems like a nice guy. He also found a great place for Wes and me, so that says a lot."

I smile. "Yeah, you're right." I switch my phone to the other ear. "So, does anyone know where Colin ended up going?"

"Uh, I think he went home with one of the guys in his band."

"Really? It's *that* bad that he can't go home for the holidays?" I ask her.

She breathes heavily through the phone. "Yeah, his family did some fucked up shit to him," she tells me. "Oh crap! I have to go, Jade! I'll call you later." She hangs up suddenly. I'm used to Reese having to hang up suddenly when she's back home, so it doesn't bother me. I go back inside, but all I can think about is Colin being stuck with people who aren't his family on Christmas. Why couldn't he just spend his Christmas in California? He could have stayed with Wes and his family.

I decided to call Wes to wish him a Merry Christmas. It also can't hurt to find out a little more about Colin and why he was so reluctant to go home for Christmas.

"Hey, Jade! Thank you! Merry Christmas to you and your family as well!" Wes says through the phone.

I plop on the windowsill, glancing at the mirror hanging on the wall beside me as I run my fingers through my messy hair. "So, how's it going there? In California?"

"Can't beat the amazing weather."

"Oh, I bet," I say as I continue to watch the snow fall. "It's snowing right now, actually."

"Is it really? I've always wanted to experience snow during Christmas."

"You are not missing much." I laugh, playing with a Santa Claus decoration by the window. I soon let out a sigh, moving my eyes back to the falling snow. "So, Wes, do you know where Colin ended up going this Christmas? I was just curious."

"I thought he was with you."

"Wait, what?" I pull out a kitchen chair to sit.

He laughs. "Yeah, that's what he told me. I couldn't believe it because you guys always seem to bicker. I heard what happened at Thanksgiving."

I roll my eyes, recalling how annoying he was at Thanksgiving. "That's so odd that he told you that. I did offer, but he quickly declined."

Wes sighs. "Yeah, I don't know what's going on with him." Laughter is booming in the other room, but my eyes are focused on the white snow falling from the sky.

"But you're his best friend. Why didn't he just go home with you?"

"I offered, but he said no, swearing he'd never step foot in Cali ever again. He doesn't exactly get along with his family."

"So I've been told."

"Reese told you?" he asks.

I tilt my head, wondering if Wes and Reese know all about Colin's secrets concerning his family. "Well, she never told me what happened. Do you know?"

"I know a little. Colin is a really closed-off guy and never talks to anyone about what he's feeling. I pretty much know the gist of it."

"Would you be allowed to tell me?" I turn and see my sister entering the kitchen. She gives me a funny look. Knowing her, it's her way of telling me to get off the phone. Still, I quickly shift my eyes away from her and back to the window—the sound of cabinets shutting rattles my eardrums as I try to focus on what Wes is saying.

I then leave the kitchen to sit on the floor by the door to the terrace. I lean my back against the hard wall and perch my elbows onto both knees.

"Oh, I don't know, Jade. I want to. I know you'd never say anything, but it's not my business to share."

"No, I get it, Wes. I do."

"Yeah, it would really crush him if I shared his business. You know how he can be."

"Yes, I do." I chuckle.

"Before I met you and Reese, it was just Colin and me, and it took him a really long time to get over what happened. The Colin you see now is a new and improved Colin. A year and a half ago, he was angry, always drinking, and depressed."

"Wow, I had no idea."

"Yeah, I'd advise you to stay away from all of that and don't ask any questions concerning his family."

Wes and I talk for another couple of minutes. He tells me about the big surprise he bought for Reese and her family because they aren't celebrating Christmas together. Three big boxes of their favorite cheesecakes, made in Pennsylvania, were shipped right to their front door. I nod with a smile, pleased to know how amazing he treats my best friend and her family.

I get off the hardwood floor as I stare at Colin's number on my screen, wondering if I should just call him to see if he's okay.

He doesn't pick up, and I decide not to leave a voicemail.

I hear my name being called, and I make my way to the living room. It's gifting time.

My dad finally comes out of the room and plops on his side of the couch.

I received some clothes from my parents and a funny mug about shopping from my sister. The clothes I got aren't so bad. They're sort of understanding the style I like, but I'll definitely have to fix them and make them more me. The bracelet on my wrist dangles, making me glance at it every so often. It makes me think of my boyfriend— the boyfriend who won't return my calls.

After we open all of the gifts, we all get into our warm clothes and head out. Every Christmas, we always go to my mother's childhood friend's house. Her name is Alla. I don't mind though because it's a far drive to Upstate New York. And they live in a lovely home. The only problem is one Christmas, I got really drunk and ended up hooking up with their son, Ollie. And by hooking up, I mean I let him grab my boob, and we dry-humped for a little bit. Nobody knows, and my little secret with red hair Ollie will be forever locked up.

"Everyone, please be nice. Okay?" my mother says. Everyone moans "okay." Then, she turns to me, "Jade?"

"Okay!" I lean my head against the car seat.

꙳

Later in the evening, everyone finishes eating the feast Alla made. My eyes were glued to my food the whole time. I try my hardest not to make any eye contact in case I am met with one of Ollie's occasional winks.

Raspberry cheesecake, carrot cake, and Christmas cookies are served. Nothing intrigues me until Jason's name buzzes on my phone. I smile wide and head outside to their patio.

"Hey!" I say, closing the door behind me.

"Jade, hey. Sorry, my phone was off, and I was so busy."

"That's fine." I exhale loudly. "How's Christmas in Vermont?"

"Lots and lots of snow." He laughs.

"What are you up to now?" I ask, touching the cold snow that sits on the outside table.

"I'm, uh, taking a walk, actually. Can't drive anywhere because the roads are pretty bad from the storm. Needed to get away from all the craziness of the family," he says.

"I miss you," I sigh.

"I miss you, too, Jade. Merry Christmas."

"You too." I smile, glancing at the bracelet he got me. "So, do you think you'll be able to come out with me for New Year's Eve?"

"Uh, yeah. I said I'll try, Jade. I'll probably just tell my family I have a work thing."

"Or you can tell them the truth? You want to spend New Year's with your girlfriend." Now he's pissing me off. There must be something I'm missing.

It is dead silent as I wait for him to respond. Something's up, and I want to know what. Maybe I should have just listened to Reese and found out for myself.

"Yeah, I'll say that." He laughs nervously. "I hate to end the call, but I'm freezing my ass off outside."

"So, go inside, silly." I bite the tip of my finger.

"I'll call you tomorrow, Jade. I promise."

"Wait! Jason, can I ask you something?" I bite my lower lip.

"Yeah, sure. What's up?"

I play with the zipper on my jacket, sort of nervous to call him out. "Well, you've been acting sorta strange lately, and I don't want you to think that I'm some psycho girlfriend—"

"I don't think you're a psycho by any means." He laughs.

"Okay, then what's up?"

"I'm sorry, what?"

All I can picture right now is the confusion on his face as we speak.

"With your family, Jason! Every time I bring them up, you look like you want to die, and I feel like I'm this horrible secret." I glance at the closed door behind me, just in case anyone is overhearing my frustration with Jason.

"No, no, not at all, Jade. I guess you can say I kinda walk on eggshells when it comes to them, and I don't want to drag you into the drama."

"So, I'm not a secret?"

Silence.

"No, of course not." He is quiet yet again. All of a sudden, he lets out a laugh. "Jade, you're not a secret."

"Okay," I sigh, feeling relieved.

"Can we please not end this conversation like this?"

"Like what, Jason?"

"Mad."

"I'm not mad," I say, already sick of this conversation.

I hear him breathe hard into the phone, almost as if he is relieved. He wouldn't be feeling this way if this conversation was face to face.

"So, I'll see you soon?" he asks.

"Yeah. I hope so."

He continues to tell me how special I am and how happy he is to be in this relationship with me. I can't help but agree with him because I appreciate how sweet he is. Even though my gut is telling me something else entirely, I push it back, walking back into the warm house.

I text Reese, telling her that I heard from Jason and that it was a bizarre conversation. She texts, "*Just give him the benefit of the doubt.*"

Okay, Reese, I'll try....

CHAPTER 12

The day after Christmas, I decided to head back home—my home. Nat stayed at my parents' place, and I'm relieved. On the way back, I couldn't help but think how well the two days I spent with my family went. It was nice to see them and enjoy the holidays with them, and I especially liked the conversation I had with Aunt Taya. I forgot how similar we are, and it was nice talking to her like we used to when I was younger. Since we are both so busy, we never see each other unless it's a holiday.

But I needed to get back home. Wanda ended up putting me on the schedule for tomorrow, so I have all of today to find something for Jason.

After I settle in for a little while, I head out. I take the subway into the city. I want to venture into the huge Macy's instead of sticking to the tiny stores in Brooklyn. I feel like there's everything I can think of and more at this Macy's—eleven huge floors worth of stuff.

I make my way through crowds of people—most of them are in

line to buy or in line to return. I look through racks and racks of clothes, but I realize that it's stupid to pick out clothes for someone you haven't been dating for that long.

"Well, hello, young lady! Do you need help?" A woman who's wearing a Macy's tag approaches me.

I look up and smile. "Um, well, I'm just trying to find something for my boyfriend."

"Oh, fun!" she chirps. "Well, Macy's is the perfect place to find a gift!"

"Yeah, that's what I thought." I smile at her.

"These shirts here, the polo button-downs are twenty percent off." She points at the shirts with a smile. "Starting today, actually. A lot of the clothes will be on sale after Christmas." She leans in closer to me and whispers, "The clothes nobody wanted to give as Christmas gifts." It's like she doesn't want the unwanted clothes to hear her, as if the clothes have ears and will be offended if they listen to her talking shit. I'm not surprised by this woman. We *are* in New York.

"Uh, thank you, ma'am," I say, and I watch her walk away. I let out a deep breath and smile to myself, walking over to the rack she pointed to. I look through the shirts and decide to get him a nice work shirt. I push the negative thoughts out of my head, the ones saying it's too soon to buy Jason a shirt. I make sure to thank the nutty Macy's lady as I make my way to the counter.

I get his shirt nicely wrapped, and I'm happy; a brick, metaphorically, has been lifted.

∼

After shopping, I get some sushi and a spring roll to go. I eat them as I watch a crazy Lifetime movie with a glass of wine. I check my phone to see if Jason has texted me back, but the message is green, which means he probably didn't even receive the message. His cellphone is probably off.

I try to stay up to see if Colin will come home, but by the time one a.m. rolls by, I decide to call it a night.

CHAPTER 13

Colin ended up coming home a couple days later. I was sitting at the kitchen table one morning, reading a Vogue magazine and drinking a cup of coffee. When I looked up randomly, I saw him walk in. He did it so casually too. Then he immediately opened up the fridge and ate my leftovers. I asked him where he ended up for the holidays, but all I got was, "Oh, you know. Here and there and everywhere."

~

Later that day, Reese calls me to discuss our upcoming plans for New Year's Eve. "So, we'll pregame at your place at around nine and then head to that rooftop party at around eleven."

"Pizza and beer?"

"Yes. Of course."

I nod then end the call with Reese.

Reese is still at her parents' home on Long Island, and I'm stuck having to work this morning. But luckily, my shift is only from nine to three. I still have plenty of time to pick the best New Year's Eve outfit.

Claire is at her usual table by the window, with her cup of coffee and chocolate chip cookie. I give her a friendly wave and head to the back. A couple of my coworkers are scarfing down their breakfasts, and I say my good mornings to them. Wanda glares at me and motions me straight to the counter. The cafe is usually pretty busy, but today it's incredibly slow. Sometimes that can be great because I don't have to deal with frantic New Yorkers needing their coffee fix, but today, I'm really missing it. I'm bored. I'm tired of all the Christmas music, and I'm tired of staring at the few faces sitting and drinking their coffees. There is also nobody really interesting or intriguing to spy on—in a non-stalkerish way, of course.

I'm actually really excited for tonight. I've always loved New Year's Eve. Reese and I always stumble upon the best parties. I don't know how we do it, but it's like the New Year's Eve gods just look after us on this particular night.

～

Later that night, Reese points to the two cases of Coronas sitting on the kitchen counter at my apartment. "Wes is picking up the pizzas, and luckily, Colin got loads of beer."

"Okay, good. I got a bottle of vodka just in case he forgot."

Reese and I high-five as we walk in separate directions.

Colin plugs in his phone into the aux cord, and rap music blasts through the speakers. I walk over to him and cross my arms.

He glances at me and rolls his eyes. "What now, roomie?"

"Is it really necessary to play this?" I shout, and all of a sudden, he plays it even louder.

"What did you say?"

I give him the middle finger and plop on the couch. Reese sits next to me and leans into my ear. "Are Suzy and Noah coming out with us?"

I shake my head no.

"Is Jason?"

I shrug. "I'm not sure. I texted him the address to the party because I doubt he'll make the pregame."

Reese nods. "I have a feeling he'll show. Remember, Jade, the gods," she says, pointing up at the ceiling.

I smile, nudging her shoulder with mine.

A few people stop by, including a few of Reese's nursing friends, some girls Colin invited, and a few of his bandmates and guy friends. As for me, the only person I want is Jason.

I walk over to the bottle of vodka and grab it. "Shots, anyone?"

Randall, one of Colin's bandmates, approaches me. He smiles without showing any of his teeth. "So, you're Colin's roommate, right?"

I pour some vodka in a red solo cup because I don't have an actual shot glass. I gulp it down, and the face I just made probably isn't the most attractive. "Yup!" I shout. "Want a shot, Randy?"

"It's Randall, and okay!"

"Whatever you say, Randy." I laugh loudly.

Reese comes over and grabs my arm. "What are you doing?"

"Taking shots with my new friend, Randy. What does it look like?"

"It's Randall!" He rolls his eyes.

"I thought we agreed we wouldn't get plastered this New Year's Eve, and we'd actually go to the beach tomorrow morning without hangovers."

"Well, fuck that idea! Who even goes to the beach in the winter?" I laugh, taking another shot and pouring one for Randy.

Colin comes over to us and grabs the vodka out of my hand.

"Hey! That's mine, Colin!"

Colin takes a swig of the vodka and makes the same face I did. "Relax, Reese. Let her have some fun," he says, handing me back the vodka.

"Thank you, Colin! Oh, oh, Colin, wait! We've all decided that we're all gonna call Randall Randy from now on! Okay? Tell your friends."

Colin shakes his head and walks away, not wanting to involve himself in my nonsense.

"Since when?" Randy shouts, looking confused. He glares at me then follows Colin.

"What's his deal?" I laugh, hanging onto Reese.

"What's *your* deal, Jade?" she asks.

I don't know if it's just me, but she sounds super judgmental. "What do you mean?" I blink a few times, pouring myself another shot.

"Jade, you've already had three shots. I think that's enough," she says, grabbing the cup and bottle out of my hand.

"Wait! Gimme that."

Reese swallows my shot and hands the bottle to one of her friends. "Take this away from her, please."

"Whatever." I roll my eyes. "I just wanna have some fun. No biggie."

"Yes, biggie, Jade. Stop feeling sorry for yourself about Jason and man up!"

"Vodka is the only thing that will help me forget about Jason, and now I'm thinking about him. All because of you! You really are a buzzkill!" I shout.

Reese rolls her eyes and walks away from me. I stand by myself until I hear Randy come beside me. "I'm gonna forget you called me Randy because I think you're really fucking hot."

I turn my head over to him, and I glance at his spiky, greasy brown hair and dirty fingernails. "Never going to happen," I say under my breath and walk away from him.

Wes and one of his friends walk in with a bunch of pizzas. Everyone passes around thin plates and piles them with pepperoni pizza. I grab two slices, stuffing my face with both of them at the same time. I think I pissed off Reese because she refuses to look at me. I think Randy got the memo that I'm not into him because he won't look at me either. I'm not sure if the New Year's gods are looking down on us this year; this night is sort of starting off bumpy, but I guess I am to blame for that.

～

Around eleven, as planned, we head over to the rooftop party in the city. Picture a bunch of drunk twenty-somethings all riding the subway together—definitely a recipe for disaster. But luckily, we all make it in one piece.

The spaghetti straps on my dress keep falling down, and it's annoying. Why did I have to pick this skimpy white strappy dress? I know why—I wanted to impress my boyfriend, who I have a feeling will be a no-show. And I'm wearing heels. I only wear them to parties, and they hurt, but I am definitely loving the height they give me. On the way to the subway, I knew I should have changed my shoes, but it was already too late. These heels go great with my dress—perfectly, actually.

I tap Reese on the shoulder. "We're good, right?"

She nods, and I smile, joining her and Wes. Everyone lingers around the bar, and eventually, we all head upstairs to the actual party on the roof. I put my blouse back on, and I let out a deep breath, moving my wavy bangs away from my eyes.

"You look cold," Colin says beside me.

"Because I actually am."

"Do you want my jacket, roomie?"

I shoot my head over to him and raise a brow. "Are you seriously offering me your jacket?"

"Yeah. This is a once-in-a-lifetime offer."

I laugh. "Wow. Okay, well yeah, if you don't mind. I'm freezing my ass off."

He half-smiles, exposing his one dimple. "I would be too if I had no meat on my body," he says, taking off his sports jacket and handing it to me.

"Did you just insult me? Am I too skinny?"

"I didn't say anything. You did," he says before walking away.

I wrap the jacket tighter around myself, smiling and enjoying the smell of his cologne.

~

Around 11:50 p.m. I've already come to terms that Jason isn't showing. There's ten minutes left until the ball drops and the New Year begins. Everyone takes a glass of champagne, waiting eagerly.

"Nice jacket." I hear behind me.

I turn around and, lo and behold, Jason is standing in front of me with the warmest smile.

I let out a breath of relief before walking over to him and giving him a big hug. "Why didn't you respond back to me?"

"That's all you have to say? I came all this way to surprise you." He laughs.

I look down at my shoes and shrug.

"Well, if it makes you feel better, I called you twice, like an hour ago, but you didn't answer."

"Oh."

"Yeah." He continues to laugh. "You look magnificent tonight, by the way."

"I do?" I blush.

"You always do." He says, giving my cheek a kiss.

Randy walks past us, giving me another dirty look.

"What's his deal?" Jason asks, raising a brow.

I shrug. "I have no idea."

I grab Jason's hand, and I lead him over to where Reese and Wes are. Reese gives me a smile and points at the sky, and I love that it's our little inside joke. I nod in agreement and laugh.

"What's so funny?" Jason asks in my ear as he wraps both arms around my waist.

"Nothing. Nothing at all." I smile, giving him a peck on his lips.

Ryan Seacrest is hosting the countdown this year, and the whole crowd gathers around a large screen to watch. Jason and I grab another glass of champagne and wait for the countdown to begin.

"Ten!" Everyone shouts.

"Nine!"

"Eight!"

The whole crowd is yelling and hollering and clinging onto each other. Jason and I latch eyes, and my smile continues to grow.

"Five!"

"Four!"

"Three!"

"Two! "

All of a sudden, Jason grabs my face in his hands and plants the biggest kiss on my lips. I can't help but giggle in his mouth. We tap our champagne glasses then take a big sip. Wes and Reese release from their kiss and give us all hugs.

"Here's to another amazing year with you guys!" I shout, doing cheers with my friends, even Colin. The famous New Year's Eve song comes on, and we all start to slow dance and love on each other.

~

At around two a.m. the six of us—including Colin's girl for the night—decide to get burgers at some diner. They have the curliest fries I'd ever seen.

"Yo, man, Jason. I'm happy you ended up showing up," Colin says drunkenly. "My roomie would've had a meltdown." I shoot Colin a look, and he smiles, taking a bite of his burger. "She looked so sad, man. I was concerned that I would've had to kiss her at midnight."

"Well, that would have been a damn shame for me, and especially for Jade's lips," Jason says back to Colin.

I let out a laugh, feeding Jason a fry.

"I'm a great kisser," Colin says, finishing the last of his greasy burger. "Right, babe?" he says, leaning in and tongue kissing his girl right in front of us.

"Get a room," I say, disgusted before throwing a fry at them.

Reese lets out a laugh. She then takes the fry that landed on Colin's shirt and eats it.

"Don't mind if we do." Colin grins. Then he and his blonde lady friend get up and head to the bathroom in the back.

We all groan with disgust and agree that Colin has no class. This is still a family place, even if it is two a.m. and nobody is in here but us.

Wes and Jason give each other high-fives and agree that Colin is still the man. That just makes me even madder. He doesn't deserve to be called that, and poor girl, she can do better.

CHAPTER 14

I stayed the night at Jason's, and it was definitely worth the wait. I stretch my arms and legs, feeling his soft blanket on my naked body.

"Good morning," I say, feeling totally relaxed. With my eyes still closed, I let out a little yawn. "I'm meeting my friends at the beach in a few. You should join us, babe. It's like our little tradition."

I finally open my eyes and realize Jason is not next to me. I sit up, holding the blanket to cover my breasts. I look around the room and finally spot Jason. He is sitting on a chair by the window, in a fetal position, biting his nails.

"Jason?" I ask, feeling very concerned and confused. "Is everything okay?"

He looks up from his lap while ferociously biting his nails. "Uh, yeah. Actually, no." He lets out a breath.

"Well, can you at least come back to bed?"

He shakes his head then grabs my clothes from the floor and hands them to me.

"I'm going to make some coffee. You should get dressed," he says curtly before leaving the room.

I sit still for a few seconds, replaying the event that just happened. Did I do something he didn't like last night? I study my hands that are now pressed into the blanket, confusion overwhelming me.

After I dress and fix my bed-ridden hair, I watch Jason scarf down a piece of toast.

"Hey," I say, walking over to him and wrapping my arms around him.

"How did you sleep?" he asks me.

"What's wrong?" I ask him, skipping the nonsense conversation.

"Why don't you sit down," he says.

I nod, planting my butt on his kitchen chair. He hands me a cup of coffee, and I thank him before taking a sip. Even sipping the coffee hurts. I'm regretting my decision to drink so much last night.

Jason wipes some crumbs off his face. "I tend to eat a lot when I'm nervous." He then laughs.

"Well, why are you nervous? Did I do something last night?"

Jason runs his hand through his messy hair then sits down next to me, grabbing my hands. "No, you were great last night, Jade. But, I can't keep doing this anymore." He takes another deep breath, then exhales loudly.

"Doing what, Jason? You're scaring me."

Jason lets out a long groan. "I can't keep lying. It isn't fair to you."

I don't say anything. I wait for him to continue, but he doesn't. He just keeps rocking his body back and forth in his chair.

"Jason?" I say quietly. I put my hand over his cheek, but he quickly moves it away. *Oh gosh. This is bad.*

"I haven't exactly been honest with you about my life in Vermont."

I nod.

He sighs. "The family I mentioned to you aren't exactly who you think they are. My mom is sick, but all the craziness isn't from her."

I nod. "So, what is it then?"

"My family. My own."

I tilt my head, not understanding what he is saying. "What do you mean, Jason?" I ask, raising my voice. Now, I'm getting annoyed.

"I have a family back in Vermont that I've been keeping from you. I thought—"

"Wait, are you saying you have, like, a wife?"

He nods. "And two kids. Heather and—"

I put my hand up to silence him. I don't want to know what his kids' names are.

I stand up and begin to pace back and forth in his kitchen, trying to process this all. So, this whole time, this entire time we were together, he had this family. Well, it makes sense why he always seemed so secretive. I think back to all the times I felt like something was off, specifically when he was on the phone with his mother that one day I came over. "So, are you and your wife separated?"

He shakes his head.

"So, are you this perfect husband to your perfect little family in Vermont?"

"Yes and—"

I put my hand up again to silence him, and he nods, lowering his head.

"And you moved here…to what? Meet a twenty-something year old and have fun with her while your wife waits for you at home? Did you even move to New York intending to sell real estate?" I yell.

"Yes, yes, of course! And I did. I was just doing my own thing. No intention of meeting anyone." He pauses. "Then I met you."

"Oh, spare me the romance shit, Jason." I roll my eyes.

"Sorry," he says, looking like a sad puppy. But I don't care. I'm mad, furious.

"When you said you were bored, Jason, were you talking about Vermont or your fucking family?" I yell, smoke practically coming out of my ears.

"To be honest, a little bit of both."

"Are you leaving your family?"

"No. I can't. Everything was fine back home. My wife and kids were doing their thing while I was working here, but when I got home for the holidays, Marybeth informed me that she's pregnant."

"I'm out." I throw my hands up in the air. I walk into his bedroom to grab my things.

Jason follows me, attempting to talk. "Jade—"

"Jason, don't. Just stop. We're done. Don't call me or text me or stop by my place. We're so over," I say as I put on my shoes.

"If you could just let me explain more," he says, a tear crawling down his cheek. It makes me want to vomit.

"There's nothing to explain, Jason. You're a liar and a user. You used me. You came back knowing that Mary-whatever is pregnant. I'm not saying that it wasn't completely messed up to cheat on your wife and lie to me, but last night, you were able to push away all the guilt. Well, enough to sleep with me that is." I shake my head in disgust. "I deserve better, and your *wife* deserves better as well," I say as I open his door. "It only took, what? A month or so to finally tell me?"

"I needed to tell you because after the night we had last night, I realized I was falling in love with you."

I laugh. "Fall out of it because this is so over. Congratulations on the baby," I say sarcastically, throwing the bracelet he got me at his chest. I run down the stairs, not even wasting any time waiting for the elevator. I then call a cab and head to Coney Island.

~

Reese sends me the location to where she, Wes, and Colin are. My head is pounding, and I'm not sure if it's the conversation I had this morning or the alcohol from last night. I just need my friend right now.

As soon as I get out of the cab, I take off my heels and walk onto the cold sand. It's brutally cold outside. Whose brilliant idea was this again?

I see my friends sitting on a blanket, in their winter jackets. They're practically the only ones on the beach.

"Hey! What took you so long?" Reese asks as soon as I approach them. She eyes my outfit and tilts her head. "What's wrong?"

"He's married," I say quietly, still trying to process it all.

"Who's married?" she asks.

I hunch my back and frown, trying my hardest not to cry in front of them.

"Babe, grab the extra blanket," Reese says before getting up and putting her arm around me. She then gestures for me to sit down. She wraps the blanket around my body, and silence fills the cold air.

"The fucker is married, isn't he?" Colin finally speaks.

I nod.

"Wait, Jason?" Reese practically shrieks.

I nod.

"And he told you this morning?" Wes asks.

I nod.

"Are you okay?" Reese asks.

I finally shake my head.

"Oh gosh. I'm so sorry, Jade," she cries, giving me a long, warm hug.

"A wife and everything," I finally say. "Two kids and one on the way."

Colin opens his mouth, but Reese shoots him a look which shuts him down. I look at each of them and fake a smile. "You guys, I'm seriously okay. Really. We ended things. I said everything I needed to say, and I'm pleased," I tell them. "I just feel bad that the guy confessed his love to me."

"Fuck that guy's feelings, Jade," Colin bites out.

"Yeah, seriously, Jade. He lied to you this entire time," Wes adds.

"What did he expect? To have a wife in Vermont and a girlfriend in New York?" Reese sighs.

"Well, he got it for a couple of months," I sigh.

I thought I'd be sadder about this, but I'm not. I feel betrayed, I'll admit that, but I haven't cried as much as I should. "I guess the gods weren't looking down on us this year. Especially for me," I joke.

Reese moves a section of my bangs away from my eyes and shrugs. "Well, they only look down on New Year's Eve, not the actual day."

I let out a sigh of relief and laugh. But I know in my heart that this is going to take some time to get over.

SPRING

CHAPTER 15

Winter has officially passed. The weather is becoming warmer, allowing the leaves and plants to blossom again. I love springtime in New York. It is almost as if all the colorful flowers make the city brighter.

My shifts at the cafe have been keeping me busy. Everything in my life has been the same—well, aside from my love life. The liar and I are completely over, and by the liar, I mean Jason! Oh, right, that's his name; I almost forgot. I haven't spoken or talked about him for a month, and I don't care. Who's Jason?

My family was pretty surprised when I told them that we were over. I spared them the drama about the whole marriage thing. They'd probably think I just made it up anyway.

I've just been working a lot, and I decided to keep my spot with Claire at her table. My flower guy is continually buying his white flowers, and I'm going to more auditions. Oh, and I've been shopping…a lot. It's like my therapy—retail therapy.

Shopping has been a lot of fun, but what isn't fun is bumping into an ex. It happened two days ago. I was lazily walking down the street with a coffee in one hand and a shopping bag in the other when I saw him. I would think the city is so big that I'd never bump into any sort of ex, but stuff like this happens, especially to me. We made eye contact, and it took my breath away. I wanted to walk the other way, but my feet wouldn't move.

"Jade. Hi."

"Jason," I said, taking a deep breath.

"How are you?"

"Fantastic."

He scratches his chin. "I'm happy to hear that."

I gave him a thumbs up and an eye roll. I turn to leave when he lightly touches my arm.

"Wait, I just want to apologize for what happened. Honestly, I didn't want to hurt you."

"You didn't."

He nods. "You don't have to say that, Jade."

I shake my head. "Well, it's the truth, Jason." I try to walk away yet again, but he stops me.

"Before you leave, I want to make you an offer."

"An offer?" I raise a brow.

"You and me. Us. We were great. Amazing. Right?"

I don't answer, so he continues. "What I'm saying is that before I told you about my marriage, our relationship, our flow, our rhythm was bliss, and I want it back."

I shake my head. "Well, you can't have it back. It's over. We're over."

"But think about it, Jade. If I never told you, there was no way that you would have found out."

I find myself stepping back from the words he threw at me. As soon as I recover, I give him a dirty look. "Yes, I would have, Jason!" I raise my voice. "And that's just a cruel thing to say."

"Okay, I'm sorry, b-but the chances were slim. My wife and kids live in Vermont, and-and they are never stepping one foot in New York, Jade. Listen, can't we just go back to how things were? I miss you so much." I watch as he comes forward, trying to grab me, but I move before he can touch me. He frowns, and it looks like he's about to cry. Typical Jason, trying to be sweet in order to win me over. Not this time, *liar*.

"No, Jason."

"I have given you enough space, Jade! Please."

"Yeah, that's to be expected, Jason. We're broken up."

"I'm just going to say it. I want you to become my New York girlfriend even though I have a wife in Vermont."

"You're a sick man, Jason. Goodbye."

I turn the other way and immerse myself into the crowd. So, that's what happened. His New York girlfriend? He's out of his mind.

～

"You guys wanna stay in tonight or go out?" Reese asks as she looks through one of my magazines at the kitchen table. The four of us are all spread out in the apartment. Wes and Colin are watching a baseball game on the couch, and Reese is in the kitchen with me. My apartment is pretty small, so if we're all in the same room, it would feel super cramped.

"I got work in an hour," Colin responds.

"Oh damn, okay. So what do the rest of you want to do?"

Wes and I are silent. Wes' tuned into the baseball game, and I'm making a sandwich. It takes a lot of concentration to create the perfect sandwich.

"You guys are unbelievable," she huffs with frustration.

"Babe, it's up to you," Wes says in a monotone voice.

"Jade?" Reese says, watching me take the first bite of my turkey sandwich.

I shrug. "There's nowhere fun to go anymore. I feel like we've been to every bar." I swallow.

"Yeah, but we need to get out," Reese groans.

"You guys should come out to my bar," Colin offers.

I laugh. "I love how you say, 'my bar.' Like you own it or something."

Colin shakes his head and gets up from the couch. "I'm bartending till three. I'll try to give you guys some free drinks."

"You always say that, but when we come, you never can," I point out.

Colin disregards my comment and disappears into his bedroom.

My phone begins to buzz, and it's an unknown caller. Usually, I'd probably let it go to voicemail, but I recently auditioned for an off-Broadway play. I'll take the chance that it might be a possible telemarketer selling me insurance.

"Hello?" I say in my classiest voice.

"Sup, bitch!"

My eyes widen at the sound of the familiar voice on the other line. "Maude? Is that you?"

"The one and only," she squeals.

"Oh my gosh! Maude!" I say, practically walking in circles around my whole apartment. I glance at Reese and Wes, who are now cuddling on the couch.

Maude is a friend of mine. Funny story. I was using the bathroom in this hip bar in SoHo that Reese practically dragged me to. She was fighting with Wes and needed to "let off steam." So, five margaritas later, and I was impatiently waiting in line with thirty other impatient drunk females. When it was my turn, I headed to my designated stall. I closed the door, and I remember just standing still, feeling my incredible buzz and the pounding music hitting my eardrum from the other room.

"Hey, you! Girl with the green platforms."

I looked around, and I realized the voice was coming from the stall next to me. All of a sudden, I hear a banging on the stall wall.

I opened the door, and this extremely tall girl was standing in front of me. I was so shocked, I forgot to pee.

"What?"

"I like your shoes. I'm the person that checks out other people's shoes when I'm peeing. Is that weird?"

"No, no, not at all. It's only weird if it's like a fetish."

I laugh when I remember that this conversation took place in the middle of the bathroom.

"Oh gosh, no. I'm a shoe guru. True story."

"Well, I'm a clothes guru. True story."

And like that, Maude and I became friends.

"Yo! What's the hold up? I have to shit!" some lady with a pink pixie haircut said behind us.

For the rest of the night, I was with Maude. She told me her whole life story, and I was intrigued by every little bit of it—from her world-traveling past to her search for old billionaire men. Also, her actual name is Brittany, but she decided that Maude fit her better at a young age. She also said Brittany was too "basic."

Reese ended up ditching me and running back to Wes as soon as he called her. Back then, when they were like a year into their relationship, they were the most infuriating couple—infuriating, meaning that they always fought over stupid shit and then made up a few hours later. Reese and Wes are the opposite of every couple in this world—they skipped the whole honeymoon lovey-dovey stuff and went straight to complicatedness. Now, they are this perfect couple.

Usually, I'd leave with her or try to stay and meet a random guy. I'm not proud of it, but I was so emotionally numb from my breakup with Noah that I thought (and I emphasize *thought*) that it would be a good idea to just hook up with guys. I called those days my "slutty days." I skipped those years that every girl says she had in high school because I was in a committed relationship. I was nineteen, gimme a break.

At the time, Maude was twenty-four. I tried my hardest to come off as sophisticated because she was in her last year of college, and I was in my first. But then I quickly learned that Maude was just as fucked up as me—and everyone else in this world—so I didn't care how I acted.

Maude was a struggling model. A runway model, to be exact. She isn't "commercially beautiful." She's runway-model-beautiful—painfully skinny with a long drawn out face that's perfect for posing and looking hungry.

I told her all about my dream to be on Broadway. She listened and eventually offered to introduce me to her boyfriend at the time, Gustavo. She said he'd take some pictures for my portfolio someday. At the time, I never thought I'd ever consider becoming any sort of a model. I've always been cute, not pretty. And I never wanted to walk in my mother's footsteps with modeling, but Maude was so convinced that I'd be this fantastic model.

"You're not runway. Too short, but I can see you in a fucking magazine. With that rounded face and those huge ass eyes." Those were her exact words. I'm not kidding.

Later that night—I'd say it was probably around three a.m.—Maude and I went to her apartment. It wasn't all hers. Tom, her other boyfriend, was luckily out of town on business. It was a beautiful, sleek, two-bedroom loft on 87th Street. It had a view to die for, overlooking all of New York and Carnegie Hall.

Tom was so in love with Maude that he gave her a spare key to his place, to come and go as she pleased. Maude was lucky because, without Tom, she'd practically be homeless. Tom was just happy to get laid whenever he wanted. Still, he was always working, so that nice apartment overlooking all of New York was pretty much Maude's.

"So, how'd you meet this one again?" I asked, looking around the loft.

"I was dating his friend, and one thing led to another, and we started hooking up."

"How many boyfriends do you have?"

"Too many to count." She gave me a wink.

Maude's philosophy was that if she shared her vagina with a bunch of men, she'd have a place to sleep every night, good food, and the most important thing to her were the gifts. And when I say a bunch of men, I mean a bunch of *rich* men—men who had money burning a hole in their pockets.

Maude practically begged me to stay over, but I was feeling wary because I had only met the girl earlier that night. My gut was telling me to leave, but the alcohol was telling me to stay. The alcohol and my youth won, and I stayed. I followed Maude up to Tom's roof. It was covered in fall leaves and cigarette butts. We danced to crazy hip-hop that boomed from the apartment building over and took many pictures on Tom's polaroid. I still have those pictures somewhere.

"So, what do you say? Come out with me tonight. I'm only in New York for a couple of days," she says.

We stay on the phone for a few more minutes, and I practically leap into my room to find the best outfit. This isn't some regular night out. Maude never has normal nights; it's either go home with two rich guys and have a threesome or jump off the Empire State Building. Maude knows what fun is all about.

"So, you're going out after all?" Reese asks, leaning her body on my door frame.

"Yeah. Maude called," I say, scanning my entire closet.

"I heard," she sighs.

"Reese, you should join us! It'll be fun."

Reese walks over to my bed and sits down, hugging my throw pillow. "Uh, I don't know. I never exactly got along with Maude. We don't have much in common."

I take off my shirt and throw on a possible blouse. "So what? It'll be fun! Just come, okay?"

With a shrug, she says, "I'll pass, but thanks, Jade. I don't want to leave Wes all alone."

I stand still for a second, studying my best friend's face. "Are you sure?"

She nods then leaves my room. I guess she won't be helping me find an outfit….

I decided to wear my black and white striped knotted hem cami with matching pants. I think this outfit looks great on me. It really accentuates my waist thanks to the knotted tie in the front. I fix my hair, making sure I brush out all the knots, and apply more lip gloss.

"Look at you," Reese says, raising a brow as soon as she sees me. I do a three-sixty spin for the three of them and smile. I'm so excited!

"So, who's this Maude?" I hear Colin ask as I walk into the bathroom to apply more mascara on my lashes.

"She's Jade's college friend," Reese says.

"Jade went to college?" Colin asks just as I walk out of the bathroom, folding my arms.

"Yes, Colin, I went to college. *Surprise, surprise,*" I say sarcastically.

"Hey, I didn't say anything, roomie. You did."

I ignore him and grab my bag that's lying on the floor. "All right, guys, I'm out. Wish me luck." I smile.

"You and your Maude friend are welcome to stop by *my bar.*" Colin winks.

"Yeah, not gonna happen."

And with that, I leave.

CHAPTER 16

Maude is sitting by the bar with a martini in one hand. We lock eyes, and she gives me a grin before eating the olive off her straw.

"Wow, Jade! You're all grown up," she sings, pulling me into a hug.

"I have to say, Maude, your outfit is unbelievable!"

She's wearing a tight printed jumpsuit and beige heels. Her chestnut hair is tied in a tight high bun.

She nods in agreement and looks pleased.

"I had to step up my game," she says, playing with my shirt.

I sit next to her at the bar and order myself a glass of rosé while we wait for a table. Maude picked a fancy restaurant in the city. It's everything I'd expect it to be—a quiet atmosphere, expensive menu, and unfriendly hostesses pointing to the bar since every table is taken. There's even a waiting list to sit at the bar.

"Did you make a reservation?" I ask, taking the first sip of my drink.

She shakes her head. "Nope. But I always have connections, honey bun."

I smile. "Which waiter did you sleep with?"

"None." She pauses. "I gave the owner a hand job once." She winks. "Mr. Ronald Birkenstein."

Ronald, the owner, walks over to us. I'm immediately disgusted by his shiny, balding head and his chunky, short body. He gives us a broad smile, then he gives Maude a big ol' kiss on the cheek. I tilt my head to the side, leaning back to watch their encounter. He says something in her ear, and she begins to fake a laugh. I glance at his little sausage-fingered hand resting on her lower back. He says one last thing, and she gives me a look—the *follow me* look.

Ronald leads us to a small table in the back; a table people have been begging and waiting hours for. This restaurant received a fantastic review in the *Daily News,* so it's always packed. Anyone who is "hip" and wants to give off the whole "I like to eat fancy food that I can hardly afford only because it's the best in the city" vibe comes here.

"Gosh, I've missed New York." She laughs, scanning the menu with her dark, brown eyes.

The waiter comes by. Of course, Maude has to do her typical flirtation with the twenty-something year old who is probably a struggling student at NYU or Columbia. She bats her long purple eyelashes and puckers her pink lips.

"So, what wine would you recommend for my dearest friend and me?" she asks flirtatiously.

He goes into all the Chardonnays and Pinot Noirs on the menu. Maude is most likely only half-listening. After all, the three things Maude specializes in are fashion, wine, and men.

"We'll have a bottle of your finest Pinot Grigio," she says, resting her chin over her hand, exposing her long, manicured nails.

"So, tell me, how's it going in the amazing world of Jade?" she asks after the waiter leaves.

I shrug and smile. "Well, I've been working my ass off, and I'm always shopping."

"Ah, how I've missed those days. When I was your age, I'd sleep all day and party all night. Dick was flying everywhere, and I was snorting coke in dirty ass bathrooms." She squeals before continuing, "I'd buy the oddest and cheapest clothes I could find."

"Please tell me you still do that."

She grins. "I only snort in clean bathrooms now."

I laugh, taking a sip of my wine. "Touché."

"By the way, I saw you in that magazine," she says.

I cover my face and groan. "Oh gosh. I'm so embarrassed by that."

She reaches over the table and grabs my wrists, moving them away from my red face. "Don't ever be embarrassed by your art. You're the art, Jade."

"Thanks," I say quietly.

"I've never seen anyone look so damn hot in an acne ad."

"Really? Maybe I should just stick to acting." I laugh nervously.

"Oh, c'mon, Jade. You belong somewhere where people can see those eyes and your perfect cheekbones," she says, grazing her long finger along the rim of her wine glass.

I smile, looking down at my hands.

"Look up, my love. Thank your momma and those bright fucking stars for that face of yours. Right, Matty?" She winks at our waiter, who is standing by our table. He looks as if he is about to ask if we are ready to order. I look up at "Matty," whose name tag clearly says Mathew. Maude has a thing for giving strangers nicknames. I think she does it so they feel more relaxed around her. Mine was "green eyes."

We make eye contact, and I immediately turn back to Maude, giving her a look. This one is called the *why-the-heck-did-you-just-say-that* look.

Matty runs his hand through his black gelled hair and smiles, showing us his long white teeth.

"You don't have to answer her," I tell him with a smile.

"Fine, you don't. But Matty, Jade and I will be at Cave tonight. Promise us you'll come and buy my friend a drink?"

Great, that's where Colin works….

"Sure thing." He is talking to Maude but I feel him staring at me.

"So, you just assume I'm not seeing anyone?" I ask her as soon as Matty walks away.

"It's just a drink, Jade. It's not a big deal even if you *were* dating Prince Charming."

"You know I'd never date Prince Charming." I grin.

"So, tell me. Why aren't you dating anyone?" She raises her eyebrow.

"Every guy in this city is horrible. It's like they keep getting worse." I shrug. "You wouldn't believe what happened with the last guy I was with."

"Oh, please give me deets."

"Well, you'd actually be proud. He was a lot older than me."

She claps her hands. "Wow, look at you. My baby is growin' up."

I laugh. "But he was married."

"And that's a bad thing?"

"I forget who I'm talking to," I say, moving my wavy bangs away from my eyes.

She pours herself another glass of wine and tops off mine as well. "Hey! It's the best of both worlds."

"Not for me. He totally lied about it and didn't confess until after we had sex. He admitted to having a wife and babies in another state."

"Wow, so he's a daddy also. Cute."

"Not cute." I laugh. "Pathetic."

"Well, Jade, you can thank me for leaving Europe and coming back to see you. It seems like you need my company after what you've been through."

"So that's where you've been hiding," I say.

"More like temporarily living."

"What exactly brought you there?"

"A little bit of *this* and *that*. But mostly my modeling and a scumbag named Gabriel."

I frown. "Oh, I'm sorry."

"Don't be! Please." She laughs. "Sometimes, I meet a guy and think that he's different, but they are all the same. Just narcissistic pricks with raging hormones and small dicks."

"Well, I am happy you're here. Seeing you is exactly what I needed to get out of my funk."

"Then I'm glad." She nods. "Also, I think this will help too." She reaches through her expensive Chanel bag and hands me a tiny baby blue gift bag.

My jaw drops and I gasp. "Maude! You really didn't have to."

"Oh please," she says, giving me a shoo-shoo. "I saw it in this small boutique when I was in Milan, and I thought of you."

She hands me the gift bag and my cheeks hurt from smiling so wide. Our food finally comes out, but Maude and I haven't even touched our steaks yet.

I open the bag and see a beautiful pair of earrings. They are emerald green, pear-shaped rough-cut edged with—

"White topaz," Maude says, reading my mind.

"Maude, these are so—"

"Glam?" She winks.

"Completely," I say, touching the green diamond.

"I knew you'd like them. They match your eyes."

"You really didn't have to."

She puts her finger over my lips and shakes her head. "Wear them in good health, my beautiful baby green eyes."

"Thank you so much, Maude." I am so touched by her thoughtfulness, I have to tell myself not to cry.

"You're so very welcome." She winks, watching me take off my three-dollar hoop earrings to put on the new pair of earrings.

"*Ahh*, they look so good on you." She claps her hands.

I move my hair away from my face, pushing the stubborn strands behind my ears.

"What do you think of Jade's new earrings?" she asks Matty as soon as he approaches our table.

"I think Jade's new earrings are very classy," he says, giving us an awkward smile.

I laugh, making eye contact with Maude, who's laughing as well.

"Yes, Matty. Classy is the perfect word," she says, cutting into her steak. "Would you be a doll and fetch me some of your most expensive ketchup?"

～

Maude and I share an Uber over to Cave. I insisted on paying for the Uber because Maude was generous enough to pay for dinner even after I had insisted on helping. Somehow, Maude is able to get us inside, and we were able to skip the line. I have no idea how she does it. Cave is already packed, and it's only ten-thirty.

"I actually know one of the bartenders," I say in her ear.

"Bonus!" She says cheerfully as we approach the bar that is already crowded with people.

"Which one?" she asks, looking around.

"Him!" I yell over the music. I point at Colin, who's shaking a drink he's making.

"Cute! Old boyfriend?"

I shake my head. "Roommate."

She bites her lip. "Even more fun."

"Not what you think," I say with a disgusted face.

She grabs my hand and leads me to the section of the bar where Colin is standing. I eye him up and down before he knows I'm here. His dirty blonde hair is messy but a good kind of messy, and his biceps are flexed from shaking and making drinks all night. He looks happy. He's even smiling and laughing with the other bartenders and guests.

We make eye contact, and he smiles, exposing one of his dimples.

"Thought you weren't coming," he says as he's handing a girl a White Claw.

"Changed my mind."

"Who's your friend?" he asks.

"I'm Maude." She grins.

"Aren't you gonna introduce me to Maude, roomie?"

"Oh, right. Maude, remember how you mentioned that all men are narcissistic pricks with raging hormones? Well, here you go. One in the flesh." I point.

"Well, I did say they also have small dicks. Do you have a small dick, Jade's roommate?"

"I think we both know I don't, but I guess you'll just have to see for yourself," he says confidently over the loud music.

She lets out a schoolgirl giggle, and my jaw drops. Is he really flirting with her? I've never seen Maude react this way towards a member of the opposite sex.

"Alright, stop it." I shake my head in disgust. "That's Colin by the way." I say to Maude who is looking at him appreciatively.

"Oh, c'mon, roomie. Do you feel left out?" he teases.

"No, you guys are just grossing me out."

Maude puts her arm around me and gives me a kiss on the cheek. "I'm sorry, baby. How 'bout a threesome?"

~

The next morning, Reese, Wes, Colin, and I share a table at a local breakfast café on Surf Avenue.

"She said what?" Reese says, letting out a laugh.

Colin finishes the last of his coffee and shrugs. "I'd be into it. Just without Jade."

"Then that's not a threesome," Wes points out.

"Yeah, no shit, Sherlock." I roll my eyes.

"Oh wow, is roomie pissed that I don't want to have a threesome with her?"

"Actually, I'm pretty relieved." I groan. "And besides, you aren't even Maude's type."

"Oh, please. She couldn't get enough of me last night. She's freaky as hell."

"And off-limits," I say.

"How long is she here for?" he asks, adding more mustard to his eggs.

"Did you not just hear me?" I ask, feeling very annoyed.

"I did. I'm just not gonna listen," he retorts before taking a sip of his water.

"For the peace of this friend group, please don't sleep with Maude. There are other vaginas you can stick your penis into," Reese says nonchalantly, cutting into her waffles.

We all stop eating simultaneously and look straight at Reese, who is by far the most prudish of us all.

"What?" she asks innocently, her tiny mouth full with waffles.

Everyone is shocked into silence, and the conversation about sleeping with Maude ends abruptly.

CHAPTER 17

There comes a time in everyone's life where a close friend of theirs starts to drift away. In my case, it started when Reese and Wes became friends with other couples. They would drink wine in each other's apartments and play Scrabble or Pictionary. They're all playing house, pretending they're married, eating fancy cheeses, and smelling their wine before they taste it. Like they have any idea what they're doing. I randomly stopped by their apartment one evening while one of these couples' nights was happening, and that was when I knew.

It's a Friday night, around nine. Ever since I became single again, I haven't been doing much. So, a typical Friday night for me is made up of drinking wine and watching reality TV. Alone.

Tonight is different though. Different meaning that Colin is home. He's usually working or performing somewhere with his band.

I pour myself a glass of white wine and grab the bag of sourdough pretzels that has been lying on the counter. I hear Colin in his room, strumming his guitar.

As I am halfway through the pretzels and finishing off the last of my wine, Colin comes out of his room. He then plops on his lazy boy, shirtless.

"Do you mind putting on a shirt?" I groan, looking away from his chiseled tattooed chest.

"Don't pretend you don't like what you see, roomie."

I turn up the volume on the television, disregarding what he said. He grabs a beer and practically drinks the whole can in seconds.

"Is this what you're doing tonight?" he asks me.

I nod.

"Pathetic."

I look at him. "Oh please, I don't see you doing anything so spectacular."

"Yeah, you're right," he says, playing with his empty beer can. "We should do something about that."

"We?" I raise a brow.

"Yes, we."

"What do you have in mind?" I ask, pausing the television.

He stretches his arms in the air, then he clasps his hands behind his neck. "Call Reese and Wes."

"I did."

"And?"

"No response."

Colin gets up and goes into his room. I unpause the television and shove some more pretzels in my mouth.

Colin walks back out and says, "So, let's just stop by there."

I laugh. "No. They're busy."

"So? They always show up here unannounced." Colin puts on a black t-shirt and rolls his eyes. "All right, fine. I will pay them a visit myself. Have a good night."

I shut off the television and groan. "Fine! You call the Uber though."

~

Colin and I walk up the few flights of stairs in complete silence. All I hear are the sounds of my strappy sandals hitting the concrete stairs.

Once we make it to their place, I knock a few times. As I am waiting for them to answer, I glance at Colin. His hands are shoved in his grey pants, and his dirty blonde hair is sort of messy. I hear him let out a huff, and instead of waiting for someone to answer the door, he decides he wants to try to open it himself by using the spare key they have allowed us to have.

"Colin!" I glare as I watch him open their front door.

The door finally opens and…there they are. Three couples sitting and drinking wine. They all simultaneously look at Colin and me, and all I want to do is leap out of here as soon as possible.

"Jade! Colin, hey." Reese lets out a nervous laugh.

"Colin insisted we just show up here, but that was obviously a bad idea. We can go since you're busy," I say, giving Colin a look.

He rolls his eyes. He then walks over to them and helps himself to a handful of chips on the coffee table.

"No. You guys can stay," Wes says, handing Colin a beer.

Reese gets up and motions for me to sit next to her on the couch. I mouth "sorry" to her. She gives me a smile while shaking her head.

"Well, we were just about to play some Charades," Reese tells us, giving one of the girls a high-five.

Everyone introduces themselves to us, but they do it in an odd way. They present themselves as a couple, and not as individuals. They say their names together and then they announce how long they've been together for, like it defines them or something. So, everyone just assumes that Colin and I are also a couple.

"Oh no, I'm single," I say. "Not at all dating that imbecile."

Colin lets out a laugh. "I'm not exactly her type, Kat. Jade's into the married ones," he mocks.

Kat and Tim, who have been dating for four years, look confused. I shake my head angrily, about to explode on Colin when Reese stands up and hands everyone a card.

"Everyone knows how to play Charades, right?" Wes asks.

"I'm not playing. I'll watch," I say.

"Oh c'mon, roomie. Don't leave me hanging here without a partner."

Reese and I make eye contact, and I sulk, looking down at my card.

Each couple takes a turn and acts out whatever is on their card. Everyone is laughing and hollering and having a good ol' time. Everyone that is, except me.

When it's my turn, everyone's eyes are on me. I fiddle with my hoop earrings as I think about what to do.

"Jade's an actress." Reese smiles.

"Yeah, this shouldn't be too hard, roomie."

I sigh and begin to act out a person shopping at a grocery store. Colin guesses a few things but doesn't get it right.

"Ten more seconds!" Reese shouts.

Suddenly, one of the girls yells out time, and I'm standing in front of everyone in silence. It's like my feet are glued to the floor. I look over to Colin who is finishing his wine.

"That's okay, Jade. You'll get it next time. Who's next?"

"Are you serious, Colin?" I say, finally speaking.

"What?"

"That was literally the easiest thing to guess." I cross my arms.

He puts his hands up. "Sorry, roomie. If it was really that easy and you acted it out well, then I would have guessed it, right?"

"Oh, so it's my fault?" I glare at him.

"No, it's mine," he says with a hint of sarcasm.

"Can you guys stop?" Wes says.

"She started it, man."

I sit back down and look over at Colin, whose eyes are glued to his phone.

Abruptly, Colin gets up from the floor and says, "All right, guys, this was fun, but I'm out."

"Wait! Where do you think you're going?" I ask him.

"I have plans," he says.

"You can't leave me here, Colin!" I glare at him. Then I look over at Reese, who looks sad and a bit angry.

Colin walks over to the door, completely ignoring my pleas. I rush over to him and practically throw myself onto him.

"I'm sorry, Reese. I'll call you tomorrow," I say as I follow Colin out the door.

"You couldn't have been more obvious," he says, laughing at me once we start walking.

"There was too much love and too many couples in one room."

"Agreed."

"So, what exactly are your plans?" I ask.

"I'm going to head to some small Getty my buddy invited me to," he says. "Honestly, Jade, you can just go home. You got out of that horrid couples' night, and now you can go back to what you were doing earlier tonight." He pauses. "And besides, it's not really your vibe anyway."

"Don't tell me something isn't my vibe," I say. There must have been some bite to my tone because Colin's eyes widen in shock.

"All right, all right," he says, putting his hands up.

I follow him a few blocks over to Greenpoint, and he tells me that his band manager/friend is hosting a little party at his place. As soon as we get to his friend's apartment building, I realize I'm already exhausted. I'm sort of regretting my decision to come when I hear the loud music playing and smell the marijuana in the air. I follow Colin like a little lost puppy when we walk into the small studio apartment. Colin slaps a few people's hands, mostly his bandmates and their girlfriends. Oh, and Randy. The weird guy who hit on me on New Year's Eve.

"Jade! I told Colin he should invite you to more things," he says, pretty drunkenly. "Might I say you look *gooood*." He laughs obnoxiously.

Colin walks over to us and drapes his arm around my neck. "Yo, Randall, I'm gonna steal Jade and get her a drink." He then leads me over to the table filled with bottles of booze, pouring me a cup of vodka mixed with something else.

"Thank you," I say with a nervous laugh.

"What are roomies for?"

"Saving you from getting hit on by a loser, apparently."

He lets out a laugh, and I laugh as well, taking a sip of my drink— my extremely strong drink, might I add.

"Jesus, Colin, what is this?"

"You don't like it?" He smiles, taking a sip of his beer.

I shake my head and grab the beer that's pressed on his lips. I then hand him my drink.

"Thank you," I say, taking a sip of his beer.

Colin lets out a laugh and downs the rest of my drink. Then he squeezes the red solo cup and throws it on the floor.

"Aren't you the toughest…" I raise a brow, not bothering to finish my statement.

"And you're just seeing that now?"

A few people approach Colin, and by a few people, I mean three girls. I leave him alone so he can do his thing. But now that means I'm left alone, trying my hardest to avoid Randy as much as possible.

"Was at your place a couple days ago. You weren't home," Randy says, sitting next to me on the couch. I guess I didn't try hard enough to avoid him….

I nod.

"Band practice. I play the bass. I'm pretty good. You should hear us play sometime."

"I have," I say, looking around the party.

"You're lying," he says, and I realize that he's a lot drunker than I thought.

"Do you think that impresses me?" I resist the urge to roll my eyes. *Why didn't I just stay home tonight?*

"What?"

"I said, do you think it impresses me that you play in some shitty band with my roommate?"

"Hey! We are not shitty!" he slurs.

"Whatever you say, Randy."

"It's Randall!"

～-

The following day, I wake up pretty early and decide to make some pancakes. My smile quickly turns to a frown when I open the refrigerator door. "Colin! Why do you always put the empty carton of milk back in the fridge?" I yell, throwing the empty carton away and pouring myself a glass of ice water.

"Hey, Jade."

The second I hear that voice, I turn around, and it feels as if my heart has stopped beating for a second.

"Maude?" I ask in disbelief.

"The one and only," she says quietly.

"Don't tell me you—" I say, pointing at his room.

She nods with a frown plastered on her face.

"Wha-what? How did this happen?" I ask her.

I glance at her outfit. She's wearing nothing but a little tube dress. When she sees me staring, she puts on the sweater she is carrying.

"I think I texted him last night."

"You *think*?" I raise a brow.

"Yeah, I was on this really shitty date, and we were texting, and one thing led to another. I mean, you can't blame me, Jade. You're not blind. He's really fucking hot."

"Do you want some coffee?" I ask, choosing to disregard what she said.

She shakes her head. "I should probably go. One rule I always stand by is to never hang out at the dude's place I just slept with. I'd like to leave before he comes back." She nervously laughs.

"Wait, he's not home?"

"No, I heard him leave early this morning," she says.

"Let's just grab some breakfast," I say to her, knowing she wants to leave my place as soon as possible. I also know that I'm first going to find Colin and give him a piece of my mind.

～

I text Wes while getting into the cab, asking him where Colin is. I'm not mad at Maude. Heck, I pity her for getting swept into Colin's web of bullshit. I'm not even mad at Colin. I'm disappointed and betrayed. The one thing I asked Colin not to do, he goes and does it. Did he hope I wouldn't find out? And to think I was actually having a good time with him last night. Then he went behind my back and was talking to Maude the whole time.

We aren't in the cab for long before I spot him. I ask the cab to pull over. He is sitting at a table at one of the cafes near our place...with another girl. *Wow.* So, he decides to ditch my friend after sleeping with her just hours before to go on a cute breakfast date with a high ponytail wearing brunette in a yoga outfit.

I grab a newspaper from a stand by the door and roll it in my hands. I tell Maude I'll only be a couple of minutes.

Then, I find myself at Colin's table, making eye contact with Colin's date while simultaneously smacking his head a bunch of times. He looks perplexed and disoriented until he realizes it's me. He then grabs the rolled-up newspaper out of my hands.

"What the fuck?" he says, throwing the newspaper on the table.

"Maude? Really? After I literally told you she was off-limits."

Colin looks at me and then at his date. He puts his finger up to silence me, and I swat it away, crossing my arms.

"I'm sorry," he says to her. "This is my roommate. We'll just be a sec," he says, grabbing my wrist and pulling me over to the side.

"What the actual fuck, Jade?" He glares at me as if I were the one in the wrong.

"Oh, don't you glare at me, mister."

"Can't you see I'm with someone?" he says.

"What about Maude?"

"What about her?" he asks.

"You slept with her, and now you're on a date?"

"Yes. So?"

"What about her feelings, Colin?"

"What about them, Jade? It was just sex. We agreed on that. I'm sorry, I'm not going to marry your friend."

"Why did you sleep with her anyway?" I ask him.

"She texted me and literally asked if I was down to fuck."

Jesus, Maude.

"I told you not to and you went behind my back and did it anyway. Why?" I can't help how disappointed I sound.

"Can we please have this conversation later? I'm sorta busy," he says, looking over at his date, who keeps glancing over at us.

I cross my arms. "Whatever, Colin. Just when I thought you were a decent fucking person, you go and screw it up."

"Yeah, I guess so, Jade. Have a good day," he says.

"You too!" I yell, giving the middle finger to his back as he walks away from me.

I let out a frustrated breath, and I realize that I am blinking back tears.

"Are you okay?" Maude asks me as soon as I'm back outside the cafe.

I nod. "Yeah, no. I'm good."

She grabs my hand and intertwines our fingers as we walk down the sidewalk. "I guess I'm just a sucker for blue eyes and large tattooed hands."

"Yoga pants must be a sucker too."

CHAPTER 18

"Are you still mad at me?"

I look away from the television. A rerun of *Friends* is playing with the volume on low. Colin relaxes in his chair and lets out a sigh of comfort.

"I said I'm not," I say curtly.

"Okay, but you seem irritated," he says.

I get up from the couch and throw a bag of popcorn in the microwave. This one is caramel and sea salt flavored. A bottle of rosé is sitting perfectly on the counter, so I grab a glass from the cabinet.

"Drinking on a Sunday night?" he asks. I don't need to look at him to know that he's probably raising an eyebrow at me.

"It's not just some random Sunday, Colin."

"What is it then?"

I open the microwave door and dump the popped popcorn into a big bowl. I savor the smell of sweet corn filling my nostrils. Tucking the wine bottle in the crack of my arm, I head back to the couch. "It's *Love Match* night," I tell him.

"*Love Match*?" he asks, sounding confused.

I nod, taking a handful of popcorn and shoving some in my mouth. Colin reaches over and grabs some of my popcorn as I pour myself a tall glass of wine. Maybe I should just drink from the bottle….

Colin seems to have read my mind. He snatches the bottle out of my hands and takes a big swig.

"It's this dating show that Reese and I always watched together when she lived here. And it just happens to air on Sundays. So, we'd do this," I say, pointing at my wine and popcorn.

Colin mutters something under his breath, then he gets up from his chair, and walks into his room, leaving me alone. It's the first Sunday he's actually home, so I understand why he's pissy that I'm hogging the television.

The theme song to *Love Match* starts to play, and I turn the volume up, singing along to the cute theme song. Richard Right comes onto the screen and shows the audience the pathetic singles searching for love. First, is a guy named Harry. He's thirty-three, still lives with his mom, and finds it very difficult to meet a woman who's okay with that. Four women are brought onto the show, and each one is crazier than the next. I finish the last of my wine then pour myself another glass.

Colin comes back into the living room then and grabs the remote sitting next to me before plopping down on the couch. He switches the channel and turns on some hockey game.

I blink a couple times, shooting my gaze in his direction. "What are you doing?"

He looks at me. "Watching TV."

I glare at him. "I was watching something." I grab the remote from his lap and put my show back on.

"I don't want to watch that shit," he huffs.

"Well, tough shit."

He doesn't respond to me. His eyes are glued to his phone. One of the girls is complaining about Harry's manners on their date at this Italian restaurant. I glance at Colin, who apparently, is starting to actually watch the show. I can hear him muttering under his breath about Harry and the girls.

~

Twenty-five minutes later, and he's hooked.

"You're wrong. He's not going to pick Bethany. I bet he's going to pick the other girl," Colin argues.

I shake my head. "No way, Colin! The other girl cares that he still lives with his mom, but Bethany doesn't."

"Okay. I'll bet you ten bucks he's not going to pick Bethany."

"All right, fine," I say, shoving more popcorn in my mouth.

Colin takes a swig of wine before grabbing a handful of popcorn.

"Reese always agreed with me, by the way," I tell him.

"Well, Reese doesn't have a mind of her own, and I do."

I sit up and turn towards him as a commercial for Chili's plays on the screen. "Admit it, you actually like this show."

He looks at me and shakes his head. "Nah. I'm just bored. Have nothing else to do."

"Oh, please. You love it!"

"The only thing I love is annoying you." He half-smiles at his own comment.

"Whatever you say." I laugh, playfully tapping his shoulder.

I stand on my feet and try to walk past him, but he kicks his legs up, blocking my pathway.

"Do you mind?"

"What's the magic word?"

"What are you, five?" I laugh.

He rests his hands behind his neck and stares deeply into my eyes.

I turn the other way, but all of a sudden, I feel his large hands around my waist, throwing me on the couch. Before I know it, I am on my back. He climbs on top of me, and his face is inches away from mine. Neither of us says a word; all I can hear is the faint sound of a pillow commercial in the background and Colin's loud breathing.

"Whoa there, what did I just walk into?" Reese says.

Colin gets up and moves over to his chair. He plops down as if nothing happened. I gradually sit up, trying to wrap my head around what just happened between Colin and me. Did we just have a moment? A moment I wasn't expecting at all….

Reese and some guy I have never met before are standing by the door. They're both wearing nursing scrubs. I make eye contact and give them both a smile.

"We were watching *Love Match*," I tell her. "Right Colin?" I'm still flustered, but my words came out surprisingly steady.

He nods but doesn't say a word.

I wonder, if Reese and her friend never barged in, what exactly would have happened with Colin?

Reese takes off her jacket. "And that's why I'm here."

She walks over to us, and her friend follows. "This is my friend, Jake. He's in my class and loves this show."

"It's the best." Jake laughs nervously.

"Hi, I'm Jade." I smile, watching him sit down on the floor next to Reese.

Jake gives me a friendly smile and a quick wave.

I can't help but admire his nice looks and muscular body. I'm a little suspicious as to why Reese brought him to my place. However, I wouldn't be surprised if she tells me he's in her class and she thought I might like him.

"Where's Wes?" Colin asks, finally breaking his silence.

"Work," she tells him. "I think he might stop by later."

"So, you like this show?" I ask Jake.

He nods with a smile. "Oh yeah, it's great. Super entertaining. Reese told me that it's like your little tradition to watch this show together."

"Aww, you said that?" I grin, looking at Reese.

Reese laughs and gets up, grabbing two wine glasses from the kitchen. She pours herself and Jake a glass.

"So, Jake, is your boyfriend coming over as well?"

Everyone in the room stops talking and looks over at Colin.

"Colin! Jake is not gay." Reese looks both angry and mortified.

"Oh, I just figured, if he watches this shit…"

"Weren't you just watching 'this shit' earlier with me?" I cross my arms.

"Yeah, and I hated every single second of it."

"You're such a liar," I sigh. Turning to Jake, I say, "Sorry for my rude roommate."

"No, it's fine." He laughs. "I'm as straight as they come."

Colin rolls his eyes then leaves us, closing his bedroom door behind him.

"I don't know what got into him." I shake my head.

"Who cares?" Reese says as she takes a seat in Colin's now empty chair. Jake then gets up and sits next to me on the couch. He smells so good, like lavender mixed with honey. He seems pretty laid back as well, considering how he handled Colin's comment. We casually glance at one another as we comment on each contestant and drink wine.

~

The next morning, Reese calls me on my way to work. "What'd you think of Jake?" she asks.

"I knew it," I sigh.

Reese laughs. "What? I thought maybe you'd like him. He's really sweet and actually single."

"Then I guess we have a lot in common."

"Besides the sweet part," she teases.

I sigh. "Yeah, you're right. I'm quite bitter."

"Well, if you're curious…he's interested."

I switch my phone to my other ear as I open the long door to Coffee Bean Express.

"How did you know I was interested in him?" I raise a brow.

"Oh, please, Jade. I watched you flirt with him all night."

I laugh. "Okay, fine. He was cute. Not necessarily my type, but he was definitely cute."

Wanda shoots me a look; we're technically not supposed to use our phones when wearing our uniforms in the cafe. It makes customers feel unwanted or whatever.

"I gotta go. Talk later."

I put my Coffee Bean hat on and begin sweeping the dirty floor behind the counter. I watch as my coworker makes a customer a drink and listen to the sound of the espresso machine rattle.

Wanda comes up behind me and gives me a hard tap on my back. I turn around to find her wearing her typical annoyed expression. Next to her, is a short blonde who I've never seen before, wearing an apron and a hat.

"Jade, this is our new trainee, Violet Sanchez." Wanda stands between us, making the awkward introduction. "And Violet, this is Jade Everly. Brandon left, so she's all ya got."

I look at Wanda and shake my head. "I love the positivity, Wan."

She gives me a wink then walks away.

"I actually just transferred from another Coffee Bean Express, so I don't need much training," she tells me. "And it's pretty self-explanatory. The espresso machine is over there and so is the blender. Always be nice to the customers, *blah, blah, blah*."

I lean my body against the counter and cross my arms. "Good, because I try to do as little as possible here."

She blinks a couple of times before letting out an obnoxious laugh. "I like you." She continues to stare at my face while stretching out each word that comes out of her mouth.

"Thanks, I like me too," I joke.

Violet plays with her long curly blonde hair as she fiddles with the stack of cups behind her. It's so blonde that I wonder if it's natural. She's pretty short, shorter than me, with a thin waist and toned legs. She also has caramel-colored skin and dark brown eyes.

"So, why did you transfer to a different Bean? You must really like it here."

She smiles. "I just moved from Queens, so I figured it'd be easy to just transfer. I needed a job as soon as possible."

"And you decided to move to Brooklyn?" I raise an eyebrow.

"Well, I'm an actress, and I was able to find a place near the subway. So it's easy for me to commute to the city and most of my friends live in this borough."

"Oh, so you're my competition?"

Her eyes open wide, and she smiles. "You're an actress too?"

"Why do you think I'm working at this shithole?"

"I heard that," Wanda says as she walks by.

"Yeah, don't care," I call out.

Violet nods and takes a sip of her water. "Well, if you're my competition, then I'm screwed."

"Oh, please. You're gonna make me blush," I say. "Have you gotten any auditions recently?"

"Here and there. It's been pretty slow, especially with moving and everything. My main goal is to land a soap opera on some Hispanic network." She pauses, then starts to scan the coffee shop. "This place is so empty compared to the one I used to work in."

I turn my head and shrug. "Yeah, the coffee sucks here, and there's a Starbucks right down the street."

"You're too funny, Jade." Violet grins. "Do you ever do improv?"

"Improv? No."

"I go every Friday night. I actually run the whole thing, and it's amazing. Think about it, ten or so struggling actors all in one room. It's spectacular."

"Here in Brooklyn?"

She nods. "Why don't you come tonight? It's on Saint Kays Street. Ya know, on the corner where the new McDonald's is?"

I shrug. "I don't know, Violet. Improv has never really been my thing."

She grabs my arm and gives it an encouraging squeeze. "Come, and I'll prove you wrong."

∼

Later that night, Colin, Wes, and Reese are all sprawled on the couch watching a stupid sports game on TV.

"You look cute! Where are you going?" Reese asks as soon as I walk out of my room.

"Oh, nowhere," I say nonchalantly. "So, who's playing?" I ask them. I want to change the subject immediately because I've always made fun of people doing improv. They all turn towards me with a suspicious look in their eyes. I guess I've never been one to be interested in sports. "What?" I ask.

Colin gets up and walks past me. "She's probably going on a date with some loser, and she's too embarrassed to tell us," he says, grabbing a couple of beers from the fridge.

"Really, Colin? That's uncalled for." I should be used to his candor by now, but lately, he's been extra rude.

"Hey! If that's what you're into, then I support ya, roomie." He gives me a wink before handing out the beers. Then, he sits back down.

"Are you going on a date?" Reese asks me, ignoring Colin's comment.

"No, not exactly," I sigh.

"What about Jake? I gave him your number."

"You're going on a date with the male nurse?" Colin laughs obnoxiously.

"I said I wasn't going on a date." I shake my head at him.

"Then, where are you going?" Wes asks.

"Well, I met this girl at work, and she invited me to participate in a little improv."

Reese laughs. "Why didn't you just say that to begin with?"

"I was embarrassed."

Colin finishes his second or third beer then crushes the can. "Yeah, I'd be embarrassed too if I were her." He burps. So classy.

Reese hits the side of his chest and shakes her head. "Don't listen to him. Have fun."

I nod then stand up. "How do I look?" I ask them. Colin opens his mouth, but I quickly walk away. I'm not in the mood to hear his insult. I decided to wear my black ripped skinny jeans, my collared floral shirt—tucked in, of course—and my favorite black boho style hat I got for ten bucks at this rad vintage shop.

They don't understand my fashion. And they never will.

I have to take the bus, and I realize that not having a car has been super inconvenient. The bus is consumed with weird people and many odd smells, smells I don't want to even talk about. I'm always surprised by the amount of filth on buses. Bus stops are pretty aggravating as well. The bus drivers only stop at their designated bus stops, and not when people ask them to stop. I know they are required to do this, so it's not their fault, but it is still a hassle. Unluckily for me, the improv place is quite a stroll from the stop.

Walking down the streets of Brooklyn at night isn't my favorite thing to do. I walk past a used phone store. It has hundreds of phones and electronics displayed in the large windows with bright white fluorescent lights. I then walk past a bagel shop with a strip club next door.

I follow Violet's directions, but I'm a little suspicious because it seems to be leading me down an alley.

"Hey, Violet—"

"Jade! Hey! Are you coming?" she says through the phone.

"Yeah, I think I'm here, but the directions you gave me are a little sketchy."

She laughs. "Oh yeah, I should have told you that. Just follow the directions. I promise you won't be killed."

I walk through the alley, jumping and walking around dirty puddles of water until I find the address. I reach a red door that is covered in black spots due to the red paint chipping away. The door opens, and a pale skinny guy rushes past me, completely startling me.

"Sorry," he says under his breath.

"Is the improv being held in there?" I ask him.

He pulls a cigarette out from his jacket pocket and lights it between his lips. Then he nods, exhaling a large amount of smoke into the air.

I open the door and turn my head, giving the smoking stranger one last look.

I walk down a long dimmed hallway, following a sign that says "improv bitches" with an arrow. I find it pretty quickly because the loud music and laughter are echoing in the hallway.

"Jade! You came. Yay!" Violet says, giving me a long tight hug. "Everyone thinks it's sketchy when they come for the first time," she says, releasing me from our hug.

I follow Violet around the room as she tells me all about what they do every Friday night.

"Yeah, so we got permission to use this room on Friday nights," she says. "All we needed was twenty people to be allowed to use this room, so we are so blessed to finally have enough people."

A couple of people approach us, and I introduce myself like it's the first day of school. Everyone's pretty chill, but it does seem a little cliquish. Also, Violet is the only person I know, and she's the leader, so she's running around like a chicken without a head.

So, I decided to sit down in one of the chairs and wait for something to begin.

"Hey, new girl."

I look up from my phone, and a girl with short pigtails gives me a small smile. I notice she is holding two soda cans.

"Violet said you might want this," she says, handing me a can.

"Thank you." I smile.

"I'm Alex."

"Jade."

Alex plops down next to me and lets out a sigh. "I've been doing improv for a few months."

"Are you an actor?" I ask her.

She nods. "I've been in three episodes of three different television shows, and I play the hell out of the good girl next door, and the girl who sits quietly in a classroom."

I laugh. "Have I seen you in anything?"

"Well, that depends." She pauses. "Have you ever watched a scene and didn't focus only on the main characters?"

I tilt my head to the side, pondering this.

"Then probably not." She smiles.

"So, who usually comes to this?" I ask, eying the room full of loud people. I turn and see the cigarette guy walking in and talking to Violet.

"People like you and me. Actors who are most likely struggling and need practice, I guess."

"Then I guess I came to the right place," I say. "I do mostly theater, but I've been venturing in—"

"Porn?" a girl says, taking a seat next to Alex.

"I'm sorry." Alex laughs. "That's Raven. She has no filter."

"I heard the word theater, and it led me to this seat," she says.

I take a sip of my coke and smile. "It's nice to hang with people like me."

"You weren't in drama classes growing up?" Raven asks me.

"Oh, I was, but it seemed like I was the only one who actually took it seriously."

Raven laughs. "Oh, that's how we feel." Raven's unique look catches my attention. She's a perfect mixture of Winona Ryder and Selena Gomez.

Violet stands in the middle of the room, and I realize that all the chairs—including the one I'm sitting on—form a large circle. The cigarette guy hands her a microphone then he slumps back down in a chair across from me.

She taps the microphone a couple of times and lets out a loud laugh. Whose brilliant idea was it to give Violet a microphone?

"Hello, my fellow thespians," she sings. "I'm Violet, which ya already know."

Everyone shouts, and she laughs, giving us a cheery three-sixty spin.

"We have a newcomer. Someone who I work with."

Oh, that's me.

"She's a great actress." Violet pauses. "Well, I assume she is. I've never actually seen anything she's been in but based on how she dresses and her quirky personality, I believe she's truly great. So, Jade, why don't you stand up and introduce yourself." She pauses. "Please tell us all why you're here."

Everyone's eyes are on me, but the only eyes I see bleeding into mine are the light blues sitting across from me. The mysterious cigarette guy with bleach blonde army-cut hair.

"Hey, guys. I'm Jade Everly, and I was born and raised in this very city. I've been acting since I was small, and I've done some commercials, theater shows that held only ten people in the room, and I've dabbled in modeling." I move my hair away from my face and give everyone a small smile. "Oh, also, I'm thankful I met Violet."

"We love you, Vi!" I hear Alex yell.

Violet gets up and gives everyone a dramatic bow. She takes the microphone from my hands and gives me a reassuring nod, letting me know that I did a great job. I sit back down, and his blue eyes are still staring at me.

"So that was Jade. Thanks, Jade. As you can see, nobody is shy here, right?"

Everyone starts to holler and yell, and I can't help but do the same, stomping my feet and clapping my hands.

"Jade, just follow along, okay?"

I nod and watch as everyone starts doing their thing. They start with some breathing exercises then they move on to making all those weird sounds to strengthen their vocals.

A few people get up and start to act out different scenes. Some are scenes they made up, and others are ones that Violet has given them, including some famous scenes from movies like *Titanic* and *Dirty Dancing*.

Afterwards, we all take a ten-minute break, and I realize that I'm actually having a really great time. I'm able to let go of my nervousness about making mistakes and have some fun. I am at the snacks and drinks table when Violet comes up to me.

"Jade, this is Montgomery," Violet says.

"Monty," a deep voice says behind me.

"I think Monty is the only one you haven't met yet." Violet smiles. "He's a bit shy."

I bite my lip and smile as well. "I thought no one here was shy?"

"I guess I'm the exception." He rubs the back of his neck, exposing a rose on the bottom of his thin arm.

"Well, if it wasn't for Monty, we wouldn't be doing this right now," Violet says, hanging onto Monty's body while his arm is wrapped around her waist. They make a cute couple.

He gives her a kiss on her head, and she giggles. "He was my right-hand man when trying to find the best place to hold our improvisation nights."

"Oh, wow, that's amazing," I say.

Another guy comes over to us and practically pulls Violet away, leaving Monty and me alone.

"I'd ask you what you've done, but you already mentioned it," he says.

"I'm surprised you actually listened." I laugh nervously.

"I listen to everything," he says. "I'm a sucker for a good line."

"Writer?"

He nods. "Screenplays. But my day job is fetching coffee and danishes for my boss, who's an actual screenwriter."

"Well, I make coffee for a living, so…no judgment here." I laugh.

"Then I guess we have something in common."

"Yeah, I work at—"

"Coffee Bean Express? Vi mentioned she works with you."

"Now, I officially believe that you're a good listener."

Monty laughs, shoving his hands into his grey skinny jeans. He bites his lip piercing, and I notice that's not his only piercing. There are two on his nose and one on his eyebrow. He even has a neck tattoo. I'm into it. And he's tall, way taller than me.

"Jade! Come here!" Violet calls.

I turn my head and see that she is with Alex.

"Go. Have fun." He smiles.

I grin and nod before walking away. I take a few steps and glance back, only to find that his eyes are still glued to me.

～

I get home around midnight with a huge smile plastered on my face. I open my front door, and I'm surprised to see Colin sitting at the kitchen table with his guitar and notebook splayed out.

"Hey," I say, opening the refrigerator door and grabbing a water bottle. "Where's Reese and Wes?"

He closes what I'm guessing is his songbook and puts his pen behind his ear.

"Dinner and probably that new bar."

I down half of my water and sit down next to him, leaning my elbows on the table. "And you didn't join them?" I raise an eyebrow.

He shrugs. "Wasn't in the mood, and besides, they probably wanted alone time anyway."

I nod. "So, what have you been doing all night?"

"This," he says with a scratchy voice, gesturing to his notebook and guitar.

"Are you expecting anyone?"

He looks at me and laughs. "No, Jade. I'm content with just myself tonight."

I finish the last of my water then let out a yawn.

"How was improv?"

I smile. "Wasn't what I expected."

"Is that a good thing?" he asks.

"Very. I met a lot of great people. People like me."

"So, weird and moody?"

I gently hit his arm and chuckle. "Good night."

CHAPTER 19

Violet and I became fast friends.

We went from being just coworkers who made small talk to actually hanging out outside of the cafe. Sometimes, we'd even meet for breakfast before our shifts start.

I am at this cute cafe a couple of blocks from Coffee Bean, waiting for Violet. She's usually never on time, but I don't mind. I like to sip on my coffee and admire the people that walk past. Since I am sitting at one of their outdoor tables, it makes it that much easier to people watch.

Violet gives me a wave and a smile as she rushes over to my table, a tad out of breath.

"I thought you were gonna stand me up," I joke.

Violet sits down and lets out a sigh before picking up her menu. "I'm so sorry. It took me forever to get a cab."

The waitress then comes over to take our order, and Violet and I both order their vegetable omelet.

"Cheers to omelets and orange juice without the liquor because we are mature adults that have work in an hour," Violet sings, tapping her glass against mine.

Our food comes out pretty quickly, and we both moan after taking our first bite.

"What's better, this omelet or sex?"

I tilt my head to the side. "That's a hard question."

She laughs. "Yeah, I know. I figured it'd be."

～

The next night, I am sitting on Violet's cushy loveseat listening to Violet and Alex singing along to some hip-hop song on the stereo.

It's around nine o'clock, and we decided to stuff our faces with loads of Chinese take-out and beer.

"Lexie just texted me. She said she's on her way to Cave."

What's up with people and Cave?

"Really? That early?" Violet asks, dipping her egg roll in duck sauce.

"Yeah, she wanted to get ahead of the line, I guess," Alex says.

I take a sip of beer and sigh. "Do you guys want to go there?"

"Yeah, it's the hottest club right now. You don't like it there?"

"I do, but it's just so loud and always crowded."

"That's every club in the city," Alex points out.

"And my roommate happens to bartend there," I say nonchalantly.

Violet stands up and lets out a shout. Since she was in the middle of eating, a bunch of food flew out of her mouth. Luckily, none of it landed on me or Alex. "No way! Can she get us in?"

"*He*, and I'm not sure."

"Well, I can't ditch Lex," Alex says, then she turns to me. "You haven't met her yet. She's usually a regular at improv."

I nod. "Is anyone else coming?" I pause. "From improv?"

Please say Monty, please say Monty!

"Uh, I don't think so," Violet says.

"Oh, too bad."

"Yeah, people are flaky and busy." Alex shrugs.

"What about your boyfriend?" I ask.

"Whose boyfriend?" Violet asks.

"Yours."

Violet and Alex look at each other and laugh.

I look back and forth between the two of them, completely confused. I figured she was dating Monty because they were all over each other that first night. I didn't have the guts to ask her because I was scared she'd tell me he's been her boyfriend for years. I have tried to let the thought go, but I can't seem to do it. I'm so curious about him. He's so different from any of the other guys I've met.

"Um, what's his name?" I say, pretending that I don't remember. Jeez, I'm pathetic.

They continue to stare at me until Alex suggests, "Robby?"

I shake my head. "The one with the bleached blonde hair," I say slowly.

"Monty!" Violet shouts.

"Yeah! Him," I say, giving them a small smile. "Montgomery."

"Oh gosh, no." Violet laughs. "Why in the hell would you assume that?"

I shrug. "You two seemed cozy with each other."

"I'm like that with everyone." She then gives Alex a kiss on the cheek just to prove her point.

They start wrestling with each other on the couch, shouting and acting drunk.

"Oh," I say. "You guys never—"

Violet opens her mouth to say something, but Alex gets up and quickly points her finger in Violet's face. "Don't lie, V!"

Violet crosses her arms and leans on the couch cushion. "There was that *one* time. We were drunk! It was at this Christmas party. It happened once." She pauses. "Fine, twice. Maybe three times."

Gosh. Was it *that* good?

"But it happened like a million years ago! We're only friends. He's one of my best guy friends."

"Yeah, seriously. I can't believe you guys hooked up." Alex shakes her head in disgust. "They could be brother and sister."

"Yeah, definitely a mistake," Violet says, finishing the remaining lo mien.

"Oh, okay. I was just curious," I say quietly.

"Why? Are you interested?" Violet asks, raising her eyebrow.

I laugh. "No. Not at all." You'd think I'd be a better liar by now, but nope….

"Oh, okay, because he's sorta taken."

Oh, great. Of course he's taken. This is just my luck….

"Chelsea." Alex rolls her eyes.

"You don't like her?" I ask.

"She's a prissy little bitch, that's all," Alex says. "They've been dating for like three years."

"On and off," Violet adds, clearly annoyed. "He's always sad and then mad and then sad again. He's always running back to me for advice. It's exhausting. But I love him, so I help as much as I can."

I nod. "Yeah, that can be annoying."

"Monty's a good guy, though. Even as a friend." Violet smiles as if she knows that I was lying about not being interested.

"Good to know." I smile back, but I know I'm not looking for another guy friend.

~

I look around Cave as I quickly put my ID back in my little clutch. The crowd is already quite thick, and I'm finding it hard to follow

Violet and Alex around. I decided to separate from them for a bit and get a drink. I approach the bar, eyeing every bartender in the place.

"Which one is your roommate?" Violet says in my ear.

I turn and see that she's leaning against the bar, lazily biting her finger.

"Oh, that's him," I say, pointing to Colin, who is talking to some blonde at the bar.

Violet nods then grabs my hand, pulling me to the dance floor. I study her face, wondering if she likes Colin too. I'll just add her to the list, I guess.

"He's a player. A hound," I say to her.

"He looks like it." She laughs.

Violet starts to dance, singing along to the song that's playing.

I raise a brow. "Wait. You're not interested?"

Now I'm really curious. I have yet to meet a single girl who has not fallen for Colin's looks.

She shrugs. "Not my type."

I suppress a laugh. Colin is most girls' type. Well, aside from me since I don't necessarily fancy him.

A tall brunette with too much pink blush comes over to us and gives Violet a hug. She tries to introduce us, but it's too loud for either of us to really comprehend her. So the girl and I just wave to each other, then I watch as Violet and the tall girl start to dance.

I need alcohol.

I head back to the bar and am approached by a much older guy. He is probably my dad's age or older.

"Hey," he says loudly, "I'd love to buy you a drink."

He's giving me a lot of flirtatious winks, and I can't help but feel grossed out. I kindly decline, using those hand movements people do when it's too loud in a room to talk.

I think he got the gist of what I was saying through my pathetic sign language because he quickly walks away. I know some girls would never decline a free drink, but I prefer to buy my own if I am not attracted to the guy. At least that way, I don't feel obligated to talk to the guy all night.

"That will be $28," Colin says as he gestures for my card.

I shake my head. "Free drinks, my ass."

Colin snatches my credit card from my fingers and motions his head over to a woman by the computer screen. "Boss," he mouths.

"Sure." I nod, knowing how full of shit he is. But damn, $28 for a drink? I look around the bar. Is the old man from earlier still around?

"Where are your friends?" Colin asks.

"What?" I pretend I can't hear him over the music.

Colin grins, crossing his arms. "Afraid I'll take another one of your friends away from you, roomie?"

I kindly take my drink from Colin, giving him an exaggerated grin as I walk away and try to navigate through this club.

I spot Violet in the distance, looking very cozy with the tall girl from before. I lazily play with the straw in my mouth, slowly walking over to them. All of a sudden, my feet are frozen, and I stop sipping my drink. The tall girl's tongue enters Violet's mouth, and they are in a full-on make-out session. I don't mind PDA at all, but *wow*. I think back to when I asked Violet if she liked Colin, and she said he wasn't her type. Turns out, she wasn't lying…. I definitely did not see this coming at all.

～

I end up calling an Uber home for myself. Violet is nowhere to be seen. She's most likely getting it on with the tall girl and Alex…well, I have no idea. I didn't feel like searching everywhere for her so I sent them both a text and shoved my tired ass into a silver Honda Civic.

As soon as I get out of the Uber, I immediately spot my neighbor. Mr. Kens is slouched down on the steps of my building. Or, I should say, *our* building.

"Jade." He grins, taking a puff of his cigarette. I don't like to engage in conversations with Mr. Kens. He's this fifty-something-year-old loser, and he sort of slurs his words. The vibe he gives off is just creepy. Colin is the one who usually talks to him if we are leaving the apartment at the same time. Somehow, Mr. Kens always seems to know when we're around and loves to pop his balding head out his door. Colin isn't here to save me tonight. I don't have a choice but to talk to him.

"Hello, Mr. Kens," I say quickly as I make my way up the stairs.

"Oh please, call me Jeff."

I ignore him and fiddle with my keys, trying my hardest to unlock the main door before I have to respond. I'm not usually this antisocial, but I try not to interact with strange men.

"Need help?" he asks, giving me a wink.

"Uh, no, I think I got it." I give him a polite smile before opening the door.

Mr. Kens gets up and follows me into the building. "Bad night?" he asks, following me up the stairs.

"Nope," I say.

"You were just leaving your boyfriend's place?"

I look over to him and nod. "Yep."

I unlock my front door and give him a smile. "Have a good night."

"You too, Jade. You too," he slurs.

I close the door behind me and immediately lock it in one quick motion. What is up with me and creepy older men tonight?

Just thinking about the guy at the club and Mr. Kens makes me feel gross, so I decide to take a shower. As I am shampooing my hair, I think back to the conversation I had with Violet and Alex about Monty. Yes, Monty, a guy who isn't creepy.

After I turn off the water a few minutes later, I decide that I'd love to get closer to Monty.

∽

The next morning, I lazily tap my fingers against the hard counter next to the espresso machine. The large swarm of relaxed New Yorkers come and go, ordering their cappuccinos and eating their pastries as they talk casually at their tables—including Claire. She holds her chocolate chip cookie in one hand, taking a small bite. In her other hand, she is lightly gripping the handle of the blue mug filled with steaming black coffee.

Brett, one of the guys I work with, taps on the computer then turns his head towards me. "Espresso! Extra cream!" he barks at me, even though we are two steps away from each other.

I nod, pushing all the buttons on our old-fashioned-looking espresso machine. Coffee making is truly a step-by-step regimen. I'm trying my hardest not to miss a step and make a customer angry. Or even worse, anger my boss, who, by the way, is eyeing me down as I quickly make the drink.

"Done!" I yell, even though nobody is paying attention to me. I carefully place the to-go lid over the coffee and slide it into the hands of the customer.

"Thank you," comes a cheerful response.

I look up and quickly take off my Coffee Bean hat, moving my sweaty bangs away from my eyes. "Oh, hi!"

And there he is, just standing there. He's wearing a loose fitting white t-shirt, a stylish dark blue denim jacket, and he has one hand casually shoved into the pocket of his ripped-up denim shorts. The other hand is holding the coffee I just made. I look into his light blue eyes as he bites his lip ring gently.

"What brings you in today?" I ask him. *Play it cool, Jade. Play it cool!*

But how? I'm wearing a puke-green apron and, just a minute ago, a stupid ball cap. I was so in my head that I didn't even notice it was Monty ordering the drink.

"I was just passing by, and I figured I'd come in and test out this coffee." He chuckles. "Violet's always raving about it."

I nod. "Oh, is that so?"

I wonder if he knew Violet wasn't working today. Did he come anyway just to see me?

"Yeah." He pauses, giving me a smile. "Anyway, it was nice seeing you again, Jade."

He remembers my name! Play. It. Cool.

"Yeah, definitely." I smile back.

"See you around," he says, continuing to stare deeply into my eyes.

I'm afraid to blink because I don't want our staring contest to end.

Monty heads over to the door. I watch as he turns around and takes a big sip. "That's some good-tasting coffee." He winks, making me laugh. Monty gives me one last wave, and I watch him cross the street through the window.

During my lunch break, I take a seat at Claire's table, poking at the turkey sandwich I made the night before.

"What's wrong?" she asks before taking a sip of her coffee.

"I don't know." I shrug, glancing out the window and watching the flower guy pick out the best bouquet. "All men should be like him," I sigh.

Suddenly, Reese comes strolling inside with the biggest smile on her face.

"Oh gosh, please tell me you aren't engaged."

Reese laughs. "Heck no. Even better. Wes surprised me and bought me the couch I really wanted. No more of that yucky couch Colin slept on for a year."

I smile. "I can't wait to see it."

"I don't even want to take off the wrapping," she gushes.

I turn my attention towards the window, watching the flower guy pick out the nicest bouquet before disappearing into the large crowd.

"Reese, it's your turn," I say.

She looks up from the cup of tea I brought her, and she tilts her head to the side. "*Hmm.* Imagine his name is Garrett."

"Okay, strong name. I like it. Go on." I nod with approval. I glance at Claire, who's smiling. She loves this game as much as we do.

"Garrett meets a nurse who's trying to work her way through her massive student debts and the crazy living expenses of New York—"

I cut her off. "Reese? Where is this going?"

She rolls her eyes. "I don't know, but just listen. It'll get better."

I nod and allow her to continue, but my mind keeps jumping back to Monty. I haven't had a crush on a guy in a while, probably since Noah. And I was young then. Those same childish butterfly feelings are coming back to me, and I'm honestly kind of scared. I semi-listen as Reese is going into depth about her perfect love story scenario. I lean my head on my hand and imagine Monty instead. I imagine him coming into the cafe with his own bouquet of flowers that he picked out just for me. He'd take my face into his large hands and stare into my eyes, which, by the way, he's very good at. And then, he'd kiss me. Not just a regular plain kiss, but one of those kisses I'd feel in my toes. The kind of kiss that would make me want to burst into a million pieces.

"Jade?"

I open my eyes and look back and forth between Reese and Claire, who are both just staring at me.

"Did you hear a word I just said?"

I nod. "Of course. Go on."

"I finished." She crosses her arms. "I can't believe you didn't listen. I always listen to yours, even when they are so unrealistic."

I rub my hand over my forehead and sigh. "I'm sorry, Reese. My head is just somewhere else today."

"Does it have to do with that boy I saw you talking to today?" Claire asks.

I look up and bite my bottom lip. "You noticed that?"

She grins. "I notice everything, sweetheart."

"Wait. Am I missing something?" Reese asks, confused. "How come you haven't told me about this guy?"

I lean my back against the chair and shrug. "Because there isn't anything to tell. I met him last week, but I can't get him out of my head."

Reese smiles. "Oh, potential new love interest?"

"Apparently." I laugh nervously. "It's just so not like me to be crushing this hard on a guy I hardly know. I've only had like two conversations with him."

"So? Ask him out and get to know him," Reese says.

I stand up, putting my hat back on and fixing my apron. "I would, but he's taken."

"Oh, wow. And you still like him?" Reese asks, the shock clear in her voice. From all the years that she has known me, she knows I don't develop crushes on guys. I find it pointless to sit around and think about them like all the other girls I've known. It's either you like them, and they like you back, and you date, or they don't want you back, and nothing happens. So I'd move on. I don't get attached.

And I'd try my hardest not to get so obsessive over some guy. It's pointless.

"Honestly, I have no idea what it is. I guess we'll find out, right?" Reese turns to Claire. "Was he cute?"

I laugh. "Reese, I'm standing right here. You could just ask me."

"Because you clearly have no idea what cute looks like," she says. "I have proof from all the dudes you've been with."

I'm a bit taken aback. I place my hand over my chest, but I don't say a word. I just wait for Claire to answer.

"Well," she says, then coughs. "I've never seen any of Jade's boyfriends, but he's definitely *different* looking."

Reese laughs. "Meaning he's exactly Jade's type."

"And that is?" I cross my arms.

"You know…those dark and secretive looking guys with lots of piercings and tons of eccentricity." Her eyes widen. "Hipsters! That's a perfect way to describe them."

"Whatever. Monty may be a hipster, but he's smart, and his face is so pretty," I say slowly. Jeez, what is wrong with me? I've never said those words in my life.

"Smart?" Reese raises a brow. "How do you know? You just said you've only had two conversations with him."

I wave away her nonsense. "That's what I've heard from Violet, who, by the way, is his best friend. And, he's a great writer."

"From what you've heard from Violet?"

I nod.

"What's his name again?" Claire asks, pulling on her pale ear.

"Monty. Short for Montgomery."

"What kind of name is that?" Reese chuckles.

"A beautiful one," I say, swooning a little.

"You must really like this guy," Reese says.

"You know what? Let's just drop this whole Monty conversation. Nothing's going to happen between us. He's happily taken by Chelsea." I give them both my fakest smile.

"So, what about Jake?" Reese asks.

I look over at Wanda, who's paying attention to someone else. I guess I have a couple more seconds left of my lunch break.

"Who?"

"Jade! The guy I have a class with!"

"Oh yeah, the male nurse. I-I guess I like him. He seems nice."

"And he wants to take you out."

"Really?"

She nods. "Should I set it up?"

"No! Just give him my number, and he and I will set something up ourselves."

Reese claps with excitement, and I wave goodbye to Claire, practically leaping away from Reese and this conversation.

CHAPTER 20

Jake ended up texting me a few days after Reese gave him my number. He seems like a nice guy based on the couple of hours I spent with him when we watched *Love Match*. I also appreciate how sweet his text messages are and how he never takes too long to reply in between each text. We made plans for Sunday morning. I never met a guy who suggests brunch for a date, but hey, I'm all for it.

～

I am at my local laundromat, pouring some soap into the washing machine. I hop onto the counter as Violet asks me a question. "Want to come with me to this thing tonight?"

A week has gone by, and the talk with Monty has become nothing more than a distant memory. Reese mentioned it a couple of times, but I dismissed it. I also hadn't seen Violet since that night out last Thursday. She then called out from work and missed our breakfast date this week.

"Hello to you too," I say.

Violet giggles through the phone. "Is that a yes?"

But before I can ask her what *it* is, she says, "Great! I'll pick you up at eight. Wear a nice dress." And with that, she hangs up.

~

The following night, I check my makeup one last time in the mirror. I pull on my tight little black dress. I didn't have enough time to really plan out my outfit for tonight. I feel kind of lazy, and maybe I was playing it safe just a little bit. I don't want to be "typical Jade" and wear something loud if I don't even know where I'm going. Even though I'm hoping Monty will be there tonight. I figure he might be because anything Violet brings me to is with her crowd, and her crowd includes Monty.

Violet texts me, saying she's downstairs. She's usually never on time, so when I glance at my watch and see that it's precisely eight o'clock, I'm impressed.

"Where are you going?" Colin asks, eying my dress.

I pull it down a little and open the front door. "No idea."

I walk down the steps of my building and spot Violet's car. She opens her window and gives me a wink.

"Nice car." I smile, opening the door to a white painted Mustang and getting in.

"Thanks, but it's not mine. It's a friend's," she tells me.

I wonder if it's the same friend she was tonguing the other night…. I turn up the radio to some Bruce Springsteen song, then we head out.

"So, where exactly are you taking me?" I turn to look at her, hoping she'll answer this time.

She smiles, her eyes still on the road. "It's a surprise."

I don't say a word, trying my hardest not to beg her to tell me.

She laughs. "I'm just kidding. My friend from college invited me to her housewarming party." She pauses and glances at me. "On the Upper East Side."

"Oh, so a super-rich friend from college." I chuckle.

"She was my roommate, and she's more like a super broke, struggling actress who married up. Like *superrrrr* up."

I play with the earrings Maude gave me and smile. "Wow, so she's like every struggling actress except she has an easy ride?"

"Marry a rich producer and live in a penthouse apartment overlooking Central Park? Oh yeah, just about."

Violet makes lots of turns then she finally heads onto the Brooklyn Bridge towards the city.

"Thanks for inviting me," I say.

She switches lanes and fixes her air vent. "No problem! I figured you'd want to eat some delicious food for free. Open bar, too."

"Sounds like a good time to me!"

"Yeah, it is. I've been to a few of her parties, and they never disappoint. And besides, I needed a date anyway."

The word "date" lingers in my head, and I tilt my head to the side, wondering if I gave Violet the wrong signal. I've never had a friend like Violet, one who likes girls, so maybe she picked up the wrong vibe from me?

"Everything okay?" She glances at me.

"Oh, yeah. Perfect," I lie.

We pull up to her friend's expensive-looking building, and Violet hands her keys to the valet. I follow her into the gigantic elevator, and we ride it all the way up to the top floor. Obviously, her friend owns the whole floor because as soon as the elevator doors open, we are practically standing in her penthouse.

"Violet!"

We turn towards the bar and see an extremely tall brunette

walking over to us in a long, silky red dress. She gives Violet one of those proper hugs with a few kisses on the cheek.

"Jade, this is my old roommate, Erin."

I look into her chestnut-colored eyes and immediately zoom in on her puffy botoxed red lips.

"Hello, I'm Jade."

We shake hands, and she gives us a smile.

"Rick and I spent months making this apartment ours. You should have seen this place when we bought it," she says. All of a sudden, a short man with red hair and freckles approaches us. He must be at least five inches shorter than Erin.

I'm trying my hardest not to laugh as she bends down to kiss her rich husband. His arm is not long enough to drape over her shoulders so he casually puts it around her thin waist instead.

"Sweetheart, this is Violet. You know, my old roommate from Rutgers."

"Oh yes, it's nice to see you again," he says, and I can tell he's trying to make his voice sound deeper than it is.

"And this is her date, Jade."

I cringe internally as I shake the man's hand. I never hated the word "date" so much in my life. We kindly excuse ourselves from the lovely couple to find some alcohol.

"You missed a vital part," I say, taking a sip of my white wine. Erin informed us that this party is a strictly white food and drink affair. Which means there won't be red wine or any foods containing the color red. Just in case anyone spills anything on her new and expensive furnished apartment.

"That Rick is a short and stocky man?"

I nod.

"Yeah, I thought it would be more fun to watch your face than to just tell you in the car."

I laugh. "You're cruel."

"I did say there was a surprise."

A waitress walks over to us, holding a platter of garlic shrimp on a little stick.

We each take one.

"Wow, these are crazy good," I say.

A few people come over to us, primarily people Violet went to school with. Every time Violet introduces me, she refers to me as her date. After a guy named Toby and a girl named Heather walk away, I finally decide to address that.

"So, I'm your date?"

Violet finishes the last of her champagne and nods. "Yeah, why?"

"I see," I say quietly.

Violet squints her eyes as if she is trying to read my face. I should have left it alone, but hindsight is 20/20.

"Is there something wrong with me calling you my date?"

"No. Well, *yes*." I pause, waiting for her to say something, but she doesn't. "Well, the other night at Cave, I saw you with your friend—"

She smiles. "Are you talking about Nina?"

"I think so. You two were, um, kissing?"

Violet raises a brow. "Does that bother you?"

"No! Of course not. I wasn't sure if I was giving you mixed messages."

"No, I get it, Jade. You don't have to explain yourself. I can understand the confusion. I'm more bisexual than I am gay if you're wondering."

I nod, feeling a bit uncomfortable. I should not have brought it up.

Violet lets out her famous loud laugh. "It's fine, Jade! I'm not insulted. I guess I was a little casual with the date reference." She takes a deep breath. "Just so you know, I was raised a hardcore Catholic. I was taught to believe that a man will always bring me happiness and a future, *but* I realized I don't have to just focus on one gender. I can truly be and feel free with myself no matter what gender my partner is," she says. "And trust me, your love life really opens up when you start dating both genders."

I chuckle. "Jeez, I can't imagine dealing with both sexes. I'm struggling here just with guys."

"I used to be like you," she jokes. "But I usually go back and forth, and it makes life so much more exciting. You should try it sometime."

I don't say anything, and Violet laughs, hugging her hands around my arm. "I'm just kidding. I knew you were straight the minute I met you. Did it freak you out when you saw Nina and me?" she asks.

"No, it just surprised me," I say. "Only because of what you said about you and Monty."

"You said what about me?" Out of the blue, Monty approaches us, hand in hand with his girlfriend, Chelsea.

Violet and I shoot our gaze over to the couple and nervously laugh.

"Nothing!" she says, going in to give Monty and Chelsea a hug.

Monty looks at her weirdly but quickly recovers as he introduces Chelsea to me. I glance at Monty, who is wearing a tight black button down shirt—tucked in, of course—a jet-black tie and black slacks. He looks good, and Alex was right, his girlfriend Chelsea does look a little stuck up. She is not someone I would assume Monty would date. Despite what I've heard about her, I can't deny that Chelsea is definitely pretty. She has brown eyes and strawberry blonde hair that's curled to perfection at the ends. She's wearing an A-line white dress and despite wearing very high heels, she is still shorter than Monty.

Violet and Chelsea begin to talk about Erin's new place, and how jealous they are because it's so beautiful. Luckily for me, that means I get some free time to talk to Monty.

"I'm glad Vi brought you tonight," he says to me.

I smile. "Me too. I haven't been to many Upper East Side apartments."

"Yeah, me neither. I can't even believe Erin lives in something like this."

Should I bring up her funny-looking husband? Or is it too soon to make jokes?

"Chelsea, Erin, and Violet all know each other from college," he says.

I nod, taking a sip of my wine.

"Yeah, I was lucky enough to have Violet introduce me to Chels."

Yes...I'll have to thank Violet for that later... "So, does your girlfriend act?" I ask.

"No," she says, intertwining her fingers with Monty's. "I work for a publishing house in the city."

"Oh, wow, that's awesome," I say.

"Yeah." She turns to Monty and fixes his tie. "I'm just waiting for my sweet Monty-bear to stop playing around and finally get a grown-up job." The entire time she was talking, she was using her baby voice.

If someone were to put a mirror to my face, all that person would see is a disgusted expression.

"I'm not playing, Chelsea. I love what I do."

"And what you do is fetch coffees all day," she bites.

"Hey! I make coffee for a living, too," I say, trying to make light of the conversation.

She glances at me but doesn't laugh. Monty and I make eye

contact though. He gives me a smile even though his girlfriend looks mad. How in the hell is Violet friends with her?

As the night progresses, we all sort of separate from each other. I move away from Violet, who's consumed with a group of friends from college, including Chelsea. I want to be anywhere but there. I decide to venture around the floor and head outside to the large balcony. The furniture outside is just as beautiful as the pieces inside, and I like how they are all covered so nicely. I make my way to the railing, watching crowds of people walking down the streets.

"Beautiful, right?"

I look behind me and see Monty shutting the door behind him.

"It truly is," I say, admiring all the trees in Central Park. Monty comes over to me and leans his elbows a few inches from mine. We are practically touching. All I can smell is the fabric softener he uses on his clothes.

"Needed some air?" he asks.

"More like a breather from all those people I don't know," I say.

"Do you mind?" he asks me as he slides a cigarette between his lips. I shake my head, and he lights it, releasing tons of smoke.

"It's pretty crazy in there and not good crazy." He smiles. "More like super-proper."

"*Too* proper," I say.

"Yeah, I noticed you were alone, so I came out here."

I turn my head slightly to face him. "You were watching me?"

Monty blushes. "Yeah, I guess I was."

"Your girlfriend seems great," I say dryly, looking ahead.

He laughs. "You don't have to lie, Jade."

I turn to him. "I wasn't! I swear."

"Chelsea sometimes comes off harsh, but she doesn't mean to. You just gotta give her time to…to relax."

I nod. "Yeah, she was definitely harsh."

"She can't help it, especially when it comes to me. I guess I'm just such a fuck up that she can't hold it in sometimes."

Are we seriously talking about his relationship? In the middle of this party, where his girlfriend is only a few feet away?

"You're not a fuck up. I'd do anything to have a job like yours, to be completely surrounded by people who are so talented and passionate about everything you love."

Silence fills the air, and I'm wondering if I said the wrong thing. Monty takes a puff of his cigarette and nods. "Well, when you put it in that way…" He looks at me and smiles.

I nudge my shoulder with his and smile back. Our staring contest has begun once again. Swiftly, the patio door opens, and Chelsea comes out. "Ew, Monty, it's humid outside! Come here," she orders.

He takes one last puff and throws it off the ledge. I watch the cigarette fall until it smacks the concrete ground. Luckily, it doesn't hit anyone or anything. I turn and watch as Chelsea glares at him as he walks past her. All I hear is, "I needed a smoke!"

~

Towards the end of the night, Violet and I are ready to leave. I get a text from Reese saying she and Wes are at my place.

"Do you want to come over?" I ask Violet as we get into her car.

"Like a play date?" she jokes.

"Ha-ha, very funny." I smile. "You were so nice to introduce me to some of your friends, so I want to do the same. And they all happen to be at my place."

She nods. "Yeah, I'm down."

I open my front door, and all my friends are sitting around watching a game and drinking beer. I drank so much wine tonight that I can't even look at beer.

"Hey guys," I shout over the loud television. Colin recently hooked up these loudspeakers, so the whole apartment is rattling. I take off my heels and Violet does the same, making herself at home. I walk in front of the television, and I get yelled at, but I don't care. "Guys, this is my friend Violet," I say. "And Vi, this is my roommate, Colin. He's the one sitting shirtless on the chair," I say, pointing in his direction. "And these are my friends, Reese and Wes."

They all say hi and exchange a few words. Violet and I both relax on the couch next to Wes and Reese.

"So, I'm not your friend?" Colin says to me, leaning back with his arms crossed.

"I knew you were gonna say that." I laugh.

"So, why did you?" Reese asks.

"I guess he became just my roommate after he fucked Maude."

Everyone starts to shout and holler and make a fool of themselves. I shrug, looking at Colin, who is drinking his beer.

"I had a feeling you were gonna say that." He winks. "But hey, it was definitely worth losing a friend over."

I let out a sigh and decide to grab a beer anyway, handing Violet one as well.

"You said your name was—what again?" Colin says, leaning forward to shake Violet's hand again. He's only talking to her to get under my skin. And it's working.

"Violet. And I like girls," she says.

Everyone starts to laugh, and I give her a nod of approval.

Colin laughs as well, finally shutting up.

~

I have a date with Jake this morning, and a very judgmental Reese is sitting on my bed. "Is that what you're wearing?" she asks.

I look down at my oversized denim overall shorts, paired with a tight white long sleeve shirt with a sunflower on it. I put my hair in a messy ponytail, and I'm sliding on my white tennis shoes.

"Yes," I say boldly.

Reese closes my Vogue magazine and sighs. "Okay. I guess I approve."

"It's only a date," I say.

"Yeah, but it's a date that I set up."

"Okay, technically you didn't set us up because Jake and I did the planning," I remind her, grabbing my boho maroon bag.

Reese rolls her eyes and follows me into the kitchen. "Just be yourself and give him a chance," she says as I lock the front door. Reese offered to walk me to this little breakfast place a few blocks from where I live. I don't mind the stroll, and it's better that I have some company. "He's super funny and loves your whole vibe."

"My vibe?"

She nods. "Yeah, he told me you're exactly his type."

"And that is?" I ask.

"I don't know, but whatever you are, he likes."

"Why are you trying so hard with us?"

"Because he's adorable! And I like him, and I want him in our group. Plus, if things work out, he'd look nice sitting next to you at Suzy's wedding."

I stop in my tracks once I see Jake sitting at one of the tables. I give him one last look before it's too late, but he sees me. "You're right," I say.

She gives me a wave, and I can feel her watching me as I approach Jake. I look down at our table and see that he has ordered us some mimosas.

"Hey!" He smiles, getting up and pulling out a chair for me. "You look pretty," he says shyly.

"Thank you," I say, taking a sip of my mimosa.

"I ordered us unlimited mimosas. Reese informed me that you like to drink."

"I do enjoy a good drink." I smile.

"Then I guess we're on the right track?"

I nod, scanning the menu. "Have you eaten here before?"

"No, I haven't. But I've passed by this place a few times, and it looks good."

"Have you eaten at this place called Bakers Delight?" I ask.

Jake tilts his head to the side. "Uh, I don't think so."

"Oh, it's literally the best! I go all the time, and their omelets are amazing."

"We should definitely go next time."

"Sounds good." I grin.

The waiter comes by and takes our orders. I order a vegetable omelet, but only because I want to compare theirs with Bakers Delight's. Jake orders a stack of banana nut pancakes.

"Those sound yummy. I may have to try them."

"Only if I get a bite of that omelet of yours," he playfully teases.

Ten minutes go by, and during that time, I've already learned so much about Jake, his three sisters, and his passion for science. Reese was right—he's very nice, and I can't help but laugh at the things he says.

Our food finally comes out. I'm so hungry, I'm considering eating this omelet in two bites. I cut it in half and watch the smoke rise. "Don't ya just love the look of that?"

Jake smiles. "It's beautiful."

I take a big bite. Even though Bakers Delight is way better, I'm definitely enjoying my meal. "How are your pancakes?"

"Super fluffy," he answers as he pours some more syrup onto his plate.

Jake asks me many questions, and I try my hardest to answer them the best I can. He asks questions about my childhood, the reasons why I've chosen acting as my career, and he even asks me what my favorite movie is.

"I'd have to say *When Harry Met Sally*," I answer. "Have you seen it?"

"It's a classic. Of course."

I grin. "And?"

"*And* I loved it."

"Good answer."

As I am finishing the last of my mimosa, I hear my name being called.

"Hey, Jade."

"Oh! Hi Monty!" I say enthusiastically. When I make eye contact with Monty, I realize I don't want him to see me with Jake.

"It seems like we're always bumping into each other," he says happily.

I can't help but smile. "It's meant to be."

I glance at Jake, who's looking between me and Monty. "Oh, sorry, I'm being rude. Jake, this is Monty. Monty, Jake."

They shake hands, and all I want to do is hide under this table.

"Chelsea is down the street at some store. I don't know how anyone can have that much patience picking out scarves," he says. "I decided to grab some coffee, and I saw you eating across the street."

"Oh, wow. I'm glad you came over."

"Yeah," he says quietly, "but I'll let you guys continue eating. Have a good day." He gives me a wave, and I watch him walk away.

"Is he a friend?" Jake asks.

I smile and take a sip of water.

As he walks away, I realize that I am definitely not interested in

Jake. All I want is Montgomery.

~

"So, how was the date?" Reese asks while taking a bite of her coleslaw. I decided to grab dinner with her, Wes, and Colin at some diner.

I shrug. "He's nice."

"She's not into him," Colin says, shoving a fork full of lettuce into his mouth.

"I didn't say that!" I shoot him a glare.

"You didn't have to," he says.

Reese leans back on the cushiony booth. "What went wrong?"

"Nothing. He's a nice guy."

"Will you see him again?" Wes asks.

I take a sip of my iced water and shrug.

Reese lets out a huff and shakes her head. "I swear, Jade. You're impossible. I'm so done setting you up."

"You always say that, but then you go and do it again. You can't help yourself, Reese."

"This was the last straw," she says.

"Thank gosh." I laugh.

Wes laughs as well, giving his sad girlfriend a kiss on her cheek.

"Monty bumped into us while we were eating," I say casually, after a few minutes of silence.

Reese looks up from her chicken sandwich and raises an eyebrow. "I knew there was something."

"It's not anything. I was just telling you."

"And? What happened?"

"Nothing. We had a brief conversation. His girlfriend was down the street or whatever. I told Jake he was only a friend. No biggie."

"So, Monty has nothing to do with you not liking Jake?"

I shake my head. "No, and I never said I didn't like Jake. He was just—"

"Safe and boring?" Colin offers.

"Yes. Exactly," I say, turning to look at him.

"And Monty's…what?" Reese asks.

"Monty has nothing to do with this at all, Reese. I'm over him."

Reese says something under her breath, but I decide to keep my mouth shut and finish my cheeseburger.

CHAPTER 21

The spring air brushes past Suzy's sundress as she walks down the sidewalk. She's darkened her hair since the last time I saw her, and her soothing voice brings me back to a time when life was much simpler for us. Suzy is very expressive, and I could always tell how she's feeling based on her facial expressions.

I silently listen to her vent as we make our way to her sister's apartment on Bedford Ave.

"I know the wedding seems so far away, which is good, right? It'll give me time to really get all I want in order. You know how I can be." She laughs nervously.

I nod. "How's all the planning going?"

I honestly don't care, but I know the right thing to do is to ask. Also, I am one of her bridesmaids. I sort of feel terrible about my lack of support towards the wedding, but in my defense, she is marrying a guy I dated for five years. It's difficult for me to be as enthusiastic as Suzy would want me to be, but at the end of the day, I'm doing this because I care about Suzy. She's been planning her wedding ever since her mother bought her an expensive notepad full of colorful sticky notes and stickers; she was ten.

"Great, actually. Noah's sister has been surprisingly helpful with everything."

"Oh, has she?" I scrunch my nose.

Suzy glances at me and smiles. "She's mean, I know, but I'll take any help I can get."

"She's mean and bossy. Terrible combo."

Suzy nods in agreement. "Honestly, I'm more scared to say no."

I laugh. "I think it probably has to do with her strong chin."

"And she's built like a football player."

After Suzy and I finish spewing hate onto Noah's lovely sister, we finally get to her sister's place. Noah's family and I have a long history, so when Suzy complains to me about his bossy sister, it's nothing I haven't seen or experienced. Let's just say I'd get an A-plus on the Noah family test.

"The door's open!" we hear through the buzzer.

I follow Suzy down a long hallway past green-colored wooden doors. Her sister's apartment is the last one on the corner, and I can't help notice the scents coming through the hallways. A few doors from Suzy's sister's apartment, there's a family that prepares food with tons of different seasonings, which has permanently given this floor the aroma of a fresh herb garden.

Suzy and I barge into the apartment, and the smell of the apple candle burning by the stove greets us. "3 AM" by Matchbox Twenty is playing on low, and we're immediately welcomed by her older sister, Grace, and her mother, Helen. They both hug us like they haven't seen either of us in years. Helen takes my cheeks into her hands, something she has done ever since I've met her. She gives my cheeks a gentle squeeze and compliments me on how beautiful I look.

Grace puts out tiny sandwiches on these rose-colored china plates for us along with some homemade raspberry iced tea.

We hear a soft knock at the door and Suzy gets up. "That must be Marni."

I let out a tiny groan, shoving the rest of my cucumber cream cheese sandwich in my mouth. Marni has been a small thorn on my side for years. I haven't seen the girl for a while, only because I don't care for her. Suzy met Marni at NYU during their freshman year. They were both going for the same major, marketing, but Marni ended up dropping out because she got married. Supposedly, the only reason Marni even got married was because she thought she was pregnant. Let's just say it is tough to have a conversation with her because her life, being married and "in love," is just so much better than everyone else's. Marni believes everything she does is right because she's so much more intelligent, and did I mention she's married? Yeah, to some guy who sells carpet. As soon as his paycheck couldn't cover them both, Marni started working for some tech company in Queens that only pays her minimum wage. But good thing she got married, right?

I hear laughter in the other room, and I shove another sandwich in my mouth.

"Honey, slow down. You might choke," Helen says, running her hand on my cheek again.

With an exasperated sigh, I watch Marni and Suzy enter the kitchen. Grace and Helen do their typical greetings, and I give Marni a fake friendly wave. After everyone is all settled, eating their sandwiches and drinking iced tea, the wedding talk begins.

"As the maid of honor, I feel so honored to take this on. Suzy, you've made an excellent choice in picking me," Marni says obnoxiously.

Relax, Marni, you don't have to sell yourself. She already picked you.

"From the perspective of an already married woman, I wanted my wedding to be perfect—"

"And it was!" Suzy sings.

Marni uses both hands to move her hair away from her bloated face. She looks pleased. I cross my arms, leaning against the chair.

"So, I brought my wedding book. Honestly, I don't know what I'd have done without it."

"I love this! You're like a built-in wedding planner." Suzy smiles.

"It's truly my calling," Marni says seriously.

Grace clears the table, and Marni opens up this gigantic book full of every other girl's nightmare. It includes budget options, venue ideas, themes, and all sorts of color combinations for flowers.

"I'm still trying to get us an appointment with Gretchen Taylor," Marni tells us, "but she's all booked."

Suzy's face falls, and Helen's hands immediately begin to rub her daughter's pale, freckly arms.

"Who's Gretchen Taylor?" I ask. They all look up, and I realize I just asked the stupidest question.

"She's one of the most famous wedding fashion designers in the country," Marni says smugly. "She designed Kate Hudson's wedding dress."

"You've never heard of her?" Suzy asks, surprised.

"No." I shake my head.

Marni says something under her breath, and I want to say something back so badly, but for Suzy's sake, I won't.

"Don't worry. I won't give up," Marni says with a smile.

"It would be a dream for Gretchen Taylor to design my wedding dress and my bridesmaids' dresses," Suzy sighs.

"Have you picked a color yet?" Grace asks her sister.

"Definitely baby blue," she sings. Marni nods in agreement, but I'm still stuck on this Gretchen Taylor lady.

"Wait, Suzy, what about the dress you picked out already? It is stunning," I ask.

"Uh, yeah. Well, if someone like Gretchen could make my dress, I'd pick hers."

"But you—"

"It's fine, Jade." Suzy laughs.

I shake my head, hating Marni so much. She's literally manipulating Suzy to think that her opinions are better because she's done this before. I'm just annoyed because I know how Suzy is; she's a follower and a hardcore one when it comes to Marni Matthews.

"I cannot believe you got a dress without telling me," Marni says.

"Yeah, I know," she sighs. "It was at some little boutique in Brooklyn. Nothing extraordinary."

"Suzy, you already have, and bought, a beautiful dress that you love. So why are you so fixated on Kate Hudson's wedding dress designer?"

"You don't understand, Jade. You're not as invested as we are," Suzy bites.

"And besides, I cannot believe you bought a dress in *Brooklyn*," Marni says, fake gagging to emphasize her point.

I turn to Marni. "Don't you live in Queens?"

"I moved, actually," she says, without looking at me. Her eyes are glued to her fake manicured nails.

"Oh, did you?" I mutter under my breath.

"Suzy said you moved to—" Helen begins, but Marni interrupts.

"Mark and I moved to the city. We were tired of life in Queens. Mark received a promotion, and I've been enjoying decorating our new apartment. And now, let's get back to Suzanna's wedding." She claps her hands.

Yeah, the carpet business is a real money maker, and that minimum wage salary too…

"I'd love to see your place." Suzy smiles.

"It's not done yet," Marni says, sniffing her nose.

I can't help but smile. Will it ever be finished, Marni?

~

I decided to head over to Reese's place after lunch with the girls. She's luckily only a block away, and I need to cool down after everything.

I use Reese's spare key that dangles on my set of keys, and when I enter her place, I find her watching *Judge Judy*.

"How was it?" she asks as soon as I close her front door.

I groan, throwing my mini backpack on the floor.

"That bad?" She smiles.

I plop down next to her and sigh. "I realize I have a lot more patience than I ever believed I had."

"What happened?"

"It's Marni. All Marni. She acts like we're in this competition to win Suzy's affection."

"And are you?" She raises an eyebrow.

"Heck no. But in Marni's twisted mind, we are."

"So, what exactly was she doing?"

"You know how she can be. Trying to one-up me as much as possible and putting stupid things into Suzy's head," I sigh. "Have you heard of Gretchen—"

"Taylor? Of course!" Reese nearly shouts.

I shrug. "Then I guess I'm the only one in this pathetic world who doesn't know who she is."

"She's amazing. I follow her on Instagram. She's like twenty-eight and started her company at like fifteen. Why? Does Suzy have an appointment with her?" Reese's eyes go wide, waiting for me to reply.

"Marni is trying to, but—"

"She designed Kate—"

"I know, she designed Kate Hudson's dress. So what?" I lean my head on my hand.

"That's unbelievable."

"Hey, Reese? Do you want to trade places with me and be a bridesmaid? You'd fit in perfectly with Suzy and her posse."

She laughs. "Yeah, I think I'll pass."

"Then get your head out of your ass and be on my side." I pout.

Reese nods, finishing the last of her water. "Okay, fine. So, Marni's a snotty bitch, and Suzy is what?"

"A follower," I say.

"Yeah, well, she's always been like that. You didn't mind when she'd follow you," Reese says.

"I just don't want her to get taken advantage of. She's willing to get rid of her perfect wedding dress just so she can wear a Gret—"

Reese's mouth opens, about to say something, but I shake my head, putting my finger up, "Don't say anything. Please."

Reese reaches up to unravel her hair out of its ponytail. Then she turns to me and asks, "Do you want to order in some Chinese? Wes is playing poker tonight with the guys."

I tilt my head to the side. "*Hmm*, order in Chinese or have my place to myself?"

Reese rolls her eyes and hits my shoulder. "Very funny, Jade."

"You didn't let me finish! Order in Chinese with you. Duh!"

"Good answer." Reese gets up and disappears into her kitchen in search of a good Chinese restaurant menu.

Suddenly, my phone, which is sitting on my lap, starts to buzz.

Suzy Boozy reads on my screen.

"Hey," I say.

"Hey."

I wait for her to continue, but she doesn't.

"Is everything okay?" I ask her.

"I just want to say that I think you crossed the line this afternoon," she says nervously. It's almost like she's afraid to start an argument, but she's too angry to let it go.

"I did? How?"

"Well, you were butting in too much."

I stand up. "Are you serious? I was only trying to help you. So, you'd rather me keep my mouth shut the whole time?"

"Jade, I don't want to start a fight here."

"I don't either, but you're accusing me of something Marni was doing. Not me."

"She's my maid of honor. She kinda has to."

"And me? What am I? Oh yeah, I'm only one of your bridesmaids."

"I guess you just pissed me off. It felt like you were judging me."

"I didn't mean to at all. I was just trying to defend you."

"You don't have to, Jade!" She raises her voice.

I sit back down. "Suzy, I'm sorry if I hurt you in any way. It's just that Marni gets on my nerves."

"I know, I know. But she's my friend, and she's only trying to help."

"I understand." To keep the peace between us, I decide to back off.

"I'm not mad. I just don't want to feel judged by you. This is supposed to be the happiest time in my life."

"It should be," I say. Reese comes back into the living room, raising a brow. I give her a slight shrug, and she nods. She then sits down next to me, handing me a glass of rosé.

I take a sip. "So, we're good?" I wait for Suzy to answer, but as I wait, I already know the answer. Suzy doesn't have an angry bone in her body.

"Yes," she sighs. "I'll call you this week."

Suzy says a few other things that I don't register, then hangs up.

"Bridezilla came out?" Reese asks.

I laugh. "Basically. Marni has it out for me and is already putting negative shit into Suzy's head."

"And she wonders why you haven't been the most cooperative bridesmaid."

"Exactly." I smack my hand against my forehead. "And thank you for reading my mind," I say, taking a big sip of my wine.

"Nothing like a glass of wine to fix a problem, right?"

"More like a bottle," I say.

Reese smiles and changes the channel to a rerun of *Sex and the City*. "I ordered our usual, okay?"

I nod, watching Miranda and Steve eat a slice of pizza.

"We need an ultimate girl gang. Like Carrie Bradshaw and her friends," Reese blurts out.

I turn my head towards her. "Like who?"

"I don't know. You, me..."

"It wouldn't be a gang if it was just us," I mock.

Reese shrugs. "Wes and Colin have a group of all guys playing poker and going to sports games. We need that."

"We can go out to fancy restaurants."

"Like the Plaza!" Reese sings. "We can go during the day and drink tea. And then we can go to clubs and get hit on by dudes and drink cosmos and not worry if our boyfriends are there watching."

"We can even go to gay bars, so we don't have to get hit on," I say, hearing my voice getting louder.

"Yes!" she yells. "Yes!"

"So, who's invited to our marvelous girl gang?"

"You and me, obviously. Um...Violet and her friend, Alex? My friend Sofia is cool, and maybe Maude? If she's in town."

"Wow, you are seriously inviting Maude?"

"I'm desperate, and you say she knows how to have a good time. And she won't always have to be there."

I nod. "What about Suzy?"

Reese scrunches her nose and shakes her head. "I'm not a fan. When the bitch didn't invite me to her wedding, it meant war." She chuckles.

I laugh as well. "I told you I'd bring you to the wedding as my date."

"Hard pass. Trust me, I'd love to watch you and Noah interact, but there's a reason she didn't invite me in the first place. She doesn't like me."

"She does! I promise you."

"It's okay. The feeling's mutual."

I shrug. "I tried so hard to push you guys together in high school. But I guess I didn't try hard enough."

"I think you did a pretty good job. Noah and Suzy wouldn't be together if it wasn't for you."

"And would that be such a terrible thing?"

"So, you'd still be with Noah?" She winks.

"Oh gosh, no. And besides, they started dating *wayyy* after Noah and I broke up."

Reese nods. "True."

"It's all this bridesmaid shit and the anxiety about bringing a date."

"Would it be so terrible if you went alone?"

"I'm not answering that." I finish the rest of my wine.

"So, what happens if you can't find a guy to bring to this wedding?"

I shrug. "I'll be fucked, right?"

"Hey! You can always bring Colin?" She laughs out loud.

"Very funny. That would be a nightmare, and besides, he'd never do it in a million years."

"Yeah, probably not. Hopefully, by then, you'll be in a relationship with a nice guy so you won't have to worry."

"Nice guy meaning Monty?" I say, covering my hands over my face.

Reese laughs and grabs my wrists, pulling them away from my face and exposing my reddened face.

"Someone's crushin' hard," she mocks me. "You *loveeee* Monty!"

"I do not!" I laugh.

"Do too."

"Nope!"

We hear a knock at the door, and Reese stands to her feet, clapping her hands. "Thank goodness the food is here. I'm so hungry!"

⁓

After three *Sex and the City episodes*, Reese and I are full of fried rice and orange chicken. We're tipsy due to the bottle of wine we shared. Reese and I have always been lightweights when it comes to drinking.

"I lied earlier. I think I love Monty. I don't know what it is."

"No shit." She laughs.

"I should just call him and ask him if he feels the same way." I pick my phone up off the coffee table.

"Whoa there, partner. Hold the brakes."

"Why? You and Claire always tell me I need to be bolder."

"I think you're bold enough, Jade. Just in the clothes you wear," she says, eying my tight flannel dress.

"Not that! I mean about my love life. I'm always so scared to take a leap."

Reese gets up, falling over a little. She laughs loudly. "We need more wine. You're killing my buzz."

"I think we're out of the buzzed stage and are now in the fucked-up stage," I say.

"You're right. Call him. Future Jade will handle the mess tomorrow."

"Yes!"

I click his contact name and place my phone to my ear. It rings twice before he picks up.

"Hello?"

"Monty! It's Jade."

"Oh. Hi, Jade. How are you?"

"You are always so polite. That's what I like the most about you." I giggle.

I can hear him exhale loudly through the phone. "Are you drunk?"

"Maybe a little." I giggle again. This is the most I've giggled in my life.

"Where are you?"

"Reese's house," I answer, giving her a high five.

"Who?"

"Reese!" I say even louder.

"Oh, okay," he sighs. "Um, Jade, you sort of called me at a bad time. Can I call you tomorrow or later tonight?"

"You can do anything you want, Montgomery."

I hear people in the background. I suddenly get nervous, ending the call immediately and throwing my phone over to Reese.

"What happened?"

"I-I heard people and got nervous," I say.

My phone starts to buzz, and Monty's name is on my screen.

"Here's your chance. Answer and tell him how you feel."

I shake my head. "I'm deciding I don't want to be bold tonight."

Reese lets out a laugh but yawns seconds later. "Yeah, that would be terrible if you told him. You should probably sleepover."

I nod, leaning my head on her shoulder. "Goodnight, Reese."

CHAPTER 22

"Reese, wake up!" I say, poking her drooling face that's leaning on her pillow. "I did something so stupid. I was hoping it was all a dream, but it wasn't, so wake the fuck up!" I shout.

Reese's eyes flutter open. She groans, trying to turn to her side, but I won't let her.

"You can't sleep!"

"Yes, I can. I have a bad headache," she cries.

"Well, so do I. I made coffee. So, get up." I pull her silky blanket off, and she groans again, gradually sitting up and taking a sip of water by her bed.

"What's wrong?" she finally asks.

"I did something that people do in movies, and you think to yourself, 'Who would ever do something like that?' But I did! I did the horrid thing," I say, following her into the kitchen.

First, she pours both of us a steaming cup of coffee. Then, she opens the refrigerator door and grabs the almond milk. "You called Monty?"

"You remember?"

"A little," she says, rubbing the back of her head as if that'll help her magically remember.

"I can't believe I'm that character that we watch and pity."

"Well, at least you got some practice as an actress."

"I know you're only saying this to make me feel better, but it's not working," I sigh.

Reese takes a sip of her coffee and shakes her head. "Do you remember what you said to him?"

"All I remember is saying something about how 'future me' will handle it all tomorrow morning. We can be so stupid."

"We?"

"Yes, we! You're the one who said it, and I remember getting all nervous and shit because I heard people around him."

"Maybe he was at a restaurant," she says.

"With whom? Chelsea? Or maybe he was with Violet, and she was listening to our call, and they were making fun of me."

"Violet wouldn't do that, and besides, you didn't technically say anything bad."

"How do you know? You don't remember," I say sarcastically. "All I know is that I drunk dialed him, and he knows what that means."

"What *does* that mean exactly?"

"That I think about him when I'm under the influence. Do you remember when Noah would call me right after we broke up? He was so drunk, always saying shit like, 'There are things I need to tell you. I'm a terrible person.' *Blah, blah, blah.*"

"Yeah, but you guys just got out of a serious long-term relationship. He was lonely and missed you."

I let out a deep breath. *How could I be so dumb?*

"Just relax, Jade. Ask Violet about it if you are so worried. Are you working with her today?"

I look up from my coffee and run over to my phone that's about to die. "Oh no! I'm so late," I whine.

Without saying goodbye, I dash out the door, sliding my black army boots on. I try to grab a taxi as fast as I can. My phone doesn't have enough battery to order an Uber, and I need my last bar to call Violet.

"Violet!" I say, out of breath, running down the busy street.

"Hey, where are you? Wanda is asking questions, and I don't know what to say," she says quietly through the phone.

"I'm running late. Tell her I'm dealing with a little emergency, and I'll be there asap," I say loudly.

Four blocks later, I'm opening the door to the cafe, sweaty and out of breath.

"What happened to you?" Wanda crosses her arms.

"I'm sorry, Wanda. I told Violet to tell you—" I stop talking to catch my breath.

"She said you had some emergency. So, let's hear it. What's the emergency?"

"It was my grandma. I can't go into the details. I'm too emotional."

"I'm sorry to hear. I understand what that's like," she says, and I can tell from her expression that she buys my story. I feel a little bad about it, but I have no choice. I don't want to lose my job.

"Thanks, Wanda."

She gives me a small smile and a pat on the shoulder before walking away.

I quickly head to the back, grabbing an extra uniform.

"Are you okay?"

I look over at Violet, who's walking up to me. "Yeah, I'm fine. Lost track of time. Thanks for having my back with Wanda."

"Of course."

I quickly get changed and put my hair into a messy high bun. "You're working registers with me, right?"

Violet nods.

A couple of people come up to the counter and order their drinks. Luckily for me, all I'm doing is pushing buttons into the computer while Violet is doing the hard part—making all the drinks.

"I'm so tired," I groan.

"You look hungover." She lets out a little laugh.

"Because I am."

Violet looks at me and smiles. "No shit, really? Getting drunk on a Tuesday night is a thing now?"

"Last night it was, but this morning I'm regretting everything."

"Regretting what?" She raises a brow.

Oh no, she knows. She definitely knows that I drunkenly called Monty intending to tell him I'm madly in love with him.

"Jade?" She smiles, waving her hand in front of my face. "How hungover are you?"

"Um, extremely, I guess."

"Don't worry about any regrets when you're drunk. It happens. Do you know how many times I've mistakenly hooked up with someone because I was so plastered?" She laughs out loud.

I nod. Okay, he definitely wasn't with Violet last night. She thinks I had sex with some random dude. This is the only time I'll let someone think I did something I really didn't do, just so my secret doesn't come out. That is unless he tells her himself.

"What did you do last night?" I ask her, just to double-check.

"Ate Ben and Jerrys and used a vibrator while watching some lesbian porn," she says nonchalantly. Luckily, a customer comes up to the counter, and I don't have to engage in that conversation.

I hear Violet chuckle behind me as I push the order for a large black coffee with sugar and milk into the computer.

~

Violet lets out a loud whistle as we wait patiently for a cab after our shift. I tug on my dress and lean my body on one hip, crossing my arms.

"Are you still hungover?" Violet asks, turning her head slightly to me.

"Slightly."

"You know what really helps with a hangover?" Violet teases.

"A bottle of Tylenol?" I half-smile.

"Something better than that," she says.

"Are you talking about that bar right across the street?" I ask, watching her eyes scan the bar door.

"No? But I'm down for a glass of whiskey." She smiles.

I stand still for a second, looking back at Violet and the entrance to the bar. "Fuck it." I throw my hands in the air, walking past her.

Violet and I find a small table in the back. The only thing I can stomach is a fruity drink. The ones with the cute umbrellas and a piece of pineapple sitting so perfectly on the rim of the glass? Yeah, that kind.

"I think we should do some shots," Violet says excitedly.

I study her thick eyebrows moving up and down. "I think not."

"C'mon, Jade, didn't you feel a sense of liberation today?"

"No, I think I felt more on the side of wanting to die."

Violet laughs and mouths *three shots* to the bartender.

"Three?" I raise a brow. "Someone's tryin' to get drunk."

"No, I'm only having one."

"So, they're mine?"

She shakes her head. "Nope."

"Then who are they for?"

Before she can answer, I see a set of familiar blue eyes walking towards us.

"You invited Monty?" I whisper in her ears.

"Yeah. Is there a problem?" She looks confused by my question.

I don't respond to that. I study Monty from afar. He's wearing a pair of white ripped jeans, which are cuffed at the bottom, exposing his hairy ankles and sockless vans.

He scratches the back of his shaven head and pulls a chair out. Monty and I make eye contact, which doesn't last very long. I wonder if he's judging me for calling him when I was so intoxicated. I lean my elbows on the table, lazily playing with the straw in my drink. The drink I haven't even taken a sip from yet.

The waiter brings over the three shots, and Violet smiles at him. Monty and Violet then gently tap their shot glasses together and immediately look at me.

"No, thank you, really," I sigh.

"Jade's a lightweight, Monty. She was practically drunk at work today." Violet laughs out loud.

I cringe. "No, I wasn't."

"Well, she was definitely hungover."

"Let's not talk about that."

Monty takes his shot and lets out a groan. "You two are terrible influences," he says, tapping Violet's shoulder.

"Hey!" She laughs, practically hanging all over him. "Life is hard, work is annoying, but alcohol and friends always mend everything, right?"

Violet glances at me, and I clap my hands, "Well said, Vi. Well said."

"You couldn't have put it any better." Monty smiles, glancing at me.

Violet gets up and lets out a laugh. "I have a small bladder, though." And with that, she vanishes into the bathroom.

I continue to play with my straw, and I wait for Monty to speak. I want him to say something, *anything* so I don't have to suffer from this terrible awkward silence and the terrible disco music playing in the speakers.

"How was your day?" he finally asks me.

I look up from my lap and smile without showing any teeth. I move my hair away from my eyes. "Well, I've had better days."

Monty nods and shrugs. "I'm sorry I was sort of cold last night."

"Oh no, you weren't. I shouldn't have called you," I say.

"I'm glad you did, honestly. I was attending one of my buddies' opening shows, and I hate to say it, but it wasn't the greatest."

I smile. "Oh, so you were happy when you saw my name?"

"I was. Gave me an excuse to leave."

"I can act pretty stupid when I'm drunk," I say with a sigh.

"Don't we all?" he says, glancing at Violet exiting the bathroom.

Violet collapses down on her chair and drapes her arms around Monty. "Wanna do another shot?"

"I think we should get you home," Monty says.

Monty and I get Violet into an Uber. We wave her goodbye as her Uber pulls safely onto the street.

"Then there were two," he jokes.

"What are your plans for the rest of the day?" I ask him.

He glances at his watch and shrugs. "Nothing."

"No plans with your girlfriend?" I ask, but he doesn't respond. Jeez, I'm such a spaz.

Monty looks at me, and silence forms yet again. I've never been this quiet with anyone in my whole life.

"I live a few blocks from here if you want to come by for a little while?" I ask him, studying his pierced lip.

"I'm just remembering that I actually have dinner plans tonight, but I'd love to walk you home."

And with that, Monty and I walk down the busy streets. Silently.

"So, have you always lived in New York?" I ask him.

Monty scratches the back of his neck and immediately puts his hand back into his front pocket. "No, actually. I'm originally from Florida."

I look at the side of his face and laugh.

"You don't believe me?" he asks, the corner of his mouth starting to form a smile.

"No, I do; it's just that you totally give off the 'I've lived in New York my whole life' vibe," I say.

"No, I get it." He smiles. "I never belonged there, honestly."

I nod. "So, I'm assuming you like it here in Brooklyn?"

"I do. I've never felt more alive. Especially with the career path I've chosen."

"Yeah, I get it."

"So, Jade, what's *your* story?"

We stop walking. Mr. Kens, of course, is sitting on the steps to my apartment building. I glance at him, but my eyes are drawn back to Monty.

"Well, it's still a work in progress." I grin.

"It's only the rough draft," Monty adds.

I nod. "Yes. Exactly."

"So, what chapter are you on now?" he asks me.

"This one is called the…" I pause, playfully biting the tip of my pointer finger.

All of a sudden, I feel both of Monty's hands on my cheeks. I don't say a word. Monty doesn't either. All I can see is Monty's blue eyes bleeding into mine.

"It's called…" I breathe, my lips almost touching his. I can smell a mixture of cigarettes and mint through my nostrils.

"It's called the 'I want to kiss you, but I know I shouldn't.'" His words come out like a whisper, almost like a cry for help.

I blink a few times and lower my head, trying not to think about how close we are to each other. Monty raises my chin and gently pushes some stubborn strands of hair behind my ear.

"I think you—"

But before I can say anything else, Monty leans in and gives me a big kiss, sliding his tongue into my mouth. My whole body feels like it's floating. The craziness around us begins to disappear, and at this moment, nothing in this world exists but Monty and me. I deepen the kiss, finally wrapping my arms around his neck. He breaks the kiss to stare into my eyes. We are so close that our foreheads are touching. I can feel his fingers running down my spine. Monty gives me one more peck like he's trying to tell me something through that one little kiss. A gust of wind hits both of us, and my hair is flying in all directions.

Monty turns around without saying a word to me. He immediately crosses the street with his head lowered, and both his hands shoved into his jean pockets. I stand completely still; it feels like ages until I can get my footing again. I feel flustered, but in a good way. My hair is messy, and I can't help but touch my bottom lip.

"That was one hell of a kiss!" Mr. Kens lets out a honk before throwing his cigarette butt past me.

CHAPTER 23

It's been one week and four days since I've heard from Monty after our kiss. It's not like I'm counting or anything, but when someone kisses you like that, you begin to wonder if they feel the same way as you do. I've been feeling a little sad recently. I hate to ruin how that kiss made me feel, but he's technically still in a relationship. And I never want to be the "other woman." Maybe that's why he created all this distance between us. I've never had such a strong pull towards anyone before, and it's getting to my head. More importantly, I haven't exactly told anyone about our little kiss. The only person that technically knows is Mr. Kens, but he's irrelevant. I guess I've been a little hesitant about spilling the news to Reese. I know she'll roll her eyes, or even worse, she'll get super excited and ask tons of questions that I don't even know the answers to. If space is what he needs, then space it is.

I hear a knock at my front door, and I put down my book and get up. I open the door and see Violet holding a tray of iced coffees in one hand and a black leather leash in the other. I look down and see a chubby, drooling bulldog panting by her feet.

"Wanna go for a walk?" she asks.

Violet and I go down the street for a little stroll. "I hope I didn't interrupt you from anything," she says before taking a sip of her coffee.

"I was just doing what everyone does on a beautiful Saturday afternoon. You know, lying on my bed and reading my book." I give her a grin.

We cross the street and walk into a nearby park. "Bella and I needed some company." She laughs, bending down and patting her dog's head. I smile, and we find a bench under an oak tree.

"I'm glad because I needed some coffee," I say, and she laughs. "I didn't think anyone actually went to the coffee shop on their days off," I say, eyeing Coffee Bean Express printed on my ice coffee.

"Well..." she says, while lazily using her pierced tongue to play with the straw. "The reason I went there was to ask for some time off so I can go to Milwaukee tonight."

"Oh, wow. You're going to Wisconsin tonight?"

She nods. "Yeah, it was a last-minute thing."

"Is everything all right? I didn't think anyone ever goes to Milwaukee unless they really have to," I say.

She laughs. "I desperately need to see someone that moved there a year ago."

"May I ask who?'"

"My ex." She pauses. "Her name is Sarah. We dated for about a year and six months, and I did something to her that I wish I could take back." She looks down at her lap.

I grab her hand, giving it a tiny squeeze.

A tear crawls out, and she quickly wipes it away, letting out a nervous laugh. "Gosh, I shouldn't cry in public."

"Let it all out," I say, moving her blonde curls away from her face. She turns her head and looks me in the eye. "I cheated on her."

I nod and wait for her to continue, not wanting to interrupt her.

"I feel so horrible about it. It was with someone I met at some bar on 5th Street. We got into this little argument, and I decided to go out and get drunk." She pauses. "And five shots later, I'm in the bathroom stall with Buck." She shakes her head and laughs. "Yeah, I know what you're thinking. How desperate am I to sleep with a guy named Buck?"

"So how did she find out?" I ask her.

"Well, when I got home, she was still there, and we talked it out. We made up, but I eventually told her, like four months later."

"Then she broke up with you?"

Violet nods then lets out a deep breath. "Yeah, and a few months ago, I found out from a mutual friend that she got a job offer. She moved to Milwaukee."

"What took you so long to want to get back together?"

"I thought I was over her completely. But everyone that I've been with since could never compare to Sarah," she cries. "I need her back, Jade." Violet grabs a couple of treats from her bag and gives them to Bella. She picks her up and begins to rub her hand on her tummy. "The only problem is," she pauses, "I can't bring Bella."

"So, what are you going to do?"

She looks at me and gives me a smile.

I shake my head. "Violet, I can't. I've never owned a dog. Actually, I've never had any type of animal before. I wouldn't know what to do."

"I'd tell you everything you'd need to know. Bella's a very well-behaved dog. Aren't you, my sweet baby?" she says to Bella in one of those baby voices.

"Don't you have a sister or brother or just any other friend to watch her? What about Alex or—"

She grabs Bella's waist and sits her on her lap like a baby. "Please, Jade! Please let me live with you for *five* days so my mommy can win back her one true love!" Violet says in a baby voice, practically shoving Bella in my face.

"Fine! Only because I'm a pathetic hopeless romantic and love epic love stories."

Violet lets out a squeal and gives me a kiss on my cheek. "*Te amo*, baby, *te amo*."

"Yeah, yeah, whatever," I say, petting Bella's back and trying my hardest not to smile.

∼

Later that afternoon, after listening to all of Violet's instructions for Bella, I'm left with a dog and an empty stomach. I walk down the crowded sidewalk with Bella and make my way to the pizzeria by my house. As I approach, I can already smell the fresh pies coming out of the oven. I open the door and allow Bella to walk in first. I want her to like me. The man with the red bandana and ponytail asks me what I want.

"Two slices, please." I point to the plain pie on the counter and pay with the only five dollar bill I have in my wallet. He nods, and I take a seat at one of the empty booths. I watch Bella sniff around, and I can't help but look at her little legs and soft tummy.

"Cute dog."

I look up, and an older man is standing in line in front of me with his hands crossed.

"Oh, thank you." I smile.

"Bulldogs are great dogs. I had one when I was a boy," he says.

"They are quite cute," I say with a nod as he starts to move up with the line. I glance at Bella and pull her in so she's not sniffing the family next to me. My order is called, and I can't wait to get home.

~

"*Mi casa es su casa,*" I say as soon as we get inside. I grab Bella's water bowl that Violet gave me, and I give her some water before I sit down and eat. I turn the television on and plop on the couch with my pizza and a glass of wine. I take a couple of bites and close my eyes. I am savoring the warmth and taste of this triangular slice of goodness. Bella jumps on the couch, and I watch her plop down beside me. I turn my attention back to the television, but all I see in the corner of my eye is this four-legged animal watching my every move. I pause the TV. "Bella? Is everything all right?"

She moves a little closer to me, and I can see that she is staring at my pizza. Oh. Can dogs eat pizza? I know for sure they can't eat chocolate, but pizza? No idea. My phone buzzes, and I see Reese's name on my screen.

"Hey," I say, taking a bite of pizza.

"What are you doing tonight?"

"You know, the norm—eating pizza, drinking wine. I have a question."

"Shoot."

"Can dogs eat pizza?"

She laughs. "Why? Did you buy a dog without telling me?"

"No, but there's a very chubby bulldog making an eye for my pizza right now."

"Whose dog?" she asks.

"It's Violet's dog. I'm watching her for a few days so she can win back her lover."

"Wow, so romantic."

"Tell me about it," I say, taking a sip of wine.

"So, what do you say about getting some drinks tonight around eight?"

"Oh, I don't know, Reese. Would it be irresponsible of me to leave Bella?"

"Not at all. People leave their dogs home alone all the time."

"I guess you're right," I say.

I glance at Bella's cute face and feed her a piece of my crust.

After I finish getting ready, I give Bella a couple of her toys and her "special blanket." It's just a ripped-up towel, but whatever floats her boat. I linger by the door, and Bella's just sitting there, looking up at me. I swear she's giving me a frown.

"Okay, Bella. Jade is leaving and will be back very soon. So, be on your best behavior," I say slowly. Jeez, I'm literally speaking to this dog like she's a human. I grab my bag and head out, trying my hardest not to look back.

∼

I spot Reese sitting alone at the bar as I make my way through the crowd of people. I squeeze in beside a man and woman having a very intimate conversation.

"Took you long enough," Reese says, taking a sip of her martini.

"Well, it's a bitch to get a cab around this time." I wave my hand to get the bartender's attention. "One Corona, please!" I call out so he can hear me.

"So, what happened to Saturday night dates with Wes?" I ask her.

She moves her hair to one shoulder and sighs. "I needed some girl time, and besides, he's going to that baseball game with Colin and Darian tonight."

I nod. "Oh right, I forgot about that."

"I wasn't in the mood to watch them pregame at my place." She laughs.

I take a sip of my beer and turn to Reese. "So, what's the plan for tonight?"

"Well, one of my friends from school is meeting us, and she's bringing her brother along. I thought we'd hang here for a while and then maybe grab some dinner later?"

Two martinis and a beer later, Reese's friend Sofie and her brother Greg eventually meet up with us. They make a straight beeline for Reese and give her a hug as soon as they approach us. "Sofie, Greg, this is my friend Jade, the one I was telling you about."

From what I heard from Reese, they're twins, born and raised in Rhode Island. Sofie is studying to be a nurse, and Greg goes to NYU, studying something to do with computers. I can't really remember what she said. I stopped listening after she said computers.

"Wow, I'm flattered." I laugh.

Greg gives me a smile and runs his hand through his auburn hair. "Shots, anyone?"

The four of us find a table by the window, and I'm standing between Reese and Greg. They both take another shot, and I casually look around the crowded place.

"Here ya go," Reese says, handing me a tequila shot.

I lick a little of the salt from the rim of the shot glass, and I wait for Greg and Sofie to come back with some more drinks.

"So, what do you think of Greg?" Reese asks in my ear.

"He seems like a cool dude. Why?"

"Oh, no reason," Reese says nonchalantly while she sways back and forth to the music.

I put my shot glass down and cross my arms. "What are you trying to do, Reese?"

She smiles. "I don't know what you're talking about, Jade."

"I know you're up to something. I'm onto you," I say, narrowing my eyes at her.

"I'm not doing anything, Jade. Relax." She pulls on my cheek and laughs.

"Okay, fine. But just admit you're trying to set me up with Sofie's brother."

She looks at me then back at her drink. "No," she says quietly. Reese is intoxicated, and I'm annoyed.

"I'm outta here," I say, but as I'm about to turn away, Greg comes up beside me and hands me a Corona.

"For me?" I ask.

"Yeah, I saw you were drinking one earlier."

I glance at Reese. Am I the only one that isn't in on this setup? Reese and Sofie are giggling like two little schoolgirls in the background.

"Thanks, Greg," I say.

"So, Reese was telling me you're an actress."

I nod.

"That's insane. My mother was a very talented screenplay writer."

I turn to him and take a sip of my beer. "Was?" I tilt my head to the side.

He looks down and nods. "Yeah, she recently passed away."

I frown. "I'm so sorry, Greg."

"It's fine." He gives me a small smile. "I know she's in a better place."

"She is." I smile. "I need some air. Do you want to join me?" I ask in his ear, and he nods.

~

Greg and I walk a little past the entrance of the bar. The big, muscular bouncer is giving a couple of people a hard time. Greg and I ignore the arguing as we slowly stroll down the sidewalk, enjoying the beautiful spring breeze.

"Wow, it was fucking loud in there." He laughs out loud.

I turn to face him. "Greg? Do you realize this was a complete set-up from your sister and Reese?"

"Oh, completely." He laughs. "But my sister did tell me she was going to introduce me to someone tonight."

"Oh, that's nice. Reese forgot to mention that," I say with a groan.

"So technically, *I* was fully aware of this sorta blind date."

"Yeah, Reese didn't tell me. Probably because if she did, I most likely wouldn't have come," I tell him.

"Some bad experiences with blind dates?"

"Sort of. Only when Reese sets them up." I laugh.

"I feel you, Jade. I was a little hesitant about this as well."

"Okay, good, it's not just me then."

There's awkward silence between us as he stares into my eyes. "I recently got out of a very serious relationship," he says.

"Oh, I'm sorry to hear that."

"Yeah, we dated for seven years, and she broke up with me two weeks after my mother died."

I nod my head, not really sure what to say. This guy seems to make all of our conversations depressing...

He smiles. "Yeah, silence is usually the most common response I get."

"Oh, Greg, I'm sorry. I just—"

"She was the love of my life. I always thought she'd be the mother of my children someday. When my mother was diagnosed with breast cancer, it was like she changed and was slowly distancing herself." He lets out a tiny sigh, placing his palm to his forehead. "And she tells me she just can't do this anymore. What about me? What about my feelings? It was always about her. And when I needed her the most...

poof, she was gone." A tear comes crawling down his cheeks, and he quickly puts his hands over his face. Is he crying? Wow, this took a spin for the worst.

I rub his shoulder. "Um, Greg, do you want to take a walk? We can stop by my place, and you can relax, maybe drink some soothing tea?" *Jade, what the hell are you doing?*

He moves his hand away from his face and nods. "Tea sounds perfect. Thank you, Jade."

∿

The walk from the bar to my place was a disaster. It was like all of Greg's baggage from when he was a child to problems he has now just exploded on me.

I really regret inviting him back to my place. He's a total mess, but I can't just send him home when he's like this. I'm not that mean. Negative points for Reese and her matchmaking skills. And besides, hanging around Greg really helps distract my mind from thinking about Monty.

"Just make yourself at home," I say.

He takes off his jacket and sits on Colin's chair. "I used to have one of these chairs when I was little," he says.

Oh, no. Please not *another* story about your terrible childhood. One can only take so much. I boil some water and walk over to him, grabbing his hand. "Why don't you sit on the couch?" I smile.

He stands up and follows, and we both plop on the couch. Bella begins to sniff, and I pick her up and sit her beside me. Just in case he owned a dog with his ex…

"I'm sorry this date—" But before he finishes, he grabs a tissue from the coffee table and lets out a big one. "I've been really out of the game, as you can see." He attempts to smile.

"It's all right, Greg," I say, looking at his pink sniffling nose.

He moves a piece of my bangs away from my eyes, and I cringe a little. If he thinks he can get all romantic and shit with me…Well, it's not happening. I'm definitely not feeling it. At first, I gave him a shot because I am attracted to him, and I was honestly a little horny when I first saw him. But now…

"You're so beautiful, Jade. Inside and out," he says, staring intensely into my eyes.

He begins making tiny circles on my cheek with his thumb, and I can see him trying to move closer to me. I grab his wrist before he tries to kiss me, removing his hand from my face.

"Greg…"

"I'm sorry, Jade," he cries. "I guess I didn't read that very well."

I stand up and pour the boiling water into two mugs and drop a teabag in both.

"You're very kind," Greg comments.

I take a sip of my tea and set it down on the coffee table, and he does the same. The front door opens, and Colin comes strolling inside. He is automatically welcomed by Bella. "When did you get a dog?" he asks, bending down and rubbing Bella's belly.

"I'm babysitting her for a friend," I tell him.

"Aren't you the cutest girl?" Colin says, with a baby voice. I discreetly smile, watching Colin rub Bella's belly as he says sweet things to her. I turn my attention back to Greg, remembering he's still in my apartment.

"Sorry, that's just my roommate."

Colin stands up and walks over to us. *Oh great.*

"What's up, man? I'm Colin."

"Greg." They shake hands.

Colin grabs a beer from his cooler and plops on his chair, totally ignoring that Greg and I are in the same room as him.

"*Ahh*," he says, finishing the can and grabbing another one.

"Don't you have anywhere better to be?" I cross my arms. This is probably one of the worst dates, or whatever this is, but I don't want Colin to know that.

Colin looks at Greg then back at me. He lets out a laugh. "Oh, I'm sorry, roomie. Am I interrupting something?"

"Well—"

Before I can finish, Greg asks, "Do you mind if I have a beer?"

"Yeah, of course not, man," he says, throwing one to Greg and giving me a wink.

"But I made you tea." I point to his mug.

"I think I need something a little bit stronger, considering."

"So, tell me, Greg, do you happen to be married? Have any kids that live in Vermont that you haven't told my roomie about yet?" Colin says with a grin plastered on his face, trying to mock me. He's trying to get under my skin, and it's not funny.

"Oh, no...what? I'm confused," Greg says, tilting his head. He looks at me strangely and then looks back at Colin.

I hit my forehead and sigh. "*Ha-ha*, very funny, Colin. I think it's time for you to leave."

Colin gets up and smiles. "Hope to see you again, Grant."

"It's Greg."

But Colin's already gone into his bedroom.

"I'm sorry. He has no manners," I say with a sigh.

"That's all right." Greg nervously laughs, then stands up and grabs his jacket. "It's getting pretty late. I should probably get home."

I nod and walk him to the door.

"Thank you for listening, Jade. I'd love to take you on a proper date, and hopefully, next time, I'll leave my worries at home."

I give him a hug. "I'd love that, Greg."

He gives me a kiss on my forehead and leaves. I let out a deep breath and sigh.

Maybe I should have taken Jason up on his offer...

~

"What the heck happened with you and Greg last night?" Reese asks over the phone the next morning. I put a few quarters into the washing machine while trying my hardest to hold my phone with my shoulder. I grab my laundry bag and sit down on the bench by the window. An older lady walks by me with her three grandchildren, who are making a whole lotta noise.

"Nothing," I say.

"Well, you guys left and never came back," she says. "Where are you? It's loud."

I move my phone to the other ear. "I'm at the laundromat. It's a zoo in here today."

"So, what happened?"

"We decided to hang out at my place."

"And?"

"Nothing happened if that's what you're wondering." I frown. "Also, why did you set me up with him?"

"I don't know. Sofie told me he recently got out of a relationship and has been wanting to meet someone."

"Did Sofie forget to mention it was a seven-year relationship, and he's not quite over it just yet?"

"What? Are you saying what I think you're saying?"

"Reese, he cried the whole time."

She laughs. "About what exactly?"

"His mom passing away and always feeling like he couldn't live up to his father's expectations, his ex, his neighbor across from him, Keven Harrlol from elementary school, a girl who stole his

Twinkie in high school. Should I go on?"

"There's more?"

"Yup. I didn't even get to the depressing shit yet."

"Oh wow. That is insane. Wow."

I laugh. "Tell me about it."

"I apologize. I won't match you up anymore. I promise."

That's what Reese always says, but she can't help herself with the need to do it again. It's nice of her, but I just wished she'd stop.

I don't tell her any of this. I simply say, "Thank you."

"Sofie had a lot of great things to say about him. She never ever mentioned that he has so many hang-ups."

"Maybe he just never shares them with her?"

"I guess not. Apparently, he likes to do that with complete strangers." She laughs.

"I'm taking Bella for a walk after I finish doing my laundry; wanna join us?" I ask as I glance out the window, watching cars pass on the streets.

"I wish I could, but I'm getting lunch with my parents. Actually, I probably should leave now. Next time?"

I smile. "Sure! You owe me for last night, by the way."

"All right, I'll treat you and Bella to some frozen yogurt."

"Ice cream, and it's a deal."

She laughs. "Deal."

CHAPTER 24

I decided to tell Reese about the kiss I had with Monty. I planned to sound nonchalant about it, but what came out was a schoolgirl squeal. A squeal that I'll never be able to live down. She was surprised, knowing that he's taken and all, but she understands why I haven't heard from him.

"He's probably confused," she sighs, taking a sip of her latte. I gently tug on Bella's leash, bringing her closer to our outside table.

I rip off a piece of my orange scone and dip it into my hot coffee. "But what about me? I'm just as confused as he is."

"Have you tried to contact him at all?"

I shake my head. "And say what? If he doesn't want to speak to me, then I guess there's nothing I can do."

"You really like this guy." Reese gives me a small smile.

"I do," I sigh.

"Have you tried talking to Violet?" Reese suggests.

I let out a chuckle, glancing at Bella. "I can't bring her into all of this while she's trying to win back Sarah."

"Maybe she already knows."

I shake my head. "Why are boys so complicated?"

"We may never know."

⌒

Later that night, I decided to ask Colin and Wes the same question. It can't hurt to get a male perspective on things. "That's easy; we're not," Colin says, putting his hands up.

"We're so simple that girls think we're complicated. They overanalyze everything, then realize, in the end, that they are the complicated ones," Wes says to Reese and me.

Reese rolls her eyes. "Oh please, not true."

"I think that sounds pretty fucking legitimate." Colin lets out a huge burp.

"You can't relate, Colin. Wes is in a different category than you. At least he knows how to be in a relationship," I say before getting off the couch. Bella, of course, follows. She's been very clingy, like one of those girlfriends who never give you space. I hear Colin say something, but I ignore him. I'm going to put this whole kiss with Monty in the past. Life's too short to constantly wonder about a guy.

I just wish the kiss had been terrible.

⌒

The next day, around noon, Violet calls to check in on Bella. "So, how's my Bella doing?"

"Oh, she's great. Not at all what I expected." I pause. "How's it going over there?"

Violet lets out a deep breath. "Not the best to be completely honest. Sarah's not the most forgiving person."

"I'm sorry," I sigh.

"Yeah. At least I have a few more days to try to get into her good graces." Violet nervously laughs.

Bella is by the fridge, sniffing the floor. I think she's trying to find food. I don't know why since her bowl, filled with food, is just a few feet from her.

I get off the phone with Violet a couple minutes later. Colin eventually comes out of his room, shirtless and with terrible bedhead. There's also some scruff forming on his face.

"Nice beard," I say as I flip the page of my new script.

"Hardly," he says, rubbing his chin. He opens the fridge and grabs some leftover pizza.

Bella runs past him and sits patiently by the door. Colin and I make eye contact, and I sigh. "I think Bella—" he begins to say, and I nod.

"Yeah, I know," I say, getting up to put my shoes on.

"Give me a second; I'll come with."

I watch as he walks into his room to grab a t-shirt. I wouldn't say I don't want him to join me; it's just that I'm a bit surprised because he doesn't usually offer to take walks with me.

Colin and I decided to take a nice walk to Seabreeze Park. We thought we'd give Bella some exercise, and we are also hoping that Bella would maybe make some new doggy friends. The park is packed—tons of families are going for little strolls with their dogs, couples are picnicking, and old men are playing chess.

"We should have brought a frisbee," Colin says, eying a frisbee that is flying past him.

Bella tries to pull towards a tree, but I see a familiar face out of the corner of my eye. Bella yanks my arm, practically throwing my whole body forward.

"Whoa, there." Colin lets out a laugh. I find my footing and get out of my daze as I pull Bella back. I grab onto Colin and use his body to block me from the familiar blue eyes coming towards me.

"What are you doing?" Colin asks, trying to turn around, but I don't let him.

"Jade? Is that you?"

The second I hear his voice, all I want to do is run away. Escape.

"Monty! Hi," I say.

"Were you hiding?" Monty asks, raising a brow.

"Oh yeah, I saw a squirrel over there, and I thought it was gonna attack me." I move away from Colin and closer to Monty.

"Yeah, it happens all the time. They must think her hair is a big, messy nest," Colin says.

I smack his arm, glaring at Colin. "Leave us, please."

Colin puts his hands up in surrender and takes Bella over to the grass.

"Sorry, that's my roommate. He has no filter."

"It's all good." Monty smiles. "I recognized Bella and remembered Violet mentioning that you'd be watching her this week."

It's like the kiss never happened. Does he realize what he's done to me this past week? Or does he do this with everyone? Kiss and then become distant? If so, I'm not into it.

"She told you?"

"Uh, yeah. She sort of came to me first, but my dog Tucker isn't the best around other dogs," he says, glancing at his huge Rottweiler.

"I can't believe I was her second option." I shake my head with a small smile.

"Well, just be happy you were an option. I've known Violet for a while, and she doesn't let a lot of people into her circle if you know what I mean."

I nod with a smile. "I do. I feel flattered."

"You should be." Monty looks down at his dog, who's trying to dig a hole beside us. "I should probably get going," he says. "Maybe we can meet here on purpose sometime? Maybe have a dog date? If that's even a thing." He chuckles.

I grin. "It's definitely a thing."

"Okay, good." He gives me a small smile. "Take care, Jade." He waves goodbye, and I watch Monty's bow-legged legs walk down the crowded sidewalk.

Colin comes up beside me and lets out a laugh.

"What's so funny?"

"Oh, nothing." He gives me a knowing smile as he hands me back the leash. "You're a goner."

"I am not!" I cover my face so he doesn't see me blush.

But Colin's right. I totally am.

On the way back home, I can't help but replay the fantastic conversation I had with Monty over and over again in my head. He finally asked me out! I can't believe it. I guess soon I'll see what his definition of a date really entails.

⌒

A couple days have passed, and the date with Monty is at the forefront of my mind. I was keeping it together quite well until I saw Monty's name on my phone screen. It buzzes a few times as I grab milk from the refrigerator at the supermarket. I walk down the aisle towards the check-out and answer the phone call. "Hi." I smile through the phone.

I put the few groceries I have onto the conveyor belt, and I switch my phone to my other ear.

"Hey, so are you up for that dog date?" he asks.

⌒

I rush home to grab Bella, dumping all my groceries into my fridge. I feel bad because she was literally snoring when I got home. She was lying on her back with her towel beside her. She really knows how to make herself at home.

"Some sunlight will do us both some good," I say to myself as we walk out the door.

Monty and his dog are sitting on a bench by a tree. His ankle is resting on his knee, and his eyes are glued to his phone. Before Monty can see that I'm here, I quickly take in this beautiful guy. But it doesn't take long for his dog Tucker to notice us. His dog starts to tug, and Monty looks up, catching eyes with me. Without saying a word, Monty gives me a quick smile, and I sit beside him.

"How are you?" he finally says.

I turn my head. "I'm great."

"So, this is what a dog date is."

"Yeah, looks about right." I grin.

Monty nudges his shoulder against mine and pats Bella on her head. "I actually helped Violet pick out Bella," he tells me.

I watch Bella plop down near Monty's feet, already tired and out of breath.

"She's a keeper." I smile. Silence fills the air, and I look down at my lap, wondering if Monty is feeling as awkward as I am.

Monty scratches the top of his head and lets out a nervous laugh. "Things in my life have been sort of crazy."

My eyes are glued to Bella as I ask, "Is everything okay?"

I finally look into his eyes, and he lets out a sigh. "Not really. I've been dealing with a lot of shit."

I nod, and he continues. "And that kiss has been on my mind. I'm sorry I've been distant from you. Something came over me that day." He pauses. "I'm extremely attracted to you, Jade." I watch his mouth move as he says each word. "But I don't do things like that, ever. And I needed time to process it all. When Chelsea cheated on me, I said to myself that I'd never go down to any level like that, but I did."

"Monty—" I say, but he shakes his head.

I touch his shoulder, but he moves away.

"If you touch me, Jade, all I'll want to do is kiss you again."

I desperately don't want to move my hand away from Monty's shoulder. I want him to take me right now, on this hard concrete bench, but I nod, moving my hand back to my lap.

"I just want to say that I don't usually do anything like that either. Kiss someone else's boyfriend, I mean."

"I respect that," he says.

"So, what now?" I ask, looking into his eyes.

Monty bites his lower lip and plays with the leash between his hands.

"Chelsea and I have always had a toxic relationship. Maybe I'm just a sucker for sticking around with her. Even after the whole cheating thing," he says. "But I realized I needed to make a change to better myself and my life." He pauses, and it feels like a million years until he finally speaks again. "So, I called it quits."

I shoot my head over to him, and we catch eyes. "How did she take it?"

"Well, there were a lot of words being thrown...and plates." He half-smiles. "But I honestly felt amazing after I did it. She wasn't right for me."

"I just want to say, Monty, that I like you. I like you a lot. I might regret saying this, but I don't care. I get it if you want to take some time to figure things out—"

Monty smiles, placing his hand on my cheek and pulling me closer to his face. "I don't. I'm willing to try this out with you. If you are."

"Yes." I grin. "I want it more than anything. I think we vibe really well together," I admit.

"That's cute. You're cute." He grins.

Monty moves his hands away from my face and spreads his fingers through my wavy hair. Once his hand is on the back of my neck, he leans in and plants a little kiss on my lips. I smile, deepening our kiss.

"You have a beautiful soul, Jade."

I bite my bottom lip and lean in to kiss him again. Monty grabs my hand and intertwines our fingers before giving my palm a kiss.

∼

Meanwhile, Colin and Wes are staring at the television, hypnotized by the game. I look back and forth at their faces, and I shake my head as I lean back on the couch. "I don't understand why you guys care so much."

"I can say the same thing when you watch those stupid runway shows," Colin says in a monotone voice.

"Well, at least it's entertaining," I say.

Reese sits down next to me with a bowl of popcorn. "I agree with Jade," she says, shoving a handful of popcorn in her mouth.

"So, what's the plan for tonight?" Wes asks, finally looking away from the television.

Colin takes a sip of his beer and shrugs. "I'm down for some wings at that bar tonight."

I groan. "We always go there."

"Says the one who got hit on there and left with the guy. Maybe you'll get lucky tonight, roomie." Colin winks.

"Jade's taken now," Reese says, munching on popcorn. All three shoot their heads towards me, and I smack my hand on my forehead.

"Thanks, Reese," I sigh.

"What? It's not a secret," she says.

"Since when?" Colin asks, raising an eyebrow.

"Since yesterday, actually," I say quietly.

"Whoa, this is huge," Wes comments.

"Why is it huge?" I ask him.

"When are we gonna meet this dude?" Colin asks, interrupting Wes.

"Soon," I say. "I just need time."

"I think Jade's embarrassed by us," Reese says as she nudges me with her shoulder, giving me a grin.

"I'm not! Monty's just reserved and kind of shy—"

"So why are you with someone like that then?" Colin asks.

I get up and walk into the kitchen, grabbing a water bottle from the fridge. "Because I like him."

"Wait, is he that punk guy I met the other day?" Colin asks me.

I don't respond.

"It is him!" He laughs.

I walk back over to him. "What's so funny? And he's not punk, Colin. He's hip."

"No one says that anymore." Reese laughs.

"And this is the exact reason why I'm not bringing him around yet. You guys are already roasting him, and you haven't met him yet."

"I just can't believe Colin met him, and I didn't. Even Claire saw him," Reese says.

"We literally just started dating." I say.

"I haven't met him yet either, babe," Wes says, putting his arm around Reese.

"And what kind of name is Monty?" Colin asks, taking a sip of his beer.

"It's short for Montgomery." I want this conversation to end so badly. I hate when they put me on the spot.

"Okay, okay. Guys, Jade's our friend, and we can't roast her man because we love her and she's happy," Reese says, coming to my defense.

"Well, I'm allowed to because, according to Jade, we're not friends." Colin smiles. "But roomie, have fun with your punk boyfriend."

"I will."

The game comes back on, and the chit-chat about Monty finally ends.

CHAPTER 25

Bella barks when she hears a knock at the door. I fix my hair one last time before walking past her and let out a little breath as I open the door. Monty's standing there with a smile on his face and a bouquet of flowers.

My eyes open wide. "Oh my gosh!"

"Too much?" He grins.

"Not at all." I smile. I let him in and grab a tall cup from the cabinet.

"I don't have a vase, so this will have to do." I laugh, glancing at Monty, who's playing with Bella.

"So, this is your place," he says.

I nod. "Yep. It's a little messy. I live with a caveman."

Monty looks around and leans his hands on my couch. "It's cute," he says, disregarding my comment about Colin.

"I have the place to myself right now. Do you want to stay in or go out?"

"I was thinking we could take a walk."

"Sounds good to me."

Monty grabs my hand, and I smile to myself as we walk down the stairs, passing Mr. Kens. He's drunk, of course. Too drunk to even acknowledge us.

The sidewalks are crowded, especially on Saturday nights, but I'm just happy to be holding hands with Monty. He talks more about his life and wants to know more about mine. We talk about music and our favorite movies.

"Trust me, they have the best hotdogs here." Monty gives me a wide grin as we approach an umbrella stand on the corner of the street—the same exact umbrella stand I walk past every day on my way to work. A man with a big rounded belly and a white shirt with grease stains on it holds a pair of tongs in his hand. He shouts, "Hotdogs, get them here," in his thick New York accent.

"I'm always down for a good hotdog." I smile.

Monty orders us two hot dogs and two cans of coke. We grab some napkins and continue down the street. "And this is the exact reason I love New York," he says.

"Buying hotdogs from a stand?" I laugh.

"Yes! Exactly. Food stands on every corner. Always hot and always good."

"You couldn't have said it any better."

Monty gives my hand a squeeze before releasing it. My smile fades, but I recover as soon as he looks over at me. I give him a smile, taking a big bite of my hotdog.

"So, what makes this hotdog stand so much better than the rest?" I ask as we walk past another identical one.

"I know the guy. He hooks me up," Monty says.

I laugh. "Smart. I need to start making connections with the hotdog man."

"Hey! Don't judge."

"It's cute," I say with a smile before taking a sip of my coke.

"I asked you about your parents, but I never asked you if you have any siblings. So, do you have any siblings?" he asks between bites.

I take a sip of my drink and nod. "Yeah, I have an older sister, Natasha."

Monty takes a bite of his hot dog, and we continue to walk down the busy streets.

"What about you?" I ask.

"Little sister, actually. Her name is Annie."

"That's a pretty name." I smile.

Monty grabs my hand and intertwines our fingers. "I'm having a great night with you, by the way. Even if it's just getting hotdogs at a corner stand."

I look into his eyes and nod. "I am too, Monty."

"Just to let you know, Annie isn't my only sibling."

"Oh no?"

He shakes his head. "I have two half-brothers."

"Wow! That's awesome."

"Yeah. My dad remarried. They're cool."

"Do they live in New York?" I ask.

He shakes his head. "No, but my sister does. She goes to KCC. She's studying to be an accountant."

I finish my hotdog and smile. "Are you guys close?"

"Extremely. Annie is a little tough to get along with, but once you do, she's great." He nervously laughs.

"I'd love to meet them."

Monty kisses my cheek and smiles. "I'm glad to hear that. Chelsea was weird and never wanted to. When she finally did, they hated her. Well, my sister hates everyone, but you get what I mean," he says.

Wait, what? No, I don't.

"But when they come to town, you're the first person I'm gonna call."

"I can't wait," I say.

"And I'd love to meet your folks as well."

"Yeah, I mean, you can," I say, picturing my loud-mouthed family meeting Monty for the first time.

"I don't have to if you don't want me to."

"No! It's just my parents are actually visiting my mother's side of the family in Russia," I say.

"Well, I'd love to meet them when they get back."

"They would love to meet you, but more importantly, my friends are dying to meet you. They are like my second family."

Monty smiles. "That's sweet. When can I meet them?"

"I'll set that up soon and will let you know."

"Is there anything I should know about them beforehand?"

I don't respond. I'm trying to think of the best answer I can give him. "Just be yourself."

∽

I invited Monty over for dinner Saturday night to meet my friends. It's really important to me to incorporate my boyfriend into all aspects of my life.

"Is there a reason you're cooking instead of just going out?" Colin asks, taking a sip of his beer. He walks behind me, taking a green bean from the bowl. I slap his hand and sigh. "I want to impress, Monty."

"She wants to show him that she can cook," Reese says.

"But she's lying to him because Jade doesn't cook."

"I cook all the time, Colin," I snap.

"When?" He crosses his arms.

"Well, right now." I give him a cheeky smile.

Wes opens the front door in a huff. "Sorry I'm late. The subway was packed," he says, giving Reese a kiss. "It smells amazing in here, by the way," he says, grabbing a beer from the fridge.

"We're making chicken, pasta, and green beans," Reese says.

"When's he coming? I'm hungry," Colin groans.

"He's on his way," I say, opening the oven to check on the chicken. "It's ready, right?"

Reese walks over to me and nods. "Looks like it."

"If my chicken is raw, I'll kill both of you," Colin says.

Wes and Colin are watching a baseball game, and I'm impatiently tapping my foot, waiting for Monty. Reese and I set the table beautifully with a floral tablecloth. I put the bread rolls in a pretty basket and set it down.

We hear a soft knock at the door, and I quickly get up to open the door.

"Hey." He smiles, giving me a hug and a kiss on the cheek. He then hands me a bottle of wine.

"My favorite red." I smile, hugging the bottle.

I introduce Monty to Reese, and they immediately begin a conversation.

"Can you guys shut that off?" I call out to Colin and Wes.

"Hey man," Colin says, doing one of those handshakes guys give each other. Wes hands Monty a beer, and we all sit down. Everyone fills their plates with chicken and pasta, and Wes pours everyone a glass of wine.

Reese raises her glass. "I'm thankful for this food and this amazing company."

"Amen," Colin says, mouth stuffed with food.

"It's delicious, babe," Wes says, leaning in to kiss Reese.

"It is," Colin says.

"Oh wow, did I get an approval from Colin?" I raise a brow.

"I was complimenting Reese," Colin says.

I hit his shoulder, catching eyes with Monty. I give him a grin, but all I get in return is a nervous smile as he takes a sip of his wine.

"I'm going to be sad when Violet comes home because I have to give Bella back," I say.

Monty looks up. "It would be nearly impossible to think that Violet would ever let you keep her."

"I can't believe that chick is a lesbian. I have a good radar for those things, and she did not look like one," Colin says obliviously.

Everyone shoots their heads over to Colin, and I smack my hand on my forehead. Colin looks at me, his mouth filled with food. "What did I say?"

"So, Monty, do you watch baseball?" Wes asks, motioning his eyes over to the muted television screen.

Thank you, Wes, for changing the subject.

"No, I don't," Monty says quietly. An awkward silence fills the air. All I can hear is the sound of us chewing and Mr. Kens' muffled voice in the hallway.

"I just want to say, I really like your name," Reese says, looking at Monty.

Monty looks up and smiles without showing any teeth. "Thank you."

"Is it a name your parents always liked?" I ask.

"Well, Montgomery is my mother's maiden name, and Ian is my last name. So, they thought it would be cool to name me Montgomery since it's usually a last name. And Ian is normally a first name for most people, but for me, it's a last name." He coughs. "If that makes sense."

"Completely." I smile. "Montgomery Ian."

He nods, giving me a smile.

A long couple of hours later, we finally finished dinner and decided to sit around and drink some beer while watching the game, of course.

"So, what do you think?" I whisper to Reese. The two of us are washing the dishes, which gives me some time to get her opinion. I glance at Monty, who is sitting awkwardly next to Wes and Colin on the couch.

"He's nice." She smiles.

I tilt my head to the side and study my best friend. I hand her a dirty plate and bite my nail. "Just nice?"

She turns her head, making sure nobody can hear her but me. "He's just a little shy."

"I honestly have never seen him so shy, Reese."

"Don't worry, he'll loosen up. I mean, he has to." She laughs, eyeing him as he takes a sip of his beer. "Do you think he can be a potential date for the wedding?"

I groan. "Reese, stop asking me that question about every guy I date. I'm trying not to think about the wedding until it's close."

Reese puts her hands up and nods. We finally finished cleaning all the dishes and putting the leftovers away. I walk over to the guys, and I squeeze between Colin and Monty. I look at Monty, giving him a smile before leaning my head on his shoulder. I finally feel him relax with his hand resting on my lower back.

After the game is over and everyone is tired, Reese and Wes decide to leave. They say their goodbyes to Monty, and I smile. I love my friends. Even though Monty was a bit awkward tonight, they still put in the effort to get to know him.

"I should probably go too," Monty says.

I bite my bottom lip and frown. "I mean, you can stay the night. If you want to."

Colin comes out of the bathroom, burping and plopping on his chair.

Monty glances at him then back at me. "I should just go; it's late."

Wait, what?

"Oh, okay," I say, grabbing his hand and following him to the door.

"I had a lot of fun tonight. Thanks for making such a great dinner." He smiles, leaning in to give me a kiss on the cheek.

I smile. "No problem."

I give Monty a hug, but it seems like he can't wait to leave. Did I do something wrong tonight? Does he not like my friends? Or worse, me? I start to worry as I watch him walk down the hallway then disappear down the stairs.

"Burn." Colin laughs.

"Stop. Please."

"I'm just messing with you, roomie." Colin frowns.

I ignore him and walk into my room, slamming the door behind me. I then throw my horny and sad ass down on my bed.

～

Violet and I haven't been on the same shift at the café in a week, so we have a lot to catch up on, meaning Monty.

"So, you and Monty, huh?" Violet asks, crossing her arms.

I am wiping down the empty tables when she asks this. I then turn around to face her. "He told you?"

"Yeah, he told me today, actually."

"It sort of just happened."

"Well, it's news to me. I'm happy for you guys, but I have Chelsea calling me non-stop."

"He was ready to move on, and we clicked."

She nods with a smile. "I love Chelsea, but that boy needed to get away from her. So, I approve."

"Thanks." I smile, still feeling uncomfortable.

"I'll walk home with you after work to get Bella."

I sigh. "Oh, okay. I'll miss her, though."

"Someone liked having a dog." She smiles. Wanda walks over to us and gives Violet the "you need to work" look. Violet nods and steps away from me.

I let out a small breath. I was tossing and turning last night; I hardly slept. I was nervous about telling Violet for some reason, but luckily Monty already did. I wonder how he told her because I was getting the vibe last night that he thought dating me was a mistake. Why are guys so confusing?

Violet ends up joining Reese, Claire, and me during lunch. She tells us all about her trip to Milwaukee.

"Ate great food and drank some good ass wine," she tells us.

"But what about Sarah?" I ask.

Violet's face saddens but then she smiles. "She wants me to regain her trust and to go slow."

"That's good, right?" I say, taking a sip of my iced coffee. Violet nods and moves her blonde curls away from her shoulders.

"I guess. It just killed me to see her being so cold and not herself."

I place my hand on her shoulder. "I'm happy for you. Does this mean you're taken?"

"Yeah." She laughs. "I can't believe I'm taken, and I'm happy to be."

"I guess I'm the only single one," I nervously laugh, desperately trying to bring Monty into the conversation.

"What do you mean? What about Monty?" Reese asks. They all

turn to me, and I shrug.

"You're Monty's girlfriend," Violet says confidently.

"I am?"

Violet looks at me strangely. "Yes, Jade. He told me today."

"And he said those words?"

"Jade, what's up?" Reese asks, tilting her head to the side.

I let out a loud sigh and cross my arms before leaning into my chair. "I don't know. I didn't get much sleep last night. I guess it's because of last night."

"What was wrong with last night?" Reese asks me.

"He seemed weird."

"Monty?" Violet asks, and I nod.

She chuckles. "Don't worry. That's just Monty. It takes him a minute to get comfortable. Especially if there are new people."

"So, he told you that he is committed to this relationship?"

"Yeah, he did."

I nod, feeling a little better. I take a sip of my coffee and turn to Claire. "Hey, Claire."

"Yes, sweetheart?"

"I'm sorry you had to hear my craziness."

She smiles. "It keeps me feeling young."

CHAPTER 26

E merson Lang is a friend I've known for years. I tend to know a lot of people since I've lived in this city my whole life. I met her our senior year in high school, and we instantly clicked. Despite being in different groups, we found a common interest: boys. Emerson always had a story to tell, and she'd always squeeze into our table at lunch to share her wonderful stories. I'd laugh and engage in the stories while Reese would roll her eyes and eat her peanut butter and jelly sandwich. Let's just say Reese and Emerson have never really seen eye to eye....

It's Friday night, and Reese and I decided to get a drink with Emerson, who, by the way, made a trip all the way over to Bay Ridge just to have some margaritas with us. Em lives in the city with five of her prissy art friends. She's currently finishing up her last semester at NYU, and she works for a talented art gallery dealer. Emerson is gorgeous, and she knows it. She wears all the designer clothes and never cares how bright her makeup looks.

"The subway, a fucking disaster," Emerson says as she rolls her eyes.

"Tell me about it," I say, playing with my bitten straw.

Reese comes back from the bathroom and immediately takes a sip of her drink.

"So, what were you saying about that guy?" I ask.

"Oh right," Em says. "I met him online."

"See, there's your first mistake," I respond. "You can't meet anyone decent on a stupid dating app."

Emerson sighs. "I'm learning this now. He seemed like a good one. Checked all of my boxes. You know—tall, good-looking, nice clean beard."

"So, all the physical boxes?" Reese comments.

"Yes, Reese, that's important." Emerson rolls her eyes. She takes a sip of her drink and leans back on her chair, moving her pin-straight black hair away from her face.

"So, what happened?" I ask.

"Well, we talked for about three weeks, which is big for me. A lot of guys I meet, I end up losing interest in or vice versa, but this guy was different."

"Different how?" Reese asks, leaning her elbows on the table. I'm not sure if Reese is actually interested in Emerson's story or if she is just pretending to be.

"He was a great texter. Always responded right away. Which is a box that definitely needed to be checked." She pauses. "But during those three weeks of communicating, we never got a chance to actually meet in person. I had family visiting, and then I got sick. Then he ended up going away for a week to see his mom in some redneck state or whatever. We'd talk on the phone a lot, and he said all the right things."

"Like what?" I ask her.

"He said he was looking for a relationship and hooking up

with different girls is so pointless and disgusting. *Blah, blah, blah.* Whatever."

"I'm assuming you fell for that?" Reese says.

Emerson looks at both of us and laughs. "Of course I did. I'm a fucking girl who wants to find love." Emerson finishes her drink and pours herself another. "When he got back from his family trip, we made plans to grab some lunch. However, he seemed distant, uninterested, and closed off. The conversations felt forced and awkward. After that, he became a shitty texter, to the point where he never responded back. I even texted him a couple days before we were supposed to meet, and he never responded to me."

"Wow, what a douche." I shake my head.

Emerson claps her hands. "Douche. He's a douche. They all are. But why? Why did this guy who seemed so fucking interested become a douche?"

"Em, he's definitely talking to other girls. Especially the ones who are on those apps. He didn't just become a douche; he was always a douche. He was just able to mask it long enough to possibly get in your pants," I tell her.

"Oh, you're so right." Em laughs. "I swear, I can't deal with all these damn douches."

I turn to Reese. "I told you that, remember? I said all guys in New York are douches!"

But before Reese can respond, Emerson opens her mouth and says, "Heck, I even considered having my parents arrange a marriage for me. Every time I see them, they are always setting me up with some Chinese man from their church."

"I didn't think people still had arranged marriages," Reese says.

Emerson blinks a couple times and rolls her eyes. "I was kidding, Reese. But whatever, fuck that guy, right? He had red flags anyway."

"See, that's the thing that bothers me," I say.

"What? Red flags?" Em asks.

"Yeah. Do all guys have red flags?" I ask both of them.

Emerson chuckles. "Of course they do, Jade. Even the good ones have some red flags. How long have you been dating this guy of yours?"

"It's been two months," I say.

"And?"

I tilt my head to the side. Of course, Monty has red flags, but I've never used those words to describe any guy I've dated. And when it comes to Monty, I'm guilty of closing my eyes to the red flags because I want our relationship to work.

"You need to be more aware," Em says to me. "Guys like to give you the song and dance in the beginning, but if you stick around long enough, the flags will fly high. You'll see."

I nod. "I guess I don't want to see them."

"I learned a lot about Wes when we moved in together," Reese says, "but if you love someone, you have to understand that no one is perfect."

Emerson leans her chin on her palm and half-smiles. "Then congratulations, Reese. You found the only good guy in New York."

"I wasn't saying that. I was just saying—"

I cut her off. We just got here, and the two of them are already not seeing eye to eye. "Yeah, honestly, there are so many guys out there. Better ones. You don't need to waste your time on a douche," I say.

"Yeah, seriously," Reese says before taking a sip of her drink.

Emerson lets out a laugh and looks at Reese. "What do you know about douches, Reese? I'm not trying to call you out or anything, but you've been in a long-term relationship for years. Heck, you're practically married."

"Hey, Reese may be in a relationship, but she gives the best advice," I say, coming to her defense.

"Thanks, Jade, but I didn't have to date a bunch of douches like you and Emerson to understand guys," Reese retorts.

I let out a sigh, already kind of cringing inside.

"And I'm not the only one who's in a relationship," Reese says, glancing at me.

"I know, but Jade has a lot of guys under her belt," Emerson says.

Reese rolls her eyes and gets up, grabbing her purse. "Okay, fine. I'm tired of feeling like I'm not allowed to be here because I'm in a happy relationship." And with that, she rushes out of the restaurant.

I look at Emerson, and she shrugs. "What's her problem?"

I shake my head and get up, squeezing myself through the crowds around the bar and front entrance. "Reese!" I call, running towards her as she speed walks down the sidewalk. "Reese, please!"

Reese stops walking and turns around. "I'm going home, Jade."

"I can see that," I joke, but she doesn't smile. My smile disappears, and I sigh. "Please come back. Em is just frustrated and is taking it out on you."

"She always does this, Jade. She doesn't like me, but that's okay. I don't like her either. I can't believe I came tonight. I didn't want to, but you practically dragged me."

"Because I wanted to hang out with you, Reese."

Reese leans half her body on one hip and crosses her arms. "I'm going home. I'm just sick and tired of feeling like I'm not experienced enough because I never dated in high school. And because I found someone who actually loves and cares about me."

"Where is this coming from?" I ask her.

"You don't get it, Jade," she cries. "You and your friends sit around and have all these stories about this guy and that guy—"

I cut her off. "But Reese, we have to date all these guys so we can find what you and Wes have. Do you think I enjoy the game? Do you think Emerson is happy?"

Reese sighs. "I guess I just get frustrated because I kinda envy you. Wes is the only guy I've ever been with. It seems exciting to experience what you have. And my mom always tries to remind me not to put all of my eggs in Wes' basket. I guess everything has gotten to my head."

"Don't envy me, Reese. I'd do anything to have what you have. Wes is such a good guy."

Reese nods, wiping a tear from her eye. "I'm going home."

"Okay, let me grab my bag. I'll leave with you."

She shakes her head. "No. Go back in. I need some time alone to think."

"Reese, it's late. I don't want to go back inside without you."

She sniffs and shrugs her shoulders, then she turns back around and walks down the sidewalk, passing a group of drunk people. I stand very still, watching my best friend disappear into the distance.

～

I wake up extra early just to surprise Reese with her favorite bagels. There's a bagel shop on the way to Reese's place, so I made sure to get there early enough to get a dozen of their fresh everything bagels and a side of vegetable cream cheese. I even got her a cup of vanilla bean iced coffee to go with her bagel.

"You didn't have to," she says leaning her body on the hinge of her front door. Despite her protest, she's smiling.

"I wanted to," I say, following Reese inside. She's still wearing her pajamas, and her hair is messy. She rubs her tired eyes and yawns, grabbing an iced coffee from the tray.

I open the bag of bagels, automatically putting one in the toaster for her.

"Is Wes home? I got him a coffee too."

"He's still sleeping," she says.

I nod, plopping down at her kitchen table that is pushed up against the wall. I lean my back on the baby blue wall and sigh. "I'm sorry I stopped by so early. It's just I felt bad about last night."

"I overreacted. I realized that when I was walking home," she says, grabbing her bagel from the toaster.

"I think Em gets jealous and takes it out on you."

"Jade, she's been doing that since high school."

"And that's my point. You were always the one who never needed a guy. And me? It was like I always needed my relationship with Noah to lean on. Which we all knew was a disaster."

"What's your point?" she asks, sitting down across from me.

I grab a bagel and the cream cheese from the brown bag. "My point is that Em always has some guy that screws with her, and you went from being single to finding this awesome guy."

She nods, scooping some cream cheese onto her bagel. "I shouldn't feel like an outcast because of that."

"You aren't. Em doesn't have the best way with words, but I never cared that you have Wes. Heck, it has given me some hope that maybe there are some decent guys in this city," I confess. "You know I'm a hopeless romantic. Emphasis on the *hopeless*."

Reese tilts her head to the side and smiles. "Thank you, I appreciate that."

I nod. "So, are you still upset?"

"I was never upset. I was just frustrated with myself, and it doesn't help that Emerson was there too. It's just been on my mind lately, but I appreciate that you came all the way here and brought me bagels."

"The good-good bagels." I wink, taking a big bite. "But I was thinking about something last night."

"Of course you were," she jokes.

"It was all the talk about red flags."

"What about them?" she asks, sounding confused.

"What do you think about them?"

"Well, everyone has red flags, but you have to decide if they are deal-breakers or not. You just have to go day by day and roll with the punches."

"What are some of your red flags?"

"I don't know, Jade. Ask Wes. I'm sure he'll give you a whole list." She laughs which makes me smile.

I shrug, putting my bagel down and wiping some cream cheese off my fingers. "Monty and I have been good. We've hit the two-month mark already, and all is well."

"So, what's wrong then?"

"Reese, you know me. You know me better than anyone else. Even my own mother," I say, which makes her laugh. "So, be honest with me, have I been blinded to Monty's red flags?"

"Jade, you guys are still in the honeymoon stage, remember? Just give him some time."

I shake my head. "Remember when you said that I should decide if Monty's red flags are deal-breakers?"

"Yes." She smiles. "I said it a couple minutes ago."

"Yeah, well, there's actually one thing…."

"Go on," she says, taking a bite of her bagel.

"He's, um, not the best in bed," I say slowly.

Reese tilts her head to the side and leans her elbows on the table. "What do you mean?"

"Well, he's sorta awkward, like a cold fish. But his kisses were no indication of this at all!" I groan.

Reese laughs. "What does that even mean?"

"Okay, don't get me wrong, Reese. My connection with Monty is undeniable. We laugh, we talk about everything, and we like the same music. There's also a strong attraction, but when it finally comes down to doing the nasty...Well, he screws it up."

"Have you said anything to him?"

"Yeah, that's what I want to do—tell the guy I'm seeing that he's a snore-fest when he's inside me."

"Wow, do I have good timing." Wes smiles, walking out of his room and into the kitchen. Reese hands him a coffee, and he thanks me while simultaneously kissing Reese.

"Girl talk starts in the a.m. I see." Wes laughs, pulling out a chair.

"Well, you do have great timing, Wes." I nod. "I need some advice from an intelligent man."

"What about Colin? He loves talking about stuff like that. People being inside of people." He coughs. Reese rolls her eyes, rubbing Wes's back.

"See, that's where you're wrong. I said intelligent and man. Colin doesn't fall into either of those categories."

Wes laughs, leaning back on his chair. "It's too early to talk about boyfriends."

"What about boyfriends who are terrible in bed?" Reese asks.

"Thanks, Reese," I say, slightly irritated. "And I didn't say he was *terrible*. He just lacks..." I pause, trying to find the right words. "The skills needed to not be so terrible..."

"Have you ever been with anyone who has rocked your world?" Wes asks.

I look at Reese and Wes before letting out a laugh. "What kind of question is that?" I shake my head.

"It's a pretty simple one," Reese says.

"Of course I have." I laugh. They both look at me, and I frown. "Okay, fine. I haven't. But has anyone ever had mind-blowing sex?"

"Yes," they both say at the same time.

"Okay, okay. But admit it, Reese, you have to say yes because your boyfriend is sitting right there," I stutter. "Shut up, guys."

Reese laughs. "Buy some sexy clothes and rock his world. *Boom.*"

"It's that simple?" I ask, leaning back against the chair.

"Pretty much," Wes says nonchalantly before taking a big bite of his bagel.

~

Back at my apartment later that night, I decided to call Reese. "Hey, Reese," I say as I pucker my lips in front of the mirror, dabbing on the new pink lipstick I bought.

"Why are you whispering?" she asks.

I fix my shirt and do a three-sixty spin to make sure I chose the right outfit—my black bodysuit and a white high-waisted ripped miniskirt.

"I'm practicing my sexy voice. How does it sound?"

Reese groans. "You're making me feel uncomfortable."

"Well, it's your and Wes' fault. All day I felt bad because I've never had mind-blowing sex."

"I swear, you need more hobbies." She laughs.

"Oh, stop. Monty's on his way here, and I want to seduce him."

"Oh, wow. So tonight is the night?"

"Apparently," I say. I walk into the kitchen and pour myself a glass of wine. I hear a soft knock on the door, and I smile. "He's here. Wish me luck."

"That's something you say when you're about to go on stage or start a new job, not—"

I hang up on her and open the front door.

"Hey, beautiful," Monty says shyly.

I hand him a glass of wine, and he smiles, leaning in to give me a kiss. We grab the bottle of wine and head to my room. Monty looks through my CDs on the shelf, and I plop down on the edge of my bed.

"What are you feeling tonight?" he asks with his back facing me.

"I don't care." I stand up, and then I try to sit back down on my bed, but in a sexy way. I'm so not good at this….

"Or we can just watch a movie," he says, finally turning around.

"Movie sounds good," I say quietly.

Monty grins then walks over to sit on the bed next to me. He nudges my shoulder and leans in, giving my cheek a simple kiss. "I missed you today," he tells me.

"You did?" I grin. "How much?"

"A lot," he says, gently kissing my lips. I drape my arms around his neck and smile, deepening our kiss. Monty places his hands around my waist, and I lay on my back. Monty nuzzles my neck, and I laugh.

"Is your roommate home?" he asks, looking into my eyes.

"Uh, I don't think so? Why? You want to take this to the other room?" I wink.

Monty looks at me strangely. "No, I just want to know if we have the place to ourselves."

"Oh, okay," I say, kissing him again. Monty takes off his white V-neck and exposes his skinny torso, full of tiny, bizarre tattoos.

"Every time I see you shirtless," I say, giving him a small kiss. "I find something new every time." I smile, eyeing the little blue bird on his shoulder to the Pokémon character on his chest.

"I was never an organized guy, so why should my tattoos be any different?" Monty says.

"Aren't you clever?"

Monty starts to pull down my skirt, and I pick up my butt to help him out.

"Teamwork," I say.

Monty laughs, finally taking off my miniskirt and throwing it on the floor.

"I like what you did with the place," he says, pointing to the few candles on my nightstand.

I look over and nod. "I read it's supposed to 'set the mood.'"

"Oh, is that so?" He smiles.

I nod, waiting patiently for him to get down to business. I reach over and open my drawer which is full of condoms. "Just in case you forgot."

Monty takes the condom from me and grins. "There's a whole lotta condoms in there."

"Just as many from the last time you were here," I say.

Monty lays down beside me on his back and takes off his skinny jeans. I take off my shirt and bra in one quick motion and immediately get under the covers. Monty and I have had sex about thirty times already, not that I'm counting or anything. Still, it reminds me of when I lost my virginity to Noah. That awkwardness with Monty never seems to ease.

"Okay, it's on." He smirks, getting back on top of me.

And there it goes, back to how it always is. Monty's perfect face goes to its favorite spot—into the side of my neck and my pillow, while I stare up at the cracked ceiling, feeling his tiny jolts inside of me. Occasionally he caresses my breast, but it doesn't take him very long to ejaculate. As soon as he does, he grunts into my neck and falls onto his back beside me, panting and sweaty.

"Did you?" he asks, motioning his fingers near my private area.

"Yeah," I breathe. "Actually…" I pause. "I didn't."

Monty looks at me with a surprised expression. "Did I do something wrong this time?"

"No! It's not you. It's me," I say.

Monty leans his hand on his palm, looking down at me. "Do you want me to?" he asks as he points...again.

"Well, would you wanna try again but do it differently?" I ask.

"Differently?"

"Yeah, well, we can like, talk about what turns each other on and stuff," I say slowly. Jeez, I'm so bad at this.

Monty smiles. "Okay."

"You first." I wink, running my thumb on his soft chin.

Monty grabs my wrist and gives it a kiss. "I think you're so sexy, and it makes me want to do sexy things to you."

"Like what?" I ask, finally feeling intrigued.

"Well, for starters, I want to tear all your clothes off...with my teeth."

"Okay, very kinky! Go on."

"You can't make me laugh." He smiles.

"I'm sorry. Go on." I smile back, covering my face with my hands.

Monty pulls them away and gives me a kiss. "I've always been into rough sex."

I tilt my head to my side. "Rough sex?"

He laughs. "Don't worry. I'm not into whips or anything, just occasional biting and scratching."

So, did Chelsea do that with him? Stop it, Jade, this is between you and Monty now. You can't think about Chelsea when you're lying in bed with her ex-boyfriend, naked.

"Okay, rough sex. Anything else?"

"I'm a guy, Jade. I like everything. I want to know what you like."

"I was thinking about that a lot today, actually." I swallow. "And I don't know. Maybe doing it in different places? And having different positions?"

"I love how you say 'doing it.'" He grins, leaning in again and kissing my neck. "Anything else?" he asks.

"What about dirty talk?"

Monty looks into my eyes. "How did I get so lucky?"

I laugh. "Don't make fun of me."

"I'm not. I am very into that."

"Okay, good." I nod.

"You know what gets me so turned on?" he whispers in my ear.

I let out a moan, closing my eyes.

"This." He breathes, biting my ear lobe gently.

"Oh, that's nice," I say.

Monty lets out a chuckle and grabs another condom from my nightstand.

"I'm down to go again if you are. Which I think you are," he says, touching my very wet area.

I nod, swallowing hard. "But this time, Montgomery, I'm on top."

~

The next day at the café, Reese gives me a devilish grin, holding her cup of coffee by her chin. "So, how did it go?"

"I can't talk about this right now." I glare at her as Violet sits down beside me.

"Talk about what?" Violet asks, taking a sip of her latte.

"Nothing," I say casually.

Reese rolls her eyes and lets out a loud sigh. "Flower guy?"

I nod, eyeing him from afar. "Claire, do you want to take this one?"

"Oh, I don't know, honey. I don't think I'm as good as you girls."

"Violet?" I offer.

Violet smirks. "Are any of you into trapeze artists?"

CHAPTER 27

"Large soy latte!" barks Rob, the new manager under Wanda. I let out a tiny groan, only to mask it with a smile as soon as Rob turns to look at me. I make the coffee in seconds, and I slide the drink into Monty's hand as he gives me a wink.

"Hey." I smile. "What brings you in today?"

"Thought I'd see the most beautiful girl today. Any takers?"

I tilt my head to the side. "*Hmm*, me?"

"You got it." He laughs. "No, actually, I thought we could have lunch together."

I clap my hands. "I love that idea. My break is in ten. Do you mind waiting?"

"Not at all." He smiles.

I watch as he walks past the counter and sits on one of the chairs, leaning one elbow on the wooden table beside him. I glance at him occasionally, just admiring him casually sipping on his coffee.

Wanda shoots me a glare, and I thankfully work the register until my break ends.

"Okay, I'm ready," I sing, draping my arms around his shoulders behind him. I give him a kiss on the cheek, smelling his aftershave.

Monty doesn't say anything. His face appears angry as if something has triggered him. He stands up and heads for the door. My feet are frozen as I watch him leave the cafe. After a few seconds, I run after him.

"Hey, is everything okay?"

Monty takes out a cigarette and lights it between his lips. "Are you that oblivious?"

I try to grab his hand, but he jolts it away.

"What are you talking about?"

"Jade, every guy that ordered coffee was either hitting on you or checking you out."

"No, they weren't." I laugh.

He takes a big puff and rolls his eyes. "Don't laugh, Jade. And yes, they were. I was sitting right there, remember?"

"Yes, but I think I would have noticed if they were, Monty."

He doesn't say anything, and I don't either. I'm waiting for him to respond, but all he does is sigh. "I just know how guys think, and I see how they look at you."

I rub both of his arms and grin. "Monty, you don't have to worry about that. They can look all they want, but I'm yours."

Monty nods, holding back a small smile. He drapes his arms around my waist, and we walk down the crowded sidewalk.

～

I follow Monty up the six flights of stairs leading to his apartment. We ended up getting lunch at this sandwich bistro a couple of blocks from the cafe, and when I had to get back to work, Monty waited for me at a table against the wall. I wasn't sure if he only did it because of what happened earlier today, but thankfully, he didn't bring it up.

Monty unlocks his front door, using multiple keys, and I lead the way into his tiny apartment.

"I don't think Rodney's home. And the three others." He chuckles.

"I think it's crazy that you live with four guys. I live with one, and it's a lot."

Monty walks over to his terrace and opens it. He's quiet, and I am too as I watch him pull out his third cigarette in the last hour. Monty leans against the wall, tilting his cigarette, so it's outside.

"I hate the smell of cigarettes," Monty says.

"But you smoke them?" I raise a brow, walking over to his couch and plopping down. His dog, Tucker, approaches me and I bend down and rub his belly.

"Yeah, it's a bitch to quit," he answers.

"What's that?" I point to a crate that's sitting beside him. It's full of different things—a medium-sized picture, a hairbrush, and it even looks like there are some articles of clothing.

"It's Chelsea's stuff that she's left behind."

I nod, wishing I didn't ask.

Monty scratches his nose and sighs. "I would be a dick if I didn't let her grab her things."

"Oh, so she's coming here to get them?"

He nods. "Yeah."

"When?"

"I think tomorrow."

"Okay." I fake a smile.

"Don't be short, Jade. All she's doing is picking up her shit."

"I get it. It's fine."

The conversation about Chelsea and her belongings ends. After Monty's cigarette, we move to his room, just in case any of his roommates return home. He said there's never any privacy since he lives with four other people, and he's not the biggest fan of them.

We lay down on his queen-sized bed, and Monty turns on his television, switching to some '90s cartoon. He seems relaxed. I am, of course, still churning from earlier.

"I mean, I can stop by tomorrow," I say quickly.

Monty looks at me. "Because Chelsea is coming by?"

"No, I just want to see you."

"Jade—"

"Okay, fine. I won't." I bite the inside of my cheek.

Monty pauses the television and sits up. "You don't have to worry, okay? Chelsea is nothing to me. Our relationship was toxic, and I'm over it."

"But why can't you just leave it outside for her?" I ask.

Monty rubs the back of his neck. I'm beginning to sense this is a nervous habit of his. "Jade, this is New York. Some looney will steal it." He laughs.

"And you care? You just called her belongings shit," I remind him.

"I'm not a dick."

"I know you aren't."

Monty shrugs and unpauses the television. Yet again, the conversation about Chelsea and her "shit" ends. This time, I leave it alone, but I'm still irritated. He doesn't care how I feel about this whole situation.

I tell Monty I'm tired and turn to my side. I'm not sure if he understands why I am upset that the girl he used to love will be stopping by tomorrow. My anger doesn't fester long because after a few minutes, I end up falling asleep.

⁓

Around 2 p.m., I get back to my apartment. I drop my keys on my kitchen counter and sigh. I texted Monty an hour ago, the second my shift ended. On the way home, I was praying I'd feel a vibration from my phone. But I didn't. All I felt was a pain in my pathetic heart. Should I be mad? Probably. But I feel scared for some reason. Maybe I'm afraid because I really care about Monty, and I'm not sure if he still has feelings for Chelsea. If he was truly over her, then why would he care so much about returning her belongings? Maybe it's because all her stuff has been accumulating there for three years during their relationship....

Everything happened so fast—from the time we met to when we shared our first passionate kiss to that conversation at the park where we made our relationship official. I never even thought about how he was able to throw away the three years he spent with Chelsea to be with me—someone he hardly knew. I just figured since she cheated on him a year ago, that maybe he lost feelings along the way. But then why did he take her back? Why didn't he just break up with her the second he found out? I still don't know.

The thought of alcohol enters my mind, and I stand up from my slouching position on the couch with my palm stuck to my forehead. I can't stop thinking about Monty and Chelsea. I also can't stop thinking about Chelsea and her three years' worth of stuff at Monty's. Suddenly, I hear a loud pound shake the front door. My feet are still, and I stare at my gray door, startled and a bit concerned.

I walk over to the door, and I look through the peephole. Is it her? I don't know why Chelsea appears in my head during the few steps it takes to approach my front door. Luckily, it's not her. It's a girl I've never seen before. She pounds again. Emphasis on the pounding—I never realized how much I respect people who kindly knock until now.

I open the door. I'm not sure why I want to because I don't know this girl, and secondly, why would I want to engage in any conversation with this angry stranger? But I'm curious, and I need a distraction from my boyfriend giving his ex-girlfriend her stuff back....

"Can I help you?" I ask the angry blonde.

She crosses her arms and leans her petite body on one hip. "Is he home?" she asks.

"Is who home?" I think I irked her with my question because we both know who she's talking about. The angry blonde becomes a crying blonde as she begins to wipe the tears that she's desperately been trying to fight back. The tears obviously won because, all of a sudden, they come all at once like a freaking waterfall.

"I'm sorry," she cries. "I don't usually do this. I should have listened to Vicky."

I swallow my pride and give in to the fact that I'm this crying blonde, and she is me. The only reason I'm saying this is because currently, I'm sitting a few inches from the crying blonde. We're both sitting on my couch, a glass of wine in both of our hands.

"You're sitting on my couch and drinking my wine and also using my tissues," I say, handing her another one. "I should at least know your name."

She looks up and nods, wiping another tear that has escaped. "I've never been in this apartment during the day, by the way. It's usually two in the morning when I'm here, and only that lamp is on." She points to the lamp that's perched in the corner of the living room. My grandmother bought us that lamp when my parents got this apartment.

I don't say a word. I watch her swallow a lump in her throat and wait for her to continue.

"You have a cute apartment. I wish I would have taken a few more seconds to actually look around. But I didn't realize at the time that I was like every other girl. You know, the girl that gets used and abused. I would tell you my name, but why should I? You'll never see me again, and you'll just be greeted by another blonde with bigger boobs."

"So why are you here?" I ask her.

"Why am I pounding on your door at three o'clock in the afternoon?"

I nod.

She lets out a sigh and sniffles her nose. "I would like to give you an answer, but honestly, I don't have one. I guess you can say I'm a sucker for punishment. I'm a sucker because I dared to even think a guy like Colin would ever want me. And I got mad and shut off my brain."

"I tend to do that too. Not the part about dating guys like Colin but shutting off my brain."

"Cheers to that." She smiles, and we tap our glasses.

"Well, if you're not going to tell me your name, then I won't tell you mine. But feel free to stick around and wait for Colin to come home. I'd rather you stay here than be alone," I say.

The crying blonde becomes a curious blonde. "I know it's none of my business, but is something wrong? Why would you rather hang out with me, a complete stranger, than be alone?"

"My boyfriend has his ex-girlfriend of three years at his place," I tell her. I'm not sure why I do, though. This is really out of character for me, to tell a complete stranger my problems, I mean. But it's sort of helping in a way. Better than when I tell Reese. Only because if I tell Reese something, there's a possibility of judgment, and I might say something that will haunt me for years on end. Telling this girl all my worries about Monty has no repercussions because I'll never see this girl ever again. Well, unless Colin gets hit in the head and decides this blonde is the one. Only then would she end up in my life longer than the hour I'm spending with her on this couch. But we both know that's not happening. She's right. He'll be onto the next blonde with bigger boobs soon. Heck, he probably already is. Sorry, no name girl. She knew what she was doing when she was sneaking into the apartment at two in the morning. Who was she kidding? But I would be mad too. Nobody wants to feel like a schmuck, especially a schmuck that gets used by a player—a player who I call my roommate.

"I think we're both on the same page. Obsessing over the opposite sex," I say.

"I wish I could agree. If we *were* the same, I wouldn't be sitting on Colin's couch, drinking wine with his female roommate." She crooks a smile.

"You have a point." I shift my body so I'm entirely facing her, taking both my knees to my chest.

"But why are you here? Shouldn't you be at your boyfriend's place?" she asks but suddenly lets out a tiny chuckle. "Maybe you shouldn't take advice from a girl who has no idea what she is doing."

"I keep asking myself that," I say. "I don't know why I'm so scared to show him that it bothers me so much that she's there."

"And if you did, what do you think would happen?" she asks.

For the first time, I don't know how to answer. I'm completely flabbergasted because ever since I can remember, I've been self-diagnosed with "know-it-all syndrome." I always have an answer. Right or wrong. But recently, I find myself completely clueless. Maybe, ever since Jason, I've cured this imaginary syndrome.

"I don't know how to answer that," I say out loud. I decided to share the thoughts that are crowding my mind.

She shrugs and finishes the last of her wine.

"Do you want another glass?" I ask her.

"Yes, but I better not. I should get going. I think I needed this. Talking to a complete stranger is actually better than any friend or therapist I've never spoken to," she says with a hint of a smile. "And I'm glad you were the one to answer the door and not Colin."

"Me too, no name." I smile back. This no-name blonde and I needed each other today. For different reasons, obviously, but sitting and talking with her this afternoon helped. It distracted me from my thoughts, and I think she realized that it was a stupid idea to just show up here to yell, do, or say things to him that she'd regret.

I open the door for her, and she turns to me and gives me another smile, exposing her straight white teeth.

"Colin is stupid to let you go. Trust me, you deserve better," I tell her.

She threads her fingers into the loops of her lavender-colored jeans and nods. "Thank you. I really appreciate that. And you should really speak to your boyfriend about how you feel. At least you have a guy that wants to be committed to you. So, hold on to that and stop worrying, Jade. Don't overthink."

"You know my name?" I gasp.

"Yeah, Colin told me." She smiles and turns away. She is already halfway down the hall before I am able to process all of this. I stand outside my door until she disappears. She knew my name the whole time...and I called her no-name blonde the entire hour I was with her.

~

Sometime later, Monty opens the front door to my apartment without knocking, which has become a thing we do. I'm midway through a bowl of Frosted Flakes as I watch him casually stroll into my apartment. We catch eyes, and he gives me a cute grin, and it makes me want to grab him and forget about what haunted my thoughts all day. Colin comes out of his room from playing his guitar. The soothing sounds of him strumming his guitar allowed me to stare at my bare refrigerator until Monty came strolling inside. Colin says a friendly hello to Monty, but all he gets in response is an awkward nod.

Monty walks over to me and takes off his denim jacket. He kisses my cheek and grabs my hand. "Can we go to your room?" he asks, discreetly eying Colin, who's leaning on the kitchen counter. He's shoving cold pizza into his mouth, and he's obviously daydreaming about something.

I glance at Colin and back to Monty and then back to my half-eaten soggy cereal.

"I haven't finished eating," I say.

"So? Bring it with you." He rolls his eyes.

"But that's how you get ants!"

Monty gently pulls my arm and walks over to my bedroom door. He opens the door before saying, "Ants are the least of your concern, Jade. It's the roaches you gotta worry about."

I nod, looking back at Colin as I get up from the kitchen table. He finishes the last of his pizza and wipes the crumbs off his hands into the sink. He's not speaking, which is odd because Colin always has something to say. He's usually quiet when he's in his room playing the guitar for hours and hours, most likely writing songs for his band. His mind is probably still consumed by the words and melodies he spills onto the paper. I leave him be and follow Monty into my room, holding my cereal that I don't even want anymore.

"Are you hungry?" I ask him, eyeing the clock on my nightstand that reads five o'clock.

"I already ate," he answers.

My heart sinks, and I bite the inside of my cheek, trying my absolute hardest to keep myself from asking if the reason he's not hungry is because he ate with Chelsea.

But I can't help myself, so I ask, "Did you eat with Chelsea?"

"No, silly," he jokes. "I grabbed a bite to eat before I came over."

"Why didn't you just wait for me?"

Monty plops on my bed and lets out a sigh. A sigh that basically says he wishes he didn't have to have this conversation with me. "I don't know, Jade." Monty lets out a frustrated huff and avoids making eye contact with me.

"I was just asking." I discreetly shrug, setting my completely soggy cereal on my nightstand. "How was your day?" I ask him.

He drapes his arms around my waist and gives my cheek a lengthy kiss. As if the kiss can prolong his answer to my question. "Boring as usual."

"Why was it boring?"

"I didn't have work today."

Is he seriously not going to bring up Chelsea? What is he hiding?

I think back to no-name blonde as the words *don't overthink* come to mind.

"Did Chelsea stop by to get her things?" I finally gather the courage to ask.

"She did," he says quickly.

That's it? Two words?

"And?" I raise a brow.

Monty smiles, and I'm already getting annoyed. Actually, worse than annoyed. I'm getting mad.

"Why are you smiling, Monty?"

"Because it's cute that you care so much about me and this relationship. When Chelsea stopped by, of course, she was trying to add doubt about you and this relationship. Still, it made me like you so much more, and it validated that my feelings for Chelsea are gone for sure."

As I take in each word he's saying, the madness I feel quickly fizzles. I'm already climbing into his lap with my arms wrapped around his neck. To think I spent a single moment stressing about today makes me madder than I was at him today. I wasted a whole day worrying. I give Monty a kiss on his lips, and he smiles.

"I want to ask you something because I know if I don't, it'll sit on my chest until I hear an answer."

"Ask away," he says.

"A nameless blonde told me to stop overthinking—"

Monty holds his finger up, confused by my words, but I shake my head. He nods, waiting for me to continue.

"Last night, when I found out Chelsea was coming over in the first place to grab her stuff, why didn't you want me to be there when she was supposed to stop by?"

Monty doesn't answer right away. I guess he's trying to find the right words before he speaks. It feels like a million years until he finally opens his mouth.

"I know Chelsea. I know how she can be, and I didn't want her to say something that would possibly hurt your feelings. She's a bitch, and I didn't want to put you in an uncomfortable situation."

"You know I can defend myself," I say.

"Yes, I know, but for your sake and even my sake, it was just easier to handle Chelsea without you being there."

I nod.

"I hope you understand. It's not that I didn't want you there. It's just—"

I put my finger over his lips and shake my head. "You don't need to explain yourself. I get it. I just needed to know for my own reasons. That's all."

Monty nods, grabbing my waist. Then he brings me back to my mattress, and I yelp, giving him a wide smile. I am now on my back, looking up at him. He hovers over me and gives my neck a simple kiss. He looks calmer now compared to how he was at the beginning of our conversation. The smile I give him definitely reassures him.

"I'm falling in love with you, Jade."

Every word replays in my head as we make love all night.

CHAPTER 28

I think about those scenes from movies when a character is so happy that they walk down a street and a whole song and dance number happens all around them. Yeah, that's how I feel in this exact moment as I casually walk to work like a dance number can break out at any moment. The birds are chirping extra loudly this morning, and the sun is shining brightly. There are no clouds to be seen in the perfect blue sky. Oh, and my boyfriend told me he was falling in love with me. I thought I'd just throw that one in there. Everything seems to be falling into place.

My smile quickly disappears as soon as I walk inside the cafe. Once again, I am greeted by a bunch of impatient New Yorkers waiting for their coffee. Wanda dramatically taps her imaginary watch on her wrist as we catch eyes. I rush behind the counter, helping Violet make drinks. She looks flustered and not her usual self, meaning she's not cracking jokes and making fun of customers behind their backs. Her blonde curls are already frizzy, and she's groaning as the manager barks at us to hurry up. By the time the crowd of people fizzles down, Violet can finally catch her breath.

"I didn't get much sleep last night," she tells me.

Yeah, me neither, Violet.

"Really? Everything okay?"

"Yeah, just been stressing over my audition this afternoon."

"You'll do great. I know it."

Violet nods and moves her long curly ponytail behind her. "It's great pay, and I'm obsessed with the character already."

But before I can ask about the audition, Wanda comes out of nowhere and disrupts our conversation—as usual.

⁓

The next night, Reese dips a tortilla chip into the salsa bowl. "Did Violet come up with another weird scenario about the flower guy?" she asks me.

"It was actually just Claire and me today."

"Oh? Where was she?"

"At an audition," I say, hoping to change the subject to anything but that. I've been feeling a little guilty because I haven't been going on as many auditions as I'd like. Don't get me wrong, it's not like I haven't been on any, but not the amount I should. The more auditions I go on, the higher the chance will be for me to pick up a gig.

I turn to Colin, who is sitting beside me. I watch as he adds way too much hot sauce to his steak tacos before asking, "So, when's your band playing their next show?"

He raises an eyebrow. "Why do you ask?"

"I don't know. Maybe because I'm curious," I say. "And I can see and hear that you've been writing a lot."

"Next weekend, actually," he answers me. "You guys are welcome to come."

"I'm down," Wes says, mouth filled with chunks of his burrito.

"Me too. You should bring Monty," Reese says, giving me a wink from what I told her an hour before we got dinner—the whole "I'm falling for you."

Colin groans and quickly bites into one of his tacos, probably hoping none of us heard him. Unfortunately for him, we all did.

He rolls his eyes, not wanting to answer any questions that are about to come his way.

"Did I just hear a groan towards the mention of Monty?" Reese finally asks. No one says anything as we wait for Colin to answer.

"Maybe." He shrugs. Everyone is still staring at him. The answer he gave us is clearly not good enough.

Colin rolls his eyes and sets his taco down, wiping his fingers with his napkin.

"I don't know what to say. No offense, Jade, but I get weird vibes from the dude." The fact that Colin actually said my name instead of his usual playful "roomie" is odd. But I'm not going to allow him to take the happiness I feel towards Monty away.

"What vibes do you get?" I ask.

"To me, he just seems a little odd. That's all. There's something I can't put my finger on that I don't like."

"Maybe it's because he doesn't like you," Wes says dryly. We all turn our attention to Wes. "Sorry, had to say it."

"Yeah, fuck that. I honestly don't care if the dude doesn't like me. Just shows his insecurities," Colin says nonchalantly before picking his taco back up.

"It's normal for a boyfriend to not like that his girlfriend is living with another guy," Reese says. "Has he said anything to you about that?"

"No." I shake my head. "But he made it clear that he doesn't like it when other guys talk to or even look at me."

"Oh, you got a jealous one on your hands, roomie," Colin says.

I turn to look at him. "I don't think he's jealous. He's just protective."

"Whatever you say," Colin says, putting his hands up. He is clearly over this conversation.

I look at Reese and shrug. She leans her elbows on the table and gives me a shrug back. Now that I'm thinking about it, Monty does show signs of extreme jealousy. But that shouldn't change how I feel about him or our relationship. Big whoop. Jealousy is normal, right?

Still, Colin's words linger in my head all night. Am I blind to the vibes Monty is apparently giving Colin? I asked Reese and Wes if they share the same feelings as Colin, but they said they don't. On the other hand, Colin does see Monty a lot more often than they do. But that's because he lives a few feet away from me. The question Wes asked me on the way home sits on my chest as well.

"Would you care if Monty asked you to move out?"

～

A few nights later, I knock a few times on Monty's front door. Something holds me back from just barging in. I'm giving myself time. Finally, I'm welcomed by one of his roommates, whom I've never seen nor have ever met. He gives me an awkward smile as I walk past him, immediately entering their kitchen. His roommate walks past me and into his room without a word. Odd. And Monty has a problem with Colin? So he says, but at least Colin has the courtesy to say hello. Tucker welcomes me by sniffing and wagging his tail. I plop on the couch, playing a game of tug-a-war with Tucker. Then, I hear Monty enter the apartment. I don't need to turn around to know that it's him. I hear him sliding in and taking off his jacket in seconds. He comes from behind the couch and gives the top of my head a little kiss.

"Hey, pretty." He smiles, walking over to me and sitting down.

"Hi." I grin, leaning in and kissing his lips.

"Sorry, I'm late. My boss is an asshole. As usual."

"No, it's fine. I didn't mind playing with Tucker."

"Tuck loves this more than you. Trust me." He laughs, beginning to play roughly with his dog. He then throws a ball across his living room. The ball accidentally hits one of his roommate's closed doors.

"Maybe that'll finally wake him up," he says sarcastically under his breath.

I turn to him. "Do you have relationships with any of your roommates?"

"*Hmm.* Lemme think. One's a druggie who sleeps all day. One is an intern at the hospital on Fifth—"

"Wow, you live with a doctor. Good to know and very convenient." I grin.

Monty shrugs and drapes his arms around me, changing the subject. I don't know why he has so much animosity towards his roommates. I never realized how lucky I am to semi-like and tolerate my roommate.

Monty stands up and feels for his wallet that's sitting in the back pocket of his skinny slacks.

"Are you hungry?" he asks.

I nod.

We decided to get some sandwiches at this diner by his place. They have great pastrami sandwiches and steak fries. I open my menu as soon as the raspy-voiced waitress hands them to us. Is it a prerequisite to have a smoker's voice when you decide to wait tables at a diner?

We're both silent, studying the menus as if we are going to be tested on it. I've eaten at this place a few times, but Monty hasn't.

"Wow, everything is so expensive," Monty says out loud.

I look up from my menu. "What did you expect? It's New York."

Monty shrugs, and I look back at my menu. But this time, I'm not reading the descriptions of each item. I'm feeling uncomfortable. I've never been to a restaurant with anyone who's pointed out the prices of the food. Only my parents, but they're old, so I understand. And this isn't the first time Monty has said something like that. A casual comment about prices, I mean. I understand the costs—they're high. But when you're on a date with someone, it's always best to keep that to yourself. It makes me uncomfortable knowing that he probably doesn't want to eat here.

"Do you want to leave?" I ask him because he's silent as he looks at the menu. I ask him in the most honest way. I wouldn't care if we grab a pizza or eat at a five-star restaurant. All that matters is that we are together.

The waitress comes by our table, and Monty hands her his menu, ordering the turkey club with an extra pickle on the side. Due to Monty's comment, I didn't have a chance to really find something, so I decided to get the pastrami again.

As we wait for our food, Monty goes into his day at work. He was fetching coffee as usual. But today, he was able to read some of the upcoming scripts for the television show. It's the first time his boss has ever let him in the room besides grabbing the coffee Monty brought him.

"It was incredible, Jade. I was the tenth person to finally read it. I wonder how it started and how much it changed by the time I got my hands on it."

"Is your boss finally coming around to being nice?" I ask.

Monty laughs. "Hell no. He's still a dick. But at least the dick is finally letting me do the job I actually signed up for."

It doesn't take long before our steaming hot sandwiches are sitting in front of us. I grab the ketchup and squeeze a ton over all my fries. Monty does the same to his sweet potato fries.

"You look different today," Monty says with a mouth full of turkey.

"Is it because my hair is straight?" I ask.

He nods. "Yeah, that's it. You look terrific like that," he says.

"Yeah, it's not its usual wavy, frizzy self."

Monty looks at me, reading my face. "Well, I obviously like it both ways. Why did you straighten it?"

I play with a fry on my plate. "I had a meeting with my agent about my acting career."

"And?"

"Nothing out of the blue. I told her that I need to step up my game when it comes to auditioning more, and she agreed."

"Atta girl." Monty smiles. "What job would make you the happiest?"

"Honestly, anything right now. But if you had asked me that same question a few years ago, I'd say Broadway. Of course."

"Is that something you still want? What about TV and movies?"

"If I wanted to be in TV and movies, I'd be living in California right now," I say. "But I wouldn't mind an acting gig like that. I've been in a few commercials throughout the years."

"I know. I've seen them."

I look up from my half-eaten sandwich and into his blue eyes. "You have?"

He nods. "Yeah. That first night I found out your name, I googled you when I got home."

"I think you're the first person who has ever seen my commercials," I say in awe.

"No, I'm the first person to *admit* it to you," he corrects me.

I wonder who else has seen those commercials and never told me. Reese and Wes? Colin?

"You looked hot in that magazine, by the way." Monty winks.

I smile. "Was that on Google too?"

"Everything's on Google, baby."

I laugh. "You're right, and I'm kinda mortified. I never thought that anyone would Google me, or would even want to Google me for that matter."

"I wanted to Google you the second I laid eyes on you, Jade. Trust me. You're talented. I can definitely see you on Broadway."

I smile at him without saying anything back. We go back to our sandwiches, and the topic of me and my commercials end.

The bill comes, and it's placed right in front of Monty. I'm a bit nervous to see how much it all came out to because we ended up getting dessert as well. I watch him carefully as he eyes the bill. Monty slides his credit card inside and hands it to the smoky-voiced waiter. Monty tends to feel awkward when we eat at restaurants. I just figured it was because he wasn't the most comfortable with me yet, but the words he told me the other night make me think otherwise. Now the money thing crosses my mind, but I'm not sure if that's the reason either. Maybe Colin is right about Monty and his insecurities, but who doesn't have any insecurities? Heck, I have tons, but I guess eating at restaurants is one of Monty's. We had good conversations this evening, sitting in this diner booth, but the constant awkward looks he gave me between our conversations were off-putting. I kept asking him if he was okay, only for him to always answer with, "Yeah, why are you asking?"

～

"So, what did you think of your sandwich?" I ask him as we walk hand in hand down the sidewalk.

"Best turkey club I've ever eaten," he says.

I give him a smile, glancing at the side of his face.

Monty's forehead is clenching like he's thinking hard about something.

"Monty?" I ask him.

He looks down at me then turns his attention back to the buildings beside us. "Sorry, I'm just thinking."

"Thinking about what?" I ask.

Monty lets out a sigh. "When I told you that I was falling in love with you last night..." He pauses.

Oh no, Monty, please don't take it back. My heart won't be able to handle that right now.

"I wanted to hear you say it back to me, so I know you feel the same. But you didn't," he stutters, then he stops speaking. I'm not sure if he's going to continue or if he wants me to speak. After a few seconds of silence, Monty finally opens his mouth. "So...do you?"

"I thought I showed you how I felt last night." I give him a wink.

Monty looks at me and rolls his eyes. "That's not the same thing, Jade."

We continue to walk down the sidewalk but in silence this time. I wasn't aware that he was yearning for me to say it back. I'm starting to really fall for him, but it's hard for me to say those three words. I guess because I came from a home where those three words were hardly said. When I dated Noah, we were so young that we threw those words out the first week we dated, but I never actually loved Noah. Before I say those three words to Monty, I really want to truly feel them.

I stop in my tracks and stare at Monty, who is a couple steps ahead of me. He turns to face me, confused by my sudden halt. I reach my hand out for him to grab, and he does, walking in front of me, so we're eye to eye.

"I am falling in love with you. And I'm not just saying that. I do mean it, trust me," I say. I watch his face as concern turns into relief which turns into happiness. Monty grabs my waist and pulls me into a hug. I drape one of my arms around his neck, and I rest my other hand on the side of his cheek before leaning in to kiss his perfect lips. Monty deepens our kiss, and we officially become the couple who says I love you—and the couple who makes out in the middle of the street.

⌇

A day later, my phone rings, and I run into my room, closing the door behind me.

"What do you say about meeting my family tomorrow night?"

"The whole family?" I ask Monty as I sit on the edge of my bed.

"Yeah. My dad and his wife are flying in tonight actually. And my brothers are flying in tomorrow morning,"

"Yeah, I'm so down to finally meet them! And your sister will be there, too, right?"

"Yes. Of course."

CHAPTER 29

My head is racing…

My audition is on Monday, and I don't know what to wear. Maybe that purple blouse? No, who wears purple? I have those pearl earrings. My audition is on Monday. Why can't I remember that line on page twenty?

Monty.

Monty's family.

Acting is what I love.

Acting is what I love to do.

Five more hours.

Dinner.

Monty's family.

Will they like me?

Will I like them?

"Alexa, change the song."

My eyes are sealed shut as the warm water falls over my face while I stand still with my fingers threaded through my hair. Thoughts are still racing through my mind as I slowly open my eyes, watching the shampoo slide down my body and into the drain. I hear a few knocks on the bathroom door. Still, I decide to ignore them, wanting this relaxation to continue a bit longer as I listen to a Beatles album. Also, this is my favorite spot to think about the outfit I'll be wearing. I know it's silly, but I'm meeting Monty's family in five hours. *Five hours.*

Five hours.

Monty's family.

Red dress? Nah.

I hug my towel around my body and clear the fog off the mirror the best I can and stare at my reflection. The door suddenly opens, and I hug my towel a little tighter.

"Don't you knock?" I yell, eyeing Colin through the mirror.

"I did," he says.

I walk past him and right into my room. I drop my towel on the floor, sliding into my silk nightgown in seconds. I eye the script on my bed and sigh, picking it up and glancing at each highlighted sentence on the page. I lean my forehead against it and stand in the middle of my room with my eyes closed, nervous and anxious. I am worried about this upcoming audition that I was lucky to get and anxious because I want it so badly. I pace around my room; pacing always helps me memorize my lines. If I sit or stand still, my mind will race with thoughts—thoughts about absolutely nothing. Sometimes being an overthinker can be annoying. I lost track of the time since I got lost in my character. My clock on my nightstand reads 6:40, and I know I have twenty minutes until Monty will be at my doorstep.

I run to my closet, still having no idea what I should wear. I brush my fingers against every piece of clothing I own. I bite my finger gently and wonder how long it's been since I met the family of the

guy I am dating. Too long, apparently. I decided to wear a dress; it's
my safest bet. I decided on my mustard-colored boho crochet wide
sleeve smock dress, paired with my brown boots. I love being specific
when it comes to putting an outfit together in my head. It's what I do
when I'm nervous.

~

"We're late, fuck. They hate when I'm late," Monty huffs as we speed
walk hand in hand up the stairs from the subway and immediately
into the city. We become swarmed by thousands of people in all
directions. Monty and I continue to walk fast, practically running to
the restaurant. I try to slow us down a little, rubbing the material on
his black sports jacket. These boots aren't the best for running.

"Monty, it's fine. We don't need to run," I say, looking up at him.

Monty doesn't respond, but he does listen. He's definitely nervous,
which isn't helping to calm my nerves. Shouldn't he be the more
relaxed one? I would assume so since it's *his* family we're having
dinner with. But I'd be freaking out as well if I knew Nat and my
parents were sitting at a table, waiting for Monty and me.

On the way here, Monty seemed fine, but he wasn't acting like
his usual self. He was tense, like his whole body was clenched.
Occasionally, he'd give me a smile, as if for a second he forgot where
we're heading to and wanted to enjoy the few minutes we had alone
together.

We finally approach the restaurant his family picked out. I've
walked past it a few times—an Italian restaurant on 3rd. Super pricey.

Monty and I are still holding hands as we walk into the restaurant
and up to the hostess. "Ian," he says.

She grabs two menus and leads us down a long hallway filled
with tables on each side. I notice that the majority of the tables were
taken. We suddenly approach what looks like a huge indoor glass

dome. It seems like it is covering half this restaurant. She opens the door to the dome, which kind of reminds me of a huge, rounded greenhouse. I look around in awe, eyeing each frame of glass that surrounds us. Vines and beautiful flowers cover each window, and there must be thirty-something tables filled with people, including the Ians. My awe quickly diminishes as I'm immediately welcomed by the whole Ian clan. After all the hugs and the handshakes, we all take our seats.

"Why were you late, Montgomery?" his dad asks.

Monty pulls in his chair and grasps his menu so hard that his knuckles turn white. "Traffic," he says nervously.

Silence fills our table, and I discreetly look around at each family member. Monty's stepmother is wearing a white blouse with a collar around her thin, pale neck. She has short hair, cut into a brown bob. She is casually nibbling on some Italian bread. We make eye contact before I'm able to move my eyes over to his father.

"So, Jade, it's so wonderful that we finally get to meet you." She smiles.

I glance at Monty before I speak; he looks so uncomfortable. His face is red, and his knuckles are still white. He seemed okay when there was that terrible awkward silence, but as soon as his stepmom, Leah, says something to me, he's mad? Nervous? I have no idea what's going on in that head of his.

"I've heard great things about you guys." I smile back.

"You have?" Monty's dad questions. I'm finally able to draw my eyes over to his father. He's wearing a navy blue, long-sleeved button-down shirt, and his hair is gelled back. Monty shares a lot of his father's features. They most definitely have the same nose and chin.

Monty lets out a groan only loud enough for me to hear and begins a conversation with his two half-brothers, Bennett and Cooke.

I guess his father liked that whole last name for a first name thing, and his stepmom didn't mind. His sister, Annie, and her boyfriend are sitting across from me. They are quietly engaging in their own conversation, hardly looking at me. I guess Monty was right about his sister; I wonder if I made it on the list of everyone she hates.

Leah begins asking me a slew of questions—about myself and how Monty and I met. When she asks about my acting career, I happily tell her all about my upcoming audition on Monday.

"Wow, that seems intimidating." Leah laughs, placing her hand against her chest. "I could never get in front of anyone like that."

"Remembering all of those lines must be difficult as well," his father chimes in.

"I used to get nervous, but I don't anymore. However, memorizing lines is still a bit hard for me." I smile at them, and they both nod. "I love this character so much. It takes place in the 1950s. The character is a divorcée trying to make ends meet with two kids," I tell them.

"You're a theater actress?" Bennett asks me, and I nod, giving him a smile. This is the first time tonight that one of his half-brothers has spoken to me.

"Well, we hope you get the part," Leah says to me, taking a sip of her wine.

"Thank you, me too. But I always look at each audition like it's practice, and I'm one audition closer to getting a part. I just focus on practicing my lines and the emotions that go into them."

"That's a great way to look at it! Positively. You hear that, son?" Monty's father turns his direction over to Monty.

Monty, of course, stays quiet.

The waiter comes by our table and fills our empty wine glasses. I feel a sense of relief as I watch my favorite alcohol friend being poured into my glass. I didn't have a chance to really look at the menu yet. One by one, each Ian member begins ordering. When it comes to me, I quickly scan the menu and order the creamy gnocchi, remembering how much I liked it when Jason ordered it for me.

"So, Monty informed me that you guys live in Florida. What part?" I ask.

Monty's father takes a sip of his wine and casually dips his bread in some oil. "Fort Myers. I run a contracting business there. But my Annie bear lives in the city."

Annie looks up from her lap and gives the table an awkward smile without showing any teeth.

"My baby girl is almost a college graduate. Still can't believe it." His father grins, placing his hand on Annie's shoulder.

I look at Monty, whose elbows are on the table. His shoulders still look clenched, and his face has reddened.

This is going to be a long night.

$\sim$

After dinner, we head back to Monty's apartment. The minute we return, he lets out a sigh of relief and lays down in the middle of his bed. His eyes are shut, and color finally appears on his perfect face again.

"Did you have fun?" he finally speaks. He was quiet the whole way back to his apartment.

"Yeah, I did," I say.

He opens his eyes and looks at me. "You can tell me if you didn't, Jade. I know how they are." He laughs bitterly.

I lean half my body on one hip and look at him. "I did. But did you?"

Monty doesn't answer me. I'm getting weirded out by his reaction towards what looked like a totally average family dinner. The only not normal thing is how they seem to rub him the wrong way. I wonder how he is with his actual mother…. I try to lighten the mood the best I can as I sit down beside him, leaning my head onto his chest. I can feel his heartbeat begin to calm.

"I have the biggest, most important question, though," I say.

His heartbeat quickens. "What is it?"

I sit up and look into his blue eyes. "I have a strong feeling that your family likes me, and I knew they would because why wouldn't they? I'm likable and cute." I laugh.

Monty gives me a smile and nods.

"But the biggest question is…" I pause. "Did your sister like me?"

Monty laughs and shrugs. "I don't know. It's tough to read Annie. She might just like you because you're an actress, and she thinks it's cool."

What he said was harsh, and it rubbed me the wrong way. Maybe unintentionally, but they still hurt me. I just wish he had lied and told me that she liked me for me.

~

The next day, Monty and I spent the whole day together—from morning sex to drinking coffee on his terrace. We then took a stroll on the Coney Island boardwalk and stopped along the way for some Nathan's hotdogs.

Monty finishes the last of his hotdog and cheesy fries without uttering a word, and I do the same as well. He seems a little worked up from last night's dinner with his family so I'm trying my hardest to take his mind off it. His family is leaving Tuesday, so he's spending the day with them alone on Monday while I'm at my audition and work.

"You guys can stop by the cafe after the museum." I grin.

Monty doesn't even look at me; his eyes are glued to the label that's printed on his half-empty ginger beer.

"They don't drink coffee," he says dryly.

I nod my head, letting out a sigh. My hair is blowing in all directions because of the strong ocean breeze, so we decided to go back to my place and watch *Love Match*, only because it's Sunday.

Monty plops on my couch as I stand by the microwave, waiting for the popcorn to finish popping. I casually sip on my rosé, eyeing him as he's sitting slumped on the couch, switching through each channel before my show starts. Luckily, we have the place to ourselves. I'm not sure where Colin is, but I'm just happy he's not home. It was the only way I could get Monty to agree to come here instead of his place. Hanging out at Monty's place is odd...and I'm only saying that because Monty's weird when it comes to his roommates. If we're in his living room, which we aren't typically, we have to be quiet. Even in his room, we have to be quiet. If my voice carries in any way, he'll say, "The walls can talk." I never realized how much I hated those four words.

"It's on, babe," I hear him say. He turns around, and I reach over to hand him the bowl of popcorn. I sit down next to him, and he immediately wraps his arm around my shoulders. We watch in silence as each contestant comes out. All I can hear is Richard Right and the crunching sound of popcorn. Then, the front door suddenly flies open. I don't need to turn around to know it's Colin. He's loud. It seems like he's carrying something heavy due to the quiet curse words he is muttering under his breath. I finally turn around and see that he's holding a box that's just as big as he is.

"Do you need help?" I ask him.

He lets out a groan, setting the box down by the front door. He's out of breath, running his hand through his messy hair. "That was a bitch to carry up those stairs." He's still out of breath.

I wonder what's in that box as I pause the television. "Why didn't you text me? Monty could have come down to help you."

Monty doesn't say anything. I can feel his body tense after my last statement.

"Nah, that's fine." He shrugs, opening the refrigerator and grabbing a bottle of water. He downs all of it in seconds.

"You guys are watching *Love Match*?" he asks, walking over to the couch and plopping down next to me. Why doesn't he sit on his chair? It's like he knows Monty doesn't like him, and he's purposely irritating him.

"I thought you didn't like this show?" I mock playfully.

"I don't, but there's nothing better to do."

I unpause the television, and we all watch in silence. Colin constantly reaches over me to grab handfuls of popcorn. Monty and Colin haven't said one word to each other. It's weirding me out, but the distraction of *Love Match* is helping. Colin lets out a laugh as the new contestant appears on the television, a thirty-year-old man who has too many fetishes for women to handle—even the three crazy women that went on dates with him.

"He's gonna pick the second girl," Colin says.

I shake my head. "I don't think so. This might be one of those episodes where he gets no love at the end."

"My guess is that he's going to pick the second girl, but she's going to decline because he's disgusting."

"I agree—"

But before I can finish my sentence, Colin lets out a laugh. "Wow, roomie is agreeing with me?"

"You didn't let me finish." I shrug but end up laughing as well. "If he is going to pick anyone, I think the third girl."

"The yoga instructor? Fuck no, she's way too hot for him."

"You just can't wait to disagree with me, can you?"

I glance over at Monty, who isn't engaging in our conversation at all. His arm isn't draped around my shoulder anymore; they are crossed against his chest. I bring my legs up to my chest, and I'm beginning to feel uncomfortable during the commercial break. Colin is on his phone, oblivious to Monty's discomfort, and he's letting out tiny sighs only I can hear.

"I'll be right back," Monty says quietly, getting up and disappearing into my bedroom. I sit still for a second, leaning my head back and shutting my eyes. Colin's still oblivious, I think.

Curious to see what Monty is doing, I get up from the couch and open my bedroom door. I then quickly shut it behind me. I lean my back against the door, eyeing Monty who is sitting on my bed. He's on the phone, nodding, and yes-ing to death. I wait patiently, my hand still grasping the doorknob as I wait for him to get off the phone.

"Is everything okay?" I ask as soon as he says goodbye.

He nods, putting his phone back in his front pocket.

"Who was that?"

He looks into my eyes. "My boss."

He seems angry, I think. I never know what mood Monty is in or will be in from one moment to the next.

"Are you okay?" I ask.

"I already said I was, Jade," he bites.

My back is still against the door. I'm not sure what is going on because he's not moving from my bed, and I can hear Colin calling for me from the living room.

"Okay, you just seem angry."

He lets out a fake laugh. "Trust me, I'm not angry."

"Do you want to go back out in the living room and finish watching the show?"

"Nah. Why don't you go and watch your show with the roommate you're fucking behind my back, and I'll stay in here and wait for you like a good little puppy."

Silence fills the room, and I'm processing each word he barked at me. Especially the "fucking the roommate" part.

"Monty, I'm confused."

"Did I stutter?" He rolls his eyes.

"Nothing is going on between Colin and me. We only live together and occasionally watch this show together."

He disregards my response. "I can see the look on his face. He eye fucks you, Jade. You may not see it, but I do. And you're just feeding into it. Flirting back with him while I'm sitting next to you."

"I wasn't flirting with him, Monty!"

"That's all you have to say?" he says, raising his voice.

"What do you want me to say?"

He disregards my comment yet again. "I don't like him, and I don't trust him."

"Do you trust me?" I ask.

"I don't think I trust anyone," he sighs.

I walk over to him and sit beside him on my bed.

"I'm sitting there and watching it with my own eyes. I can't even imagine how it is when I'm not around," he says slowly.

"You could have been a part of the conversation. What were your thoughts on *Love Match*?"

Monty stands up, which startles me a tad. "Fuck *Love Match*, Jade. It's been bothering me for a while." He pauses. "Probably since the day we've been dating, when I found out you live with a guy. And you say he's just your roommate, and that's it? Bullshit, Jade. The guy was eating dinner with us the first night I met your friends. So, don't tell me you don't have a relationship with him."

I remain quiet. Frankly, because I don't know what I should say. Or maybe it is because there isn't anything to say back.

"So now you're silent?"

I shrug. "I'm not sure what you expect me to say. I love you, and I want you to trust me. Nothing is going on between Colin and me."

He rolls his eyes, obviously not satisfied with my answer. "Whatever, I'm leaving."

"Where are you going?" I ask.

He walks past me and leaves my room. I quickly get up and follow him into the kitchen. He grabs his denim jacket and opens the front door in one quick motion. I glance at Colin, who's staring at us, confused.

"Where are you going, Monty?"

"My buddy's," he says harshly.

"I'll come," I say.

"Don't bother."

I watch Monty leave the apartment, and I want to cry. I feel so misunderstood. I hear Colin say something to me, but my head is so fuzzy. I want to run after Monty, but for some reason, my feet won't move.

~

Monty and I officially had our first fight. And of course, it happened the day before a huge audition. Getting ready for my audition was stressful. I forgot to set my alarm clock the night before, so I woke up like a freaking crazy person. Luckily, I set out my clothes, so at least I did something right.

I'm sitting in a stuffy room full of women who all resemble me. I cross my legs and close my eyes. I repeat my lines in my head, trying my hardest not to look down at the script. I'm also trying my hardest not to replay the conversation Monty and I had last night. As soon as I say the line in my head, Monty's face appears, and I rest my hand on my forehead. I'm exhausted.

"Jade Everly?"

~

As I leave the audition room, I'm unsure about how I did, but at least they let me finish my lines. I impatiently tap my fingers against my blue jeans as I wait for the elevator door to open. I then pull my phone out and call Monty.

"Hey," is all he says.

"So, I just finished my audition, and I'm running late for work. I guess I didn't time that out well." I laugh nervously. I'm not sure if I'm more nervous that I might be fired or because Monty and I are speaking post-fight.

Monty doesn't say anything. All he does is breathe heavily through the phone.

"So, what are you doing now?"

"Are we seriously doing this?" Monty asks abruptly.

My heart drops. "If doing this means our relationship..." The elevator doors open, and I walk inside, clicking the lobby button. "Then, yes."

"No, I mean pretending what happened last night didn't happen?"

I lean my body against the elevator wall. "I don't know what to say about last night, Monty."

"I do. I don't want you talking to him or even looking at him anymore. I get that you can't move out, or whatever, but I don't want you interacting with him."

I don't say anything. I'm just processing the order he just barked at me. "And how do you expect me to do that? Not speak to my roommate, I mean?"

"You're a smart girl; you can figure it out. But knowing that this guy is living under the same roof as you and that he wants to fuck you, I don't like it."

"Can you stop saying that?" I'm trying my hardest not to cry. The elevator doors open, and I walk into the lobby. "I have to go. I'm about to run to work."

He doesn't say goodbye. He just hangs up. A tear crawls down my cheek, and I quickly wipe it, trying to push aside my feelings towards all of this and get to work as fast as I can. My heart is beating out of my chest, and I'm sweating as I run full speed to the subway.

SUMMER

CHAPTER 30

This past week has been challenging. Monty's words continue to linger in my head, even though we made up. We had long, meaningful make-up sex, although nothing was resolved.

The other thing that has been bothering me is that I've been avoiding Colin. It's hard when his room is only a few feet from mine, and he technically doesn't know that I'm avoiding him. When he approached me Friday morning with his money for rent, I kindly accepted it. And also, when he asked me what time it was one night when he stumbled into the apartment, I told him. Otherwise, I think Colin is oblivious to my sudden avoidance of him. I wonder if he even cares.

Well, there is some light at the end of the tunnel: At least I got a callback for the Off-Broadway show.

~

"How can you stop being friends with Colin just because Monty demands it?" Reese leans her back against the chair and crosses her arms. I had to fill Reese and Claire in on my sudden avoidance of my roommate. See, I didn't even use his name. That's called progress.

My fingers are tightly gripping my coffee cup as I let out a long sigh. I study Reese's frustrated demeanor towards me. I can feel my armpits starting to sweat. I don't know why I'm so nervous about having this conversation with her.

"Were we ever friends?" I finally speak.

"Oh c'mon, Jade. You guys kid around with each other about not being friends, but I know you guys really are. You care about Colin."

"What am I supposed to do, Reese? Monty's very stern about this—"

She cuts me off. "Since when do you care about listening to your boyfriend?"

I nod. "I know, but I love Monty."

"What about Colin? You're so selfish."

I let out a loud laugh. "How am I selfish?"

"You're deciding on a whim to end your friendship with Colin…." She pauses, leaning on the table. "Knowing my birthday is in two days."

Oh right, Reese's birthday. How could I forget? I guess the stress about the audition and Monty's sudden ultimatum made me totally forget about Reese and her surprise party. The party that we have practically every year at her favorite restaurant in Bay Ridge. It's not really a surprise party anymore. Wes let us know that he arranged it, but my job is to get all the balloons, so I guess I know what I'm doing after this….

~

Later in the afternoon, after ordering twenty blue and yellow balloons, I grunt as I use my hand to block the sun that's shining too damn bright and hitting my pale skin. I drag my water bottle all around my face. Luckily, it's helping cool me off. I'm in a bad mood.

I'm irritated, and all I want is peace as I walk home.

I want Colin in my life. I admit it. It's strange to even think about knowing how irritating that guy is, but I guess Reese is right; I care about the selfish prick.

I drag my body up the stairs leading to my apartment. The only good thing about today, besides getting a callback, is Colin not being home right now. I let out a sigh of relief, and I immediately jump in the shower. That's how it is during the summer months in New York—a lot more showers.

I stare at my reflection through the mirror, feeding my fingers through my somewhat knotty and drenched hair. I open the bathroom door, glance around, and walk into the living room, only wearing my towel. I glance at the front door and lower my head as I walk into my room to change into my comfy clothes.

Once I've changed, I come back into the living room. Monty's face pops in my head as I nibble on a scone I took from work. I close my eyes, and Colin's face pops into my head as well, making me shove a bigger piece of scone in my mouth. My eyes begin to scope out the whole apartment. That's what I do when I want to make mental notes to straighten up something, or I'm just bored, and I want to admire my beautiful apartment. But something catches my eye...Colin's door is slightly open.

It's never open when he's not home. *Never.* He always remembers to close it, even when he's home, and he's not returning to his room anytime soon. It's something we both do. I know Colin wouldn't take anything from me and vice versa, but it's a way to say, *don't go in my room*, and *don't let any of your guests go in my room either.* I bite my finger slightly as I eagerly tap my foot, staring at the door to his room. Eighty percent of me would never in a million years go in there and snoop around. Still, the other twenty percent wants to so badly, just to get the inside scoop on Colin. Maybe this is a good thing. Like it's meant to be. This can be the reason I never speak to Colin, and we become "hey" and "hello" roommates.

Wow, that twenty percent is really kicking that eighty percent's ass right now. I stand up and walk over to his room. I place my palm against the brown wood door and push it softly. The door slightly creeks as it opens more, enough for me to slide my body inside.

I stand very still as my eyes do a quick scan, and my nose takes in any foreign smells. There aren't any. I'm shocked, and I'm surprised by many things—one being that his bed is made. I never met a guy that took time in his morning to actually make his bed. Also, it's decorated—guitars on one wall next to a tall bookshelf full of records and old CDs. I knew Colin was into music, being a musician and all, but I never realized he was into the good stuff like Fleetwood Mac and Elvis Presley. I never asked because every time he plays music, rap songs are blasting through the speakers.

I walk over to his bed and sit down. I glance at his nightstand and see a picture in an actual frame sitting horizontally next to the lamp. Before I snoop through his nightstand drawer, I pick up the photo. I tilt my head to the side as I study the smiling faces next to Colin. The smiling faces are two adorable kids. A boy and a girl; they must be around five or six years old. I can't make out where this photo was taken, but they look comfy, smiling next to Colin. I wonder who these kids are. Maybe he paid their parents to take a cute picture just so he can place it on his nightstand to woo the next girl he brings home.

I put the picture back and immediately scrunch my nose when I see a box of condoms and lotion sitting in the drawer. I get on my feet and smooth out my butt print on his blanket before I make a run for it. I walk over to his door and turn around, giving the room one last scan. And I'm happy I did. My eye catches a crumpled-up piece of paper lying next to the garbage can. I step over to it, and I can already see that this paper has words written on it from the ink that's bleeding through. Before I can open up this mysterious crumpled-up paper he wanted to throw away, I hear the front door slam shut. I let out a nervous gasp and run all the scenarios in my head that could possibly happen in the next thirty seconds if I don't do something and hide. I shove the ball of paper in my sweatshirt pocket and dash into his tiny closet.

I can hear Colin whistle in the kitchen as I curse myself and my curiosity. His bedroom door swings open, and his whistle becomes a soft hum as he turns the light on. I squint my eyes, looking through the wooden slats of the closet as I hide between his hanging clothes. I'm praying he doesn't need anything in the closet. His bed squeaks as he plops down, looking down at his phone. I try to relax my breathing. What if he hears me? All of a sudden, Colin stands up and takes off his shirt, exposing his perfect physique. Oh gosh...not his shorts too. I try to close my eyes as he pulls down his cotton shorts. I place my hand against my forehead as I watch my roommate—while I'm in his closet—get undressed. He walks over to a part of his room where I can't see, and I let out a sigh of relief. Why do I suddenly hate myself for yearning to see him naked? Seconds later, he comes back to where I can spy, I mean to see. He's wearing gym clothes, and he already has his music blasting in his ears. His door swings open again, and I touch my chest, feeling my heart begin to slow down. I wait a couple more minutes until I hear the front door open and close.

Never in my life have I ever been that scared and nervous at the same time.

～

Over dinner, a couple of nights later, Monty asks me, "Is it done?"

"Is what done?" I ask as I take a little sip of my Chardonnay. Monty gives me a look, pressing his chest against the table. Tom comes by and casually picks up our empty plates used for cheese pizza only an hour ago. Monty leans back into his chair as if Tom distracted him or he didn't want to reveal his top-secret plan in front of Tom, the waiter.

"Your roommate," he finally says.

"Is what done? Are you asking me if I killed Colin and hid his body where you asked me to?" I joke.

Monty finishes off his glass of wine and leans his elbows on the table. "Very funny."

"Hey, I thought it was." I laugh. "We don't talk if that's what you're asking."

He nods, looking pleased. "I didn't want to be a dick about all of this, but you can see where I'm coming from, right?"

"I guess."

"You guess?" he asks. "What do you mean 'you guess'?"

"Monty, I'm not trying to start something here. Especially in Vince's Pizzeria." My eyes do a quick scan around the small restaurant. There are five small tables, including ours, that line the wall next to the counter. A man only a few inches away from our table is waiting patiently for his to-go order. Even though it's small and stuffy, people still come here because their cheese pizza is the best.

"I'm not either, but you wouldn't like it if I was friends with Chelsea."

"No, I wouldn't. Only because Chelsea is your ex-girlfriend. Colin and I never dated. It's the same thing with you and Violet. And I know you guys hooked up."

Monty doesn't respond. I guess he knows he's being an asshole and a hypocrite. I get up to use the bathroom. Maybe I just need a little breather from our pizza date. Monty's been moody lately. I'm not sure if it has to do with me and the whole Colin situation or if he's just grumpy about other things that don't involve me. Monty's moods come so randomly. I can't keep up. That's why I'm constantly rubbing his back and asking if he's okay.

Luckily, when I got back from my little breather, Monty already paid so we can get the heck out of this stuffy pizzeria. Walking hand in hand, Monty and I decided to take a walk toward Greenpoint for some ice cream. The sidewalks are pretty busy due to the beautiful summer evening. Monty and I get in the long line for this famous ice cream spot known for its homemade scoops. The line is unsurprisingly out the door.

We make small talk as we wait for the line to move.

Jade? Jade Everly? Is that you?"

I look up from the menu I'd been eyeing into a pair of dark brown eyes. Those eyes are familiar to me. I've seen them before. And that face. I know that face. Eric Fletcher.

"Eric?" I smile.

"Yeah! My gosh, how are you?" He gives me the biggest smile, leaning in and giving me a tight hug. He's not as skinny as I remember him. I can feel his muscles as I hug him back.

"I'm good; it's been a long time. Probably since high school." I smile, glancing at Monty, who is standing quietly next to me.

"Oh, I'm sorry. Eric, this is my boyfriend, Montgomery," I say. They shake hands, and I turn to Monty.

"Monty, this is Eric. We were friends in high school. We had art class together." I smile.

The light breeze hits Eric's curly brown hair, and he shoves his hands into the pocket of his jeans. "It's nice seeing you. How's Reese?"

"I love that you assume we're still friends." I grin.

"How can I not? You guys were inseparable." He laughs.

"And they still are, by the way," Monty butts in, wrapping his arm around my waist. I'm not sure if it's because of Eric or if he feels the need to show affection right at this moment. I never know with him. I know Monty is being fake nice to Eric, and for some reason, I'm slightly pissed.

"Yeah, I bet." Eric smiles at him. Eric is so friendly and social now. Eric was extremely shy in high school. It took me practically half a semester to finally break down those artsy walls of his, but I did. Even though Eric was a grade below me, we had art together for two years. We'd always sit next to each other. He'd make me laugh and draw the funniest pictures of our mean art teacher; I have no recollection of her name. I wonder if he still paints; Eric always painted the best pictures, better than everyone in the class, even our teacher.

"Tell Reese I said hello, and it was nice bumping into you." He smiles. "But I'm late for something, so enjoy your ice cream." Eric glances at the big, flashy ice cream sign, and we say our goodbyes. I give him one last look as he continues down the sidewalk, attaching his phone to his ear.

I turn to Monty. "Wow, that's crazy."

"What's crazy?" he asks, placing his hands on my hips.

I shrug. "Bumping into Eric Fletcher."

"Was he like an old—"

I shake my head, already knowing where his question is going. "No. He was always a friend. Just a nice guy."

Monty doesn't respond, and we finally move up the line.

⌒

I had hardly heard from Monty since our date last night. I keep reminding myself that he's been working hard lately, and that's why he hasn't had the chance to text me back. But I can't help but shake the feeling that he's pulling away as a reaction to something I did. I never know where I stand with Monty.

When I get home from a long day at work, I can't wait to take a nice long shower. The warm water pushing on my skin gives me my second wind. I get a call from Reese asking me if I wanted to meet her at this new bar in the Village. She's going with a couple of her nursing friends to play Connect Four as they drink strong apple martinis. I kindly decline and tell her I'm waiting for Monty to get back to me. I pace around my room, and I hear Colin leave the apartment—probably off to pick out the girl of the night. I decided to call Monty for the third time and, of course, there's no answer. I'm starting to get angry.

I walk over to my closet and brush my fingers along the fabrics of some new shirts and dresses I recently bought. I begin organizing my closet when I hear my phone vibrate on the dresser.

"Hey," Monty says through the phone.

"Hey, babe. What are you up to?" I ask enthusiastically. Maybe I'm in my own head, and I'm making up these problems between Monty and me.

"I'm about to head out."

My stomach drops. "Head out? To where?"

"I'm going to the movies with Violet."

"The movies?"

"Yeah. She invited me last minute, and I've been dying to see this movie," he tells me.

I sit down on the bed and sigh. "I thought we were hanging tonight."

There's some silence through the phone, and I wait for him to respond. "Did we have plans?" he finally asks.

"No...but it's Friday night, and I assumed we'd just figure something out."

"You can come to my place for a little while before I have to go." He pauses. "I just knew you didn't want to see this movie. When I mentioned it the other day, you made a face."

"Okay, but why would I go to your place if you're leaving?" I'm not annoyed anymore; I'm mad.

"To see each other, you silly willy," he starts to joke with me. I hang up on him. I toss my phone on my bed and let out a loud groan. I don't know why he's playing these games with me. My phone vibrates yet again, and I sigh, putting it to my ear. "Hello?"

"Did you hang up on me?"

"Yeah," I say.

There's silence between us as I wait for him to respond. "You know, Jade, we don't have to hang out every weekend. You shouldn't make me feel guilty because I want to see a movie without you."

"I'm not, Monty."

"All right," he says, probably rolling his eyes. "What would we do anyway? All we do is lay in your bed every weekend."

A tear rolls down my cheek. "That is not true! It doesn't matter what we do. What matters is that we're together. And I don't care that you're seeing a movie with Violet. But what I do care about is that you didn't even care to see what I was doing before you made those plans," I say, already out of breath.

Monty exhales loudly through the phone. "I don't know what you want me to say."

"You wanted to hurt me, Monty. That's why you said it."

"Well, you hung up on me."

I wipe my eyes. "Have a good night, Monty."

"Are you mad at me?" he asks.

"No."

I end up meeting Reese and her friends at the board game bar in the Village. I tell her all about my little exchange with Monty—how he made plans without me and purposely said something to hurt my feelings. Reese shakes her head, then she immediately buys me a drink.

CHAPTER 31

My eyes fly open when I hear glass shattering from the other room. My door is shut, but since our apartment is so small, I can practically hear everything. I get up to quickly investigate the situation.

"Be careful!" Colin says as soon as he sees me out of the corner of his eye. He turns his back to me as he kneels to pick up big pieces of glass.

"What happened?" I ask him.

"I was trying to juggle too many things in my hands and accidentally dropped a glass mug." He pauses. "Shit!"

Colin stands up and walks over to the sink. From where I am standing, I can see the water running onto his bloody cut. I rush over to him and try my best to help.

"I'm fine. It's just a little cut."

I nod, letting him take care of the cut on his own. Instead, I walk over to our supply closet and grab the broom. I then return to where the glass mug lies and begin to sweep the kitchen floor.

Colin turns his head over to me. "You really don't need to help. I'll do it."

"It's okay. I got it."

"Thanks." He gives me a soft smile. "So, what are you doing the rest of the day?"

"I'm busy," I say, keeping my head down and gathering all the little pieces into a small pile.

Colin turns around and leans his body against the kitchen counter, dabbing a dry paper towel against his swollen finger.

"I need to get Reese a gift," he says. He then walks over and kneels in front of me, holding the dustpan for me to sweep the tiny little pieces onto it.

"You haven't yet?" I continue to look down at the floor.

Colin lets out a little laugh. "No, I haven't. I have no idea what she likes to be honest."

"Have you asked Wes?" I ask.

He shakes his head. "No, but I'm asking you."

I finally look up into his eyes, and we both simultaneously stand up. "Come to the store with me. It won't take long if you're with me," he says. Colin then turns around and dumps the glass into the trash can. I have a few seconds to think of the best excuse as to why I can't go with him.

"Well, I..." I start to say, but I stop as soon as I see Colin roll his eyes. "What?"

"This whole ignoring me thing is getting in the way of my day."

My jaw drops and practically falls to the floor. "I'm not ignoring you."

Colin pats my shoulder. "Whatever you say, roomie."

Colin walks over to his chair and plops down, then he grabs a beer can. "I'm ready whenever you are," he says.

I walk in front of him and cross my arms. "Didn't you hear me say that I'm busy?"

"C'mon, it'll only take an hour or so. I'll treat you to whatever you want. I know you can't resist free food," he says, clasping his hands behind his neck.

～

"What about this?" I hold up a plain pink blouse Reese would definitely like. Emphasis on the *plain.*

Colin walks over to me. "Nah."

I groan. "We've been in this store for hours, Colin. Pick something so we can go."

"Lies, but fine." He laughs, snatching the blouse out of my hand. I follow Colin as we make our way towards the checkout counter. I let out a deep breath as I bite the top of my fingernail. I hate that I feel like I'm doing something wrong, even though I know I'm not. Monty and his controlling ways toward my relationship with Colin are unsettling. I know that something as innocent as us shopping for Reese's birthday gift would absolutely kill him. And that's why I won't tell him. Ever. He's working in the city, so I made sure we stayed in Brooklyn.

"Just so you know, it's not that I'm not allowed to talk to you. It's just I'm respecting Monty," I say as we leave the store.

"Whatever you say." Colin is dismissive, and I can't say I blame him.

"Colin, I'm serious," I add, but he doesn't respond. I don't know why I feel pissed. Maybe because I feel judged by Colin. Heck, I feel judged by everyone. The way Reese was looking at me last night absolutely killed me.

"How did you know?" I ask.

We walk down the sidewalk on our way to burgers on Fifth. "Reese told me."

Did she? Why would she do that? She's lucky it's her birthday today or she would have received a rude call from me.

"Don't worry," he says, scratching his chin. "I'm not judging you. We don't have to talk anymore so you can keep this amazing relationship you got going." He laughs.

"I can do anything I want, Colin! It's not that I'm listening to Monty or anything. If I want to talk to you, I can."

"Okay, Jade. Do what you want. I just don't want to be involved," he says calmly.

I feel a fire burn inside of me, and I don't even want to look at Colin right now. It's not him; I'm madder at myself for giving in. I'm not acting like myself anymore. Never in a million years would I ever listen to a boyfriend who asked me to do something like this. I walk faster, a few steps ahead of Colin, so I'm not walking next to him. All I want is to go home, so I don't have to be around him anymore. Thank gosh we're only a block from the apartment. All of a sudden, I feel a hand pulling me back.

Colin turns me around so we are eye to eye. "I'm just messing with you, roomie. I honestly don't give a fuck what you do, but I was serious when I said leave me out of it. If you want to talk to me, talk to me. If not, then don't. Doesn't bother me," he says, giving me a crooked smile.

I lean my weight on one hip and cross my arms. "What are you doing?"

"I'm being honest and real with you," he says.

"Then stop. You being all serious and shit freaks me out."

"Do you hear yourself right now?" He raises a brow and touches my ear.

I swat at him and grin. "You know I hate you, right?"

Colin puts his arm around me and nods. "Hate you too, roomie."

We continue down the sidewalk, and I'm able to push that horrid conversation and my guilty feelings to the side, for now.

"Are you still treating me to—" but before I can finish my question, I'm distracted by the look on Colin's face. I've never seen that look on him before. It's one of pure surprise. But I can't tell if it's good or bad…

"Addison?" Colin's arm is still hung over my neck. It's as if the sight of this woman's back made him forget how to use his arms. He knows exactly who this stranger is. It's crazy that he is able to identify her just by her perfect posture. The unknown woman turns around, making her long, glossy pin-straight hair fly in the soft breeze. She gives Colin a smile, exposing the familiar dimples that are identical to Colin's.

"This is your building, right?" she asks, without saying hello to him. Either she's oblivious to Colin's shocked expression, or she's just very comfortable in her own skin.

Colin swallows hard but doesn't answer her question. I'm still wondering who she is and why his arm is still on me.

"Hey, Collie." She laughs, walking over to us and giving Colin a big hug. Colin releases his hold on me and wraps his arms around her. I stand quietly, wondering if I should just walk away or stand awkwardly beside them. Before I can make a quick decision, they pull away from their tight hug.

"Hi, sorry. I don't mean to be rude. I'm Addison." She puts her hand out, and we shake hands. "Colin's sister."

Now that makes sense. I knew this beautiful blonde wasn't some ex-girlfriend or anything based on the look on his face when he first saw her. It wasn't annoyance or anything like that. He had a soft look on his face, like he was fond of her.

"I'm Jade." I smile back at her.

Addison turns her body away from us and lets out a loud whistle, which startles me. A little girl with two long blonde pigtails skips over to her, and she picks her up in one quick motion. Addison gives this little girl a kiss on her cheek and turns her body towards us again.

"Who's that?" Addison asks the little girl in a baby voice.

The little girl looks at Addison and places her hands on both of Addison's cheeks.

"Uncle Colin!" she squeals.

I glance at Colin, and my heart warms from his reaction towards his niece.

"Emma, this is Colin's friend, Jade. Can you say, 'Hi, Jade'?"

"Hi, Jade," Emma says shyly, placing her head into the side of Addison's neck.

"She's a little shy," Addison says to me.

Colin walks over to his sister and places his hand on Emma, saying things that I can't make out. Then it hit me. The picture. The picture in Colin's room with the two adorable kids. The little girl has grown since that photo was taken, but her familiar blue eyes and blonde hair are the same.

"Emma and I are starving," Addison says. "Anyone hungry?"

$\sim$

I don't know how this happened. It's a blur as to how I got to this restaurant with Colin and his sister. It was like Addison's eyes hypnotized me to say yes to coming out to lunch with them, and Colin stayed quiet as if he wanted me to join.

My hands are tightly clasped as I sit beside Colin in this tiny bistro on Fourteenth Street. Addison orders a bottle of white wine for the table to go with our sandwiches and soups. I haven't said a word yet. I'm admiring Addison from afar. Well, not technically, because I'm sitting across from her. Every single thing about this woman is classy, from the way she holds her wine glass to the way she leans her chin on the front of her palm. Addison's eyes look like they forever glisten.

Colin on the other hand, isn't acting like his usual self. By that I mean, he isn't being goofy or making sarcastic remarks. He's not tense or anything; he's just calm and serious.

"The drive to the city was surprisingly nice. Wasn't full of too many cars," Addison tells us as she sticks her fork in the bowl of lettuce she calls a salad.

"Where do you guys live?" I ask. I decided I want to engage in the conversation and not be my intimidated, awkward self.

"New Jersey," she says. "The suburbs. So, we're not used to all this hustle and bustle." Addison grins, looking out the window.

"Emma, tell Uncle Colin about the song you're going to sing in the choir," she squeaks, moving a little piece of hair away from Emma's eyes. Emma doesn't say anything. She remains quiet as she plays a game on her iPad.

"Kids and their electronics." Addison laughs, shaking her head.

"Emma's singing a song?" Colin finally speaks.

"Yeah, she's singing 'Mary Had a Little Lamb' in her choir. We're very excited." She claps her hands. Addison turns to me. "I run the PTA, and I made sure we had a choir for the children at the school."

I nod and smile. "That sounds really nice."

"Look at you, Addi, running the PTA. No more hospital?" Colin asks.

I stay silent and wait for Addison to respond.

"Nope. I'll let Harry take care of the finances for this family." She rolls her eyes.

Addison turns to me. "Colin's just a little moody because he's the only one in the family without a Ph.D.," she says.

"Wow, there's a lot of doctors in the family." I smile.

"Yeah, well, it was either become one or marry one." Addison laughs, glancing at Colin. When she sees that he doesn't seem amused, she frowns. "What's gotten into you?" she says, taking a bite of her salad.

Colin looks up from his untouched soup and gives her a fake smile. "Oh nothing, sister."

"My brother is usually such a talker. Which you probably already know," she says to me. I look at Colin then back to Addison with a smile.

"So, what brings you into the city, Addi?" Colin says, finally sitting up and engaging in the conversation.

"Oh, you know, a little bit of this and a little bit of that." She grins. "And you know, I really wanted to see my little bro." She rips off a piece of Emma's grilled cheese and feeds her while Emma's eyes are glued to whatever she's playing on that iPad.

"Where's Ethan?" Colin asks, taking a sip of his lemon water.

"He's with Harry. They are at some sports game. So, Emma and I needed something to do while they are at the game, and all she wanted was to see her amazing Uncle Colin, who lives in the Big Apple. Right, Em?"

Emma looks up and nods. "The biggest apple," she says, looking around.

Colin smiles. He definitely has a soft spot for his niece. I've never seen this side of him before. "Well, it is nice to see both of you."

"I don't see you enough, Colin. Ever since you moved, it's been really dull."

Colin rests his hands under his chin and nods.

"Oh, I thought you lived in New Jersey?" I say.

Addison looks at me and then back at Colin. "You didn't tell her?"

I look around and wait for more clarification.

Addison rolls her eyes and turns to me. "Colin lived with me in Jersey for a couple of months when he moved from California," she tells me. "And then Wesley begged him to come to the city, and now I never see my little brother," she says with a sigh.

"Oh, I had no idea. Colin doesn't exactly tell me anything," I joke.

"Excuse me," Colin says. He stands up, throwing his napkin on his soup.

"Where are you going?" Addison sighs.

"I need a smoke," he says before walking out the door.

"Sorry, he gets this way." Addison shakes her head.

I give her a smile and glance out the window to see Colin lighting up a cigarette between his lips.

"I always thought he moved in with Wes as soon as he moved down here," I say.

She shrugs. "Well, Wesley was the one who got Colin to finally pack his bags and leave California. He decided he needed some comfort from me before he moved to New York."

I nod.

"Yeah, it was a great couple of months. The kids loved him living in the guest room." She smiles. "Even my husband, Harry. I mean, who doesn't love a built-in babysitter?"

Addison takes a sip of her wine and sighs. "It was unfortunate when he decided to leave. Besides Colin being a little depressed from what happened back in California, we had some really great memories with all of us as a family. I knew…" She pauses, looking out the window. "…That once he moved to New York and embraced that life with Wesley, he wouldn't ever want to come back."

"You seem like a really great sister." I give her a smile.

She looks at me and moves her daughter's hair away from her eyes. "I wish I could have been a little better."

But before I can ask her why she looks up and smiles. "And you seem like a great girlfriend!"

I open my mouth, about to tell her I'm actually not his girlfriend, but Colin interrupts me. He plops down on his chair, folding his arms.

"It's getting pretty late, actually," Addison says, looking down at her expensive watch. She throws down some money, and we all get up.

"Well, it's really nice to see you, Collie," Addison says, giving Colin a long hug outside of the cafe.

She walks over to me and gives me a hug as well. Through Addison's long blonde hair, I watch as Colin picks up Emma, giving her a hug and a kiss goodbye.

"It would mean the world to us if you took a drive to see us one night. I'd love to have you over for dinner," Addison says to Colin. She then turns to me. "And Jade, please come as well. I'd love for you to meet my other little one."

I give her a smile and a nod. She says one last thing to Colin, which makes him shake his head sternly. She looks at me up and down, as if she's about to say something to me. I stand still, watching Colin and his sister engage in a serious conversation. Then she gives Colin a peck on the cheek and turns the other way with Emma. We watch them disappear into the crowd of people.

"She was very nice," I say to Colin as we walk down the busy streets. I move my hair away from my face and sigh. "Um, Colin?"

"Yes, Jade?"

"Why didn't you tell her we aren't dating?"

He turns his head towards me. "Because I didn't want to answer a million and one questions. It's just easier to not address it and let her assume," he says casually.

"Oh, okay. I guess that's fine."

"Why? You have a problem being my fake girlfriend?" He raises a brow.

I smile. "No problem with it at all."

Colin nods, and that's that. We walk the rest of the way home in silence.

CHAPTER 32

"We have to be at the restaurant in fifteen minutes," I say to Monty, who is lying on my bed with my pillow on top of his head. I hear him groan underneath the pillow, but I decide not to engage. I touch up my makeup and apply more of my plum-colored lipstick. I slide my red heels on and touch the pearl earrings sitting on my ear lobes. It's something I've always done right before I leave the house, just in case I forgot to put one in. That's how far my forgetfulness can go. Also, I've been stressed this entire evening, trying to get ready and reminding Monty we have to leave soon. He hasn't moved.

"Monty, we—" But before I can finish, he sits up and leans his back on the headboard.

"Do we have to go?" he asks.

I stand still and study his face as I blink a couple of times. "To Reese's birthday dinner? Yes."

Monty groans again and slowly gets up like a small child that doesn't want to go to school. "I have a stomachache."

"You do? From what?" I ask him.

He shrugs. "I don't know."

I walk over to him and sit down on the side of my bed. I lean my chin on his shoulder and sigh. "I'm sorry, but I have to go tonight. You can stay here if you want."

"I don't want to be alone." He pouts.

I sit up and grab my little clutch by my nightstand. "Monty—"

"Okay fine," he huffs, getting off the bed. He walks over to my little mirror and fixes his button-down shirt. He runs his black painted fingernails against his shaven head and turns his head slightly over to me. "Let's get this over with." He gives me a smile, but it isn't very convincing.

I walk over to him and run my fingers along the side of his arms, leaning in and giving him a kiss. Monty looks into my eyes and shrugs, moving away from me, not allowing me to kiss him.

Odd. Did I do something?

Monty walks past me and exits my room. I frown as I replay what just happened.

~

"All right, there's a speech I want to make, so here I go." Wes laughs as he holds a glass of wine in one hand. I can tell he's nervous. He clears his throat as he stands to his feet, turning his head over to Reese, who is sitting beside him. Reese moves her pin-straight hair behind her ears as she laughs and looks up at Wes. I lean my chin on my palm as I watch Reese and Wes from across the table. I try not to glance at Monty. He's quiet as usual and seems uncomfortable in the chair next to me. He's exceptionally stiff and motionless. Unlike everyone around us who's laughing and making fun of Wes' lovey-dovey speech about Reese. Colin says something that makes everyone laugh.

"Okay, okay. I won't make this long." Wes playfully glares at

Colin. He turns his head back to Reese and takes her hand, giving it a simple kiss.

"To many, many more, my love. Happy twenty-fifth birthday. I love you."

Everyone begins to cheer and holler for Reese as we watch them kiss dramatically. I glance at Colin, and he looks over at me, giving me his famous grin as he holds up his glass of wine in the air. I look down at the empty plate in front of me and turn my head over to Monty. He's looking at me without a smile or anything. His hands are clasped in his lap, and I reach under the table to grab one.

A few waiters come by the long table that's filled with all of Reese's friends—some nursing friends and Reese and Wes' couple friends as well. And then there's a few stragglers like Monty, me, Colin, and his flavor of the week—a tall blonde with big boobs. The girl he brought looks like she's having tons of fun, laughing and leaning her body against Colin as she whispers nonsense into his ear. I think she's already on her fourth glass of wine. The few waiters give all of us a friendly bow as they pour each one of us a steaming cup of green tea. I stay quiet as I wait patiently for any type of food to come to the table. I haven't eaten since breakfast, so I'm not in the best mood to make small talk with Reese's friends. I look at Reese as she's talking and laughing with her friends from game night. My stomach begins to growl, and I pick up my chopsticks, anticipating the food that will eventually come. I start to casually play with the chopsticks in my mouth. I'm a little bored so I turn my head to Monty as I play with the sticks in my mouth, doing impersonations of a silly walrus. All of a sudden, Monty grabs the chopsticks between my teeth and pulls them out of my mouth before slamming them onto the table. He gives me a stern look as if he's my father and I did something wrong. I narrow my eyes at him and tilt my head to the side. What the heck was that all about? I pick up the chopsticks and put them in my mouth yet again, staring into his eyes. I don't know what he's trying to do, but I've had it.

The food finally arrives in this gigantic boat filled with every sushi I could think of. But I don't feel as hungry anymore. I am annoyed and a little embarrassed by Monty's harsh reaction.

"Excuse me." I get up, needing to take one of my breathers in the bathroom. I stare at my reflection and try my hardest not to cry. I hate when this happens. I don't understand why he reacts so intensely to such trivial things. I let out a deep breath and fix my bangs, sweeping them away from my eyes.

I leave the bathroom and I shake my hands, splashing away the excess water since there are no paper towels.

"Your food is getting cold."

I look up to find Colin leaning against the wall. His hands are shoved in both pockets of his dark blue pants, and his neck is extended, exposing his prominent Adam's apple.

"Were you waiting here just to tell me that?"

"Come with me," he says as if he were taking me to a secret place. I stand still, not knowing what to do. Colin gently grabs my hand, and I realize how odd it is to be holding hands with my roommate. He leads me to the back door and pushes the tall glass door open with his shoulder. We are both silent. All I can hear is the chatter coming from our table and the faint music playing in the speakers.

"What are we doing?" I ask him as we step out of the restaurant and into the back alley. "Is this where you kill me?"

Colin smiles and pulls out a cigarette from his pocket. "I needed some fresh air."

"When did you start smoking? I noticed that you were smoking outside the restaurant that one time we ate with your sister." I cross my arms.

Colin rolls his eyes. "I didn't invite you out here with me to judge what I'm doing."

"So why did you invite me out here?"

Colin licks the corner of his mouth and places the cigarette between his lips without lighting it. He runs his hand through his messy but gelled hair and shrugs. "I thought you needed a breather outside rather than just hiding in the bathroom."

I part my lips slightly, but I can't find any words to say, only because I'm not sure what he means.

Colin lets out a little chuckle and takes the cigarette out of his mouth. He begins playing with it between his fingers. "Are you in there?"

"I should probably get back in," I stutter. I turn away from him and head towards the door. I reach for the handle, but his words stop me in my tracks.

"Choose happiness. Don't settle, Jade."

I turn my head slightly and squint at him. "What?"

"You know what I'm talking about, roomie," he says, nodding his head in the direction of the restaurant. Monty.

"Are you seriously giving me relationship advice?" I laugh at his audacity. "Dating a different girl every week shows you are not relationship material."

"Yeah, but at least I'm happy," he says condescendingly.

"I am happy!" I throw my hands up, completely turning away from him.

"You don't have to convince me. Only yourself."

I laugh. "Wow. Thank you, Doctor Colin."

I leave him in a quick huff, and those tears that I was able to fight off earlier come back, but this time, in full force. I lean my back against the terrible wallpapered wall and let out a huge breath as I wipe the tears from my cheeks. I head back to the table, and it was like I never left. Reese and Wes are talking and laughing with their friends, and Monty is on his phone as he drinks his wine.

"Did you fall in?" he says as I sit down.

I look at him and laugh. "You're so funny."

"I try," he says, leaning in and giving me a peck on the cheek.

⌒

I decided to wake up early and go for a walk the next morning. A walk meaning I walked over to my favorite bagel shop a couple blocks from my place. I casually sit by the window as I eat my everything bagel and sip on my iced coffee. Breakfast is the only time in the day where I don't care if I'm sitting at a table by myself. People are too consumed with the busyness of the morning to even notice me. Monty and I didn't spend the night together last night. I told him I had a headache, which wasn't true. I just needed some time alone to catch up on some sleep that I desperately needed. And I'm glad I lied. I feel refreshed as I finish the last of my bagel. A solo breakfast is an excellent time for me to think. I decide to not let Colin annoy me with his judgment about Monty and our relationship. I love Monty a lot, and I want our relationship to work. I can't be so fixated on everything I don't like. Instead, I need to focus on my second audition. Which is exactly four days from now.

⌒

"I quit smoking by the way," Colin says to me later that night as soon as I leave my room. He's sitting slouched on one of the kitchen chairs as he eats a banana.

"Well, that was quick," I say, sitting across from him.

"Yeah. Quick recovery too." He smiles.

"Why the sudden need to quit?"

"I believe the smoking was affecting my singing voice," he says nonchalantly, the corners of his mouth lifting slightly.

My stomach begins to growl so loudly that I think our neighbor can hear it from next door. Colin raises a brow, and I let out a little laugh. "I haven't eaten since breakfast."

Colin reaches over to the counter and grabs his last banana. Without saying a word, he hands it to me.

"Really?" I ask.

He nods.

"So, what did you do with your cigarette pack?"

"Why? Are you calling dibs?"

I laugh as I take my first bite. "No chance."

"I gave it to Randall. He was pretty happy."

"You mean Randy?" I grin.

"Oh right." He laughs. "Randy."

I play with the little strings on the banana as I lean my arms on the table.

"So why did you start smoking in the first place?"

"Why are you so fascinated with my sudden smoking habit?"

I shrug. "Just making conversation, I guess. Monty also smokes, and I hate that he's so addicted. They're cancer sticks."

Colin nods. "I'd always have a cigarette when I was out with my band. I thought it was something I could do socially, but it ended up becoming something I did by myself."

"And you had a terrible smoker's cough?"

"I wouldn't go that far, roomie." He chuckles. "I didn't smoke them long enough for that."

Silence fills the table, and all I hear is us chewing.

"Thanks for sharing by the way." I smile, taking another bite of my banana.

"That's just who I am, roomie." He pauses. "A sharer."

I laugh. "Okay, Colin, don't be too full of yourself."

I hear a soft knock at the door. "That must be Monty," I say.

I get up and open the door in one quick motion, taking another bite of my banana.

"Hey." I smile, waiting for him to kiss me. But he doesn't. He walks past me like he's a detective in search of his top-secret case.

I close the door and watch as he eyes Colin and his banana.

"What's wro—" I begin to say but I stop when Monty turns his back to me. He rushes to my room, slamming the door behind him. I stand still for a moment, trying to understand what just happened.

"Honeymoon stage over already?" Colin asks smugly.

I throw the rest of my banana away and shrug.

"What the fuck just happened?" I ask Monty as I close my door behind me.

"I can ask you the same question," he spits.

I tilt my head to the side and wait for him to continue, but he doesn't. "Monty, I'm confused."

"Of course you are." He rolls his eyes.

"What is that supposed to mean?"

Suddenly, Monty starts to unbutton his shirt, taking it off and throwing it on the floor.

"Give me a fucking blowjob," he barks.

I stare into his eyes, shocked. "Excuse me? Monty, are you on something? Because if you are, then you need to tell me."

"I'm not on anything, Jade. If you think it's okay to eat a sexual fruit with your male roommate, then we have a problem."

"A sexual fruit?" I raise a brow.

"The fucking banana, Jade!"

"Are you serious?" I glare, throwing my hands in the air. "You are seriously mad because I was eating a banana with Colin? I was hungry."

"Can you please not say his name? And if you were *sooo* hungry," he mocks, "instead of filling your mouth with his fruit, just fill your fucking mouth with my dick."

"You know what? That was really disgusting and disrespectful. Now I'm not even allowed to say my roommate's name? Monty, I don't understand what you want from me."

"What I want is for you to not speak to that guy again."

"We've discussed this. I'm not friends with him, but I can't do that. I live with him."

"I know what he's thinking, Jade. He wants to fuck you."

Why does he keep saying those words?

"And so does the stranger that passes by me down the street and my dentist. Should I not speak to them either? Because they're men and have raging hormones?"

"You're unbelievable," he spits. "The way you're acting really makes me believe you probably already fucked him."

I laugh at his craziness, trying my hardest to keep myself from crying. "Then I guess you really don't know me."

"I guess not."

"And who do you think you are? The way you stormed in here, acting like an infant and being so damn disrespectful to me was not okay. I thought this was a relationship. Am I only good for a blowjob?" I cry.

"No." He lets out a long breath, rubbing his hand against his chin. "I'm just sick of feeling like you're doing something behind my back."

"Maybe that's what Chelsea did, but not—"

"Don't fucking bring her up," he bites.

I lean my back against my door and stare at his sulking face.

"I need time to think."

"Think about what? *Us*?" I ask, but he doesn't say anything. "Monty."

Silence fills the air. Monty then picks up his shirt and puts it back on. "I didn't think tonight was going to end up like this."

"Like what?" I ask.

He shakes his head and walks past me, reaching for my doorknob.

"So, you're leaving?"

"I said I need to think."

I watch his back as he reaches my front door. "You know what? I think this is over," I say softly. "I love you, but I can't keep fighting like this."

He turns around, and a tear falls down my cheek. I quickly wipe it away; I never want Monty to see me so vulnerable.

He stares into my eyes and leaves my apartment. My feet are frozen, and I stare intensely at the gray door.

"Jade?" I hear behind me, but I can't find the strength to answer.

"Are you okay?" Colin asks.

"I don't know."

∼

I hear a knock at my door. I haven't heard from Monty since last night. I figured we were broken up until I see him standing outside my door, leaning against the wall awkwardly tapping his fingers along the sides of his black ripped skinny jeans.

"Hey, can I come in?"

I nod.

He walks past me, sitting on my couch. "I'm sorry about what happened last night, Jade. I really got out of hand. I can be an asshole, but I don't mean to be. I hate dragging you into my moods."

I nod. If I try to speak, I know I'll cry and come off weak.

"I don't want to hurt you. Ever. You deserve so much better.

Things just aren't the same between us." He pauses. "I hate to say it, but it's obvious."

I let out a sigh, and he shrugs. "So you're on the same page as me, good."

I nod again.

"I just keep dragging you around like this, and it's not right. I was hoping I would change, but I seem to stay the same. I wanted to change for you, Jade." He grabs my hand and gives it a gentle squeeze. "I'll always care about you. I hope we can still be friends."

I look up from our hands and nod. "Of course, Monty." My voice comes out hoarse from crying all night long.

Monty stands up and walks over to my front door. "Be well, Jade. You deserve better," he says again. And with that, I watch Monty leave my apartment and my life all at once.

⁓

The morning after the breakup, I meet Reese and Claire at the café. Luckily, I'm not on shift today, so I'll have enough time to have an uninterrupted conversation with them.

"Friends? You don't want that, right?"

I breathe. "Of course not. I think that's what people say when they break up with someone."

"So, he broke up with you officially?"

"Well, I officially said it first, and then he ultimately flat out said he can't do it anymore."

Reese nods. "Are you upset?"

"A little. I think what really bugs me is when he said things aren't the same as when we first met."

"Why does that bug you?" Claire asks me.

I lean my back against the hard chair and stare out the window. "I think it's because I blame myself in a way. Like it's my fault that things aren't the same as when we first met. We were so happy back then. I don't know what changed," I say, watching the flower guy walk into the crowd of people, holding his white bouquet. I turn my head back to them and sulk. "Am I crazy for thinking that?"

"Extremely." Reese smiles softly. "Jade, did you ever think that it was Monty who changed?"

"No, I thought it was me."

"Monty was *extremely* insecure, and you know that."

"I just feel like as soon as I let down my walls with him, things went haywire."

"Then he obviously wasn't right for you," Reese says.

I let out a fake laugh, trying my hardest not to cry. "He said I deserve better. That's the classic way to break up with someone."

"If the man you're with says you don't deserve him, and you deserve better, it's because he sees your worth, but he is not willing to fix himself to be better for you." Claire looks into my eyes and gives me a stern but loving look. "You really do deserve better."

CHAPTER 33

I 've been listening to sad music.

I didn't realize how much my breakup with Monty would affect me.

There are times when I'm totally fine, but then all of a sudden, his face pops into my mind, and I feel sad. When that happens, I listen to music. I am also constantly reminded of him. Who knew shitty Mexican food on the corner of Fourth Avenue would make me think of my ex-boyfriend?

I try to remind myself how I felt during the tail end of our relationship, which seems to help a little. Then I think about each and every word Claire said to me.

"I do deserve better," I tell myself.

Work has been really slow. Slow, meaning that there isn't enough work to keep my mind occupied. I'm bored, even during the morning rush. When I don't have enough to do, my mind goes back to Monty and that isn't good.

Violet and I haven't talked much either. Maybe because we haven't been on the same schedule for a while.

After work, I decided to take a walk over to Violet's place. During the walk from the cafe to her front door, I feel uneasy.

I knock a few times, and I can hear her on the other side of the door but her words are muffled. She opens the door wide, but as soon as she sees me, she walks out into the hallway and closes the door behind her.

"Hey," she says.

"I was leaving work and was craving a hotdog, and I thought of you. Do you want to join me?" I smile.

Violet leans her back against the door while her hand is still grasped around the doorknob. "I can't."

I nod. "I'd love to catch up—"

"Jade, I know that you and Monty broke up. I'm not picking sides or anything, but I have some people over now so…" she says, cutting me off.

"People, meaning Monty?" I ask.

"Like I said, I don't want to pick sides or anything."

"It almost seems like you are, Violet."

"Well, Monty is over now, and he's a good friend and—"

I put my hand up and shake my head. "You don't have to finish that sentence. I get it. I'll see you at work."

"I switched to a different Coffee Bean location," she says without any emotion in her words.

"Oh wow. That's news to me." I fake a laugh. "Because of me?"

She shakes her head. "No. I-I just thought the other location was closer."

I nod. "Okay. I get it. See you around, Violet."

I turn around and continue down the hallway without waiting for her response.

CHAPTER 34

Butterflies and all sorts of other creatures are dancing and twirling in my stomach as I grasp the subway pole. I swallow hard as the doors open, and I follow a ton of people up the flight of stairs to the city. I squint my eyes as soon as I step outside, and I fix my purse that has slid off my shoulder. I speed walk as I make my way over to Ryders Avenue. My heart feels like it's beating out of my chest. I let out a deep breath as I open the long, heavy door and walk down a very familiar hallway. I glance at the maroon carpet as my uncomfortable heels push into both of my pinky toes. Walking fast through the city probably wasn't the best idea, but I was so anxious.

I tell the receptionist my name, and he nods as his eyes do a quick scan of my appearance. Yes, I know I look a little disheveled. The receptionist hands me a glass of water, and I kindly thank him before continuing down the hallway towards the tinted glass door.

I knock a few times and open the door without waiting for a "come in." The swivel chair is faced towards the large window that covers the back wall of this tiny office. I slowly walk to one of the chairs and plop down, waiting for the chair to turn. This could be a scene in a movie. The one where the chair slowly turns, almost in slow motion, to reveal an evil man holding a white cat. But this isn't a scene in a movie, and I'm not James Bond. The chair turns, and Rita is shoving a big forkful of lo mein in her mouth from an old take-out box. She wipes the grease from her mouth with the palm of her hand and lets out a burp.

"Oh, Jade, I'm glad you came," she says, placing her fork in the empty carton. She takes off her headphones that are blasting music, and she lets out a little laugh. "I can't hear anything. Gotta love Chinese pop. Right?"

I blink a couple of times then smile. "Of course, Rita. If you call, I'm here," I say, completely disregarding her music comment.

She nods, tapping her long fingers against her desk. "I got good news, Everly. Good news."

I sit up a bit and wait for my agent to speak again. "Did I get it?" I swallow hard before taking a sip of my lemon water.

Rita leans back on her chair, and I stare deeply into her dark brown eyes. The black leather chair squeaks as she crosses her short, thick arms.

"I remember the day you walked in here with your mom," she says, leaning her chin on the side of her palm. "You were so cute, with your long pigtails and those eyes. You hadn't grown into them yet."

"I still haven't." I smile, moving my hair away from my face. "Rita, please just tell me. It's been one month and one week of anticipation. Did I get the part?"

Rita bites the corner of her lip and grabs the empty carton, throwing it into the garbage can.

"You got it!"

~

I lay on my couch as I lazily snack on popcorn and read my lines for the first day of rehearsals tomorrow. My stomach is still churning from nervousness. My phone buzzes, and it's my mother, reminding me to bring sunscreen in case the rehearsals are outside. I let out a groan and turn my head over to Reese who is reading one of my fashion magazines.

"I'm going to be single forever," I cry.

Reese rolls her eyes. "Jade, stop. You need to relax and that was totally random."

"It is not random because this is what I do. Something happy is happening in my fucking life, and I have to ruin it because all the guys I've met have turned out to be douches. It's too much for one girl to take. It would have been nice to share my big news with a guy that I like or even love."

"Whatever happened to that guy you met?"

"Which one?" I ask. "I meet a lot of people." I tease.

"Glasses," she says. "Shakes Bar."

I stick my tongue out. "Gross."

Reese laughs. "What happened? I thought he was adorable."

"Oh, he was. Emphasis on the *was*."

"What did you do?" She crosses her arms.

"Okay, why do you assume it was me?"

"You're so picky, Jade. Admit it."

"I am not! I dated Monty for too long, remember?"

"That doesn't mean you're not picky. That just means you stay complacent or you're desperate. It's one or the other." She shrugs.

"Ouch, but desperate sounds about right," I say.

"So?" She nudges my shoulder.

I sigh. "Well, it's a little embarrassing."

"Listening."

"Okay, well, he took me to Chipotle, and long story short, he shouldn't have ordered sour cream." I put my hands up.

Reese tilts her head back and lets out a loud laugh. "Please explain."

"Let's just say I got grossed out by the way he ate his Chipotle bowl."

"Wow. You can't wait to find something to complain about." She shakes her head but ends up laughing seconds later.

"What is that supposed to mean?"

"It means *exactly* what it sounds like."

"I don't appreciate that. I don't have to defend myself to anyone." I cross my arms. "The sour cream was everywhere."

Reese covers her face and laughs.

"See! You're grossed out."

"Okay, a little. You know how I feel about sour cream."

"See, I would have disagreed with you last week, but after seeing it on his horrid mouth, I don't think I can look at sour cream the same way again. Honestly, I might need a break from Chipotle." I shrug. "So, that's what happened with Shakes Bar guy."

"Speaking of Shakes, wanna go tonight?" Reese asks.

"Sure," I say, grabbing my script. "Oh shit. I can't."

Reese groans. "What now?"

"I promised Emerson I'd go check out the gallery she's managing for the night. It's a big deal for her. She needs all the support," I say.

"No." She shakes her head. "Not gonna happen."

"Oh, c'mon Reese! There will be free champagne and those yummy sandwiches you like so much. It'll be fun."

"Fun? I don't think so. Art is not my thing."

"But you love me, and I want you to be my date. Besides, I need a distraction from my nervous stomach acting up about tomorrow."

"Have Emerson be your date." She rolls her eyes.

"Emerson's not really my type."

Reese looks at me and laughs. "Fine. But you're paying for the Uber."

"Deal."

⁓

"You almost ready?" I ask, knocking on Reese's door later that same evening. I hear her groan, and I tilt my head to the side, opening the door.

"I'm coming in," I say.

"I have nothing to wear."

"Since when do you care about that?"

Reese turns to look at me. "I always do. And I put on five pounds."

"No, you didn't," I say, watching her as she pulls on her tight dress.

"Are you blind?" She rolls her eyes then grabs a sweater out of her closet.

"We're so late," I say.

"Since when do you care about being late?" She crosses her arms. "It's a stupid gallery full of art. Nobody will notice that we're not there."

"Well, Em will, and I want to show her I care about her stupid art." I laugh. I fix my bun and my bangs, which are already getting frizzy from the lack of air conditioning in this room. "It's hot in here. Too hot," I say.

"Okay, okay. I'm ready," she groans. Again.

⁓

Wealthy New Yorkers with perfect posture stand tall with a permanent tilt to their heads as they nod and drink Pinot Grigio, eyeing each and every painting on the pale white walls of this big gallery in the lower east side. Reese and I head over to the table filled with glasses of wine and tiny sandwiches. I look around for Emerson as I shove a tiny sandwich into my mouth.

"You made it," she smiles widely, giving me a hug and a kiss on the cheek. "Here." She hands Reese and me a glass of wine. "The finest glass of Bordeaux. The best red wine imported from France."

I take a sip and smile. "This gallery is hopping," I say.

Emerson lets out a sigh of relief and touches her hands to her chest. "This is the most stressful but exciting night of my life." She laughs. "Take a look around. I spotted some wealthy clients walking in." She winks, walking away from us.

"Shall we look at some art?" I wink at Reese.

Reese takes a sip of her wine and smiles. "We shall indeed."

After a few minutes of tilting our heads and drinking our fancy wine, we walk away from a painting with two black dots to another similar painting with three red dots.

"*Hmm*. This painting really speaks to me," I say, standing up straight and taking a sip of my wine. "This one would look great in my bedroom, right above my bed."

"Ah, yes. The other one would look great in my living room."

"You two are hilarious." We hear laughing beside us. I glance over to find Eric, wearing a black hoodie and black jeans. He has both hands clasped behind him as he smiles at Reese and me without showing any teeth.

I let out a nervous laugh and move my eyes away from his. "I'm considering purchasing this painting," I say.

"Good choice," Eric speaks. "'The Lonely Heart.'"

"What?" I ask him.

Eric points. "This painting is called 'The Lonely Heart.'"

"Okay, and this is why I don't understand art. Why in the hell would the artist name this terrible and, may I add, extremely dull painting, 'The Lonely Heart'? First of all, there are absolutely no hearts in this painting, and secondly, why would I buy a painting that costs over five hundred dollars?"

"Jade—" Reese coughs, discreetly tugging my arm to shut me up.

"No, I get it." Eric smiles. "It is extremely dull, and there are no hearts either. But when I painted this, I was very high."

I shoot my head over to him and back to the little sign under the painting that states his name. Eric Fletcher.

I look at Reese, and she looks at me before taking a sip of her wine.

"I'm sorry, Eric, that's what I do."

"What you do?" he asks.

"Say stupid things, and I tend to sometimes shut my brain off at terrible times."

Eric shakes his head. "I thought it was quite amusing."

"Amusing?"

"Anyone with eyes who doesn't have anything to prove to their rich, art-loving friends can clearly see that this is a very boring painting and with a name that doesn't make sense."

"But didn't you paint this? Aren't you supposed to love what you paint?" I ask him.

"I do but not this. This isn't my style," he says with a shrug.

Reese laughs. "So, what is your style?"

"I love colors and when paintings have meaning. I like to look into my painting's eyes and see it looking back at me. I like to watch people and radiate their happiness or sadness when I paint. Two dots on a canvas are just depressing and overrated."

I nod, taking a sip of my wine.

"Emerson begged me to bring a few of my paintings to her

opening night, but she made sure to inform me to not bring any of the art I usually make. She said some schmuck would buy my boring painting, and I may make a few bucks tonight."

"The same schmuck you were saying has to prove something to their rich, art-loving friends?"

Eric looks into my eyes and smiles. "Yes. Exactly."

A couple walks over to us and nods and hums as they look at Eric's painting.

"And my point exactly." He winks, walking away from us.

"What the total heck just happened?" My eyes go wide as I look at my best friend.

"I think Eric Fletcher was flirting with you."

"No way. He's like an adult who has paintings on the walls of this gallery."

"And who are you? You're an actress in an off-Broadway play. The boy couldn't take his eyes off of you."

"Maybe it is because just minutes ago, I was insulting his art." I laugh.

"Yeah, that was pretty funny and kinda cringy."

I take a sip of my red wine as I eye him from across the gallery. His hair is longer and bushier since the last time I ran into him with Monty. Eric's hands are still clasped behind his back as he talks to Emerson and a few other people. Reese and I make our way over to them, grabbing another glass of wine on our way.

"Jade, have you seen any particular paintings you're keen on?" Emerson asks. It's pretty amusing to see Emerson in this setting— so poised and using words like "keen." I'm used to Emerson talking about every guy who played her while she's taking a shot.

"Well, to be honest, Em, I love them all," I say, glancing at Eric. He gives me a small smile and takes a sip of his champagne.

"I know, right? I'm so relieved. Everyone seems to be loving the gallery."

"Eric, you remember Jade and Reese, right? From high school."

"How can I forget?" he says. "It's nice to see you both again."

"All these years," I say, giving him a half-smile.

I turn to Emerson and give her a hug. "Reese and I are gonna head out. Thanks for inviting us."

"Of course! Thanks for coming," she says.

"Leaving already?" Eric asks with a pout.

The way his dark brown eyes glisten under the white lights of this gallery is a picture that should be hung. My lips are suddenly feeling dry, and I'm at a loss for words, which is very unlike me.

Reese and I give Emerson and Eric one last wave as we head to the front door. I glance back at Eric; he gives me a nod.

"See, that was fun, right?"

"Totally," Reese says dryly. "But I'm hungry."

"Cheeseburgers?" I ask as Eric's brown eyes are still on my mind.

"Cheeseburgers," she agrees.

～

White walls surround me as I stand in the middle of about fifty people, holding a black cup of coffee. Everyone's making small talk as we wait patiently for the director to come and greet us. I look around and study the faces I'll be working with for the next few weeks. An exceptionally tall man comes beside me and lets out a huff as he fixes his scarf. I glance at him as I casually, but also nervously, sip on my disgusting coffee.

"Let me guess, Rosalina?" I hear him say.

I look at him and study his face. "Oscar?"

"Are we so predictable that someone can guess our characters just by how we look?" He rolls his eyes as a small smile forms on his perfect and clear, tan face.

"I'm Chaz. And you are?" he asks, reaching his hand out towards me.

We shake hands, and I smile. "Hi, Chad. I'm Jade."

"Oh, honey, no. I said Chaz. With a 'z.'" He rolls his eyes.

I let out a laugh and place my hand on my chest. "I'm sorry. I heard wrong."

"Clearly," he says.

"I get it. People always assume my name is Jane."

Chaz places his hand over his chin and nods. "Yes. I like Jane. I might call you that. May not. Haven't decided."

I nod. "Whatever you say, *Chad*."

Chaz lets out a laugh and nods, clearly enjoying our little game. "By the way, this coffee tastes like a butthole."

～

I drag my heavy feet up the flight of stairs leading to my apartment. I don't think I've ever been this tired. I guess anyone who has been rehearsing since six o'clock in the morning until almost midnight will probably feel like a zombie. My body may feel like it weighs a thousand pounds, but my mind is on a different level. I feel so liberated—heck, I feel like I'm on cloud nine. I'm finally doing something I've always envisioned doing. I pull my keys out of my bag, and I gently bite my lip from the excitement and happiness rushing through my body.

I open the door, and my smile automatically turns into a frown as soon as I see Colin and his band rehearsing in my living room. Scratch the whole happy and excited feeling. I'm not saying Colin's band is terrible—they are actually outstanding—but seeing Randy in my living room at eleven-thirty doesn't exactly make me wanna cheer.

I release a tiny huff as I open the fridge for a little snack before bed. Luckily, they are in the middle of a song, so I get the privilege of not getting hit on by Randy, their bass player. I grab my leftover sushi and practically run to my room, but before I can vanish, Colin calls my name. I turn around, leaning my body against the door.

"How was your first day?" Colin asks as he lazily strums a couple of cords on his guitar. I'm actually surprised he remembers and wants to hear about it all.

"It was great, actually. A month of rehearsals and then showtime," I say.

Colin nods, but before he can say anything, Randy steps in the way. He literally moves his body in front of Colin so we're eye to eye.

"Colin told me the awesome news," he says to me.

I nod. "Yeah, it's very exciting."

"Trust me, I'll be front row for every show," he says quickly. Randy has a problem with talking too fast. His words tumble into each other.

Colin comes up beside Randy and gives him a hard slap on the side of his neck. "That's exactly what Jade wants," he says.

I let out a laugh when I see the expression on Randy's face. I then walk into my room, closing the door behind me.

CHAPTER 35

The wooden chair scrapes against the mahogany wood as I move closer to the table, leaning my palms against the table.

"Is it weird that I come here on my days off?" I ask Reese and Claire as I glance at the flower guy buying his usual bouquet of white flowers. It's been a month since I started the play, but I can't help but come here.

"Not at all." Reese smiles, taking a long sip of her iced coffee.

"Heck, the coffee may be shit, but it's cheaper than Starbucks. Besides, who doesn't want to see the flower guy?" I say.

"I think it's your turn with a scenario," Reese says, taking a bite of my blueberry muffin.

I shake my head. "I have a better game actually." I smile mischievously.

"You look extra cheerful today, my dear." Claire smiles at me.

"Oh, maybe it's because I have these." I grin, reaching into my bag and handing them tickets to the opening night of my show.

Reese lets out a gasp and studies the ticket in her hand. "How did I not know this? I'm usually on top of these things." She hits her forehead and reaches for my hand to give it a squeeze.

"Well, it worked out because I got to see your reaction. All those tiresome rehearsals are finally over, and now I get to show people what I love to do."

"Oh honey, this is beyond amazing," Claire says enthusiastically. "But are you sure you want me to be there? You must have other people you'd rather have come to your opening show."

I shake my head. "You two are my favorite people. Of course, I'd use my two tickets for you guys," I say.

~

A burst of adrenaline rushes through my body as the maroon curtain closes. The cast and I give our finishing bow to the cheering audience. My heart feels like it's pumping so hard through my whole body as everyone congratulates each other with hugs. We all sigh in relief, knowing the last show tonight is over and was "spectacular," as my director says, throwing her arms in the air.

"Have you ever given an autograph?" Chaz says as soon as he approaches me.

"Never," I tell him, finishing the last sip of my water.

Chaz puts his arm around me and another actress as we walk down a long ramp, leading us to a back door.

"Well, you will now," he squeals as we approach a bunch of people who are very eager to meet us all. I let out a laugh and begin signing my name on the cover of some people's playbills.

"Hi, excuse me, can we have a picture, please?" I turn around and see Reese. She is standing next to Wes with her arms out, waiting for me to hug her. I let out a sigh of relief and a grin.

"You came!" I give her a big hug and smile.

"Of course we came, silly. You were amazing, by the way," Reese gushes.

I rub the back of my neck. "Really? I was?"

"Is that even a question?" Reese asks, looking at me and then at Wes.

"Yeah, Jade. Fucking brilliant," Wes says, giving me a hug. I look between my two friends and wonder why Colin isn't with them. I didn't necessarily expect him to come, but I'm not sure why I surprisingly care so much that he isn't here.

"Have you seen Claire?" I ask Reese, removing my thoughts away from Colin and his absence.

She shakes her head. "Nope, I haven't."

Chaz stands beside me and drapes his arm around me again.

"Chaz, these are my friends, Reese and Wes."

"Well, hello," Chaz says, batting his eyelashes at Wes.

"You were so good up there. Both of you." Reese smiles.

"Thanks, darling." He blows a kiss at her then walks away.

Reese lets out a laugh and grabs my arm. "C'mon, let us treat ya to a burger or something. Your pick."

"Oh, I wish," I say. "But I promised I'd get some celebratory drinks with the cast."

Reese nods. "I get it. Have fun."

They both give me a hug, and I watch them walk down the sidewalk into a crowd of people getting autographs.

I walk back to the small crowd and sign a few more autographs. I can totally get used to this. I think I might have a permanent smile on my face after tonight, but it quickly vanishes when I see Eric Fletcher approaching me. He's wearing a navy polo shirt tucked into beige slacks. One hand is shoved in his front pocket and the other is holding a bouquet.

"Girl, a cute guy is walking towards you." Chaz gives me a wink.

Yes, I can see that Chaz. I sigh and internally punch myself for not taking an extra ten minutes to look a little less sweaty and maybe check my makeup? *Jeez, Jade.*

"Hey, stranger." Eric laughs as he comes in for a hug.

"Eric! Hello," I say too loudly. *Chill, Jade. It's been a long night.*

Eric smiles and puts his hand back into his pocket as he leans his body on one hip. He seems so relaxed, unlike me.

"Did you watch the show?"

He nods. "Yeah, I actually got a free ticket."

"Really? People are already pawning out these tickets?" I laugh.

"Not quite. My grandmother gave me hers." He pauses. "And these flowers."

I nod. "That's nice of her." He hands me the bouquet. I bring them to my nose, and I close my eyes for a split second until I hear his soft laugh. I look into his eyes and tilt my head, wondering what's so funny.

"Yeah. She's great. Really cute. Loves coffee and cafes in Brooklyn."

Eric tilts his chin up, giving me a kind smile while waiting patiently for the wheels in my brain to turn.

My eyes open wide, and I place my hand over my mouth. "Wait, is Claire your grandma?"

"She is." He laughs.

"Please fill me in on how you know I know her and vice versa?"

Eric smiles and nods. "I was walking through Sea Breeze Park one day with my grandmother. We saw you sitting on a bench with, I'm guessing a friend of yours, and she pointed you out, and I was like, 'I know her, it's Jade Everly.'"

"You two are super sneaky." I cross my arms, grinning.

Eric grins. "What can we say? We like a little drama."

I laugh. "I get it. I like drama too. As you can see."

"Oh shit, yeah. You were fantastic up there. I was only focused on you."

I look down at my dirty converse and try my hardest not to show him my blushing face. I've never felt this way towards Eric. The way the streetlights are hitting his perfectly rounded face is making me feel things. Good things. Things I'd like to feel again. A couple of people come up to us, asking for an autograph, and I smile, signing my name the best I can.

"Well, I should probably get going. It was really nice seeing your pretty face," he says, reaching in and giving me a kiss on the cheek.

Wait, did that just happen? I stand still, my feet frozen on the dirty concrete sidewalk.

⁓

I haven't seen or spoken to Eric since he surprised me at the opening of the show. It feels like forever because this week is the last week of the show. Everything from the day I got cast to this very moment feels like a blur, even though this has been the happiest and most exciting time in my life. I even got a warm congratulations from my sister the other day. She was able to watch it online.

I've also been so preoccupied with everything that when I finally received my bridesmaid's dress, I shoved it in my closet, barely looking at it. It will be a surprise at the wedding. I've decided not to bitch about it. I guess you can say I've matured.

I haven't even seen Claire since I invited her to the show a few weeks ago, but more importantly, I haven't seen my friends either, only Colin here and there.

⁓

The last show was bittersweet. We were all hugging and crying but also laughing and congratulating everyone at the same time. It was very emotional. I ended up having a nice dinner with the whole cast after the show. We ate filet mignon at a nice restaurant in the city and drank red wine all night.

I slept for a few days. I used two of my vacation days to really catch up on my sleep. I'm a little nervous to go back to my life before I got that part. Not saying my life was so bad, but I definitely got used to being on stage. Also, I'm dreading going back to auditioning. It was nice having a little break from all of that.

My phone buzzes on my bed, and it wakes me up a bit. I rub my tired eyes and turn over. Reese texted me a few times, asking me to meet her for dinner. I'm trying to decide if I feel like getting up or if I'd rather just stay in bed until I actually have to get out of bed. But my stomach begins to growl, so I guess it decided for me.

I take a quick shower and change into a pair of high-rise capris and a sleeveless tank top. I call Colin's name as I linger by the front door to see if he's home. When he doesn't answer, I assume he's already with our friends.

I get to the restaurant pretty quickly, and I spot my friends sitting at a high-rise table. I make a beeline over to them. We're eating dinner at this wings place on Fifteenth Street. It's right near the meatpacking district. They have a deal where if you order fifteen of their famous hot and spicy wings, they'll throw in a beer, all for only $9.99. But no one ever drinks just one beer...

"I ordered you a beer," Reese says.

"You know me too well," I say, and she giggles.

I glance at Colin and Wes as they study the soccer game intently, giving me the perfect opportunity to tell Reese about my little exchange with Eric a few weeks ago.

Reese lets out a loud gasp as I tell her every detail. Colin and Wes tear their eyes away from the screen and their chit-chat about the game and focus on us.

"Wait a second. So, you're saying Claire's grandson, who she always brings up, is the shy art guy from high school? The one who you reconnected with later on?" Reese says enthusiastically.

I nod with a massive smile on my face.

"Wow. Just *wow*," Reese says. "And then he shows up to the opening of your show...wow."

"Romantic, right?"

Reese nods. "But how did you know he was Claire's grandson?"

"He told me she gave him the ticket I gave her," I explain. "And he got me flowers."

Reese begins to play with her hair. "How did Eric know you knew his grandma?"

"Well, he said he was walking through Sea Breeze with her one afternoon, and they saw Violet and me in the distance."

"*Wow.*"

"Romantic, right?" I practically shout.

"So romantic," she sighs.

"I hate to interrupt, but when are you seeing this dude again?" Wes asks.

"Well, we spoke for about ten minutes after my show, but so many people were coming up to me that I had to end our conversation quickly."

"Well, if the stars are aligned, which I know they are, then you'll meet again," Reese tells me.

"Jesus, Reese, you sound like a Nicholas Sparks novel with all the shit coming out of your mouth," Colin growls.

"What's your problem?" I ask him.

"If the stars are aligned," he says, totally mocking Reese and ignoring my question.

Wes laughs and orders another beer.

"Oh, shut up, Colin. I'm just so happy for my best friend," Reese squeals, giving me a hug.

The waiter comes by our table and hands everyone a basket of chicken wings. I dip a piece of chicken in some chunky blue cheese as I glance over at Colin, who is shoving the whole wing in his mouth, eating every last bit as if he is starving. He doesn't even bother to wipe the sauce that is now all over his mouth.

I wipe the hot sauce off my fingers and turn to Reese. "I'll get his number from Claire. No biggie."

"Doesn't that make you look a little desperate?" Colin asks.

"Um, no? He came out of his way to see me. So, no, me asking his grandma for his number isn't desperate, Colin. Right?" I turn to Reese.

She shakes her head. "No, not at all. Ask away."

"I'm just sayin', roomie."

"I don't need any advice from a guy who has hot sauce all over his mouth."

He rolls his eyes. "I'm saving it for later. Hot sauce is hot, and I'm hot. We just work well together." He winks.

I pretend to vomit, but it only makes Colin laugh louder.

"You're throwing away that romance shit if you ask for his number, by the way," Colin says. "If the guy wanted your number, he would have asked."

"I thought you didn't believe in romance?" Reese says.

"Oh, I don't."

Hmm. Does Colin actually have a point? Am I jumping the gun here? If he really does like me, he definitely would have asked for my number the other night. Also, he wouldn't have let three weeks pass after our little exchange. Maybe I need to pull the brakes a tad and not dive in headfirst. After what happened with Monty, I should know better.

~

Reese and I end up leaving and the boys continue to watch the game. We're all "beered" out, and we are especially done with all the table slamming and shouting.

We find a cute gelato place a couple of blocks from the restaurant and decide to stop in for dessert. Plus, it's been weeks since I've seen Reese, and I think we needed some catchup time.

I dip my little plastic spoon into my Nutella gelato and bring it to my lips as I listen carefully to Reese's update. She talks about how the last semester of nursing school is almost over, and she believes it has prematurely aged her. Going further into her theory of aging, she found a couple of gray hairs the other day.

"Wow. I really did miss a lot." I smile, sort of mocking her a little.

Reese smiles back and takes a bite of her raspberry gelato. "It's traumatic to see, Jade."

"I'm just upset you didn't call me as soon as you found them," I say.

"Well, I wasn't sure when would be the right time to call, ya know?"

I nod. "Yeah...This has been a crazy month, but I'm glad I'm back," I say.

"Me too. I really missed you."

"I missed you and Wes," I say.

"And Colin?" She laughs, already knowing the answer.

I bite my bottom lip and finish the last of my gelato without answering her question.

CHAPTER 36

I hum along to the song playing through the speakers as I punch in the tall muscled man's coffee order into the computer. I ask for his name as I eye Claire from afar. She's glancing at the newspaper in front of her. Her red polka-dotted glasses sit on the ridge of her nose as she holds her coffee mug. She takes little sips and occasionally breaks off pieces of her chocolate chip cookie. I check the clock and groan inwardly. My lunch break isn't for another hour. It's been bugging me that I don't know the whole story about why Eric surprised me at my show. Was that her way of setting us up?

Before I can think of hundreds of other questions to possibly ask her, I see a familiar blonde walking into the cafe. Her chin is raised high as she looks around for an empty table. She walks past Claire and sits at the table right behind her. She pulls the chair out, and the scraping sound against the hardwood floor sends a chill down my spine. The same chill and uneasiness I felt the first time I met her.

Chelsea.

She anxiously taps her pale fingers against the table and

occasionally looks out the window. *Hmm*, she is probably waiting for someone since she didn't even wait in line to get a drink. I stand frozen next to the rattling cappuccino machine. As I run scenarios in my head, a bleached blonde with blue eyes walks in.

I turn around and pretend to be working as I fiddle with the empty cups behind me.

"Soy cappuccino, Jade," one of my coworkers barks at me, and I look up. He's here. That has always been his drink. I turn around and spot those blue eyes I once loved so deeply. He looks at me and then quickly looks away as he hands my coworker his credit card. I turn to Shelby, who's sweeping behind the counter.

"Hey, can you make the customer a soy cappuccino, please?"

I guess she can hear the desperation in my voice because she nods and hands me the broom. I sweep the floor with my back to Monty. I hear his soft voice saying thank you as I stare at the bare blue wall, wondering why they came here. Of all places, why would he come to the place I work at? I turn in their direction and watch as he walks towards her and sits down, his back to me. She gives him a slight grin as she leans her chin against her palm. I always knew he was never over her, and I was right. And here they are. I shake my head and thank Shelby again. If I wasn't over him yet, I know I am now. Chelsea can have him and his moody ass.

∼

Another day passes, and I still haven't spoken to Claire. She left before Monty and Chelsea did, and I didn't want to sit with Claire and possibly eavesdrop on their conversation. I'm over Monty, but I don't need to put myself in that kind of situation.

I stumble into the apartment, throwing my Coffee Bean hat on the couch. I open the fridge and grab a loaf of bread and some jelly. I then sit down at the table and casually read an issue of *Vogue*.

"Oh good, you're home." I look up and see Colin rushing towards me. I swallow the last of my sandwich and tilt my head to the side.

"Where else would I be on a Wednesday night?"

Colin runs his hand through his hair and looks around. He seems nervous and sweaty.

"What is going on with you?" I ask, but before I can say anything else, he pulls a chair out in one quick scrape and sits down.

"Do you remember that one time I did something for you, and you said you owed me?" he asks, staring into my eyes. His phone starts to vibrate, and he quickly declines it, waiting for my answer. But I don't have one. I have no idea what he's talking about, and I'm not sure if this is some sort of a joke.

"Colin—" I begin to say, but he shakes his head.

"Fuck," Colin says under his breath as his phone starts to vibrate again.

"Can you please tell me what the heck is going on?" I say loudly. I've never seen him like this. So flustered, I mean.

Silence begins to form between us as I wait for him to speak. But he doesn't. He leans his back against the chair, rubs his hand against his face, then looks at me. "I fucked up," he says.

I wait for him to continue. He is going to need to give me a lot more than that.

"My parents are coming, and they sort of think you're my girlfriend."

That entire sentence takes me a minute to fully process. "Wait, what did you say?"

Colin sighs and crosses his arms. "My parents, who I haven't spoken to in two years, are coming in from California to see me." He pauses and looks at me. "And apparently you."

I laugh. "Why me?"

"Because my sister assumed you and I are dating, and she fucking told them, and I didn't correct her!" He rolls his eyes. "And when I told them you were too tired to meet them at the restaurant for dinner, they insisted on coming here."

"Here? To the apartment?" I ask, and he nods. "When?"

"In about twenty minutes."

My eyes open wide, and I shake my head. "No way! I'm not pretending to be your fake girlfriend," I tell him.

"Fuck, I know," he sighs.

"Why haven't you spoken to them in two years?" I ask. Through Wes and even Colin's sister, I've heard that there's tons of animosity between Colin and his immediate family. But no one has given me the full explanation as to why Colin doesn't speak to his parents and why he moved to New York so abruptly. There was so much pain in Addison's eyes that I know the reason can't be good.

"It doesn't matter," he bites. "What matters is that they are coming here and expecting to see you. Trust me, they couldn't give a shit if they see me or not," he huffs.

"Oh please, you—"

"Just forget it," he says. He then gets up and walks over to the fridge to get a beer. "You need to stay in your room."

"What?"

"Or leave."

"Won't they wonder where I am?"

"Does it matter?"

"Yes, I don't want them to think badly of me, even if I'm your fake girlfriend," I say.

Colin looks at me blankly, and I stand up.

"No more band practice when I'm home. Randy and your other bandmates can't eat my food or smoke in the apartment. And I want more space in the medicine cabinet," I say, crossing my arms.

"Wait, you're gonna play along?" A small smile forms on his face.

"Yes, but you have to agree to all those things." I nod.

Colin puts his hands up and grins. "Deal."

I'm not exactly sure as to why I agreed to this family dinner. I guess I'm a little curious to see the people who raised Colin.

"What are we doing for dinner?" I ask him as he fixes the pillows on the couch, tossing my work hat at me. Of course, I don't catch it, and it falls on the kitchen tile.

"Already covered. Ordered Sandos," he says.

"Oh, how fancy."

I have never seen Colin like this. Nervous. It's definitely a sight to see. I'm not sure if I like it though. I like the calm and confident Colin more, but maybe he'll relax when they're here. I pick up my hat and myself and walk into my room. I don't have time to shower, but I might as well look presentable as Colin's fake girlfriend. I throw on my violet-colored summer dress and throw my frizzy hair into a cute messy bun. I apply a little lipstick and a pair of my purple earrings. I hear the front door open and close, and I peek out of my room and watch as Colin sets up the dinner he ordered for us.

"Does it look like I cooked this?" he asks nervously.

I walk over to him and can't help but notice the outfit he's wearing. A thin long-sleeved button-down—perfect for the summer—and a pair of light blue shorts paired with white shoes. He could be in a catalog. He hands me four glass plates, and I silently place them on the table in front of each chair.

"Is this okay?" I ask him and wait for him to turn his head to look at me. When he meets my eyes, I point to my tight-fitted dress.

Colin lets out a slight cough and nods as his eyes rake up and down my body. "Yes. Perfect."

I smile and sit down at one of the chairs, watching him transfer the green beans from the plastic container to a glass bowl.

"Is there a reason why it's so important that you have a girlfriend here? Even though it's fake?" I ask.

"If you're here, they won't bring up shit that I don't want to talk about. Also, it'll be easier since all their focus won't be on me," he says.

I nod, wondering what "shit" he's referring to.

"Do you need help?" I ask.

He shakes his head. "They should be here any minute," he says as he paces in the kitchen, finishing his third beer.

A loud knock at the door gets our attention. Colin looks at me before he goes to open it. I stand up and slowly walk towards the loud voices I so desperately want to meet.

Colin lets his parents in, and I can finally examine the two people in front of me.

"You must be Jade." A woman with straight blondish gray hair smiles as she reaches for a hug. She appears tall, but it could also be the four-inch heels on her feet. She's beautiful. Absolutely beautiful. And Colin looks exactly like her—the same blue eyes and dimples.

She gives my body a tight squeeze. "I'm Rebecca," she tells me. "But everyone calls me Bec."

We release from our hug, and I smile. "It's nice to meet you."

"Bec, would you stop hogging Miss Jade," Colin's father jokes as he reaches his hand out for me to shake. "You sure are pretty. Didn't expect to see those huge, round eyes. I'm Clint."

Wait, was that a compliment?

"It's so nice to meet you." I smile. I'm not sure if I should say that I've heard many great things about them, so I decided to keep my mouth shut.

"It smells wonderful in here," Bec says, and I smile as we all sit down at the table.

"Why haven't you shaved?" Bec asks Colin, and I glance at his stubbled face. Colin doesn't respond to her, and there's an awkward silence at the table. Bec clears her throat and gives me a smile without showing any teeth.

"Do you live here with Colin?" Bec asks me as she looks around our apartment. My mouth opens, but before I can answer her question, Colin answers for me.

"No. But she's here all the time."

"Well, I'd hope so if she's your girlfriend, son," Clint says.

I wonder why he didn't want to tell them I live here. Is it because they would think we were really serious?

Everyone begins to fill their plates with garlic-covered green beans and breaded chicken. Colin then pours everyone a glass of wine.

"This tastes great, Collie," his mother says, and I can't help but laugh at her nickname for him. I remember that Addison used that nickname as well.

"Yeah, Colin's a great cook," I say, rubbing my hand on his muscled arm. His parents narrow their eyes to my hand, and I quickly move it away. I'm not sure why I did that.

"So, how long has this been going on?" Clint asks the both of us. I glance at Colin, and he glances at me. I take a sip of wine and wait for him to answer.

"Six months," he says dryly.

"I take it that you two are getting pretty serious?" Bec asks her son.

"What does it matter to you?" Colin bites.

His reaction catches me off guard.

"Do not speak to your mother like that," Clint raises his voice intimidatingly.

Colin slumps in his chair and rolls his eyes.

"Colin's never been one to be open about his relationships. Heck, we're just happy he's in one." Bec laughs. "My Colin never settles."

Tell me about it. Do you know how many blondes I see leaving the apartment, Bec?

An awkward silence fills the room. Bec clears her throat and puts her fork down. She clasps her hands, looking at Colin and me.

"How's Wesley doing? We had dinner with his folks the other night," Bec says.

Colin doesn't say anything.

"He's good, actually," I say.

"You've met Wesley?" Bec asks.

I nod. "Yes. He's dating a good friend of mine."

"Would you look at that? Wesley has always had a good head on his shoulders. Smart too because being a mechanical engineer is hard work," Clint says between bites. I look at Colin, and he's slouched in his chair, utterly disinterested in the conversation. There's a tinge of anger in his eyes.

"Just say it, Dad. I know you want to."

Clint takes a sip of his wine and shrugs. "All I'm saying is that Wesley isn't wasting his time messing around in some little band and bartending."

Bec glares at Clint, and I'm picking up that this is a sensitive subject. But before Colin can respond, Bec turns her attention to me. "So, what do you do?"

"Jade's studying to become a nurse," Colin answers for me.

I nod. I guess I'm a nurse for tonight.

"Oh, how delightful," Bec happily responds. "Did you hear that,

Clint?"

Clint lets out a laugh. "I'm sitting right here, honey." He looks at his wife in awe before turning to look at me. "We're a family full of doctors, so it's nice to hear that my son is dating someone in the medical field."

I guess they would have negatively judged my career choice the same way they are judging Colin's. Soon, everyone goes back to eating, and silence creeps back up to the surface.

"We ended up selling your Ford Bronco," Bec says, looking at Colin.

Colin shoots his head up from his untouched food. "You did what?"

"The poor car was sitting in the driveway for so long, and god knows I can't drive a stick." Bec laughs, placing her wrinkly hand against her chest.

"Why would you sell it without asking me first?" Colin's back is rigid, and he's mad. Really mad.

"Well, your—" Before she can finish her sentence, Colin smacks the table, making it rattle. The sound of the table rattling takes Bec and me by surprise.

"I fucking knew it," Colin stands to his feet, throwing his napkin onto his plate.

"Watch your language!" Clint yells.

"I knew you were still talking to that piece of shit!" Colin practically has smoke coming out of his ears.

"Colin! That is enough. Sit down," Bec cries.

"No. Fuck, I thought maybe there was a chance I was wrong, but I was right. I'm always fucking right," he says harshly.

"Colin, there's nothing we can do." Bec sulks into her seat. I'm assuming they aren't talking about Colin's old car anymore...

"Bullshit!" Colin tears his eyes away from his parents and looks at me. "Jade, would you please ask these liars to leave?"

I look at them and back to Colin, completely puzzled.

Colin runs his fingers through his dirty blonde hair before storming into his room and slamming the door. I look down at my lap, trying to process everything that just happened. I'm trying to put the puzzle pieces together, but I have no clue what to do. Whatever happened, I know it must have been big. I have never seen Colin so angry and…hurt. It's disturbing to see him like this.

Clint clears his throat and looks at Bec and then at me. "We are very sorry for our son's behavior tonight, but it was a pleasure to meet you. Addison told us great things about you."

I nod and smile, unsure what to say back to him.

"But knowing my son, he won't be coming out of that room, so I believe it's time to call it a night."

They both simultaneously stand, and I do the same, walking them to the door. We hug goodbye, and I'm left alone to clean up tonight's dinner. As I clear everyone's plates, I can't help but wonder if Colin's okay. I want to check on him, I know I should give him some space to breathe. After I'm almost finished putting the leftovers away, I hear Colin come out of his room.

"Hey," he says.

I turn to face him. "Hey."

Colin grabs a beer and walks over to the couch, turning the television on. I walk over and sit on the couch next to him. There's comfortable silence between us as we watch a Kevin Bacon movie.

"Thanks for cleaning up," he says.

"It was no biggie."

Colin turns his attention back to the television, and our little exchange ends.

~

The next morning, I stumble into the bathroom to get ready for work. I open the medicine cabinet to grab a tampon, and I see another shelf has been cleared off. I guess Colin removed his stuff earlier this morning before he left for the day. I smile to myself, knowing that the man with soft blue eyes has thanked me for last night.

CHAPTER 37

*A*merica's *Next Top Model* is playing quietly in the background. I
lick my finger and swipe through one of my magazines as I sit
slouched on one of the kitchen chairs in the middle of a hot summer
day. A shirtless Colin stands quietly by the stove, sautéing peppers
and onions. I study a tall model as she walks elegantly down the
runway in an outfit the critics call the "new wave of fashion." I tear
my eyes away from the hem of her olive-colored dress to the half-
soggy cereal I forgot to eat beside me on the table. Colin softly hums
a song I'm not familiar with as we sit in comfortable silence. He adds
some raw chicken to the pan, and the sound of it sizzling along with
the other delicious aromas makes my cereal even more unappealing.

I move my spoon playfully around the daisy-printed bowl as I
continue to watch the show.

"It's not nice to play with your food, roomie," I hear Colin say. I
look at him and sit up straighter, just in case he starts nagging about
my posture too.

I let out a huff and push the cereal away from me. Colin's broad, muscular back is facing me. He begins to "top chef" his chicken in the pan, picking it up and shaking the chicken and vegetables.

"The food you ordered from Sandos was delicious," I say. "Too bad I didn't get to eat much of it."

Colin turns his head slightly over to me and shrugs. "Should have eaten faster."

"Can we talk about Wednesday night?" I ask him.

He tenses but quickly recovers. He then transfers his meal to a glass plate. "No," is all he says.

"Why did you tell them I was a nurse? What if your dad had asked me specific questions about nursing?"

Colin pulls a chair out and forks a big piece of chicken before shoving it in his mouth. "He didn't though."

"But he could have."

Colin rolls his eyes and takes a sip of his seltzer. "My parents don't give a shit about anyone but themselves. Anyone else, especially fucking doctors, would have asked a million questions. But not them. They couldn't care less, and I know that. That's why they don't know about half the stuff I really do with my life."

I nod, watching Colin practically finish his meal in minutes. The conversation about Colin's parents ends, but there's so much more I want to know. Days have passed, and I wonder if they are still in town or if Colin has apologized for his sudden uproar at the table. I learn not to push when it comes to Colin, and it's definitely not my place to poke.

I stand up and dump my soggy cereal into the sink. This conversation is obviously over.

A soft knock grabs both of our attention, and we simultaneously glance at each other, telepathically asking if either one of us is expecting company. Colin shakes his head and goes back to his meal, grabbing the remote and changing the channel to some golf tournament. I walk over to the front door, and my mouth falls to the floor when I see Eric Fletcher standing in the hallway. Both of his hands are shoved in a pair of his loose-fitted cotton shorts. I can't help but glance at his extremely hairy legs. He's wearing an orange creamsicle-colored shirt, and he has a black backpack on his shoulders.

"Eric?" I ask, crossing my arms as I lean against my door.

He removes his hands from his pockets and places them onto the straps of his backpack. "Hi, Jade." He gives me an awkward smile.

"So, how do you know where I live?" I raise an eyebrow.

"Well, let's just say I have connections."

"Connections?"

"Yeah, it's secret spy shit. I can't get you involved."

"I'd invite you in, but you probably already know what's inside," I say.

He nods. "Yeah, I'm really liking the new couch and new pj's." He jokes.

I laugh. "Ah, good one."

Eric runs his hand through his messy brown hair, and I can't help but stare at his long fingers and dark brown eyes.

"I bumped into your lovely friend Reese, and she told me," he says quietly.

Of course, Reese… "So, what brings you to my place at three o'clock on a Saturday?"

"I thought we could go on a date," he says confidently. Then he quickly backtracks, "If you're not busy that is."

"A date?" I say, eyeing his backpack.

But instead of responding, all he does is nod.

"Um, okay. Should I change?" I ask, glancing at my floral button-down dress.

"Please don't." He smiles without showing any teeth.

I walk back into the apartment, leaving the door wide open as I grab my bag and my white tennis shoes. "I'm going out!"

Colin obnoxiously gives me kissy noises from the couch. I give him the middle finger and hear him chuckle as I close the door behind me.

Eric leads us all the way to Central Park. On the way there, I couldn't help but ask him what the plan was. However, he was being super secretive for some reason. "You'll see," was all he would give me. So, by the fifth time, I finally shut up.

The subway ride wasn't as awkward as I imagined it might be on the walk there. He filled me in on his life since high school, and it amazes me how much he has changed. He graduated from some prestigious art school, and for the last couple of years, he's been painting all over New York. I finally ask him for more details about his sudden surprise at my show. He blushes as he tells me it was Claire's idea to have us reconnect because she knew he always had a crush on me. I can't help but blush as well when I hear this.

Eric takes my hand, leading me to an empty area of grass overlooking a pond. He takes his backpack off and looks into my eyes as he unzips it, giving me the cutest grin.

I can't help but be in complete awe as he lays a sheet out on the grass. My mouth opens, but he shakes his head, putting up one finger to silence me.

"Not yet," he says, reaching into his backpack and taking out containers of fruit. He kneels to take out another bag, then he dumps out different color paints, paintbrushes, and two small canvases.

He takes my hands, and I kneel beside him, taking in all that's in front of me.

"So, I was lucky enough to attend one of your shows and see you in your element," he begins. "So, I thought I'd show you mine. My love, my passion."

"We can't forget when I completely embarrassed myself at Emerson's gallery." I awkwardly smile, replaying the uncomfortable exchange I had with Eric before knowing it was his painting.

Eric laughs and shakes his head. "That stupid painting doesn't even come close to showing you what art really means to me."

I nod and smile at him. "Wow, Eric, all of this is so great."

"Yeah? I'm glad you like it."

He opens all the containers of fruit and hands me a sliced kiwi. "Now, as the French say: *Peindre votre petit coeur.*"

"Is that supposed to impress me?" I raise a brow, grabbing a couple of paint colors in front of me.

"Yeah, did it work?" He looks into my eyes.

"A little," I say, giving him a playful smile.

I hear Eric chuckle, but I decide not to get caught up in his adorableness…yet. I can't fall for him too fast. I don't want another Monty moment.

"So, what should we paint?" I ask him.

"Whatever you see. Whatever inspires you," he practically sings.

I smile. "Just so you know, I haven't painted since we were in art class together."

Eric places his paintbrush behind his ear then he grabs a handful of grapes and shoves them in his mouth. "How about this? We can't show each other until we're adding the finishing touches," he coos.

"I like that idea," I say, playing with the paintbrush between my fingers. Eric and I lean our backs against each other, and I smile when I feel his back against mine. Eric plays some soft rock from his phone, and we continue our conversation from earlier as we paint. I decide to paint the first thing I can think of and piercing blue eyes enter my head. I dip my paintbrush into the black paint and begin outlining my mysterious blue eyes. I fill Eric in on the little bubble of my life, and he nods and laughs along as he listens to some of the ridiculous stories that have happened to my friends and me.

"I live in Chelsea," he tells me. "I live alone in a tiny studio apartment. Emphasis on the *studio* part because it's literally my little art studio."

I smile. "How long have you been living in Chelsea?"

I feel Eric tilt his head. "*Hmm*…let me see… I believe about a year now. I went from growing up in a three-bedroom apartment in Brooklyn, to a little dorm room, to this studio, so I'm pretty thankful for the no roommate thing."

I shrug, and I hear him laugh behind me.

"Sensitive subject?"

"Sort of." I laugh. "I live with a roommate right now, and sometimes I imagine living alone and seeing how that feels."

"You get to live by your own rules," he says.

I nod. "Exactly."

"Grandma Claire helped me out with my apartment, actually. Because heaven knows I'd never be able to afford the cost of my apartment alone," he tells me. "I mean, I do all right selling my artwork. It has saved me plenty of times."

"Your grandma is a special woman," I say, grabbing a strawberry and taking a big bite.

"She is. She's the only family I have here."

"Where are your parents?" I ask him.

"They moved to North Carolina to be closer to my sister after she had a baby. I do miss them though. I'm very close to them, especially my mom. I'm a huge momma's boy," he says proudly.

I smile, picturing Eric and his mother together. It's probably a beautiful thing to see.

"That's really cute."

I dip my paintbrush into the cup of water and finally dip it into the sky-blue color. I feel Eric's body shift, and I look over to see his eyes trying to get a preview of my painting.

I gasp, which only makes him chuckle. "You can't cheat," I tease.

Eric grabs a cookie from a Ziploc bag and takes a bite. "I can't help it," he says with a cookie in his mouth.

An hour passes quickly. I'm adding some more blue to make my eyes pop a little more, then I apply some white around the sides to add a slight glisten. I'm pretty surprised by what my hands can do to what was once a plain white canvas. I'm very pleased with how it came out until I see Eric's painting. We reveal them simultaneously, and mine looks like complete rubbish compared to Eric's exquisite portrayal of a beautiful woman crossing the street with a bouquet in her hands.

My eyes open wide as I take in every detail of his painting, from the rich colors of New York to the woman's deep brown hair and pink roses.

"Wow," I say as I tear my eyes away from what looks like a photograph into Eric's eyes. "Is that supposed to be me?"

He nods as he blushes. "Claire told me how much you like flowers. And now I'm currently regretting not bringing you flowers."

I shake my head. "This is better." I smile at him.

"Well, I think your painting is outstanding." But I know he's only saying this to make me feel better.

I playfully roll my eyes and shrug. "You're too nice, Eric. But my painting doesn't compare to yours."

"Yeah, I know," he says nonchalantly. I gasp, softly hitting his shoulder and he laughs.

"How about this? I keep your painting, and you keep mine."

"Okay, but mine costs big bucks," I joke.

"Tell me how much, and I would be happy to pay for it."

⁓

Eric and I settle on some dinner after going back and forth about our paintings. Who knew painting could work up such a big appetite? We find a little restaurant a couple of blocks from the park that Eric has been to many times. On the way there, Eric tells me an intriguing story about these customers he had a few months ago from Norway. As he is telling his story, I notice he likes to use a lot of hand gestures with his free hand. His other hand is holding our paintings. We stop to watch a man paint the tall buildings in front of him, and I listen as Eric quietly explains each technique the man is using. I nod and smile as I watch Eric's eyes study the painting in front of us.

When we get to the restaurant, we are lucky to have the hostess seat us immediately by the front window. We set the paintings facing forward on both chairs and decided to play a game, asking each waiter and busboy which one they think is better. Most of them said Eric's, but I think one busboy felt sorry for me and said mine was better.

⁓

"I can show you my artwork if you'd like. You know that tiny gallery I have?"

"You mean the tiny gallery you have at your apartment?" I tease.

Eric looks down at his feet as we casually walk along the sidewalk after dinner. "Yeah, it just *happens* to be where I eat and sleep as well," he says flirtatiously.

"I didn't peg you to be a guy who brings a girl back to his place on a first date." I raise a brow.

He turns his head over to me. "There's a lot you don't know about me, Everly."

I take him up on his offer to go back to his place, and he looks pleased.

"Follow me," he says.

Eric opens the door to his one-bedroom studio apartment filled with drawings and paintings on every wall. Every corner of his place is covered in art. Paint is splattered on the walls and floors as well.

"Sorry, it's sorta a mess," he says, moving one of the canvases away from the open pathway. "Do you want anything to drink?"

"Water is fine." I smile. I walk to his bed—which isn't made—and plop down. He quickly fixes his blanket and pillows and lets out a deep breath, resting one hand on his hip. He then hands me a glass of water.

"Eric, I love it here. Relax." I laugh, grabbing his hand and giving it a squeeze. "You can really tell when someone is an artist by looking at their hands," I say, intertwining our fingers.

He looks down at his hands and laughs. "It's a bitch to get the paint off."

"I'm glad. I like it," I say, looking up at him. I blink a couple of times, never leaving his eyes. He licks his lips and moves his hands to my cheeks, giving me a little laugh.

"What?" I tilt my head to the side.

"Speaking of paint, you have some blue on your face."

I gasp and stand up, handing him my glass of water before bolting to his bathroom, leaving the door open. I hear his shoes tap against the hardwood floor as I grab a washcloth from a shelf sitting on the white wall. I hear him chuckle and I look at the mirror to find him leaning against the door with his arms crossed.

"I can't believe you didn't tell me the whole time we were at dinner."

"Oh c'mon, I thought it was cute."

I shake my head and rub the washcloth harder on my skin, but it will not come off.

"Allow me," I hear him say. I turn around, and he picks me up and sets me on top of the sink. He bends down and grabs a bottle of soap I've never seen before. He puts the washcloth under the water for a second then adds some of the soap to the cloth. He bends his knees a bit to meet my eyes and smiles as he softly removes the paint from my cheek.

"That will do it." He smiles. "It's a painter's secret weapon to remove the stubborn paint from our skin."

I turn my head and touch my paint-less cheek and then look back at him. I pick up his hand and point to the paint there. "Why don't you use it on your hands?"

"Because it smells awful, and it's supposed to give you nasty blisters."

My eyes open wide, and he lets out a loud laugh. I hit his shoulder playfully.

"I use it a lot, but I paint so much that it's tiresome to keep using it. And it doesn't help that I'm lazy, and this stuff is hard to find for some reason."

"Well, thanks for using some on me." I half-smile.

"Of course." He blushes as we continue to stare into each other's eyes. I thread my fingers through his curly hair, and I can sense that his heartbeat has quickened. I bite my bottom lip, and I can feel his hands attaching to my hips. We stay like this—gazing into each other's eyes for what feels like hours, but it's only seconds. Suddenly,

Eric's lips are attached to mine. I place my arms around his neck, and he deepens our kiss by sliding his tongue into my mouth to meet mine. I let out a tiny moan inside his mouth, and he squeezes my hips a little harder. I wrap my legs around his waist, and in one quick motion, Eric picks me up off the sink and carries me over to his bed, all without releasing from our kiss. The bed's old springs squeak as he puts me on my back and lies on top of me. He releases from our kiss and moves down to give my neck some attention. His soft touch makes me close my eyes. I feel his hand move from my hip up to my stomach to near my breasts.

"Eric?" I say, my voice coming out hoarse.

He gives me a "*hmm*" and moves his lips over to my jaw, giving me small kisses. He moves his hand away from my chest. "Sorry if I made you uncomfortable in any way," he says quietly, catching his breath.

"Of course you didn't. I just—"

He shakes his head, giving me a kind smile. "I like you, Jade. I always have. Which I know you had to know. It was obvious."

"I did." I bat my eyelashes. Not going to lie, I had a tiny crush on Eric too, but I was never able to act on it because I was dating Noah.

"If you want to take it slow, let's take it slow," he says, moving my hair behind my ear. I bite the inside of my cheek and nod. It takes all of my self-control not to take him right now on this bed. It's hard not to give in after he just said those words.

"We can still make out," I say. He lets out a little laugh and nods, leaning down and attaching his lips to mine again.

～

An unfamiliar alarm goes off early in the morning. I shift my body and squint my eyes to take in my surroundings—Eric's apartment. I lay on my back, bringing his white blanket to my chin as I look over to a lightly snoring Eric lying on his stomach. His thick curls are practically covering his eyes, and I can't help but take in this picture beside me. I check the clock, seven-thirty. I'm meeting Reese and Claire at the cafe in an hour, and I'm all the way in Chelsea. I quickly put on the clothes I wore yesterday and use some of his toothpaste on my tongue.

I climb on his bed, forgetting how noisy the springs are, and give his temple a little kiss before leaving.

"Bye, Eric. I had fun last night." I smile as I replay all the events from yesterday. I hear him let out a breath, and I decide to let him sleep.

On the subway ride home, I bite the inside of my cheek as I think about what happened after we agreed on just kissing. It didn't last very long because our clothes were on the floor twenty minutes later. I squeeze my legs shut as I feel my panties getting wet. I think about Eric and how good he was compared to the few guys I've had sex with. I probably shouldn't have rushed into it and had sex with him on our first date, but my philosophy is to never look back and to also thank the orgasmic gods.

I get to the cafe a little late, and I spot Claire and Reese at our preferred table by the window. It offers the perfect view of the flower guy. The second I sit down, I have two pairs of eyes on me. They're both grinning, of course.

"So, how was it?"

The date or the sex? I want to say, but I'll spare Claire some of the details.

"One of the best dates I've ever been on." I smile to myself.

Reese claps her hands. "*Aww*, Eric Fletcher for the win!"

Claire gives my hand a gentle squeeze and smiles. "I always knew you would end up with my Eric. You just needed to kiss some frogs along the way."

I let out a laugh. "Why didn't you set us up earlier?"

"You needed to get that punk boy out of your system to really enjoy my sweet Eric," she says nonchalantly.

I look at Reese, and she looks at me. Both of us are laughing.

"I really was obsessed with Monty." I roll my eyes. "And he had the audacity to come into the cafe the other day."

"I noticed," Claire says. "I kept giving the blonde bimbo dirty looks."

I laugh. "That's great."

I go into all the details about our date—from him surprising me to painting in Central Park. I look at Claire, and she seems pretty pleased with herself.

After drinking an iced coffee and eating a slice of quiche, Reese and I head over to my apartment.

"So, how was it?"

I look at her, baffled. "I told you and Claire everything. Weren't you listening?"

"No, I mean the sex."

My eyes open wide, and I hear her laugh beside me. "How did you know?"

"Oh please, you're wearing what looks like yesterday's makeup, and your hair says it all—sex hair."

I cover my mouth. "Do you think Claire figured it out?"

"Probably not." She laughs. "But who knows?"

"It was amazing, though. Like best sex I've ever had. I came twice."

Reese nods with approval. "Wow. Eric Fletcher for the win. *Twice*."

I let out a laugh and hook my arm with Reese's as we walk down the sidewalk.

CHAPTER 38

A few weeks have passed, and there hasn't been a day where I haven't seen Eric. I was worried I wasn't going to hear from him after that one night. I guess all the douches I've met in the past made me think that, but Eric proved me wrong. He showed up at my door the day after with a painting he made me in one hand and a flower in the other. It warmed my heart. I knew he wanted this as much as I did.

"What are you thinking about?" Eric asks as he gently runs his finger along the outline of my jaw.

"Nothing," I lie. He is lying on his side, perched on his elbow. I mimic his position which makes him smile.

It's around seven o'clock on a Friday night. We practically stayed in bed all day just talking, laughing, and eating greasy Chinese food.

I hear voices outside my door and decide that is our cue to get up. I lean in for a kiss before hopping out of bed. I throw on a sports bra, even though I've never actually worked out in my life, and a pair of sweats. It's still technically summer, but Colin likes to keep the apartment as cold as an icebox. Hence, sweats are a must.

I open the door, and Eric follows me outside. We immediately see Reese and Wes sprawled on the couch, ready to watch the game.

Eric has met Wes a few times. He obviously knows Reese, but he never officially met Colin since we've mostly been hanging at Eric's.

Colin's wearing a soccer jersey, which I've never seen him wear before, but it somehow works for him. Wes throws us both a beer, and I watch Eric approach Colin. A small part of me is nervous about this encounter due to the feud he had with Monty.

"You must be Colin, right? Jade's roommate?"

Colin looks up from his chair and gets up. They are eye-level now. They both shake hands and automatically begin small talk about sports. Reese and I look at each other, and I'm in awe as I watch Eric and Colin actually get along. I sit beside Reese, and I tug on Eric's arm, gesturing for him to sit down with my eyes. The guys turn the volume on high, and all I hear is all three guys shouting and talking about each play. Reese orders two pizzas, and when it arrives, Eric insists on paying.

"You really don't have to," I whisper in his ear.

He gives me a smile and a shrug. "It's really no biggie."

Everyone thanks Eric, and we all enjoy our slices as we continue to watch the game. After the game ends, we all decide to hang out some more, talking and drinking beer. Reese asks Eric about his opinions on a few people from high school, making all of us laugh.

Eventually, Reese and Wes leave, and I'm left alone with Eric and Colin. Thankfully, it isn't awkward at all. Colin rubs his eyes and lets out a yawn. "Fuck, I'm tired for some reason."

"Past your bedtime?" I joke. I look at Eric, who is laughing. I hate to compare Eric to Monty, but it's such a breath of fresh air to see Eric so relaxed around Colin.

"*Ha-ha.* Very funny, roomie. You two have fun." He gives me a wink. "And Eric, let us know if you're down to go to that Yankees game."

"Yeah, will do, bro."

I can't help but laugh at their little exchange as I watch Colin walk into his room.

"What's so funny?" Eric asks, turning his head towards me.

I go over and sit on his lap. "I just can't believe my roommate is stealing my boyfriend," I joke, but my smile dies on my lips when I realize that I just called him my boyfriend. Wow, this is *so* embarrassing. He never even asked me to be his girlfriend. I guess Eric can see how mortified I am because he smiles and caresses his hand against my face.

"Don't be embarrassed. I like that word. You should say it more often." Then, he attaches his lips to mine.

⁓

Eating dinner at Claire's small but cozy apartment in Brooklyn is something I thought would never happen. The smell of fresh garlic mixed with cinnamon fills my nostrils as Eric leads me inside. We're automatically welcomed by Claire and her orange-colored cat as we sit down with a glass of wine in our hands.

"Dinner should be ready any minute," she says, sitting down on a green suede chair across from us. Eric picks up Rusty the cat and begins playing with him. Claire reaches over and grabs a beautiful cloth that is resting on her armchair.

"I'm making a blanket for my great-granddaughter, Caroline," she says with a smile. "She's about sixteen months." Claire picks up a picture frame that is sitting on the coffee table and hands it to me. "This picture was taken when Caroline was born. That's Eric's sister, Elizabeth."

"Wow, this is beautiful." I trace my finger around the Fletcher family picture. "You guys look alike." I grin, looking at Eric, who has moved to the floor. He looks up at me with a smile.

"I believe I'm the better-looking sibling."

We all laugh. Eric then holds up a mouse toy for Rusty to try and grab.

"Was this taken in North Carolina?" I ask. She nods before getting up and walking over to the oven. She opens the oven door with an oven mitt in one hand, grabbing what looks like meatloaf. I stand up and walk into the kitchen, leaving Eric and Rusty in the living room.

"Do you need any help?" I ask.

"Thank you, Jade. I would appreciate that," she says, handing me three plates. "Eric and I took a long drive to North Carolina. We decided we wanted a nice road trip," she tells me, placing the dish filled with meatloaf on the table.

"Oh, that sounds so fun!" I say. It warms my heart that Eric and Claire are so close.

Claire places forks, napkins, a big bowl of green beans, and dinner rolls on the table. The second she plops the dinner rolls on the table, Eric walks in.

"Are you ladies finished preparing dinner?" Eric jokes as he walks past us, putting his finger into the green beans. Claire rolls her eyes and smacks his hand, ordering him to sit—for all of us to sit. We all take our seats, and Eric fills our glasses with the wine I brought over.

"It all looks delicious," I say, practically drooling from the look and smell of the spread in front of me.

"Dig in but save room for some dessert," Claire says as we all fill our plates.

"How do you like the meatloaf?" Claire eventually asks me after my third or fourth bite.

"It's amazing. Best meatloaf I've ever eaten."

"I'm glad to hear that because it's actually meatless," she tells me, and I stop chewing. I look between Eric and Claire as they wait for my reaction and my commentary.

"Oh really? Wouldn't have guessed that," I say, and they laugh. I squeeze some more ketchup on my plate and take another piece of meatloaf.

I didn't listen to Claire about leaving room for dessert because I'm incredibly full. We all help clear off the table and dishes. By the time we finish, all I want is to try what Claire baked, even though I'm stuffed.

"You're gonna love it," Eric says quietly to me. I look at him and back to Claire as she walks over and places what looks like an apple crumb pie on the table.

"Wow," is all I can say as I watch Eric cut into the pie. Claire gives me a scoop of vanilla ice cream, and we all dig into our pie in silence.

"Claire, you have to give me this recipe."

"It probably would be a good idea to write it down, right?"

Eric and I quickly turn to Claire, who is casually eating her pie.

"You memorized the recipe?" I gasp.

"Yeah, Grandma, you should probably write it down."

"I guess it has been drilled into my head. I came from a family full of great bakers. What if I write it down and it gets into the wrong hands?" she asks us.

Eric and I glance at each other and smile. Claire is too cute.

Eric turns to his grandma. "I guess we'll cross that bridge if it happens. I want my future kids to be able to enjoy my grandma's apple pie," he says before going back to his pie.

I can't help but imagine myself with Eric. How would our future kids look if we ended up together? Claire and I make eye contact, and I quickly look away. The thought of me even imagining it scares me. I take a big bite of the pie so I don't have to respond.

Eric and I say our goodbyes to Claire, and I thank her for the hundredth time for everything, even the leftovers she put in a container for me to take home. I give her one last hug and tell her I'll see her tomorrow.

Eric intertwines our fingers and pushes the elevator button. "I can't get over how adorable you are."

The elevator doors open, and we walk inside as Eric pushes the lobby button.

"And why's that?" I smile.

"Because you are friends with my grandma, that's why."

I jump on my tippy toes and kiss him on the cheek. He puts his arm around my waist, and we head over to my place.

～

Colin is spread across the couch when Eric and I come strolling in. I head over to the fridge to put away the leftovers Claire gave me. I then grab a Jell-O cup.

"How can you possibly be hungry?" Eric asks, shaking his head. I give him a cute grin as I take a bite of my lime-flavored Jell-O.

"I'm always hungry."

"I'm pretty hungry too," Colin groans, picking his head up and shutting the television off. He stands up and fixes his baseball cap that's sitting backward on his messy head.

"You guys down to get some food?" Colin asks, looking between Eric and me as he strolls over to the door. Before I can say no, Eric chimes in with a yes. I groan as we head out. We walk a couple of blocks over to a McDonald's—it was the only thing we could agree on—so I decide to get a milkshake and call it a day. The table is filled with everything on the menu as I watch Colin and Eric devour what's in front of them.

I wrap my arms around Eric's waist, resting my chin on his shoulder. "How can you possibly be hungry?" I say.

He laughs, fries sticking out of his mouth. He squeezes my nose and feeds me a fry.

"So, is this getting serious?" Colin asks, leaning his back against the hard booth.

Eric and I look at each other and nod.

"I definitely dig this," he says. "Eric, you are so much cooler compared to the last fucker."

I shoot him a glare, and he lets out a laugh, clasping his hands behind his neck. "Roomie, ya can't lie."

I sigh, placing my hand in Eric's. Why is Colin bringing up Monty?

"I think I met that guy. At least...I think it's the guy you're talking about," Eric says.

"Oh, right. We ran into each other way before we ran into each other again at the gallery." I had forgotten all about that. I remember how mad Monty was when he saw Eric approach me.

"Yeah, he seemed a little off. But who am I to judge?"

Colin looks at me and takes off his hat, running his hand through his messy hair. He nods but doesn't say much after that. We go back to finishing the rest of the food, and Eric changes the subject by asking Colin about his day. I'm not sure what Colin was trying to do by bringing up my ex-boyfriend, but I'm glad Eric didn't feed into it.

～

The next morning, I crack a couple of eggs into the pan and add some salt and pepper as I casually nibble on some bacon. The toasted bread pops from the toaster, and I quickly throw them on a plate. Then, I add the scrambled eggs onto each plate. I juggle the two plates plus two cups of orange juice as I saunter back to my room. Eric is spread across the whole bed; his face is nuzzled into my pillow as I walk inside.

"Breakfast in bed?" he groggily says as he sits up, exposing his bare chest. He leans forward, giving my cheek a little kiss as he takes in what's in front of him.

"Breakfast in bed," I repeat with a smile. "Scrambled eggs, bacon, toast, and some orange juice." I point to each item as I name them off. Eric rubs his eyes and gives me a kind smile but doesn't touch any of the food.

"What's wrong?" I ask.

He sighs. "I don't eat meat."

"Oh," I say, but he reaches for my hands, giving them a gentle squeeze. "All of this is amazing, Jade."

"I don't know how I didn't catch that you're a vegetarian." I laugh.

"I'm actually a pescatarian. No meat, but I dabble in fish," he kids.

"So, what made you become a pescatarian?"

"Well, for the longest time I was a vegetarian, but recently I ventured into the pescatarian side, which is—" he pauses. "I guess you can say another branch of vegetarianism. I haven't eaten meat in the longest time, but I needed more protein in my diet. I was really getting tired of eating every type of bean you can think of, and tofu just isn't for me," he says, taking a big bite of his toast.

I nod. "I think it's great that you don't eat meat."

"Do you eat meat?" he asks.

"Well, I'd like to say I don't, but I do. I try to stay away from it as much as possible though."

He laughs. "Meat-eaters always feel judged by vegetarians for eating meat. If you enjoy eating meat, by all means, eat it."

"Yeah, I am feeling judged by you." I laugh, taking a bite of bacon.

Eric runs his hand through his hair and smiles. "Why are you so damn cute?" He pushes some of my hair behind my ear and rubs his thumb in circles on my cheek.

"Are we really doing this?" I tilt my head, giving him a grin.

"Doing what?" he whispers, eyes glued to mine.

"You see...I woke up early just to make you some breakfast in bed, and you already want to get into my pants."

Eric can't help but smile as he places his hands on top of my bent thighs. "It's all your fault. You just look so good bringing me food that all I want to do is ravish you."

"Ravish me?" I raise an eyebrow.

Eric licks his lips and moves his hands around my waist, pulling me closer to him. I wrap my arms around his neck and wait for his answer.

"I thought I wanted eggs, but you're looking like a pretty good meal right now," he says. I laugh as he tickles the sides of my stomach, throwing me onto my back.

CHAPTER 39

Eric playfully taps on the glass window outside of a corner bakery in Brooklyn. He left my place early in the morning to help Claire with something in her apartment, so we agreed to meet at a bakery that's known for its huge and fluffy croissants. I smile at him as I watch him open the door for a woman and her young child. He walks over to the table I'm holding for us and gives me a peck on my lips before he takes a seat across from me.

He thanks me for the iced coffee I ordered for him and smiles wide as he rips off a piece of his croissant.

"How's Claire?" I ask him.

"She's good. Her refrigerator is fine. She thought it was rattling, but it's just old," he tells me.

"I think she just wanted to see you this morning." I smile at him as he takes another bite of his croissant.

"I believe she wanted to see *you* more because she was upset when she saw it was only me walking in." He laughs.

I smile, intertwining our fingers across the table. "You know, I would have come with you. I love seeing Claire."

"I didn't want to wake you. You looked so peaceful." He squeezes my hand.

I take a sip of coffee and tilt my head to the side, casually using my tongue to play with the plastic straw. "So, answer me this...What was always a staple in your house growing up?" I rest my elbows on the table, leaning closer to him.

"M&Ms," he says without even thinking.

"Oh, wow. I definitely wasn't expecting that."

"My grandma never told you?" he asks, running his hand through his hair.

"No." I laugh. "Tell me what?"

"My grandma loves chocolate, especially M&Ms. But for some reason, she never buys them, so on Thanksgiving, when we're all together, we always surprise her." He pauses with a smile. "Which isn't a surprise anymore, I suppose. But she only eats the green M&Ms."

"Wait, why? Don't they all taste the same?"

"Trust me, my whole life, I've been trying to convince her of that. We've tested her by having her close her eyes, but she always knows."

"Oh, that's why she never orders the M&M cookie at the cafe." I wrinkle my nose.

"What does she order?" He laughs.

"Just plain ol' chocolate," I say.

"See, now you know the reason. But I'd like to try that M&M cookie sometime." He grins, bringing my hand closer to him to kiss my palm.

"Are you sure?" I tilt my head to the side. "This M&M syndrome doesn't run in the family, does it?"

Eric shakes his head, keeping my hand close to his lips. "Don't tell anyone, but I only like the red Skittles."

I laugh. "What do you do with the other flavors in the bag?"

"Can't say."

"So, it's not M&Ms, but it has to be the same shape as M&Ms? Got it."

"Ding-ding-ding."

I reach over to pull his earlobe and smile. "I like learning about you and your family."

Eric beams as he places his hands against my cheeks, meeting my face in the middle of the table as we kiss passionately in the middle of this crowded bakery.

~

I watch Eric from across my room as he throws on a black t-shirt, making his already messy hair even messier. He gives me a wink as he strolls over to me, sitting beside me on the bed. "Hey," he smiles, wrapping his arms around my waist.

"Hey," I say, moving some of his stubborn curls away from his forehead.

Eric moves in closer and gives my neck tiny kisses, making me extend my neck. I let out a slight moan as I feel his groin area get tighter through his pants.

"Don't you have to go?" I ask him.

Eric groans and nods his head, giving my neck a gentle bite.

I let out a laugh and push his chest. "The guys are waiting for you."

"What are you gonna do tonight?"

"You know, the usual. Stay home and miss you tons."

Eric doesn't respond as he moves his lips back to my neck.

I nudge him away again. "I told you, Reese is coming over, and we're gonna attempt to bake."

"All right," he says, then he walks out my door. I get out of bed and follow him into my living room to the front door. "Have fun. But not too much fun."

I laugh, giving him a hug. Eric kisses the top of my head, and I lean against the door hinge as I watch him disappear down the stairs.

Reese comes by a half-hour later with our favorite brand of French rosé and a box of cookie mix. We then begin to bake. Reese reads the instructions on the box as I mix all of the ingredients.

"Is it sad that we can't bake?" Reese laughs as I grab the box from her hands, making sure she read the ingredients correctly.

"Don't say that," I say, putting the terrible shaped clumps of cookie dough in the oven. I pour myself and Reese another glass of wine as I prop myself onto the counter. Reese plays with her blonde hair as we wait patiently for our cookies to finish baking.

"I hope Eric can handle himself with the guys." She grins. "You know how they can be."

"He'll be fine." I laugh. "He's hung out with them before."

"They must really like him," she says, taking a sip of her wine.

"It's just weird not being with him," I say.

She grins. "We should bring them the cookies when they're finished baking."

"Crash boys' night?" I raise a brow.

She nods, tapping her glass against mine.

⌒

Reese and I walk through the crowded bar with a container of cookies. We probably look pathetic as we navigate through a slew of people, looking for the boys. We eventually find them at a standing table, watching some UFC fight. Eric seems surprised when he sees me but quickly recovers as he pulls me in for a tight hug. He gives my lips a tiny peck, and we proudly show off our cookies.

"They taste good but look like shit," Colin jokes as he takes a bite of one.

I roll my eyes and playfully hit his shoulder.

"Such a baker." Eric laughs in my ear, and I grin, wrapping my arms around his neck. I move my lips to his neck, and he looks at me. "Jade—" He nervously laughs, pointing to the fight on the television. I give his neck a gentle bite and move my lips to his jaw. "Jade, I'm watching—"

All of a sudden, Eric lets out a loud *woo*, making me jump a little. I move away from him and watch him and Colin watch the fight. They are basically in their own little world. I roll my eyes at my boyfriend's lack of attention towards me. I walk over to Reese and grab her arm. "Come get a drink with me."

She follows me to the bar, and we wait for the bartender to make our drinks. "What's wrong?"

I shrug. "Do you see them? They're leaving us out because we're not obsessed with each fighting move."

Reese lets out a laugh. "Someone's jealous that Colin is stealing her man."

I take my beer and Reese's martini from the bartender's hands. "I'm not."

"Just be happy that everyone's getting along."

"I am, Reese," I say through the loud music.

We walk back, and I don't even think they noticed that we had left in the first place. Eric puts his arm around my waist, and I smile, leaning into him.

Two hours of Colin and Eric's eyes being glued to the television and three cookies later, I've had enough. I want to go home. Eric takes his hand in mine, and we follow the group through the crowd of people outside the bar. Everyone starts talking about the fight we just watched, and I gently tug on Eric's arm. He looks at me and smiles before leaning in and kissing my temple.

"Let's go," I pout.

He looks at me then back to the group. "Oh, I thought we were going to Cave."

"Now?" I ask him. Then, I turn to the group. "You guys are going to Cave?"

Everyone answers me with a simple "yes." I sigh, turning back to Eric. "I don't want to go."

"Where do you want to go then?" he asks me.

"Home," I simply say.

"But it's Saturday night, and we're already out," he says as I hear Wes call an Uber.

I look down at my uncomfortable heels and let out a sigh. I'm so over tonight. "I think I'm gonna call a cab and go home," I say. Before he can respond, I take a few steps over to Reese to give her a goodbye hug.

"Wait, you're leaving? Is everything okay?"

I try to provide her with the fakest smile I can muster. "My feet are dying in these shoes. I can't last another minute."

I think she believes me because she smiles at me. "I totally understand."

"Not coming with us, roomie?" Colin asks me.

I shake my head, and luckily, I spot a cab pulling over by the curb in front of us. A man and woman stumble out mid-laugh, and I'm sort of envious of their happy spirits.

I give everyone one last wave goodbye and open the cab door. Just before I'm able to climb inside, I feel a familiar hand touch the middle of my arm.

"Are you mad?" Eric asks me, running his hands through his hair.

I shake my head. "No, silly. I'm just too exhausted to deal with Cave tonight."

Eric continues to study my face. I linger by the opened door, wondering what's running through his head. Eric doesn't say anything, and I give him a half-smile. "If you want to go with them, don't let me stop you."

"I know, but I feel bad letting you head back alone. I feel like that makes me a bad boyfriend."

I place my hand on his chest and shake my head. "It doesn't, but I have to go. I'm pretty sure the meter's already running."

Eric looks at me and glances at the group. I plop inside the cab and feel a slight sting as Eric closes the cab door for me. I give him a little smile without showing teeth and move my eyes to my lap, playing with my fingers. As I tell the cab driver my address, I'm trying my hardest not to cry. Before the driver can pull away, I hear the other side door open and see Eric jumping in. I look at him, confused, and he gives me a kind smile.

"I'd rather be with you."

We drive down the street in silence. I'm not sure how Eric feels towards me at this moment, but when I feel his hand touch my thigh, I feel a sense of relief. Eric follows me up the stairs and into my apartment, walking towards my couch. I pour the last of the wine Reese brought over and plop down next to him. He turns the television on, and there's still this awkward silence between us.

"Eric?"

"Jade?" He gives me a cheeky smile.

I can't help but grin as I caress my finger against his cheek. "Are you mad that you didn't go to Cave?"

He gives me a puzzled look. "Of course not. Why would you think that?"

I shrug. "Because I know you wanted to go. And now you're here, watching TV, on a Saturday night."

"Honestly, Jade, I'm already over that. I wanted to go at the moment, but now that I'm here, I don't care. All I care about is that I have you by my side. Cave wouldn't be fun without you anyway."

"Really?"

Eric looks at me and pushes a piece of hair behind my ear. He runs his thumb along my chin, tilting it up, so we're eye to eye. "Yes. There is no place I would rather be than here with you. Whether it's at Cave or even a supermarket. What matters is that you're there with me."

I can't help but smile. I move my body closer to him, and I feel his arm wrap around my side. "I'll admit I was a little upset when I thought you'd go without me."

Eric gives my lips a lengthy kiss. "I know," he says, leaning his forehead against mine. "I never want to make you feel upset, ever. And if I do, I want you to know that it's not intentional."

I nod, smiling at him. I feel his hand wrap around the back of my neck. "There's the smile I always want to see."

I wrap my arms around Eric, giving him a long, tight hug. I nuzzle my face into his neck as I feel a wave of happiness and relief wash over me all at once.

～

"He said that last night?" Reese enthusiastically asks, nudging her shoulder with mine as we sit slouched on a park bench, eating two-dollar popsicles we bought from a cart.

I stare at my grape-flavored pop and back at Reese. "I just can't believe how lucky I am to have met someone so special like Eric. No matter how I am feeling, he is able to calm me down."

Reese turns so she's facing me, and I do the same, propping my elbow on top of the bench.

"What a difference between Eric and Monty?" Reese says, biting into her lemon-flavored pop.

I laugh. "I know. I was thinking about that the other day. I should stop though, right? Monty's old news, and it makes me mad whenever his weasel face pops into my mind."

Reese lets out a loud laugh, tapping my shoulder. "He did look like a weasel."

I can't help but laugh as well.

"Eric is great, though. I know I've said that before, but he really is."

I nod. "I want to tell him I love him, but we haven't hit the six-month mark yet. I feel like I rushed into the 'I love you' with Monty, and look what happened."

My popsicle starts dripping onto my hand, and I quickly lick it off my finger. I'm waiting patiently for these summer months to finally end. I want autumn to come already.

"So, you're saying if you rush into saying I love you with Eric, something bad will happen?" Reese tilts her head to the side.

I nod. "This whole relationship is freaking me out a little. I mean it's *too* perfect, Reese. *He's* too perfect." I pause. "There's nothing wrong with him! He even has good morning breath."

Reese laughs, but I continue, "Maybe he's just the biggest bullshit artist. No pun intended."

"I thought the same thing about Wes when I first met him, but don't worry. There's always something."

FALL

CHAPTER 40

The long branches on the trees in Central Park have changed from green to red. There is a slight chill in the air, and there are a lot more people out and about, wearing the jeans that have been shoved in the back of their drawers all summer. Eric and I walk hand in hand down the gravel pathway through the park as we casually snack on caramel popcorn. We pass a woman pushing a baby in a stroller and walking a golden retriever. I tell him about the time I babysat Violet's bulldog, Bella. Eric beams as he tells me about his dogs growing up.

"So, you had two pugs named Apple and Cinnamon?" I ask with a smile on my face.

Eric glances at me. "Yeah, it was my sister's idea to name them that. When I got home from school, they were already named."

I laugh. "So, what would you have named them then?"

"Something tough like Buster and Titan," he says confidently but laughs seconds later.

"What happened to Apple and Cinnamon?" I ask.

"My parents took them to North Carolina." He shrugs as we find a bench overlooking the leaves falling off the tall trees. "I'm excited about tonight," Eric says as he puts his hand on my thighs.

I look at him and touch his cold nose. "I am too. I can't wait to see you in your element, teaching wannabe artists how to paint."

Eric smiles. "A couple of my buddies from college are coming to the class."

"Are they painters like you?"

Eric shakes his head. "Conner and Blake are sculptors, actually. They work for a gallery in the city. They are extremely talented."

"Not as talented as you," I say, kissing his cheek.

"I don't know." He laughs. "I guess we'll see how well they'll do."

"I'm just happy there's wine, and I'll be living out one of my all-time sexual fantasies."

Eric looks at me, and I can't help but laugh. "Go home with my teacher," I whisper in his ear.

"Oh, you're bad." He laughs, putting his arm around my shoulders and pulling me into his chest.

I laugh as I nuzzle my face in his neck. "What can I say? My boyfriend/teacher is hot."

Eric shakes his head, a small smile forming on his handsome face. "Why don't you leave the compliments to me?"

"You don't like being called hot?" I laugh.

"I do...but I'm getting a boner in the middle of Central Park," Eric whispers, and I look up at him. He looks into my eyes, and I giggle, poking his cheek with my finger.

～

Sometime later, I linger by the front steps of my apartment building as I wait for my Uber to pick me up. There's a sharp crispness in the air as I fix my white hat. I told Eric I wanted to meet him at the class because I needed to get some things done before going tonight, like the dishes Colin refuses to do and my laundry that has been sitting in the basket for a few days now. An old Honda Civic pulls over a few inches from me, and I get inside.

I feel the excitement as I walk inside the room full of long tables. Each chair has medium-sized canvases with cups filled with paintbrushes. Eric and I make eye contact immediately, and he gives me a wide smile. "You look beautiful," he says from across the room.

"How long have you been here?" I ask as he puts a paper plate next to each canvas.

"About twenty minutes. I wanted to fix up my painting with some fresh paint. They sent me a picture of the painting everyone is expecting to do tonight. I quickly painted it before I met you today," he says casually. I glance at his painting sitting up front and smile. His painting that he quickly put together will definitely be better than mine, even if I try my best.

"Do you need any help?" I ask.

Eric looks at me and smiles. "Yeah, actually. Can you grab the tray of paints and put a medium-sized glob of each color on the white plates?"

I nod and do what I'm told as Eric touches up the elephant on his canvas. As I squeeze the blue-colored paint onto the last plate, I notice that my hands already have paint on them. I feel Eric's large hands wrap around my waist, and I lean into him, my eyes still glued to my hands.

"I didn't get my kiss," he whispers in my ear, and I smile, turning my head and allowing his lips to meet mine.

The loud slam of the door breaks our attention away from each other. Eric turns his teacher mode on, and I sit in awe as I casually sip on my wine. Five more people walk inside, including Eric's college friends, Conner and Blake. They make a straight beeline over to the two chairs beside me, and we quickly introduce ourselves.

"You must be Jade," one of them says to me. He smiles as he holds out his hand for me to shake. We make eye contact. "I'm Blake, and that's Connor." He beams as he points to his blonde-haired friend. Blake scratches his reddish beard and takes a sip of his wine.

"I don't know about you guys, but I'm so ready to paint." Blake grins at me, and I laugh, looking at my empty canvas.

"So, how long have you been friends with Eric?" I ask as we wait for Eric to begin. I figured we might as well get to know each other a bit.

Blake looks at Connor then back at me. "I'd say for me, about three years. And Connor, two?" He looks at Connor, and he nods, smiling at me without showing any teeth. I guess Blake is the talker out of the duo.

"Connor's really shy. Especially around a pretty girl like yourself," Blake says as if he read my mind.

I nod, giving both of them a kind smile. We hear Eric's voice carry across the whole room as we sit silently, listening to Eric's words as he describes the painting. Eric demonstrates the first step, and I pretend to understand as I follow Blake and Connor's direction. As I try my best to cover my white canvas with blue and gray colors, I feel Eric's hands touch both of my shoulders. I look up, and he gives me a cute grin and begins to laugh as soon as Blake says something to him.

"Your lady has good technique," Blake jokes as he points to my canvas. I laugh as I add blue to the darker part.

"Jade, make sure you keep an eye out for Connor. Shit goes down when he drinks too much."

"Oh yeah, that one time at Lake Tahoe." Blake laughs as Connor rolls his eyes.

"Shit got crazy," Eric says as he walks away.

I laugh. "What happened?"

"This man right here started a fire while nude. Can you believe it?" His eyes open wide as he points to Connor with his thumb.

I shake my head. "No. I can't." I laugh. "Have you been on a lot of trips with Eric?" I ask him.

Blake tilts his head to the side as he softly adds some more paint to his canvas. "*Hmm*. Define a lot? I'd say five or six. We actually planned for one this fall, but with Eric's move happening so abruptly...I guess we'll just have to visit him."

"Move?" I ask.

Blake looks at Connor, who looks at Blake, and then they both look over at me. I stare at them dumbfounded as I wait for one of them to answer my question.

"Eric mentioned that you're a theater actress. Are you using your acting skills with us right now?" Blake raises a brow.

"No? What move?" I ask again.

Blake coughs and looks down at his lap as if he said something he shouldn't have. I glance at Eric, who is talking to a middle-aged man, and then I shift my gaze back to Blake.

"Eric's moving," he says quickly. His eyes move to Eric, who is laughing and helping someone new with their painting. "He's, um, moving to California in a couple of days."

I let out a laugh. "No, seriously. Eric mentioned that you like to kid around—"

"I'm not," he says sternly, and his tone says it all. The small room begins to spin, and I can't get it to stop. I hear Eric's laugh in the distance and the sound bleeds through me. I turn my head over to

Blake and Connor, and they quickly turn away.

"Excuse me." I fake a smile and practically dash out of this stuffy room.

As I quickly walk down the white-fluorescent hallway, I hear my name being called. I turn around to face a very worried-looking Eric. I stop in my tracks, and I cross my arms as if I can shield myself from whatever I'm about to hear.

"I'm guessing Blake told you?"

"Told me *what* exactly?"

Eric runs his hand through his bushy hair and sighs. "About California."

"Ah, yes. I'm glad I got to find out about your exciting news through one of your friends!" I raise my voice. "Is it true? Are you really moving to California?"

Eric nods, and my heart feels as if it is bursting into a thousand pieces. "Since when?"

"Since a few days ago."

"So, you knew and decided not to share?"

"Jade, it's not like that. I wasn't even sure I was going to take it, but when I got the second call." He pauses. "Which I received when I was hanging out with Blake, I knew I had to take it. An art studio in LA offered me a chance to showcase my art in their gallery for a year or so."

"Why couldn't you have told me?" I try my hardest not to cry but fail as a tiny tear crawls down my cheek.

Eric notices and walks closer to me. "And say what? I was nervous..." But he trails off and doesn't finish his sentence.

"That I'd ask you to stay?"

He nods.

I don't say anything, and he doesn't either. I feel his thumb brush against my cheek, and I close my eyes at his touch.

"This isn't how I wanted you to find out, in this smelly hallway." He smiles. "You have no idea how all of this has been laying on me. I wanted to tell you myself. I just wasn't sure how. I'm sorry you had to find out through Blake."

"So, what now? Is this the end for us?"

Eric shakes his head dramatically. "You didn't let me finish. I want you to come with me."

I stare at his face blankly as I repeat the words he spoke to me in my mind. Minutes feel like hours until I can find the right words. "Come with you? To California?"

Eric nods and waits patiently for me to continue, but the look on his perfect face tells me how scared he really is.

"Eric, I don't know what to say."

"Say you'll come. I knew the second I saw you that I wanted you. I needed you," Eric says as he wraps his arms around my waist. This time though, I pull away, making his smile disappear.

"I need time to think, Eric. I need to go." I turn around and head to the door without waiting for him to respond.

"Jade!" He calls after me as I open the tall green door. I turn my head slightly over to his direction to hear him say, "I love you."

I pace around my whole apartment as I wait for Reese to come over. I called her during the cab ride home, practically telling her it's a 911-emergency-guy-crisis. It's around eleven-thirty, and she told me she'd be right over. I knew I couldn't have all this information lying on my chest all night. I needed to talk this out with someone.

Reese bursts into my apartment with a bag of chips and a bottle of vodka. I thank her and the alcohol gods as we simultaneously plop on the couch.

"Spill. What's going on?"

I let out a loud sigh, and she looks concerned as she waits for me to talk.

"He's moving to California," is all I say. I guess the reality of it all hasn't hit me yet because it sounds bizarre.

"Who? Eric?"

I nod.

Reese's eyes widen, and she pours me a shot of vodka. I throw it back and grimace as it burns down my throat.

"Eric Fletcher is moving to California? When and how did all of this happen?"

I go into every detail of tonight, starting with how Blake accidentally told me Eric's little secret. She listens closely but stops me when I tell her how he wants me to come with him in a couple of days.

"He said that?"

I nod. "Yeah. I didn't really know what to say. I told him that I needed time to think, but when I was leaving," I say with a sigh. "He told me he loves me."

Reese doesn't say anything. I watch as she plays with the fabric on her sweater.

"Do you love him?" she asks me almost in a whisper.

I shrug, and Reese nods but doesn't respond.

"What?"

"So, that's it, right? You're gonna go with him."

"Why do you say that?" I ask her.

Reese looks at me. "Jade, the guy confessed his love for you tonight, and I know for a fact that you feel the same. Eric's the best thing that has come into your life so why would you want to end that?"

I lean my back against the cushion and shrug. "Maybe because

I don't want to give up the life that I have built here in New York to follow a guy I haven't been dating for very long?"

Reese nods and mirrors my position on the couch. "So, what are you gonna tell him?"

"I don't know," I whisper.

We sit in silence as the sound of my vibrating phone goes unanswered.

⌒

A soft knock on my bedroom door immediately wakes me up. I glance at the clock—six a.m. I groggily sit up as I watch Eric close the door behind him. He hands me a cup of steaming hot coffee and my favorite pumpkin Danish from a bakery near my place.

"Sorry I'm here so early," he says as I take a sip of my coffee. He hands me the brown paper bag, and I smile, setting my pastry to the side.

"It's okay," I say.

He leans in for a kiss before saying, "I missed you."

"I missed you too."

"I couldn't sleep last night."

"Me neither," I say as I play with the coffee lid.

"Jade, I want to apologize again for last night. I didn't want you to find out like that, and I wanted to tell you the news as soon as I found out."

"So why didn't you?"

He sighs. "I don't know, really. I was nervous. But now I'm more nervous that you're gonna tell me to get out, and you never want to see me again."

"I was considering that."

Eric looks into my eyes and grabs my hand. "Did you think about what I said yesterday?"

"All night, actually." I exhale loudly.

"And?"

"Eric, you have no idea how much disarray you put me in last night—"

"I know, and I'm sorry for that, Jade. I really am."

"My life is in New York. My family, my friends, my job—"

"You can have all of that in California. There are great opportunities for actresses in L.A."

I nod and sigh. "I know. But I don't think, at this point in my life, that I'm ready to take on a move like that."

Eric nods. "But what about what I said to you last night?"

"That you love me?"

Eric nods.

"I feel the same, Eric. I do."

Eric smiles, but it quickly disappears as he looks into my eyes. "I'm not ready for this to end."

"Me either."

"So, where do we go from here?" he asks.

"The only thing we can do is long-distance until you come back. If you decide to, that is."

"Of course I would. For you, I will."

I look down at my lap as I grin. I feel Eric's hand touch my chin as he lifts it. I smile at him and wrap my arms around his neck. "Are you sure you're okay with my decision?"

Eric nods. "Of course. It'll be tough, but I know we'll get through it because our love is strong."

∼

Eric moved a couple of days later. We spent every moment together, mostly putting his things in boxes, and I went with him to the airport. I stared into those eyes I adore so much and said goodbye.

We've been apart for two weeks now, but I still feel hopeful as I lazily tap on my kitchen counter, waiting for my coffee to finish brewing. It'll work. I know it will. As Eric said, our love is strong. And it is. It really is. We speak every night and text all throughout the day. Eric's been thriving in L.A, and his art has expanded to new horizons. He looks truly happy, and I am too.

~

It's been a month. Eric and I haven't been talking as much as we did. It went from FaceTiming every night to texting every moment of the day to calling once in a while and sending one or two texts throughout the day. Something sort of switched in our relationship, but for some reason, I haven't really cared. Maybe it's been me that's causing the distance between us. I've been busy lately, and I know he has been too. I guess people are right when they say long-distance doesn't work, but I still don't want to give up on our relationship. Distancing myself a little from Eric shouldn't change how I feel about him, but I guess when you can't see the person as much as you did then it kind of is out of sight, out of mind.

Even my friends agree that long-distance isn't usually the best.

"It never works," Colin says as he bites into his slice of pizza.

I cross my legs and lean my elbow onto them. "Well, it's working for us."

"When was the last time you spoke to him?" Wes asks me, and I tilt my head to the side.

"See, if you have to think about it, then it's practically over," Colin comments.

"How would you know? You've never been in a real relationship."

"Doesn't matter if I have or haven't, roomie. Those are the facts. He's probably cheating on you right now."

My eyes open wide, and I turn my head to Reese, who throws her empty beer can at Colin's chest.

"Eric would never do that to Jade. But long-distance does suck." Reese shrugs.

As I get up off the couch and go into my room, I hear Colin laughing behind me. I immediately call Eric, but it goes straight to voicemail. I bite my nails, and I replay all of my stupid decisions about slightly pulling back. "No, I can't video call tonight," I said to him three times in a row. He doesn't even ask anymore. I lay on my bed and place my hand on my forehead.

I hear my door open, and I know it's Reese. She sits beside me and sighs. "Don't listen to Colin. He's only saying that to get under your skin."

"Well, it worked," I groan.

"Did you call him?" she asks.

"He didn't answer. I think his phone is off. He's so bad about charging his phone." I nervously laugh.

"Don't let Colin ruin your night. You'll speak to him tomorrow."

"It might be too late," I say, slowly rising so we're eye-level. Reese gives me a small smile, and I let a breath out as we make our way back to the living room.

～

"Can you believe this is my view? And I bought this couch. The place came furnished, well, with everything besides a couch. Can you believe that?" Eric laughs as he sets his laptop back down on the desk.

I smile. "It looks so good. Are you getting along with your roommates?"

Eric gives me a funny look, and I laugh, leaning my cheek against my palm.

"We are. Only took a month, though."

I let out a deep breath, and Eric does the same as he fixes the curls that lay on his forehead.

"Eric?"

"Jade?" He half-smiles.

Colin's words have been lingering in my head since last night and all throughout work today. This is the first time I've spoken to him all day, and even our conversation tonight seems off. It's not us.

"So, do you think anything has been different with our relationship?"

Eric tilts his head and sighs. "Our long-distance relationship?" I nod, and he shrugs. "I mean, it does suck that we're so far away and we can't see each other in person."

"Across the country," I say.

"What are you thinking, Jade?"

I shrug. "I don't know." I have so many thoughts running through my head, and it feels like they are sitting on my chest as well. I'm finding it hard to express myself when I feel this way.

"Did you meet someone?"

"No! Of course not," I say to him.

Eric nods but waits for me to continue.

"I don't know where my head is. I'm so confused," I groan.

"I think I know what you mean," he says.

"You do?"

He nods, "Yeah. I guess I'll admit that I've been feeling it too."

There's silence between us as we sit in front of our screens, staring intensely into each other's eyes, waiting for the other to speak first.

"So, what now?" I finally say.

CHAPTER 41

E ric and I officially broke up. Three long hours later, we settled on being just friends...

The next day, I felt fine. I don't think it has hit me yet. I worked, had coffee with Reese and Claire, and even that wasn't as painful as I thought it would be. Claire stayed quiet as she nodded and listened to the reasons why Eric and I broke up.

Later that night was fine too. I laughed and drank wine with Colin and Reese. Eric was hardly on my mind.

Until it hit me.

I'm walking home with my coffee in hand, and I pass a young couple sitting at an outside table at a cafe on Third. They're sitting close together, and she's laughing at something he said as she feeds him a bite of pastry. A tear crawls down my cheek as I compare that couple to what I had with Eric. We were that cute couple, and I might never find someone as unique as Eric. As soon as I get home, I immediately climb into bed. The breakup has officially hit me. Full force.

I cry for three days straight, thinking about Eric and everything I miss about him.

Reese tried dragging me out of bed one night, but it wasn't happening. Then it was Wes' turn to try, and even Colin attempted, but nothing worked to heal the pain aside from sushi and melted ice cream.

~

My bedroom curtains are pulled closed, and I don't have any idea what day or time it is when I feel a hand rub my back as I groan into my tear-filled pillow. The hand moves to my head, and I suddenly feel fingers softly run through my hair. I flutter my eyes slightly open to see a familiar brunette staring down at me.

"Maude?"

"The one and only." She grins as she moves my bangs away from my eyes.

"Why are you here?" I ask, sort of feeling a sense of happiness as I see her familiar face looking at me.

"Colin called me actually and said you hit rock bottom. His words, not mine," she says, holding back a smile. Before I can even think about Colin contacting Maude for me, she stands up and opens the shade.

"Do you know there's a beautiful sunset right now, missy?" She beams as she opens the other shade. Maude grabs one of my long-sleeved dresses, tights, and brown high heeled boots. "Being sad and depressed over dick is just not acceptable, Miss Jade," she declares, throwing the dress at me. "Sit up!"

I groan as I slowly sit up. "What are you doing?"

"Getting you out of this stuffy—and may I say, slightly smelly—room." She scrunches her nose.

"Look at me, Maude. I've been crying for three days straight. I look like a crack addict."

"Get dressed and meet me in the living room in ten," she orders, then leaves the room. I stare at the dress Maude picked out for me, a dress I love so much. I decide to listen to her. Maybe I have hit rock bottom.

Maude claps as I walk out of my room in the dress and boots she picked out for me. I've been in my baggy pajamas for the past few days, so much so that I forgot I even had a body. Maude applies some makeup and practically sprays a whole bottle of perfume on me.

We then head into the city. She tries to keep my mind off of Eric by filling me in on what she's been up to these past several months—traveling and modeling, of course. Maude orders two apple martinis at a bar called Tavern Hip. I take my first sip and groan as I look around the crowded bar full of happy and cheerful twentysomethings.

"Why am I here again?" I sigh as I lean my head against the palm of my hand.

Maude yanks my wrist, making my head jolt. "Look around, Jade. Everyone is dealing with all sorts of shit. They're just better at hiding it. You need to mourn your breakup with what's his face." She pauses, taking a sip of her drink. "Which you clearly did, baby." She rolls her eyes. "And you need to live your fucking life again! There are too many places to see and people to do to be hiding out in that god-forsaken room."

"That's easy to say when you're not heartbroken like me," I say over the music.

"Do you think I've never had my heart broken? I have, but I never let them win. Do you think he's crying? Probably not."

I nod, taking a long sip of my drink. The familiar feeling burning down my throat feels good. "You're right," I say.

Maude takes a bite of her apple slice and winks. "Of course I am. I don't like seeing you like this. Those big beautiful green eyes should never dim."

I nod. "Thanks for coming. I needed this more than you know."

"Well, thank your hottie roommate. He comes with many surprises, right?"

Surprises? What is she talking about? I decide not to dive into that since I have enough to worry about as is.

I look at her and smile as I picture Colin contacting Maude. Was he actually worried about me? Or did he just want to get brownie points from Maude? I guess I'll never know the real reason.

~

A couple of weeks have passed, and I think Maude was precisely what I needed. I ended up seeing her the next day after we got drinks. We drank pumpkin spiced lattes as we casually walked through Central Park. Reese ended up meeting up with us, and we got lunch at a cute restaurant by the park. By the time I got home, I was exhausted. I didn't even realize how much Maude and I had walked. I put my leftovers in the refrigerator and decided to watch some television. I got a call during my three-day pity party from my agent about an audition for a part in an ice cream commercial. Definitely the opposite of what I wanted, but work is work, and I'll take what I can get.

A movie I've seen a few times plays in the background as I casually read a couple of lines out loud until I hear a loud knock. I throw my two-page script on the coffee table and get up to open the door. A man about six feet tall is standing directly in front of me. He tilts his head to the side, and I recognize the sparkle in his grey eyes.

"Can I help you?" I ask the stranger.

"Yes, you can." He smiles. "Does Colin live here?"

"Yes, he does," I say, crossing my arms.

"Oh great, I'm Kirk." He pauses. "Colin's brother. Is he home?"

My eyes widen, and I shake my head. "Uh, no, he's not. I think he's at the gym. Do you want to come inside and wait for him?"

"Thank you." Kirk smiles as I let him in. Kirk looks around our place before walking over to our couch. I study the back of him as I try to relax my features, especially my eyes. Colin's family continues to surprise me. He never mentioned he had a brother. Any other siblings, Colin?

"I can text him and let him know you're here," I say.

Kirk looks up at me. "I want to surprise him, actually. He doesn't know I'm in New York."

"Oh, okay."

I walk over to the kitchen, open the cabinet, grab a glass, and scoop some ice inside. I pour some water into the glass and walk back to Kirk.

"Here you go," I say.

"I think you just read my mind." He laughs.

I take a seat on Colin's leather chair, and we sit in silence.

"I'm sorry, I didn't catch your name," Kirk says, setting the glass on the coffee table.

"Jade." I offer him my hand, and he shakes it.

"That's a beautiful name," he says. "My parents informed me that you're the one who swept Colin's feet off the ground."

I look into his eyes and laugh. "Sure, if you want to put it like that."

"I felt sort of left out. My sister even met you."

"Addison is great."

Kirk rubs his pointy chin. "Do you live nearby?"

I gulp. "Uh, yes. But I'm here mostly."

"Colin never usually gets attached."

"You know him very well." I smile.

"He was my best friend."

I'm surprised that he said "was." I'm assuming Kirk has something to do with all the animosity between Colin and their family.

"So why are you suddenly in town?" I ask.

"I'm a cardiovascular surgeon back in Pasadena, and I got sent over here to perform a surgery," he tells me.

"Oh wow, how exciting."

"What do you do?" he asks me.

"I'm an...." I pause. I was about to say actress, but then I remembered what Colin told his parents. "I'm a nurse."

"Wow, a nurse. Great profession. Now I know why my parents liked you so much."

"I can definitely see the resemblance between you two," I say, trying to change the subject before he asks me any specific questions about nursing.

Kirk takes a sip of his water. "Really? Colin has always been the better-looking one. The girls always seemed to follow my little brother around."

"Oh well, you guys look the same to me." I laugh.

We suddenly hear the sound of a key entering the lock. Soon after, the door opens in one quick motion. Kirk downs the rest of his water. I watch Colin carefully then look back at Kirk. I'm not sure if Colin even knows Kirk's here until I see Colin's eyes widen. He takes his earbuds out of his ears; his music is so loud I can hear it all the way from where I'm sitting.

Kirk stands to his feet and claps his hands in front of him.

"Little brother," Kirk says.

Colin's jaw tenses, and it looks like every hair is sticking up on his sweaty skin.

"What are you doing here?" he finally says.

"I wanted to surprise you." Kirk walks slowly over to Colin. "Surprise."

"I didn't invite you here, Kirk. You can't just come to my home, unannounced," Colin says through his teeth.

"I'm your brother, Colin."

Colin looks over to me and then back to his brother. "I'm ending this conversation here."

"So...what? You don't want to see me at all?"

"No, I don't."

Kirk turns around and smiles at me. "Gotta love him, right?"

Before I can say a word, Colin says, "Don't you dare talk to her, Kirk. I want you to leave."

"I just can't believe you are still holding resentment from something that happened years ago. You have to let it go, Colin."

Colin grabs Kirk's shirt collar and stares deeply into his eyes, like a lion would stare at an antelope. I stand up and grab Colin's arm, trying my hardest to pull him back before this whole confrontation can escalate any further.

"Okay, I get it. I'll leave," Kirk says with a frown as he fixes his shirt.

He walks over to the door and turns around. "I'll be in the city tonight for dinner. I'd love for both of you to join me. I don't know anyone here. I'll be at that steak restaurant on Fifth Street." And with that, he opens the door and leaves.

Colin grabs a water bottle from the fridge and walks into the bathroom. He turns the shower on before taking off his shirt.

"Colin—"

"Butt out of it, Jade. This doesn't involve you," he snaps, closing the bathroom door behind him. I stand in silence, replaying the events that just happened. I guess I found another piece of Colin's crazy family drama puzzle.

∿

I'm feeling super anxious. It's around six p.m., and I can't focus on the script I need to memorize. I didn't give myself much time due to my self-loathing. I keep glancing back and forth from the script to Colin's bedroom door. He's been in there since Kirk left, and I'm worried. I finally stand up and walk cautiously towards his door. I knock a couple of times. No answer.

"Colin? It's me, Jade. You've been in there for hours. I'm going to that sushi place down the street." I pause. "I was wondering if you wanted to join me?"

Still no answer. I wait a couple of seconds before trying again. "Colin? Just say something, so I know you're alive."

"Go away," I hear through the door.

"I know you don't want to hear this, but things always get better. I promise you. And I know we have our differences sometimes, but I'm always here if you need me."

I wait for a couple of seconds, but he doesn't respond. And with that, I leave him alone.

∿

The next morning, I lay in bed for an extra hour. I gradually get up when I hear Colin in the kitchen. I grab my sweater and pull it over my head before opening my bedroom door.

"Hey," I say.

Colin turns his head and gives me a small smile. He pours some milk into his bowl of cereal and sits down at the table.

"How are you feeling?" I ask him.

"I'm fine, Jade. Just drop it, okay?"

I nod and sit down across from him. I bring my knees to my

chest and let out a sigh.

"Why so blue?" he jokes. I look up, and Colin's famous grin appears on his face. Last night, he was so out of it, and now he's totally back to being himself. Weird.

"I have an audition today, and I'm sorta nervous," I tell him. And I'm still totally heartbroken and also curious about you and your brother. No biggie.

He takes a big bite of his cereal. "You'll be fine," he says with a ton of Frosted Flakes in his mouth.

"I just didn't get much sleep."

"That's why they invented coffee."

I get up and pour myself a cup from the pot. "You're right."

"How was sushi?" he asks.

"Oh, you remembered." I smile. He doesn't say anything, and I take a sip of coffee. "It was delicious."

I walk over to the coffee table and grab my script before heading back to the table. I put it in front of me as I sip on my coffee, but before I begin rehearsing my lines, Colin snatches it.

Colin lets out a laugh. "Hey, bunny, taste this hopping chocolate ice cream bar. It's for bunnies like you, and I can say it's definitely yummy," he mocks.

I try to grab it back, but he stands on his feet and sits on top of the counter.

"You're talking to a purple bunny," he laughs, "about an ice cream bar that's shaped like a rabbit."

I frown. "It's a commercial that will air on national TV, Colin. This could be huge if I get it."

"You have to run after the bunny because he's hogging it all."

I stand up and grab the script out of his hands. He lets out a laugh, and I feel his large hand squeeze my waist, pulling me towards him.

He puts both of his hands around me and doesn't let me go.

"Colin, let go of me!"

"I wasn't done," he says stubbornly.

I breathe in his warm sweet breath, and for a second, we stand close to each other in silence.

Colin lets go of his hold and jumps down. He then walks past me and goes into his room. A couple of minutes later, he puts on his jacket and leaves the apartment.

What the heck just happened?

~

I'm sitting in a room full of brunettes wearing a pink button-down shirt just like mine. My nerves start to kick in full force as I hear the woman sitting next to me get called. My palms are sweating, and I try to steady my breathing. This is probably my hundredth audition, but every time I sit and wait for my name to be called, it still feels like the first audition I went on when I was nine years old. I tug on my shirt, and I try to flatten my hair. I straightened it this morning, but the humidity in this tiny room isn't helping.

The woman with the tight bun enters the room. Her posture is impeccable as she holds a chart between her pale, white hands.

"Jade Everly?"

I look up at her before getting to my feet. It's my turn to show them what I have to offer.

I enter the baby blue-painted room. Six people are sitting at the long table. They turn on the camera, and I swallow hard. It's happening right now. I introduce myself and immediately begin.

The man sitting at the table starts the first line, and I get lost in the script. Midway through, they stop me, and I'm done. I never finished, and that's not a good sign.

I walk down the long winding hallway, slumped over. The elevator ride down feels long, and I stare at the million buttons on the wall. *I'll get the next one*, but I say that every time.

"How did it go?" Reese asks through the phone.

I let out a sigh.

"That bad?"

"I'd rather not talk about it."

The elevator doors open, and I watch a guy in a black vest walk inside. We do one of those "hello" smiles without saying a word.

"What happened?"

"I didn't finish," I tell her.

He glances at me and takes a sip of water from his plastic water bottle.

"So what? You've gotten roles when you didn't finish your lines before. Don't worry about it."

I nod. "Okay yeah, you're right. I'll see you tonight."

"Okay," Reese says and we both hang up.

"Feels like we've been in this elevator forever," the guy says to me.

I look over to him and give him a quick smile. "It's a tall building."

"I'm assuming you auditioned for that bunny commercial," he says.

"How did you know?"

"Your shirt." He smiles.

I look down and sigh. "It isn't the most flattering look."

The elevator doors open, and he motions his hand out, allowing me to walk out first.

"I'm sorry, I didn't mean to be some creepy guy in the elevator." He laughs, following me out of the elevator, into the lobby. "I just hate awkward silences, especially in an elevator."

"No need to apologize." I smile.

"I'm Zack. And you are?"

Zack opens the front door of the building for me.

"Thank you, and I'm Jade."

We step into the middle of the sidewalk. "It was nice talking to you, Jade. Hope to have more awkward conversations in an elevator some other time."

"I can't wait," I say.

He smiles, showing his somewhat crooked but white teeth. "I hope you get the part."

"Me too," I say.

He lets out a whistle, and a cab pulls over. I can't believe that move actually works. I've only seen it done in movies.

He gives me a wink and hops in. I watch as the cab drives away, then I continue down the street.

I treat myself to a cinnamon bun at this cute mom-and-pop shop. Thankfully, the audition was in Brooklyn, and I didn't have to travel all the way into the city. I sit down at one of those outside tables and enjoy my pastry. Autumn is the best time of the year in New York. The leaves change to yellow and orange, there is pumpkin spice everything, and the chill in the air makes it almost tolerable to sit outside in the mid-afternoon. A lot of people pass by, and I love to watch their interactions.

After I finish my pastry, leaving behind the boring pieces without any frosting, I get up and continue my way back home.

"Hi, Jade," I look up and find Kirk sitting on the last couple of steps leading up to the front door of my building. "I buzzed, but no one answered." He frowns.

"It doesn't work." I shrug, giving him a small smile.

Kirk stands up and wipes his hands on the back of his khaki pants. This guy doesn't look like the type to sit on dirty stairs.

"He's not home," I tell him.

I walk by him and unlock the front door that leads into the hallway with all the mailboxes. I open mine and look inside; nothing.

"I figured," he says with a sigh. "Do you know when he'll be back?"

"I'm not sure," I say.

Kirk says something under his breath, and I turn to him.

"He'll be at this bar tonight if you want to check it out?"

Kirk gives me a grin and nods. I'm not sure why I want to help Kirk out; I guess it's the look in his eyes.

⌒

"Should I wear this or this?" Reese holds up two boring blouses that I'd never wear in a million years. I shrug.

"Jade!" she says in an obnoxious voice. "You're the fashion expert; help me."

"Everything I ever recommend, you hate."

She looks at me, and I guess she's thought about what I said and agrees because she doesn't say anything else. I discreetly sigh, slightly disappointed that Reese and I have never had the same style when it comes to clothing.

"I'll wear this," she finally says, putting the other blouse away in her closet.

"Is that what you're wearing?" she asks.

I decided to wear my black and white checkerboard high-waisted pants and a red long-sleeved crop top. "Yeah, why?"

"No reason," she says under her breath as I walk over to her mirror and apply a little mascara.

"I wish I had your body. I hate mine," she whines.

"Stop that. You have a beautiful body, Reese."

"I just hate my thighs. You have long, skinny ones."

"Yeah, well, I have no figure. I'm like a board. You at least have an hourglass figure," I tell her.

We hear a knock at the door, and Wes pops his head in. "Are you guys almost ready?"

Reese fixes her bun and turns to me. "Ready?"

I nod, and we head out.

The drive into the city seems long. It doesn't matter what time of night I drive into the city, there is always traffic. Wes drops Reese and me off at the entrance, and we head inside. It will take Wes some time to get a spot. As soon as we enter the bar, my eardrums practically fall out. The music is blasting, and I have to get used to it. It's like an obstacle course here—so many people everywhere, and all I want is a drink.

"I sorta invited Kirk tonight," I say as casually as I can.

Reese's eyes open wide, and she takes a sip of her rum and coke. I guess I was the last one to know that Colin had a brother named Kirk. Wes approaches us and automatically puts his arm around Reese, following up with a peck on her cheek.

Reese whispers something to Wes, and he turns to me.

"You invited Kirk tonight?" he yells over the music.

I nod and take a sip of my whiskey sour.

"I'm gonna need a drink," he jokes, and Reese hands him hers. I watch him take a big sip. I stand awkwardly, fiddling with the stem of the cherry in my drink.

"Not good." He shakes his head. I stand closer to them, trying not to get pushed into by drunk twentysomethings.

"He stopped by today, and he looked all sad," I tell them.

Wes leans into me. "They don't exactly get along."

"I can tell. I definitely regret inviting him."

"Hey! He probably won't show," Reese shouts over the music.

Wes and I both nod, and the conversation about Kirk ends. We walk over to an empty table by the stage and stand, waiting for

Colin and his band to come on.

Wes and Reese begin their PDA, and I stand there awkwardly, trying my best to not look.

"I'm getting another drink," I tell them, but before they can say anything, I walk away.

Every seat is occupied at the bar, but I'm able to squeeze in the middle of the crowd.

"Elevator Jade!"

I turn my head to the left, and I spot Zack in the crowd. He gives me a broad smile and walks over to me.

"Are you following me?" he says.

I laugh. "I could ask you the same thing, elevator Zack."

He grins. "What are you drinking?"

"Whiskey sour."

He lets out a whistle and gets the bartender's attention. Zack seems to whistle a lot.

"I'm good friends with the bartender," he says in my ear. "I work here part-time."

"And you come on your days off?" I raise a brow. But who am I to judge, right? I practically live at the cafe.

He orders our drinks. "This is the best bar in the city, and because of this bar, I get to see you again." He winks. "Can't beat that, elevator Jade."

He hands me my drink, and I smile.

"Thank you."

"No problem. So, did you come alone?" he asks me.

"No, I came with a couple of friends," I tell him. "My roommate is performing tonight with his band."

"Botox Barbies?"

I shake my head. "No, The Flight."

"Ah, nice. I've seen them play plenty of times. Which one is your roommate?"

"The lead singer/guitarist."

"I like them a lot. Much better than the Botox Barbies."

"Who cares about the Botox Barbies?" I joke.

"Exactly!" Zack grins.

"My friends are probably wondering where I am." I give him a small smile as my eyes do a quick scan towards the direction of my friends.

"I'll stop bothering you. I hope to run into you again, elevator Jade."

I smile and watch him walk away, getting lost in the crowd of people.

"Where did you go?" Reese asks as soon as I approach our table.

"I needed another drink," I say, raising my glass.

"Colin's coming on any moment."

"Have you seen Kirk?" I ask them, and they both shake their heads no.

I nod. *Everything will be okay.*

A girl with short purple hair walks onto the stage, and the loud music shuts off. She taps on the microphone a couple of times and clears her throat.

"How's everyone doing tonight?!" she yells, and everyone begins to yell and holler.

"All right, all right! I like the enthusiasm." She laughs. "Tonight, we have one of my favorite bands. Are you guys ready?"

I look over at Reese, and she begins to clap and scream, following with a few jumps here and there. I can't help but laugh.

A couple of Colin's band members walk onto the stage, including Randy and the guy who plays the drums; I can't remember his name.

The stage lights are off, and I finally spot Colin. He's the last one to walk on the stage.

The lights turn on. "Hey everyone, this is The Flight," Colin says with his strong deep voice.

With his long rocker hair, the drummer hits his drumsticks together, and they begin to play. Everyone at the bar faces the stage and enjoys the music, even me. There are many things I don't like about Colin, but whenever I listen to him and his band play, it's like I forget about all the annoying stuff, and I'm able to enjoy the music. That boy can definitely sing.

They finish their first song, ending with an incredible guitar solo by Colin.

"What's up, everyone? I'm Colin, and we are The Flight."

Everyone begins to scream and yell. Colin lets out a laugh, and I can't help but admire him up there. He looks really good, even though his hair is sort of messy and he's sweaty. Not in a disgusting way, but the sweat makes his face and his chiseled jaw shine. He plays a couple of strings. "I think they liked the first song," he says into the mic while looking at the other guitarist next to him. Colin seems so relaxed up there. I admire that.

They start to play again, song after song. I'm getting into it. I sway back and forth while I lazily drink from my straw with not a worry in the world. That is until I spot Kirk walking towards us. He approaches Wes first, giving him a handshake and a hug. Reese looks at me, and I look over to Colin, who's in the middle of singing.

"You came!" I say over the music.

Kirk smiles and leans into me. "I thought I'd check it out. I've never been to a bar in New York." He looks at Colin then back at me. "He's always been so good up there," he tells me, "always been a natural."

I look at Kirk. He's wearing a button-down shirt tucked into his khakis. The man definitely doesn't know how to dress for the bar scene.

"You look great tonight, Jade," he says in my ear.

I smile. "Thank you, Kirk."

Reese tugs my arm. "Come to the bathroom with me."

I nod and follow her. There's a line, of course.

"So, he came," I say. We both lean on the dirty wall and wait.

"Maybe Kirk will leave by the time Colin is done," Reese says.

I shrug. "No one has told me why Colin despises Kirk so much."

Reese looks at me and sighs. "I hardly know myself. Wes sorta told me a little. I know as much as you. Basically, Colin can't be in the same room as him."

"This is all my fault. Me and my big mouth," I sigh, gently smacking my palm against my forehead.

"It's fine. Don't worry. We'll figure it out."

"I need a drink."

Colin and I have been good lately. We haven't been fighting as often, and we are sort of getting along in our own way. He isn't annoying me as much, so I think that's progress. I just don't want to mess that up with my stupid invite. Colin's going to find out and hate me forever.

"I feel like this line isn't moving," I say with a yawn.

"Why do the girls always have a line, but the guy's bathroom never does?" she asks as we watch a guy walk into the men's bathroom.

"Because they have long rods coming out of them, so it's easier for them to pee," I explain.

Reese laughs. "Please never say long rods again."

"LONG RODS!!" I shout, and the girl in front of us turns around. Reese hides her face and hits my arm.

Reese and I head back to where Wes is standing, alone. *Where did Kirk go?*

"Where did Kirk go?" Reese asks before I can.

"He got an emergency call from the hospital and had to leave."

I feel a sense of relief rush through me, and I practically beg Reese and Wes to not tell Colin about what I did. Of course, they agreed.

Another band eventually comes on, and Colin makes his way over to us, downing the last of his cup of water. Randy desperately flirts with a girl behind us as we rave and rave to Colin about how great the show was. We stay for another hour and eventually head out for some late-night pizza.

"Heard about Eric," Colin says from across the booth.

I look up from my half-eaten pepperoni slice. I let out a sigh that can only be heard by me, and I simply nod.

"Sorry, roomie," he says.

"Thanks for calling Maude."

Colin gives me a grin as he leans his back against the hard bench. "My pleasure."

I give him a small smile. Our short little exchange ends, and we both turn our attention back to the group.

CHAPTER 42

"Can you believe it's already the end of October?" I ask Reese and Claire as I take a sip of my piping hot coffee and glance at the Halloween decorations around the cafe. The chill in the air has gotten colder, but only a light jacket is needed for now. I glance out the window as I watch busy New Yorkers make their way down the street.

"Time really flies when you're having fun." Reese grins at me.

I smile as I lean my elbows against the hardwood table. "More like crying yourself to sleep every night."

Claire looks at me, but as soon as we make eye contact, she looks towards the window. "Flower guy seems to be on time, yet again."

I nod. "*Ahh*, yes. There he is." I smile to myself.

"I'm still upset that we didn't celebrate your birthday."

I groan. "Reese, enough with that. I don't enjoy celebrating birthdays. I'm not like you and most people."

"Oh dear, I missed your birthday." Claire frowns.

"Jade is an unusual species. She hates birthdays."

"Yeah, especially my own," I sigh. "Eric and I planned to go away for my birthday this year."

Claire and Reese's faces soften, and I let out a laugh. "Guys, I'm fine. Totally over Eric. I promise."

"Whatever you say." Reese smiles as she shoves some muffin in her mouth.

～

Later that night, Colin passes me a beer as I receive a text from Suzanna's horrid maid of honor, Marni. She informs me that Suzy's wedding is in a few months and only a few preparations are left. I groan to myself as I look down at my hand in the potato chip bowl beside me on the couch. I move the bowl away from me as I pout, leaning my back against the sofa.

"I should have checked 'single' on Suzy's wedding invitation," I quickly say.

Everyone looks at me, including Colin's new conquest, Shelby.

"Where did that come from?" Reese asks as she bites into a breadstick.

I groan again as I imagine myself being the joke of the wedding—alone and watching all the other couples. "Marni texted me," I say.

"And what did she say?"

"That I'm the only one who has been distant throughout this whole process, to the point that Suzy doesn't even know if I'm bringing anyone. I guess they're finalizing the seating arrangements," I say, mocking Marni's obnoxious voice. "She needed to know if I accidentally checked off 'guest' because Suzy's too scared to ask me." I pause. "I guess it's obvious to everyone that I'm a lonely single who can't find anyone to love me."

Everyone in the room blinks a couple of times to make sure I'm done with the self-loathing. I stand up and pace in front of the television, which is, of course, playing some hockey game. Colin rolls his eyes but gets distracted as soon as Shelby nuzzles her face into his neck.

"And the worst part is, I put on weight." I flail my hands into the air. "I can't look like this when I go to the wedding. I just can't."

"You didn't put on weight!" Reese laughs.

"I did."

"So, go to the gym," she says.

I begin to laugh. "Gym? Never been to one. And besides, they are too expensive."

"Go to Colin's; he has a buddy pass. Right, Colin?" Wes gives Colin a wink.

"Roomie, you don't need the gym."

I raise a brow, crossing my arms. "Says who?"

"Says me. Trust me. You're too clumsy. I live with you, and I've never seen anyone fall as much as you," he jokes. "Now, can you please move away from the TV?"

I put my hand up and shush him as I think about what he said. Colin lets out a loud groan as I shake my head. "No, take me to the gym with you."

"Are you serious?" Colin asks.

"Do I look serious?" I yell.

"You look crazy."

I nod with a smile. "Then it's settled. I'll start going to the gym. Gaining some muscle for the wedding can't hurt."

∼

I hear Colin in the kitchen the next morning around seven a.m., the time I usually hear him leave for the gym. I quickly get out of bed and hear him laugh as soon as he sees me walking towards him in my wannabe gym clothes. If I had more time to plan, I would have bought some appropriate gym clothes, but these will have to do—an ex-boyfriend's baggy t-shirt and a pair of yoga pants.

"So, you were serious?" Colin says as he shakes a thermos in his hand.

I nod as I put my sneakers on. I knew these would come in handy someday.

"I'm ready whenever you are." I smile as I grab a Rice Krispies Treat off the counter. Colin raises a brow at me and nods, giving in to my pushy ways about the gym.

We head down the stairs to the outside of the building. I linger by the stairs and watch him stretch his legs and twist his body.

"So, should we split a cab?" I ask.

He laughs. "No, roomie, I walk to the gym."

"What gym is it again?" I ask him.

"NY Fitness on Twelfth."

My eyes open wide. "That's twenty blocks!"

"Exactly. A good way to get your blood pumping. Are you already having second thoughts?" he mocks.

"Of course not! Let's go." I scoff as I walk past him, already wishing I didn't agree to this plan.

By the time we arrive at NY Fitness, I'm already exhausted. My legs feel like Jell-O, and I'm already tired of every song on my phone. Colin helps me sign in at the front desk, and I practically follow him like a puppy through the whole gym. Colin stops in his tracks and turns to me.

"Roomie, this isn't personal, but when I go to the gym, I prefer to be by myself. So, you need to either pay for a personal trainer or figure it out yourself." And with that, he walks away and leaves me alone next to the StairMasters. I linger by the machines as I eye the parameter of each section of the gym—from people running on treadmills to huge muscle men pumping heavyweights. I take a deep breath before making my way over to an empty machine. I study the directions on the green painted machine and plop down on the seat. A couple of girls who look like they're around my age walk by me, and I study their tight leggings and crop tops. I thought the gym was the only place where people didn't have to dress slutty, but I guess I was wrong. I frown as I tug on my baggy t-shirt.

I try to use one of the machines to the best of my ability, but I get pissed off with it and move to another machine until I have to resort to the treadmill. I start slow as I look around; a few people are running, and an older woman two treadmills away from me is walking at the same speed as me. I huff and decide to leave early. I send Colin a text saying I had to leave for work, and I don't look back as I throw my tired self into a cab.

～

A few days have passed. The machines didn't work for me, and I hated the treadmill. Maybe a personal trainer could work? I step inside the gym again, and it has the same stuffy smell it did the other day—metal and sweat.

Thankfully, they remembered me from a couple of days ago and give me Colin's buddy pass. With the buddy pass, I am able to sign up for a personal trainer. I'm told to wait for the trainer by the entrance. I sit patiently until I see a familiar face walking towards me in the same shirt that all the workers are wearing.

"Elevator Jade!" I hear enthusiastically. My eyes open wide, and I thank the heavens I actually look presentable today. I stand to my feet, reaching my hand out for Zack to shake. He gives me a big smile, practically showcasing every single tooth in his mouth. We shake hands, and I follow him through the gym.

"What a surprise," he chirps as he leads me to a machine against the wall.

"Small world." I smile.

Zack leans his elbow against the machine and gives me the same smile from the last time I saw him at the bar. "So, how long have you been coming to this gym?"

I tilt my head. "Not very long," I trail off.

Zack claps his hands and nods his head. "Well, let's get started."

An hour later, after working every muscle in my body, I'm exhausted. Zach is a great trainer. He complimented me and encouraged me throughout the whole lesson.

He shows me where the elaborate water fountains are, and I thank him. As the cold water enters my mouth, I close my eyes, savoring how good it tastes. I must be so dehydrated after that workout.

"I think it's meant to be."

For a second there, I forgot that Zach was next to me. I look up and study Zack's face as I quickly wipe the water dripping off my mouth and chin.

"That we keep bumping into each other," he says.

I nod with a smile and wait for him to continue.

"Maybe we should meet on purpose sometime?"

I move my sweaty bangs away from my forehead and bite the inside of my cheek. I study Zack's face, his pointy gelled hair, and his long, athletic torso. He waits for my response, and I quickly give him a nod before I can second-guess myself.

"Cool. So maybe if you come back tomorrow, we can do something after?"

We exchange numbers, and I smile to myself. Maybe hanging around Zach will motivate me to work out more. Oh, and I definitely need to buy some cute gym clothes.

~

"How does this look?" I ask Reese as I turn away from the mirror to face her.

She's sitting on a lounge chair with her legs crossed as she studies my navy-blue leggings and matching colored sports bra. "It looks good, but are you really going to buy clothes you'll probably never wear again?"

"Never say never, Reese. The gym may be my new thing." I grin.

She raises an eyebrow. "I've known you way too long to believe something like that."

I shake my head and turn back to the mirror, admiring the way the bra makes my boobs look bigger than they actually are. "I have to look good on this date with Zack."

"The guy you met in some elevator?"

"Yep, that's the one," I sigh as I touch the soft fabric. "I think I'll get it."

Reese and I decide to get lunch before she has to get back to the library to study for a big exam. So, two bacon cheeseburgers and a plate of curly fries later, we're sipping on raspberry cheesecake milkshakes in a booth against the wall.

"So, are you sure you're over Eric? I know you, and you always like to jump on the first guy you see after a breakup," she says as she rips off a piece of her napkin.

I sigh as I casually use my tongue to play with the plastic straw. "I am…I think, but Zack keeps popping up, literally. And besides, what's so bad about using Zack to help me get over Eric?"

"I guess there's no harm," she sighs. "I just don't want you to get hurt."

I laugh. "Of course I won't."

~

The next day, Zack pulls up in front of the gym in an old Cadillac. I needed to freshen up a tad before our little date, so he said he'd wait for me out front. He also gave me a wink and a thumbs up. There's something a little odd about Zack, but I can't put my finger on it... yet. He pulls down the tinted window as I walk up to the cream-colored car.

"Like the car, aye?" he says as I put my seatbelt on.

I smile at him as he fixes the rearview mirror before pulling away from the curb. "It's really nice, actually. Super cool."

"Thanks. It's vintage," he says. "It's my dad's, technically, but I use it more. It's my baby."

Zack futzes with the radio as he pulls into a parking lot. I look out the window, clueless as to what exactly he has in mind. Zack puts the car in park and lets out a tiny breath as he looks at me. We make eye contact, and I give him a smile. "You hungry, elevator Jade?"

I follow Zack to another parking lot that is separated by a fence. There are a lot more people than I had expected. I look around to find twenty or so food trucks in the perimeter of this concrete lot. Long lines lead up to each food truck, and purple-painted picnic tables are surrounded by families and people in work attire eating.

Zack touches my hand, and I look up at him as he gives me a toothy smile. "I bet you've never been here before."

"How'd you know?" I grin as we walk past a taco truck.

"By your face." He laughs. "Every year around this time, a bunch of different food trucks come here for a month so everyone can enjoy their delicious cuisine."

"I'm surprised I've never heard of this before."

"Yeah, only true New Yorkers have," he jokes. "That's why I wanted to take you here. It's super remote."

After waiting in two long lines, Zack and I find an empty picnic table under an oak tree. Zack tells me he grew up in Queens, but his whole family is from Canada. They moved to New York when Zack was nine. I watch him as he takes a big bite of his pulled pork sandwich, barbecue sauce dripping down to his chin as he continues to speak with tons of food still in his mouth. I lick my thumb and wipe the sauce from his chin. Zack looks at me and smiles as he swallows his big bite.

I dip a French fry in some ketchup as I lean my elbows on the rough wooden table. "I never asked you. Why were you in that building the first time we met?"

"The day I got super lucky?" He grins.

I can't stop myself from blushing.

Zack lets out a little laugh as he takes a sip of soda from his glass bottle. "My dad has a firm on the thirtieth floor. I visit him a lot because he pays me to," he says.

"Wait, your dad pays you to hang out with him?" I laugh.

"Sort of. My dad's a real stick-in-the-mud type of guy and work always comes first in his eyes, so the fucker pays me to organize papers or answer calls."

"So technically, you're his receptionist, without him actually calling you one."

Zack smiles. "Yeah, pretty much. He knows if he pays me to hang out with him as I help him with his work shit, I'll actually come instead of him just hiring me for a job."

I nod. "So, you're an exercise trainer and receptionist by day and a bartender by night?"

"I guess I'm a jack of all trades." He laughs loudly. I study his perfectly symmetrical face as the breeze hits his pointy gelled hair.

"So, what about you?" he asks as his eyes bore into mine.

"What about me?"

"Do you work, elevator Jade?"

"I'm an actress, which you already know," I say, and he nods, waiting for me to continue, "And a barista."

"How fancy."

A couple of kids run by our table, distracting us from our conversation. I play with my cold fry as Zack finishes the last of his sandwich.

"So, tell me, elevator Zack—"

"Anything," he says as I try to find the words I want to say.

"Do you always hit on wannabe actresses that come for auditions in the same building as your dad's office?"

Zack raises a brow as he gives me a flirtatious grin. "Oh, so you're admitting that you thought I was hitting on you."

"Well, were you?" I tilt my head.

Zack doesn't answer right away. He leans his chin against his hand as a small smile begins to form on his face. "Yes."

I give him a smile as I cross my arms. Zack lets out a laugh and shrugs. "What can I say? You're a babe."

I blush from his words, and I surprisingly have a better time than I anticipated. Also, I'm more attracted to him now than I was when we first bumped into each other. There is definitely something cute about him.

"So, why did you agree to this awesome date? How can someone be this pretty and still be single?" he asks me.

I let out a sigh, and the look on his face shows that he detects my sadness. "Well, I was in a relationship, but now I'm not."

"That's it? That's all you're giving me?" He laughs. "C'mon, elevator Jade, you can do better than that."

I smile. "Well, if you must know, I was in a really great relationship, but he got a job offer in California. We tried the long-distance thing, but it just didn't work for us."

"I'm pretty sure long distance doesn't work for most people."

"So I'm told." I laugh.

"I can see that you're definitely a relationship girl," he says as he crosses his arms, studying my face.

"Guilty." I nervously laugh.

"I respect that," he says.

"So, what about you?" I ask him as I play with the zipper on my jacket.

"I'm more of...I guess you could say...go to work, hang with friends, and go home with the same girl type of guy," he says casually as he continues to study my face.

"Oh, I see...So, you're not a player, but you're also not a label guy."

"I guess when you put it in that way...Why have labels when we're young? Not saying I want to bring home a different girl every night, but at this point in my life, I just don't want to be tied down with the label of a girlfriend. You get it, right?"

I nod. "So, what are you saying?"

"That I'm not big on labels, and I just wanna have fun." He pauses. "With you."

～

Later that night, after Zack dropped me off at home, I thought more about his philosophy on dating. No labels. I can understand how that might work out for him, and if he had asked me a year ago, I probably would have laughed at his proposal to have some fun with him. As I lay on my back, looking up at the ceiling, I think about Zack. I think about what he said to me and wonder if I could be interested. I mean, I've never had a friends with benefits type of thing before, but I know plenty of girls that do. I've been trying hard to find and keep a relationship, but that always seems to just bite me in the butt.

It never works out. As I run all the scenarios in my head, I feel sort of liberated yet naughty at the same time. I like the idea, and it sounds almost freeing to see a guy with no strings attached. A police siren passes my street as I imagine Zack's hand touching my body, and my eyes shut as an ambulance speeds by.

~

I hold the subway pole tightly, standing near Emerson as we make our way to the city. There's a bar she swears by in the East Village that plays crazy techno music. I haven't seen Emerson since the night I got dinner and drinks with her and Eric. When I tell her that Eric and I broke up as we stand between two strangers, she seems pleased with the news.

"Don't get me wrong, I've always liked Eric. He's a great artist. But I prefer single Jade," she says with a grin.

"I'm not sure if I've met her yet." I laugh as the subway doors open. Emerson hooks her arm with mine, and we walk up the steps leading up to the city.

"Oh c'mon, post-break-up with Noah, remember? I had you for a little while."

"Oh right. I was single for a while until I met Brock."

"Brock! What happened to him? He was really cute."

I laugh. "No idea. He hated New York when I met him, so I doubt he still lives here."

I can already hear the loud techno music Emerson was talking about from a couple of blocks away. She lets out a squeal as she grabs my hand, leading me towards the bar. Thankfully, there isn't a long line, and we get in reasonably quick. The bar is packed with every kind of face I can imagine—I guess the types of people that come to this type of bar, Emerson's crowd. I feel so plain as we find two seats by the bar, squeezing next to a man with every kind of piercing and a woman with purple and pink hair.

"What can I get you girls?" the bartender asks sweetly. I study his red mohawk as I order two martinis for us.

"Cool bar, right?" she asks over the crazy loud music.

I give her an enthusiastic nod as I grab our drinks. "I think I like single Jade, too."

Emerson looks at me and nods. "Thank gosh. You hang out with Reese too much. I think she is giving you the 'relationship syndrome.'"

I laugh. "I suppose. That's why I needed to hang out with you tonight. Judgment-free zone."

"Oh, completely, girl." She smiles as we tap our glasses.

"I just wanna have fun, not think about what my boyfriend wants or needs," I shout. Emerson takes a sip of her martini, nodding at what I'm saying.

I'm not sure if she knows what I'm talking about. I haven't told her about Zack and his no-label type of relationship. I'm not the type of person who likes to keep things to myself, and I think that's why I asked Emerson to get drinks with me tonight. Reese would definitely tell me to forget it, and I'm not sure if that's the advice I want to hear.

A man with big muscles and short arms approaches us with one of his friends. He introduces himself, saying his name is Graham. I watch as he eyes me up and down, leaning into my ear.

"Why haven't I ever seen you here?" he asks me. "I've definitely seen your friend."

I smile. "Maybe you just didn't look hard enough."

"My bad, right?"

I give him a shrug as I glance over to Emerson who is flirting with Graham's friend.

"Can I buy you a drink?" he asks.

I shake my head, showing him the martini in my hand.

"Okay, then will you come dance with me?"

I look into Graham's blue eyes, and I think about single Jade. Relationship Jade would never dance with some strange guy she just met at some techno bar.

"Sure, why not?" I yell over the music. I hand Emerson my drink, and I follow Graham to the dance floor. How can people dance to this horrid music? Graham tries to mirror a couple of people dancing beside him. I find myself just watching them in complete confusion. Graham looks at me and smiles. "There's a certain dance people do to this type of music. You've never been to any music festivals?"

I shake my head. "No, I haven't. Have you?"

"As much as I can," he says in my ear. "I'm a tourist, by the way. Been here for three weeks."

My eyes widen. "When are you leaving?"

"Tomorrow, actually." He shrugs. "I live in England," he says in my ear. Am I drunk, or is it so loud in this bar that I couldn't even tell that the guy currently hitting on me is British?

I give him a smile and continue to watch him as he dances. Suddenly, I feel his hands touch the sides of my waist, but I don't move them. It feels nice. I sway back and forth, trying my hardest to not feel awkward and let go. Graham's hand moves to my neck, and I feel his face getting closer to mine. I look into his dilated pupils as he reaches in for a kiss. His lips feel foreign on mine, but it doesn't feel bad. I can taste the beer he was drinking earlier as I open my mouth for his tongue to slide in. Graham's fingers wrap around my hair as we sloppily make out in the middle of the dance floor. I hear Emerson's voice beside me as she dances with Graham's friend. I'm not sure how long I was making out with Graham for, but my lips feel a little swollen as soon as we release. Graham goes back to dancing like everyone else as I stand still, touching my lips.

"I'm gonna get another drink," I say in Emerson's ear. I walk slowly over to the bar as I think about what just happened. A stranger's tongue was down my throat minutes ago. A stranger I'll probably never see again. The bartender hands me another martini as I simultaneously receive a text from Zack.

Wanna hang? I read the text a couple more times before downing my martini. I leave the bar before I can second-guess myself.

I shoot Emerson a text as I jump into an Uber. Zack sends me his address, and I swallow hard at the thought of casual sex.

I had to knock a couple of times until Zack opened his door with a smile.

"Jade, it's a pleasure." He bows as I walk inside. I let out a laugh at his weirdness and look around as he takes my jacket off.

"You look very nice, like always. Did you go out tonight?"

I nod. "To that techno bar in the East Village."

Zack makes a face that makes me laugh. "Never was into that bar," he says as he pours himself and me a glass of red wine. "Never get lucky there."

"Oh really? I was," I say as I take a sip of my wine.

Zack tilts his head as he leans his body against the kitchen counter. "Is that so?"

I nod. "*Mmm-hmm.* His name is Graham, and he's from England."

"Graham from England," Zack repeats. "Are you trying to make me jealous, elevator Jade?"

"Maybe. Is it working?" I ask, taking a seat.

Zack strolls towards me without moving his eyes away from mine. "A little."

Zack places his hand gently around my neck. He lowers his head and leans in to give my neck tiny kisses. I can't deny that I'm liking how this feels. I wrap my arms around his neck as he moves his lips up to my jaw. "You're so hot, Jade. I want to do so much to you."

I let out a tiny moan as I close my eyes. His mouth moves to my lips, and I open my mouth so our tongues can touch. Zack picks me up off the chair, and I wrap my legs around his torso without releasing from our kiss. He lowers me onto what feels like a bed as I watch him take off his long-sleeved shirt, exposing his muscled stomach. I give him a grin as I seductively take off my shirt and bra. Zack eyes my bare chest as he licks his lips. I lay still, watching him stand in front of me.

"I figured we'd watch a movie," I joke as he pulls down my skinny jeans.

"I'd rather watch you." He licks his lips.

I squirm when his cold fingers touch my hip bone. "Do you have a condom?" I shyly ask as he pulls down his pants and boxers.

"Yes, ma'am," he hums. I wait a couple of seconds while he runs to his bathroom to grab a couple of condoms. The October breeze rattles his window, and the only light in his room is the reflection from the moon.

"Are you ready for the best sex of your life?" he smugly says as he slides a condom on.

"Aren't you confident?" I say as I perch myself up with my elbows.

Zack looks into my eyes. "Do you mind if I take you from behind?"

～

A couple of hours later, Zack gives me a kiss on my nose as we linger by the front door. He's only in a pair of loose sweatpants as he orders me an Uber at two in the morning. I zip up my denim jacket and give him another kiss before leaving his apartment. Everything seems like a blur—from the second I walked into Zack's apartment to now as I jump into the Uber. I lean my head against the car window as I contemplate whether or not I like casual sex. It felt good at the time. Really good. And also exciting.

CHAPTER 43

There are two types of people in this world. The first keep their personal stuff to themselves and the second likes to share every detail with their judgmental friend. Yeah, I'm part of the latter group.

Reese's eyes go wide as she listens to my story. "You left his place at two in the morning?"

"Oh please, don't look at me like that." I cross my arms. The waitress comes by our table and refills our water glasses. Wes lets out a laugh as he feeds Reese a fry.

"Wes, don't laugh. This isn't funny," Reese says as she chews on the fry.

"Jade can do whatever she wants, babe. You can't stop her."

"Thank you, Wes." I nod as I poke at my hamburger bun.

Reese rolls her eyes and shrugs. "Well, how was it at least?"

"It was good. I think the beginning part of leaving the bar and going over to his place was more fun." I laugh as I spot Colin walking into the restaurant. Drenched from the pouring rain, he runs his hand through his dirty blonde hair as he walks over to our table.

"It's fucking cold in here." He's practically out of breath as he takes off his jacket. Colin slides into the booth next to me and orders a beer immediately. "So, what did I miss?" he asks us.

"Jade had her first one-night stand," Reese blurts out.

Colin gives me a surprised look but gets distracted by the beer that is put in front of him. "Way to go, roomie. Didn't think ya had it in you," he mocks as he takes a big sip of his beer.

"Yeah, yeah, whatever. It'll probably be a one-time thing anyway." I look at Reese, but I'm not sure if she believes me.

"Shelby and I heard you come in," he says.

I grin as I rest my cheek against my knuckles. "Shelby from the other night? I thought these girls have expiration dates," I say.

Colin rolls his eyes as he takes a fry from my plate.

"You've been seeing Shelby for a couple of weeks now," Wes says, sounding very surprised.

"That's like two years in Colin's world," Reese jokes, making us all laugh. Well, all of us except Colin.

"It's casual. She's cool, and we're just having fun." He shrugs, taking another fry. Do all guys say that? Everyone continues to focus on Colin, which makes him annoyed. "Hey guys, remember when we were all talking about Jade's one-night stand? Yeah, let's go back to that."

I let out a laugh as I study the side of Colin's face. Could Colin possibly have...a girlfriend?

∿

It wasn't a one-time thing. I ended up hearing from Zack the next night. I wasn't sure if I wanted to "hang out" again, but it made me feel good that he likes the sex with me. I sound pathetic, I know, but I keep reassuring myself that all of this is fun and I need to stop overthinking everything.

"I'm close," Zack moans as I ride my body onto his. "Oh, Jade." Zack comes undone, eyes fluttering back as he leans his head back on the couch. His chest moves up and down as he tries to catch his breath. "That was amazing."

I turn my head, leaning my chin on my shoulder, and I smile without showing any teeth. "It was." I climb off of him and quickly get dressed.

"It's kinda early for us. You don't have to leave so soon," he says, still naked on his tan-colored couch.

"I didn't think we'd actually hang out." I laugh.

"Well, I'm not doing anything tonight, so if you want, you could stay."

Zack gets up and walks into his bathroom. I sit in silence as I lean my back against the soft cushion. Zack comes out seconds later in a pair of sweats and a t-shirt and gives me a smile. "So, you're staying. Cool, lemme grab some wine, and I'll make dinner."

I nod, taking off my jacket. I move my sweaty bangs away from my eyes and get up, following him into the kitchen.

"I make a delicious baked ziti," he says charmingly.

I grin. "Love baked ziti."

Zack pours me a glass of wine and begins to grab all the ingredients for dinner. He opens the cabinet, and I can hear him curse under his breath.

"What's wrong?" I ask.

"I have the wrong type of pasta. I need penne, and all I have is bow ties." He sighs.

"Bow ties work, right? I don't mind."

Zack looks at me then back to the pasta box sitting in his cabinet.

"My buddy down the hall usually has every type of pasta in his place. I'll stop by real quick and ask him for his."

"Really? Isn't that too much?" I ask as I take a sip of my wine.

"Nah. I'll be right back. Just sit and look pretty." He smiles as he leans in for a kiss. I nod as I watch him leave the apartment.

Twenty minutes passes. I check the clock one last time and groan as I eye my empty glass. I finally hop off the barstool and pace in front of his front door before leaving his apartment. I walk down the hallway and call his name a couple of times until I spot a baldish man walking up the stairs. He turns into the hallway, and I can hear his keys jingle in his pocket.

"Hi, sir. This might be random, but have you seen a guy named Zack? I don't know his last name, actually." I laugh to myself. "But he lives on this floor. He left me in his apartment alone and hasn't come back," I say way too quickly.

The man looks puzzled as he scratches the top of his balding head. "Zackary Baker in 3C?"

"Yes. That one," I say.

"Yeah, I actually saw him down the road cleaning his car."

Now I'm the puzzled one. The man studies my face as I thank him. In complete confusion, I rush down the stairs to the outside of his building. I realize I don't have a jacket the second I step out into the sharp breeze. I spot Zack down the street where his Cadillac is parked.

"Zack?" I say, watching him vigorously wiping down his already clean car.

"Oh hey," he sings, continuing to clean his car.

"Zack?" I say louder.

He finally looks up and waits for me to speak.

"Did you forget about me?"

"Of course not. I remembered that I didn't wipe her down today. I'm done now if you wanna eat."

"What about the specific pasta? I really don't care about bow tie."

We finally make it back to his apartment. I literally had to drag him away from his car. I'm not sure if I should be mad, frustrated, or maybe just confused. I think I'm a little bit of everything. Zack seems a little spacey at times, but I guess I didn't realize the extent of it.

Zack makes the baked ziti with the bow tie noodles, but something seems a little off with him tonight. Actually, I shouldn't say that because this is the first time we've hung out instead of just having sex. When I say off, I mean he seems super hyper. He would lose focus and change the conversation topic every couple of minutes. I can't believe I haven't noticed that the guy suffers from ADHD.

Two bottles of wine later, Zack and I climb into his bed. I feel pretty tired from the bottle of wine we shared. My head sinks into the soft cushion of his pillow. I feel him plop beside me, letting out a moan of comfort. I turn to my side, back facing him. He moves in closer to me and begins to stroke his fingers up and down my leg. My eyes feel heavy, and I feel them starting to close.

"Why are you so far, baby?" he breathes, pulling my waist closer into him. He wraps his arm around me and begins to kiss my neck. All of a sudden, his mouth moves closer to my ear, and he starts to softly bite my earlobe.

"I want to make sweet, sweet love to your ear."

⁓

"He said what?" Reese lets out a laugh while playing with her straw. I glance at Claire, but she refuses to make eye contact with me. Instead, she takes a sip of her latte and stares out the window.

Claire has been quiet about the guys I've been seeing post-Eric. Okay, well, there haven't been that many guys after Eric. Just Zack and that British guy from the techno bar. I'm not proud of myself.

I place my hand over my forehead and let out a deep breath.

Reese didn't have class today, so she met Claire and me during my lunch break.

"How could this happen to me? I'm a good person," I cry. "Guys like Zack make me miss Eric so much."

"Well, you could have had Eric," Claire says.

Reese gives me a small smile. "Maybe he was just intoxicated?"

Thank you, Reese, for steering the conversation away from Eric. I need to remember to not bring up Eric in front of Claire.

"Oh yeah, he definitely was," I say. "We drank a lot that night."

"Why do you care? I thought Zack was some rebound and 'a good lay,'" she says, reiterating my words from the other night.

"Oh, he is. It's just...I got a little hopeful that *maybe* I could bring Zack to the wedding and call it a night."

I look over to Claire. "Claire, please tell me what you're thinking." I sigh.

She looks at me, resting her latte down. "Zack is one kinky motherfucker."

Reese and I glance at each other and can't help but laugh at Claire's choice of words.

You're right, Claire. Zack is one kinky motherfucker.

⌣

Later that night, I decided to surprise Zack by stopping by his place. I really want to make sure that what he said about my ear was just the alcohol speaking. I stopped by this Italian bakery on Bedford Avenue and picked up some chocolate cannoli. They've been calling my name every time I pass by, so it's the perfect excuse to stuff my face.

"Now, this is what I like to see outside my door," he says as soon as the front door swings open.

"I brought cannoli." I smile.

I sit down at his kitchen table, and he pours some steaming water in one of his *Star Wars* mugs. He hands me his box of different types of tea bags, and I pick the ginger flavor.

"It's great that you're here," he says with his back to me. "I was just going to enjoy a cup of tea and watch some baseball tonight."

"How proper of you," I say.

"What'd you do today?" he asks.

"I worked in the morning and went shopping with my friend Reese for a little while."

"Nice! Did you get anything special?" He turns slightly, giving me a wink.

"I bought some earrings," I say, looking at his thin frame.

He turns around and walks over to me, putting the plate of cannoli between us. "I bet they look beautiful on you," he says, leaning in and giving me a kiss on my cheek.

I smile, grabbing a cannoli. "Last night was fun."

He takes a sip of his tea and nods. "I never realized how much I like just staying in and opening a bottle of wine with you." He runs his finger over my cheekbone.

"You got pretty drunk, though." I raise a brow.

"Yeah." He laughs. "Wine makes me feel like an eighteen-year-old girl that can't control her liquor."

"Do you remember anything from last night?" I ask him.

"Oh gosh, what did I say?" He laughs with cannoli in his mouth.

I fiddle with my teabag. "You mentioned something about my ear."

Zack leans back in his chair, arms folded and lips slightly parted. He doesn't say anything, so I begin to ramble about how it's okay to have fantasies. I said I might be interested, but I need time. *Blah blah blah*. Word vomit. Typical Jade.

He puts some of the cannoli cream on his finger and smears it over my top lip. He wants to shut me up. And it worked. I lick some of it off, and I wait for him to talk.

"What did I say, Jade?"

"You told me you wanted to make sweet love to my, um, ear," I say quickly, wanting this conversation to end. I should have just left it alone, but no, I had to bring it up.

Silence fills the air, and I want to die from the awkwardness between us.

"Jade, I really hope you didn't overthink that because I don't want to do that…I was drunk," he says slowly. "Unless you're into it."

Silence fills the room yet again.

"Do you tend to do that?" he asks me.

"Tend to do what?"

"Overthink about nonsense."

"Well, *uh*, no. Yes. Well, I don't think it's nonsense per se."

"But you spent the whole day thinking I wanted to eff your ear." He laughs.

"Yeah, I guess I did. I guess I tend to overthink at times."

He grabs my hand and gives it a gentle squeeze. "You really need to be aware that you're doing it because it's really not healthy. Trust me, Jade. I would know."

Wait a second, what is he doing? He's trying to make me feel uncomfortable for thinking what he said was weird. Even though it was! It's like he's turning it on me…*Ohh*, he's good.

"You know what, Zack? Let's just forget that all of this happened, okay?"

"What happened?" He grins.

I shake my head and smile.

"So, do you wanna fuck or what?" Zack says with a grin plastered on his face.

~

I ended up staying the night at Zack's. I laid wide awake in his bed for about an hour, just staring up at his pale white ceiling as I listened to his soft snoring. I left his apartment as quickly and as quietly as I could before he woke up. Zack and I aren't in a relationship. We're just having crazy good sex everywhere in his apartment. No biggie. I can't do another relationship right now. And waiting for him to wake up, only to have awkward conversations we both don't want to have, is exactly what I'm trying to avoid.

A thought occurs to me as I am walking down the empty sidewalk in yesterday's clothing. This whole time, I was putting myself down, feeling like a slut for sleeping with Zack and randomly making out with Graham. But maybe this is just what I need right now. I tried the whole relationship thing, and clearly, that didn't work out.

~

Colin is eating a bowl of cereal at the kitchen table when I get home, still in his drawstring pajama bottoms.

"How was your night?" he asks.

"Great." I smile from ear to ear. "It was great!"

"Wow, I bet it was," he says, folding his arms and leaning back on his chair.

"I had an epiphany walking home this morning."

"An epiphany?" He raises a brow.

I nod and plop on the chair next to him. "This whole time, I thought I needed to be in some sort of relationship to make me feel whole, but now that I'm having mind-blowing sex, I'm happier! I want to be more like you," I shout. "I know, crazy, right?"

Colin tilts his head to the side. "More like crazy eyes." Colin points to my widened eyes.

I tilt my head as I cross my arms against my chest.

"Jade, listen. You don't want to be like me, okay? You're just heartbroken over Eric, and you feel like you'll never find anyone as good as him."

Wow, he's good.

"No, I don't want to be in a relationship."

"Okay, that's fine. Then don't be in one right now, but don't sleep with every guy in New York and think they'll fix your broken heart. The girls who end up doing that just end up getting hurt, even more than they already are," he says simply.

"That's what you do, Colin."

Colin stands up and sighs. "Jade, I'm a dude. It's different."

I stand up too. "How is it different? Girls like to have sex just as much as guys."

"Yeah, but we don't get attached the same way you females do. It's just how it is. I'm not making this up. It's true."

Colin then walks over to his lazy boy and sits down.

"I'm going to prove to you that what you just said isn't true!" I say, pointing my finger at him.

Colin rolls his eyes as he gets up and walks towards his bedroom door. "Please don't, Jade. You'll only get hurt." And with that, he closes the door behind him.

"You'll see!" I then walk into my room, slamming the door behind me.

CHAPTER 44

I grab a handful of candy corn from a big bowl on the coffee table. I glance at Reese who is wearing kitty ears as she looks through the movie channels for a horror movie. We decided that we are too old to go to some rooftop Halloween parties in October. I mean, who in their right mind wants to get drunk in some slutty costume? I know I don't this year.

I shove the handful of candy in my mouth as I spot Colin from the corner of my eye. I let out a laugh as he walks over to us.

"Nice costume, Colin," I say as I sit up to get a better look.

Colin gives me a grin as he reaches for a beer in his cooler. "Thanks, roomie."

"So, tell me, Colin, what exactly are ya going for here?" Reese asks.

"Werewolf, obviously. Can't you see my ripped shirt?"

"Oh, it's ripped all right," I tease.

Colin lets out a laugh as he finishes the last of his beer. "So, this is what you guys are doing tonight? Sitting around like two hobos?"

"We are watching scary movies and eating candy," I say.

"Lame," Colin says as he walks past us.

"Jade, don't do it." Reese looks at me sternly; she knows me all too well.

I stare at the television and back to Reese. "I have to," I whine.

I get up from the couch and cross my arms as I watch Colin linger by the door.

"Are you going to that party?"

Colin nods.

"It's not lame to stay home on Halloween, Colin."

"Whatever you say, roomie."

I hear Reese get off the couch and walk over to us. She walks past me and begins to put on her boots.

"What are you doing?" I ask her.

"Wes is going now, and he's pissing me off," she huffs.

"Oh, so now both of you are going?"

They nod.

"But I'll be like the third wheel," I pout.

"What about Colin?" Reese laughs. I look at him and back to Reese. "But I thought we were gonna hang back tonight. Remember, we're too old to get drunk in slutty costumes in the cold?"

"Wes is going, so I want to, Jade. Why don't you call your boyfriend?"

"I'm out," Colin says, but Reese stops him by grabbing his arm. "Wait for us."

"Boyfriend? If you're referring to Zack, he's not my boyfriend."

"Okay then, call the guy you're sleeping with," Reese says.

"Should I?"

"Yes! So I can leave," Colin groans.

"Uh, okay. Give me five minutes to throw something on," I say before running into my room.

I close the door behind me as I dial Zack. He answers in seconds. I search my closet for something, anything, to wear.

"Hey, cutie," he says through the phone.

"Hey, so what are you doing tonight?" I ask him.

"Nothing. Why? Want to come over?"

"Well, it's Halloween, and I'm getting pressured to go to some rooftop party. I was wondering if you wanted to come?" I say way too quickly.

There's silence between our phones, and I bang my forehead as I throw on a black sweater.

"Dressing up for Halloween is really not my thing. Just not into it, but if you decide to leave early, my door is open."

"Okay, but my friends want to meet you—"

"And what should I tell them?"

"No, I get it," I sigh and wait for him to continue, but he doesn't. There's an awkward silence between us, and all I want to do is escape and pretend that I never called him. Zack and I hang up seconds later. I feel a little hurt, but I knew what I was getting myself into with him.

I walk out of my room, and Reese and Colin are settled in the living room, waiting for me. Colin probably is on his third or fourth beer by now.

"Done?" Colin asks.

"Do I look like I'm done?" I yell. "I have nothing to wear!"

"Oh please, all your clothing is unusual—not in a bad way. Oh, you know what I mean," she says when she sees me glaring at her.

"Roomie, just put some antennas on."

"Why?" I cross my arms.

"They'll complete your whole 'I look like a bug' vibe. You got those beetle eyes," Colin cracks up.

Reese glances at her phone. "Wes said it's really packed already. We really need to go."

And Wes was right. The three of us waited an hour in the cold just to stand on a roof, in the cold. I'm not happy. And I'm especially not happy with what I'm wearing. They convinced me to wear my work uniform. So, apparently, not only am I a barista by day, but I'm also one by night.

As soon as we get upstairs, the three of us head straight to the bar. Wes meets up with us, and I'm jealous that he's actually wearing a costume. Also, Shelby, Colin's new girl, ends up coming too. I'm apparently the only single one now.

I walk away from them in a huff as I down half my drink.

"Strong?"

I look up from my vodka soda and quickly wipe the bubbles off my lips.

"Excuse me?" I ask the stranger in front of me.

The stranger is wearing a leather jacket and one hanging earring. He lets out a laugh and points to my drink. "I was asking if your drink is strong," he says.

I look at my drink and back at the short, sort of chubby man in front of me. "Not really," I say dryly.

"So, are you like a waitress or something?" he asks, pointing to a couple of coffee stains on my apron.

"Yes, exactly. Excuse me," I say as I walk away from him. I hear him say something, but I'm already too far away to comprehend. I see Reese and Wes dancing to some Halloween song in the middle of the dance floor. I finish my drink then grab another one from a waiter in an alien costume. I gulp my second drink, and I make my way to my friends as the alcohol burns down my throat.

"Hey!" Reese shouts, grabbing my arm and giving it a gentle squeeze. "This is so much better than being home!"

I give her a half-smile as I move my bangs away from my eyes. "I'm heading out."

"What?" Reese yells, pointing to her ear.

"I'm leaving!" I shout, showing her an example of someone leaving with my two fingers.

"Oh c'mon! Don't be sad that your loverboy isn't here. Screw him!" she says. I spot the leather jacket man walking towards us, and I shake my head. "I have a headache. I'll call you tomorrow," I say and leave before Reese can respond and the leather jacket guy can talk to me again. I call a cab immediately, and I'm relieved as I make my way to Zack's.

"Nice costume," Zack says as he leans against the door hinge.

I walk past him and take off my smelly apron.

"Well, you would have seen it if you went to that party with me," I quickly say.

Zack raises a brow and sets his beer on the table. "Someone's sassy tonight."

I let out a sigh, wishing that the "spooky" champagne I was drinking all night wasn't making me sound so desperate. I need to find the strong and liberated Jade that came out yesterday.

"Take off your pants," I say with force, then ending it seconds later with a small burp.

Zack tilts his head. "I've always liked a woman in charge."

I watch as Zack slowly pulls down his cargo pants, exposing his blue cotton boxers.

"Now your shirt."

Zack laughs and takes off his shirt playfully, tossing it towards me.

I study his lean torso as my eyes travel to his bulge that has suddenly grown. I hear Zack's rapid breathing as he slowly walks over to me like he's a wolf, and I'm an innocent lamb. Suddenly, I feel his arms wrap around my waist, and he picks me up in one quick motion. I let out a little shout that's mixed with laughter as he carries me to his king-sized bed in the other room.

"Your turn," he says as he climbs on top of me. Zack peels off the rest of my clothes as his cold fingers run along the sides of my inner thigh. I moan as I feel him enter me. Zack's eyes are glued to mine as he stares deeply into my eyes. He then leans in and kisses me deeply. I'm a little surprised as he continues to lay on top of me, staring into my eyes as he slowly pounds, making us last a lot longer than we usually do. I've never had sex like this with him. It is as if he's turned our usual "fucking" to "lovemaking." I continue to be confused as he finishes, his eyes never leaving mine.

I hug his white blanket as I watch him get dressed. His bed creaks a little as he sits on the edge, giving me a kind smile.

"Zack?"

"Yeah?"

I sit up, still covering my naked body. "That was fun," I say. "The sex seemed different though, right?"

Zack looks confused, and I mentally smack myself. "It felt more like we were making love rather than our regular fucking."

Zack shrugs. "I guess I'm more into you than I thought I was?"

I'm not sure if that's a compliment, but I give him a smile. "I like you too, Zack."

"I mean, like, I'm not really seeing anyone else right now, but I still don't want a relationship."

I nod. "Oh yeah, me too. Definitely on the same page."

"Cool." He smiles again and gets up.

"Hey, Zack? I know this is really out of the blue, but I have this thing in May, and I was wondering if you wanted to join me? I promise it'll be fun." I laugh nervously.

Zack freezes. "Uh, I'm not sure if that's a good idea. You know, making plans so far in advance."

I nod. "I get it."

"You know what? I'll let you know." He smiles and walks out of his room, leaving me alone with my thoughts.

~

It's been two weeks since I've heard from Zack. Reese had a brilliant idea to take my mind off things. She decides to drag me to a fancy restaurant in the city. Her Aunt Leah is in town from Florida and needs some gossip. My tight black dress bunches as I cross my legs, watching our waiter pour each of us a glass of red wine. Leah is dressed in black as well. Her tiger-striped blonde highlighted hair is pushed away from her caked face. Leah rips a piece of bread and takes a big bite, moaning as some oil drips down her lips.

Leah laughs as she wipes the oil from her chin. "I haven't had bread since I met Dan."

"It's that Florida living," I say as I take a sip of wine.

Leah was born and raised in New York, and about three years ago, she caught her husband of fifteen years screwing some twentysomething. So, she packed her bags, moved to sunny Florida, and met her boyfriend, Dan. Dan is a fitness instructor from Boca Raton. I think she's happy though; she has a glow that I never saw when she was married to Kyle.

"I'm having dinner with two models," Leah says as she finishes ordering her shrimp dish. She leans her chin on the palm of her hand as Reese and I order our meals. Reese's face turns red as the waiter compliments us as well. I let out a laugh as I casually check my phone that's sitting on the table. Reese and I catch eyes, and I shrug, finally shoving my phone back in my clutch, forcing my thoughts to do the same.

Our meals come pretty quickly, and we immediately dig in. Leah lets out her famous moan as she takes her first bite of shrimp. I watch her carefully as I slowly cut into my sirloin steak. Leah smacks her lips dramatically and nods her head. "*Hmm.* White wine, garlic, black pepper, and fresh ginger," she says in her thick Brooklyn accent. Reese and I glance at each other as we listen to Leah's special talent of naming the very specific ingredients in her food. I take a big bite of my steak, trying my hardest not to giggle at how seriously Leah takes her first bite of shrimp.

"How's your food?" Reese asks her, biting her lip.

"Let's just say the restaurants in Florida don't even come close to how good this place is," she says before taking another bite of her food and scraping her teeth against her fork. Leah is never one to ever mess up her lipstick. She's been doing this since the '70s.

We eat in pure bliss as we listen to Leah tell us about her retired life in Florida. My mind keeps jumping back to Zack, and I groan, taking a sip of my wine.

"I'm gonna say it," I breathe. "I think I scared Zack off."

"Who's Zack?" Leah flutters her eyelashes.

"Trouble." Reese rolls her eyes. "Jade, I told you. He's not boyfriend material."

"I know that," I say, setting my fork and knife down.

Reese plays with her mashed potatoes and asks, "You still haven't heard from him?"

I shake my head. "It's been two weeks. He ghosted me on Halloween. How ironic is that?" I cry. Reese lets out a laugh, and I can't help but laugh as well.

It's already mid-November, and it feels like this wedding is closing in on me. "I guess I came on too strong." I shrug.

"I don't think you did. He's just an ass, Jade."

I nod, taking another bite of my steak. I look up and study Leah's confused face. She squints her eyes and looks back and forth at Reese and me. "You have no idea how many times Dan has ghosted me. Every time I walk into the kitchen, the son of a bitch is always scaring me." She laughs as she places her hand against her chest. Reese and I glance at each other as we smile at Leah's cluelessness.

~

I throw a box of apple-filled muffins in my basket as I casually look at all the pastries that are sitting so perfectly in the middle of this farmer's market. As I hand the lady in the apron my credit card, I spot Colin talking to some blonde who is wearing jeans that are a little too tight. I shake my head as the girl flirtatiously giggles at whatever Colin just said to her. I can't help but laugh at how pathetic this girl is.

The wind pushes my hair over my face, and I turn my head as I move my wavy hair back. My expression turns serious as soon as I spot *her*. This familiar face I'm observing is smiling. She's standing up straight as she nods at whatever the person who is selling fruits is saying. The wind blows her long hair, and all of a sudden, we catch eyes. Her eyes bleed into mine, and it seems like she's trying to identify me without making it obvious. I give her a wave, and she smiles, walking towards me, wearing white jeans and a long flannel button-down shirt.

We finally approach each other, and I'm hoping she'll remember our little exchange when she angrily stopped by the apartment to find Colin.

"Hi, no name," I say, breaking the silence.

She lets out a laugh and leans in, giving me a short hug while holding her basket on her forearm. "I remember you." She smiles.

"How are you? Funny to see you at this farmers market."

No-name-blonde smiles and playfully plays with the greenish-yellow apple in her brown basket.

"I know! I've been great, Jade. Honestly."

Wow, she still remembers my name.

"Colin's around here somewhere if you want to make a run for it," I kid, leaning in and telling her as if it's a secret.

"No need," she says. "Colin and I are good, and besides, I have a boyfriend now."

A handsome guy with silky dirty blonde hair approaches us. It's as if he overheard our conversation and finally had his cue to come over. He automatically puts his arm around no name's waist and gives me a kind smile.

"I took your advice, Jade. I stopped with the players and the losers who only used me, and I met a guy who wanted to know the real me." She smiles. "I was single for quite a while, but then I finally met Mark." She looks up at him, and he kisses the top of her head.

"Wow, I'm so happy for you, no name."

Mark looks kind of confused by my choice of words. After talking to them for a bit longer, we part ways, and I watch no-name blonde, and Mark walk away hand in hand. Almost immediately, Colin comes beside me. His arms are crossed, and he is facing the same direction as me.

"How do you know Janet?"

I turn to him and smack his chest. He looks at me, completely confused. "*Ouch*. What was that for?"

"I wasn't supposed to ever know her name, and now you've

ruined it forever! She was no-name-blonde!" I groan, walking away from him.

Colin follows me. "I swear, you always seem to surprise me."

"Is that a good thing?" I stare into his blue eyes. My wavy bangs move with the wind as we stand in the middle of the crowded farmers market.

"Yes," he says as we make our way over to the kettle corn line.

WINTER

CHAPTER 45

Autumn has come and gone, and that's the one thing I'm thankful for. Zack is officially out of the picture, and I realized one day while I was drinking my morning coffee that the player played me. I definitely didn't have him sitting in the palm of my hand. I hate to say it, but I think Colin was right. I'm definitely not cut out for hooking up without any strings attached. Zack was fun for what he was worth, and I guess deep down, I knew that. I laugh to myself as I open the front door to my building—I actually thought Zack would come to Suzy and Noah's wedding with me? How blind was I?

I hear Reese's voice saying the word "desperate" to me, and if she did, I would nod and agree. The heavy door shuts behind me as I'm immediately welcomed by the heat of this lobby. I quickly check my mailbox, dragging my body, covered in three layers of clothing, including my work uniform, up the long staircase leading to my apartment.

An unfamiliar man is leaning against the blotched painted wall right beside my door. The zipper to his puffy winter jacket is open, and he's holding a black beanie with California State University stitched on it. His brown hair is sweaty, and I watch as he lets a breath out, causing his pink pudgy cheeks to move in and out. I get to the top of the stairs, and we make eye contact as I grab my keys out of my bag.

"Are you waiting for Colin?" I ask him as I put my key into the lock.

The guy's face lights up as he moves away from the wall. "Are you Colin's girlfriend?"

I shake my head. "Roommate." I'm not sure if I should have lied and told him I'm dating Colin. Why not, right? I guess it's a force of habit to automatically answer no to being Colin's girlfriend. It's surprising how many people ask me on a daily basis.

"Oh, okay, great. I was worried that I might have been waiting at the wrong apartment." He laughs nervously.

"Does Colin know you're here?" I ask this stranger as we stand awkwardly outside my door.

"Yes and no." He smiles. "I was supposed to arrive next week, but I decided to come a week early and surprise him." I'm not too sure if Colin's really into surprises. Mainly based on what happened with his brother...

"Do you want to come inside and wait for him?" I ask, and he nods with a smile. As soon as we walk inside, both of us simultaneously take off our heavy winter jackets.

"I didn't catch your name," I say, walking over to the couch. Colin's friend follows me and plops onto the Lazy Boy chair.

"I'm Duke, Colin's friend from Pasadena. I've known him since we were kids." He smiles.

"Hi, Duke." We shake hands. "I'm Jade."

"So tell me, Jade, is this what a New York apartment looks like?" he says.

"Are you referring to how small it is?"

"Maybe." He laughs. "Just can't picture Colin living in one of these. Being a trust fund baby and all. You should see the house he grew up in," Duke tells me as he continues to look around, making my already small apartment feel even smaller.

"So, Colin's family is wealthy?" I ask Duke as I cross my legs and grab the open bag of pretzels on the coffee table. I offer Duke some pretzels, warning him that they may be stale. Duke kindly declines with a laugh.

"Wealthy is an understatement."

I nod as I munch on pretzels, asking Duke as many questions I can think of before Colin returns home. I seem to be the person who waits with Colin's guests. I'm surprised that I actually don't mind.

"Yeah, I've known Colin for as long as I can remember. We lived down the street from one another. We were always close."

I nod as I wait for Duke to continue.

"When we were fifteen, I broke my lower back from a bad jet ski accident," he begins. "I was stuck in the hospital for practically the whole summer. You can imagine what that can do to someone, especially when you know all of your friends are at the beach surfing and meeting girls." He laughs. "But Colin was the only one who visited me every day, for hours. We'd watch movies and play poker. He was truly there for me when I needed someone the most. That man is a true saint."

I tilt my head to the side as Duke's story sinks in. Are we talking about the same narcissist that is named Colin? Because the Colin I know would never do something that nice. Before I can ask him any more questions, the front door flings open, and a cold Colin walks in. His eyes suddenly go wide, and a giant smile appears on his face.

"D-Dog, my man!" he shouts, walking over to Duke and giving him a strong bear hug. They do one of those handshakes all guys seem to do, and I watch them be all buddy-buddy as I sit on the couch.

"Why the fuck are you here?" Colin laughs as he reaches into his cooler and hands Duke a beer.

"Dude, I needed to get away from Cali, man. Needed to see New York and all the hype."

"Fuck, man, I'm so happy you're here. You have no idea. I'll call Wes, and we'll give you a proper tour," Colin says, pulling his phone from his pocket.

Duke takes a big sip of his beer and lets a happy sigh out. "Rebecca broke up with me, by the way. You were right, man."

Colin smiles and looks at me. "Roomie's guy left her too, so you two will get along just fine."

I roll my eyes as I watch Colin walk over to the terrace. I turn to Duke. "Don't listen to that buffoon."

Duke laughs and studies my face. "So, this is just a roommate relationship, or is it more?"

I shake my head. "We're just roommates." I glance at Colin, who is walking over to us.

"Colin, you never told me that your roommate Jade looks like—" But before Duke can finish his sentence, Colin abruptly interrupts him. Part of me wonders what Duke was about to say, but I get easily distracted by the guys' plans for tonight. I grab my fashion magazine on the coffee table and flip through the pages as I listen to Colin give Duke a small tour around the apartment.

They stop by the kitchen table, and I can't help but overhear their conversation. Maybe because I'm a few inches away. Duke is raving about our little circular kitchen table that Colin eventually replaced a couple of months after he moved in. This brown wood table is a definite upgrade from the kitchen table I shared with Reese. The old kitchen table had one deformed leg, so it was never straight. I turn my head and watch as Duke slides his hand across our table. I have no idea what is so great about this table; I just figured Colin picked it up at some second-hand store. My phone vibrates beside me, and I get up from the couch, walking away from Duke and Colin's deep conversation about our lovely table.

"Wes and I are on our way to your place," Reese says.

I glance at the guys. "Cool, I think Colin said he wants to show Duke that pub on Fourth."

"Okay, great. See you soon."

~

Colin and I have decided to purchase a real Christmas tree this year. It's the first year neither of us has any Christmas plans, so we're both willing to take the nine-block walk in the freezing cold. I had a long and dreadful conversation with my family about why I chose not to join the Everly family Christmas gathering this year. Dealing with my drunk father and judgmental sister isn't high on my list these days. After an hour of convincing, my mother and father finally threw in the towel, leaving me alone to enjoy my warm apartment. The only problem with my plan to stay home and have a relaxing Christmas this year is Colin. Despite that, we agreed to try to get along as best as possible, and the first thing on our list is getting the Christmas tree.

Colin stands with his finger below his bottom lip as he studies two identical trees. I cross my arms, swaying from hip to hip. "Colin, we narrowed it down to these two, and they look exactly the same," I sigh, watching my breath form in front of me. "I thought we agreed on the left one?"

Colin glances at me then looks back to the trees. "I think I like the one on the right more."

I sigh, cold and irritated that even picking out a tree with Colin can get under my skin. A man that resembles Santa Claus approaches us, and I point to the tree Colin has chosen.

"No, that's okay. Let's go with yours, roomie," Colin says with a grin.

We watch the man with a thick white beard cut the tree for us. I glance at Colin, who walks to the counter to pay. His heavy, black winter jacket lays perfectly on his lean muscular body, along with his pants and winter boots. A grey beanie slouches around his head, and I can't help but admire the red around his cheeks. Colin catches my stare, and his dimple is exposed from smiling. I turn away, sort of embarrassed that he saw me looking, even though I'm not entirely sure why I was staring. Why am I admiring Colin's smile anyway? What is going on with me?

"Ready, roomie?"

Colin walks past me and grabs the heavier part of the tree. I groan as we take a few steps down the icy sidewalk.

"Whose brilliant idea was this again?" I cry, holding the tree as best as I can, dreading the long and cold trek back home.

Just as my fingers feel like they might fall off, we finally make it home.

"Okay, let's set it over here," Colin says, out of breath. He practically throws his hat across the living room. The tree lays by the front door as I dramatically fall on the couch and sigh. I think my toes have fallen off from the cold. Colin takes his jacket off, and I hear him turn the shower on. I get off the couch and take my coat off as well, getting some water for tea. I hear the shower turn off as I walk into my room to put on some warm pajamas.

Colin is putting the tree in the tree stand when I walk out of my room. I walk into the kitchen and pour some steaming water into a mug, grabbing my favorite tea from the cabinet.

"Now all it needs is decorations." I smile as I take the first sip of my tea.

Colin walks into the kitchen and grabs a shortbread cookie Reese brought over before leaving for her parents' house.

"That's your department," he says while shoving the whole cookie in his mouth. I run into my room for the box of decorations I've accumulated over the years, from cute ornaments that I've bought to red and white lights for the tree.

After convincing Colin to help me decorate, we decide on Chinese takeout, a bottle of Pinot Noir, and Colin's pick of a movie. That was my convincing strategy. I pay the delivery man as Colin looks through all the movies.

"That movie is good, Colin," I say, as I put our food on the coffee table. I pour us each a tall glass of wine and dump popcorn in a big bowl.

"My choice, remember?" he says, eying the string and needle I'm making for us to decorate. I sit on the couch and set the decorations to the side. I grab my lo mein and chopsticks as Colin finally decides *Rocky*.

Midway through the movie and our food, we finally get to the decorating part. I show Colin how to properly thread the popcorn into the string.

"This is called a homemade garland," I say, watching him grab a kernel from the bowl. His back is against the couch's armrest, and mine is too, on the opposite side.

"You never helped with decorating as a kid?" I ask him.

Colin shrugs. "Not really. My mother always hired someone to do it."

I sigh as I listen to Colin's last statement. I study his face and choose not to question it. "My sister and I always decorated when we were little, so I guess she's doin' it by herself this year."

Colin looks up from his popcorn garland. "I know I'm like your favorite person ever, and you love spending your time with me." He smiles, and I laugh. "But why would you choose to spend Christmas with me instead of with your own family?"

"I guess they're a lot, and this just seems more relaxing to me," I tell him. "And besides, you're not the worst person to spend Christmas with."

Colin smiles. "Same to you, roomie."

"Is your family all in California right now?" I ask, but he doesn't respond. Nervous that I ruined our little moment, I watch as he eyes Rocky Balboa on the screen. I grab my glass of wine, feeling a bit awkward.

"I believe so," he finally answers. "I know my sister is this year."

I nod, not sure what to say next. We stare into each other's eyes, and I'm wondering what he's thinking at this moment. I want to know so badly.

"I think I'm done." He gives me a small smile, and I stand up, grabbing the garland from his hands. "Don't you trust me to hang it?" he asks tenderly.

I nod with a wide smile. I've never seen this side of Colin before, vulnerable and sweet.

We stand by the tree, and I watch as he lays the popcorn garland around the tree. I grab the box of the other decorations, and we silently decorate our Christmas tree. I hand him his glass of wine after we finish the last of the decorations.

"Cheers to an amazing Christmas," I say.

We tap glasses, and he gives me a wink. "Cheers, roomie."

SPRING

CHAPTER 46

A half-eaten cheesecake is sitting on my coffee table. I shove a big bite into my mouth as I slouch on my couch with Reese. Reese dips one of her chicken nuggets from McDonald's into some ranch as I moan with tons of blueberry cheesecake in my mouth.

"Is the cheesecake helping at all?" she asks.

I give her a face and shake my head. "It's making me feel worse, actually," I groan before standing up to do some jumping jacks in the middle of my living room. I stop halfway because I am out of breath. I lean my hands on both knees as Reese laughs. I then take a big sip of my wine. You always have to stay hydrated when you work out.

"I don't even want to know." Colin shakes his head at me as he sits down in his chair.

I wipe the sweat off my forehead and take a spoonful of cheesecake from the middle.

"Jade is acting like a child about this whole wedding fiasco," Reese explains, shoving a bunch of fries in her mouth.

I turn to her. "Says the girl eating a happy meal right now."

Reese rolls her eyes, and I stand back up, pacing in front of the television.

"Jade, you've lived in this city your whole life. There isn't one guy you know that could possibly take you?"

I cross my arms and lean my body on my hip. "Hmm, lemme see. No." I blink a couple of times. "There's a reason that all of these guys never worked out. Either they're crazy, weird, have girlfriends, or are *married*."

"Then what? It's either you go alone, or there's always your cousin…" Reese laughs.

"I don't appreciate you being so calm about my situation. The situation that is happening in one week!" I glance at Colin, who is weirdly silent, just sitting there.

I then look at Reese. "Even if I did contact someone, it's in a week, Reese. It doesn't give me enough time to catch up with any of them," I sigh.

"I bumped into your little friend Trevor the other day. Maybe he's a possibility?" Reese lets out a tiny laugh.

"Are you serious right now?" I glare at Reese before sitting back down on the couch.

"Wait, who's Trevor?" Colin asks.

"Some guy Jade dated. He's an engineer."

"Reese, you're forgetting that he's a five-foot-three, kind of round asshole who I dated because he drove a nice truck." I turn to Colin. "I was going through my truck phase, obviously."

"A truck phase?" Colin raises a brow. "Is that even a thing?"

Reese lets out a laugh, and I shake my head. "Well, the fucker broke up with me the morning of New Year's Eve, even though we had plans that night."

"Yeah, it was a low blow," Reese says.

"We're moving on." I shake my head, trying my hardest not to relive that horrid time in my life.

"Why don't you go with Colin?" Reese grins as she bites her straw gently. I look at Reese and then to Colin, who is dramatically shaking his head.

"What? Would that be the worst thing?" I ask.

Colin laughs. "Are you seriously considering asking me to be your date? Jade, c'mon. Just stop."

"What do you mean, just stop?" I turn to him. "I don't know if you know this, Colin, but I'm pretty desperate here."

"There's just no fucking way I'm going to your ex-boyfriend's wedding." Colin shakes his head again.

"If I had a choice, I wouldn't either, but I have to for Suzy," I say with a sigh. "And it will be humiliating to go without anyone."

Colin looks at me and lets out a groan. I realize my pity party might just work. I'm either drunk, or I've completely hit rock bottom to consider bringing Colin as my date. The date who will have to pretend to be my fake boyfriend, but I'll tell him on the way there—no need to freak him out, especially when he hasn't even agreed yet.

"Fuck, fine."

I jump enthusiastically as I simultaneously clap my hands. Colin holds up his finger, which makes me stop in my tracks.

"Under one condition." He pauses. I wait for his following statement, holding my breath.

"My band can practice anytime and anywhere we want in this apartment. I can smoke in the apartment if I want, and you can't have random dudes in the apartment."

I cross my arms. "Anything else?"

"As of right now, no."

Ten or twenty bricks have suddenly fallen off my chest, and I can breathe again. I just hope Colin has a tux.

CHAPTER 47

I help Colin load up Wes' car that we've borrowed for the weekend. We only have a couple of bags, including my bridesmaid dress and Colin's tux. Reese and Wes stand by the curb and watch us bicker as we throw all of our things in the trunk. They look like our parents, waving us off and reminding us to have fun. We give them one last wave as we drive away. I let out a dramatic sigh as Colin makes a turn down the street.

"Relax, roomie." Colin glances at me.

I kick my legs up on the dashboard as I imagine how this weekend will go. This past year, I've been pushing thoughts of this wedding to the side, as if it didn't exist. Now that it's here, I finally feel the nerves flood through me. I'm hoping I don't regret bringing Colin with me.

Twenty minutes into our drive—which consists of a big bag of potato chips, the radio blaring, and silence between Colin and me—I finally decide to tell him the truth about this weekend.

"Fake boyfriend?" He looks at me strangely.

I nod. "Just for this weekend. It's not like we've never pretended before."

Colin doesn't say anything. I guess he's regretting his decision, but I don't care. I need this. I need *him*.

"Okay," is all he says.

"I was thinking we can tell them that we've been dating for two months, and we met at a get-together, and—"

"Oh wow. You've put a lot of thought into this."

I turn to look at the side of his face. "What do you mean? We can't go in there blindly, Colin."

There's silence between us yet again, and the conversation ends immediately. I'm just glad I got that over with, and there's enough time for him to let the plan sink in. He raises the volume on the radio again, and I glance at his lips as he sings along to the song that's playing.

"So, your friend is marrying your ex-boyfriend?" Colin asks as he changes lanes.

I look at him, and he glances at me. I'm not sure why he's suddenly curious, but I nod as our eyes meet.

"Yes, exactly."

"And you're one of her bridesmaids."

I nod again.

"And you're okay with all of that?"

"Yes, I am," I say.

Colin glances at me before looking back at the road. His eyes seem to want to ask me a question.

"What?"

"Oh nothing," he says casually. "Just can't see you as a bridesmaid, that's all."

I lean my head against the window and let out a sigh. "Me neither."

"So why did you say yes?"

"Well, because I've known both of them for a long time. Suzy and I go way back. And she doesn't really have many friends."

Colin takes one of his hands off the steering wheel and rests it on my thigh. I look at his large hand and then back to the side of his face.

"Do you have a brain aneurysm or something?" I ask, shooing his hand away from my thigh.

"Well, if I'm going to be your boyfriend for the weekend, then I have to get used to how you feel, ya know?"

"No, I don't know. You are not going to touch me at all this weekend."

He lets out a laugh. "How can I be your *boyfriend* if I can't touch you?" he asks, glancing at me.

I nod. "All right, fine. You can touch me, but only my hands, thighs, and back. No kissing."

"Fine with me."

We fall silent once again, the only sound being the soothing music on the radio.

~

We pull up to Suzy's grandmother's white colonial three-story house. The neighborhood is just as quiet as I remember as we make our way to the front door, holding our heavy bags. The door creaks open, and a friendly Suzy approaches us. She gives me a hug as I set my bag on the wooden floor by the spiral stairs. Suzy wraps her arm around me as she waits for me to introduce her to Colin, my boyfriend.

"Suzy, this is—"

"You-you must be Jade's boyfriend." She coughs, trying to catch her breath as she takes in Colin.

"Colin." He smiles, reaching his hand out to shake hers. Suzy gives me a look, and I bite the inside of my cheek, thanking the gods I brought Colin.

We follow Suzy up the winding staircase as we make our way to a room on the third floor. "You guys are the last to arrive, so everyone else had the first pick of rooms," she tells us, opening the brown wooden door. "So, the guest room on the third floor is the only one that's available. The bed is smaller, and sadly there is no TV."

I look around the small, old-fashioned room and nod, dumping my bags onto the white linen bed.

"So, take all the time you need to get settled in then come downstairs because that's where everyone is gathering for cocktail hour. The rehearsal brunch will start in an hour." She beams, giving Colin one more glance before closing the door behind her. Knowing Suzy, I let out a sigh, realizing how detailed this whole wedding will be.

I walk over to the bathroom and close the door. I run the cold water over my hands and throw some onto my flushed face.

I'm able to take a shower and change pretty quickly. Colin, being the caveman he is, changes his shirt and is ready to go. We walk down the long staircase, and I feel Colin's hand touch my arm. We stop as soon as we hit the bottom floor.

"What's wrong?" I ask him.

"How did we meet again?" He gives me a kind smile.

"From a mutual friend," I say. I can hear everyone in the other room. My heart starts to beat even faster.

"What's your go-to drink?" he asks me.

I give him a look. "You know what I like to drink."

"Yeah, generally speaking. But as your boyfriend, I should know your go-to drink."

I look into his blue eyes and nod. "Good thinking. *Uh*, I'd say rosé or champagne."

Colin nods and walks past me. I glance in the mirror that's hung on the wall, and I fix my bangs as I follow Colin down the hallway, leading us to the room full of laughter and spoken words I can't make out.

The large open living room is full of long, white painted windows, floral couches, rustic wooden floors, and a brown brick fireplace on one of the pale white walls.

"Please tell me that's not your ex," Colin jokes as he grabs two mimosas from a tray by the archway. My eyes move around the whole room as I scan the familiar face by the fireplace. His elbow is perched on top of the wooden shelf of the fireplace, and the other is wrapped around Suzy's waist as she casually sips on her mimosa. I feel Colin's hand touch my wrist, and I rip my eyes away from the familiar sharp chin, thin frame, and short, gelled blonde hair.

I take a big sip of my drink, and I follow Colin across the room. We stand by one of the large windows, and I glance at the tall, beautiful oak trees in the backyard.

"Are you surprised?" I look up at Colin. He's standing confidently in his navy-blue pants and white polo. Colin always has a way of looking so comfortable in his skin. I envy that.

"Just didn't peg you for a girl who would like a guy who wears New Balance sneakers."

I roll my eyes, glancing at Noah's terrible taste in clothes.

"Does everything I say annoy you?" Colin says, taking a sip of his drink.

I look up at him and smile. "Yes."

Colin shakes his head but ends up giving me a little crooked smile. I move my frizzy hair away from my shoulders and let out a deep breath as I hook my arms around Colin's muscular bicep as if that sudden deep breath was my boost of confidence. Colin looks down at me as I look up at him. He doesn't move or say a word about what I just did.

"In my defense, Noah looked way better when I dated him," I whisper in his ear. "And besides, we were young. I had no idea what my type was."

My attention is immediately interrupted by Helen, Suzy's mother. She's standing by the bar a couple of feet away from us. She's wearing a loose sundress, and her long red hair is tied neatly in a perfect bun. She calls out my name as she waves her hand gracefully for me to come to her. I give Colin a look to follow, and we make our way over to the mother of the bride.

"If it isn't Jade's date. Hello, young man. I'm Helen, the mother of the bride. It's a pleasure to finally meet you," Helen smiles wide as she places her hand against her chest.

Colin puts his hand out, giving the back of her hand a simple kiss. What is this? The 1940s, Colin? Helen lets out a little giggle as Colin releases her hand.

"The pleasure is all mine, ma'am. I'm Colin Chase." He smiles kindly at her.

"Oh please, call me Helen," she says. "What I'm wondering is, where in the world has Jade been hiding you?" She lets out a loud laugh as she famously pinches one of my cheeks. I give a fake laugh as I try to find the best answer for her, but I'm utterly speechless as I take a big and long sip of my mimosa. Why am I so nervous? Colin lets out what I'm guessing is a fake laugh as he firmly attaches his arm around my waist, pulling me in closer.

"I guess Jade wanted me all for herself," he says to Helen.

They both look at me, and I put my hands up enthusiastically. "Guilty!"

Helen laughs and pinches my other cheek.

"Jade has always been so funny." She smiles. Someone comes from behind Helen, and she kindly excuses herself from us, thankfully.

I release myself from his hold, and I look at him strangely as he turns and orders another drink. Colin leans against the bar, and I study the blank look on his face.

"What?" he asks, grabbing the drink from the bartender.

"Since when is your last name Chase?"

Colin looks up at the ceiling as if he's trying to find an answer to a question he already knows. "*Hmm.* For about twenty-seven years," he says sarcastically.

I frown. "Okay, why haven't you ever told me?"

He looks straight into my eyes and says dryly, "You never asked."

"And by the way," I say quietly, just in case anyone can hear me, "cool it with the body grabbing."

Colin takes my hand into his and pulls me to an area with fewer people. "Aren't we supposed to pretend we're in a relationship?"

"Yeah, so?" I cross my arms.

"That's how you do it then, Ms. Actress," he mocks as he tries to pinch my cheek, but I quickly swat him away.

"What? You don't mind when Helen does it."

"I don't because Mrs. Lodge is the sweetest woman alive. Unlike you," I say.

"*Ouch.* I'm going to pretend you didn't just say that," he says, leaning in and grabbing my butt. I hit his hand and push him away.

Colin lets out a laugh. "I get full reign this weekend, roomie," he says as he walks away, leaving me alone. My heart feels like it's beating a mile a minute as I stand frozen, watching Colin's broad shoulders leave the room.

"Well, well, well. Look what the cat dragged in," I hear behind me. I finish the last of my drink as I turn around, meeting eyes with

Marni Mathews. She laughs obnoxiously as she playfully taps my bare shoulder.

"If it isn't, Marni," I say, trying my hardest to not look disgusted as I scan her face.

"Be careful, Jade, it's only eleven o'clock. You don't want to be plastered for the rehearsal brunch."

I give her a fake smile. "Don't worry about me, Marni. Don't you have maid of honor duties to worry about?"

"Oh, I have plenty, actually. Including everything I did before the wedding, like the bridal shower you were too busy to attend." She glares at me as she says this.

I wasn't able to go to Suzy's bridal shower a couple of months ago. It was during the time I had a lead role in an off-Broadway show. Suzy understood, and that's all that mattered. I think she was just happy that I sent her a lovely gift. Suzy's sister told me that the bridal shower was a flop anyway. It was nice that they were all together celebrating Suzy, but Marni's party planning wasn't one for the books. I guess ordering every type of sushi and having that be the only food available isn't always the move. Everyone at the party ended up going to some diner after the party, which I think is hilarious.

"Perfect timing," I say under my breath as a waiter holding a tray of mimosas walks by. I give him my empty glass as I take a big sip of my next drink.

"So, where's your mystery man?" Marni crosses her arms.

"He's, um…"

"Right here," Colin says as I feel his arm around my waist. I look up at his chiseled face, and I watch Marni's pathetic grin turn to a frown.

"Colin, this is—"

"Marci, isn't it?" Colin says, staring into her eyes.

"It's, um, it's Marni." She looks down, pushing her brown hair away from her face. "I'm the maid of honor."

"Oh, right." Colin laughs. He looks at me, gently touching my chin. "You were right."

I let out a laugh as well as I study Marni's confused and insecure face. She abruptly turns around as she grabs her short, chubby husband away from the hors d'oeuvres table.

"This is Neil, my husband," Marni mutters, smacking her husband's chest as he chews the little quiche sloppily in his mouth. He gives us a cheeky smile as he wipes the crumbs off his fingers. Then, he offers me and Colin his hand.

"I'm Neil," he sings. Marni rolls her eyes and smacks the rest of his crumbs that landed on his curly beard.

"Babe, let's get another drink. Excuse us," I say, grabbing Colin's hand away from Marni and Neil.

"Babe?" Colin laughs as we walk away from them.

"Sorry." I gently bite my lip. "Gosh, did you see her face when you said the wrong name?" I laugh, bumping my head against his chest. "How did you know I hate her?"

Colin shrugs. "I know a bitch when I see one. Don't underestimate me, roomie."

The rehearsal "brunch" is a complete breeze. It's going way better than expected, even though I have to completely improvise a speech in front of everyone. I can see everyone's faces—Noah's parents especially and his lumberjack sister. They're wondering the same thing I'm thinking. Why am I here?

Luckily, I have not yet had that awkward encounter with Noah. Well, except the moment when we accidentally made eye contact when everyone was getting settled at the table. We stared into each other's eyes for a split second. Noah gave me a tiny smile as he looked down at his empty glass plate and waited for Suzy to come and save him from across the table.

~

I set out my black evening party dress onto the bed for the bachelorette party, set to begin in one hour. I hear Colin in the bathroom as I quickly take off my tank top and denim skirt, leaving me in only my bra and panties.

The bathroom door flings open abruptly, slamming against the yellow wall. It gives my body a slight jolt as I quickly cover my half-naked body with my hands. Colin comes strolling out in only a pair of navy-blue slacks with his hair soaking wet and his beard slightly trimmed. He grabs his black cotton shirt that's hanging on the desk chair as he softly hums a song.

"Colin! Do you mind?" I yell as I grab the blanket from the bed.

"What's the problem?" he asks nonchalantly. I point to my lack of clothing, and he gives me a tiny grin.

"My bad, roomie. Let's just call it even because I'm half-naked as well."

I let out a loud huff, grab my dress, and run past him into the bathroom. I then slam the door behind me. I lean against the door, breathing heavily. I can hear Colin laugh on the other side of the door, and I remind myself that Colin was the best choice, fondly thinking back to all the looks and stares he got at brunch. Everyone's a sucker for blue eyes and dimples. Even Noah couldn't acknowledge Colin from across the table. Whenever Colin said a word, I watched as Noah's face peered down into his scrambled eggs.

~

Suzy and the rest of her bridal party, including Marni and Noah's sister, Madison, are standing by the stairs. I walk down slowly as I watch them mingle and giggle, holding glasses of wine in their hands.

"Sorry, I'm a little late; I was getting ready," I say to Suzy as I walk down the last step, eyeing Suzy's veil and sash that reads "bride" in beautiful script.

"Shocker," I read Marni's lips as she rolls her eyes.

"The limo's here," Suzy squeals as she looks out the tall window. I follow the girls out the door. As I'm being shoved into the limo, I wonder what Colin and the guys are doing tonight. A glass of champagne is immediately welcomed into my hands and loud music and woos from the girls are ringing in my ears.

Suzy orders all the girls these delicious fruity mixed drinks the second we walk in. She said it was called the pineapple sunrise surprise, and it is their speciality here. It even came with a cute umbrella, a bendy straw, and a slice of pineapple on the rim! I'm barely a quarter way through my drink, but I am already feeling it. My already tight dress is sticking to my body, and my frizzy bangs are wet from the sweat from my dripping forehead. I fan some air with my hands, and I make my way over to the bar for some water. I'm lucky to find a seat by the edge of the bar to catch my breath. We've already been to three clubs tonight, but I didn't drink at the first two because I was too busy taking care of Suzy.

A sweaty and intoxicated Suzy suddenly approaches me, clinging to me as she sits on the barstool next to me. Suzy wraps her arms around me and lets out a loud laugh in my ear. "I'm so happy you're here, Jade!" she yells over the music.

"Cheers to you, Suzy!" I raise my glass up.

"Cheers to me." She laughs as we take a sip of our strangely strong drinks... Suzy moves a piece of my hair away from my face as she leans half her body onto the bar. "Sometimes I wonder if I'm even marriage material, ya know?"

I look at her and tilt my head. The music is blaring loud, and I'm not sure if I heard her correctly.

"Noah's great. I love him and all." She burps and, seconds later, laughs. We don't call her Suzy-Boozy for no reason...

"I know you do," I say as her arms are still wrapped around me.

"I'm gonna be a wife. Can you believe that?" she slurs. "Like, Noah's ding dong is my forever ding dong." She laughs, making me laugh as well.

She gently points her finger into my cheek. "You're different, Jadey. You date lots and lots of men." She smiles. "That's what Noah says."

"Noah says I date a lot?" How would he know that? Even if that's true.

She nods obnoxiously. "Sometimes I-I get second thoughts, and I tell him and-and I always bring you up because you have the life, Jadey. Noah says you're just different from me."

"Different in what way?" I say over the music.

Suzy holds one hand up in the air and takes a long sip of her drink. She almost finishes it before she continues to talk. "You date extremely hot guys like Colin. Everyone's jealous." She covers her mouth with her hand as she laughs.

I give her a smile. If only she knew...

"He's just so beautiful. Tell me, Jadey, how's the sex? I need to know."

I laugh, playfully hitting her shoulder. I've never had conversations like this with Suzy. I guess because I never wanted to hear about her and Noah's sex life. "It's mind-blowing."

"Noah's family hates me," she says in my ear. "I get compared to you all the time. They want me to be like you. But-but we all know I can never live up to you, J-Jade."

"Suzy..." I stare into her big green eyes.

She shakes her head, giving me a small smile. "I love that we can always be so honest."

I nod, but before I can say anything more, she speaks again. "Noah makes me go *shhh*." She laughs, putting her finger to her lips. I want to ask more questions, but Suzy leans in and gives my cheek a kiss. Soon one of Suzy's friends, Shannon, comes over to us and drags Suzy away from me.

～

I stumble into the room at three a.m. and try my hardest not to wake up Colin, who is sound asleep on his side of the bed. My feet feel so heavy that my balance isn't really the best. I accidentally hit something with my right hip and, of course, it makes a loud sound.

"Jade?" I hear from the bed. Colin sits up a little, and due to the large bare window in our room, the moonlight is hitting Colin's shirtless body. I swear he looks like a Calvin Klein model with bedhead.

"*Shhh!*" I say to the glass frog that I bumped into by the side of the bed.

"Are you drunk?" he asks, turning on the little lamp by the bed.

"No, are you drunk?" I laugh.

Colin rolls his eyes and gets up. I turn away from him because all he's wearing is boxer briefs. Suddenly, I feel two large hands around my waist, leading me to the bed. I plop on the soft mattress and lower my back horizontally on the bed. Colin picks up my legs and fixes my body so I'm on my side.

I rest my palm against my forehead and let out a laugh when I feel him taking off my strappy heels.

"Why are you being so nice to me?" I ask.

"What?" he asks.

I laugh. "Well, you're usually an asshole to me. Like the biggest one."

He doesn't say anything, and I let out a big breath, blowing my bangs away from my eyes.

"Remember when we were set up?" I laugh. "You were such an asshole. A dick, to say the least. You thought I was ugly. But I'm not ugly," I cry. "I was a model. I can show you my port-folio."

"Maybe another time," Colin says, walking into the bathroom. I hear the sink faucet turn on and off. Seconds later, Colin hands me a cup of water and insists I take a sip.

"I thought I'd never see you again, but no! You became my roommate." I laugh. "The asshole who thought I was ugly shares the same bathroom with me."

Colin takes the cup of water from my hands and sets it beside me on the side table.

"Colin?"

"Yes, Jade."

"W-why were you such an asshole to me?" I yawn.

"I was an asshole because you weren't like every other girl, and it scared me."

And with that, I fall right to sleep.

~

The next morning, I wake up feeling like shit. Colin's gone, probably already downstairs eating breakfast. I slowly get up and finish the last of the water that's next to my bed. I walk into the bathroom and rest both of my hands on the counter, staring at my messy hair and the dark black circles under my eyes. *I look like who did it and ran.* How much did I drink last night? I don't remember much from last night, besides the mixed drink Suzy ordered for us and the one tequila shot with those guys in sombrero hats.

I take a quick shower and throw on one of my sundresses. I am so hungover that putting on a bra requires too much energy.

I head downstairs, and the smell of all the different breakfast foods makes me want to throw up. Speaking of throwing up, I now remember doing that a lot in the middle of the night. I'd say three or four times. At least I got a couple of hours of sleep.

"Good morning, sleeping beauty," Suzy teases, taking a bite of her omelet.

"I need coffee," I sigh, "and Tylenol."

Ella, who works in the kitchen, hands me a black steaming cup of coffee and a couple of Tylenol. I thank her and plop on one of the kitchen chairs with Suzy and Colin.

"Ella will make you anything you desire, and we have delicious mimosas as well," Suzy tells me.

I shake my head. "I'm too hungover for mimosas. Remind me to never drink again," I say, lowering my head onto the table.

"You were pretty drunk last night," Colin says.

About that...

"Hey Suzy, what was in those fruity drinks you ordered for us yesterday?" I can't believe I feel this hung over after barely drinking the entire night.

Suzy laughs and shakes her head. "Pineapple juice, apple juice, and...seven shots of tequila."

"Seven?" Colin and I ask at the same time. No wonder it got me so messed up.

I take a sip of my coffee, and the caffeine makes me feel a little better.

"And how are you not hungover too? You drank just as much as me, Suzy."

"I guess I was a tad hungover this morning, but after some yoga and one of Ella's famous kale smoothies, I feel like a million bucks." Suzy smiles widely.

I groan and rest my head on my hand. My head seriously feels like it weighs a thousand pounds. "I swear I haven't been this drunk since junior year of high school."

"Colin is such a great boyfriend. He told me that he held your hair when you were throwing up last night."

I look up and stare at Colin. "You did?"

"Yeah, it's no biggie." He shrugs it off.

"Yes, it is! Noah would never do that for me. He'd probably walk away seconds after if he saw it." She laughs.

I tilt my head to the side and give him a small smile. "I had no idea you did that for me, Colin. Thank you."

"Everyone needs someone to do that for them once in their lifetime," he says, giving me a smile back.

Suzy shakes my arm and stands to her feet. "Jade, hurry up and eat. There are a lot of activities planned for today."

She hands me a schedule and walks out of the kitchen. I look at the cover sheet of the schedule, which is a large picture of Suzy and Noah just gazing into each other's eyes.

"It's a little much." Colin laughs.

I grin. "It's a typical Suzy thing to do."

I scan through each page, and my eyes catch a couple of things like ceramics and towel folding.

"This is just too much right now."

Colin shrugs, cutting into his eggs Benedict.

"What did you and the guys do last night?" I ask him.

"We went wine tasting," he tells me.

I raise a brow. "And how was that?"

"Fine. We didn't get as lit as you and the girls."

I touch my chest, trying my hardest to forget last night. "How was…" I pause. "Noah?"

"He was fine. I realized towards the beginning of the night that he was staying far away from me," Colin says with a laugh.

"I wonder why he's so intimidated by you."

Colin runs his hands through his dirty blonde hair and shrugs nonchalantly. "Have you looked at me?"

"You're so full of yourself."

"Noah's just low-key jealous that I have what he used to have," he says casually.

"What do you mean? He's happy with Suzy."

"Yeah, he is, but it's human nature to be jealous of another guy being all up on your old girl."

"Old girl?" I raise a brow, folding my arms jokingly.

"You know what I mean."

"Yeah, yeah, yeah," I say, taking a sip of my coffee.

⁓

An hour after breakfast, Colin and I head back to our room. "You should really make your bed. It sets the tone for the whole day." Colin burps, biting into his second egg sandwich, which he brought back to the room. I glance over at him; he's leaning his shirtless body against the door hinge. "Don't you have anything better to do today?"

"Well, today hasn't exactly begun," he says, throwing Suzy's wedding schedule onto the bed.

"Okay, well, if it sets the tone, then can you at least help me? You use fifty percent of this bed, right?"

Colin finishes the last bite of his sandwich and walks over slowly with both hands shoved in his cotton shorts.

"So, tell me, how are my acting skills so far?" Colin asks,

reaching over to grab one of the sides of the quilt.

"Not too bad," I say.

Colin raises a brow. "Wow, is Jade, aka roomie, complimenting me?"

"Ha-ha, very funny," I say uncomfortably.

Colin puts his hands up and smiles. "I'll take it. But you know, we can practice if you want."

"Practice?" I cross my arms.

"You heard me."

"Yeah, I did, but I'm a bit confused as to what you mean."

Colin lets out a little chuckle, and I'm silent as I watch him throw a few pillows by the headboard. He runs his fingers along the lines of his abs and walks over to my side of the bed. Colin plops down and stretches his neck to look at me. I'm still silent. He reaches over to me and wraps both of his large hands around my waist. "I was thinking more along the lines of something like this."

He runs his tattooed hand up my arm, and I want to move away. I don't want Colin to see how much my body is reacting to his touch. Colin licks the corner of his mouth as a small smile begins to form. I feel Colin's strong arms wrap around me as he lays me on the bed beside him. My breathing becomes still, and I stare into his eyes, waiting for him to surprise me again. We hear a soft knock at the door, and I try to get up, but he shakes his head, his arms are now on both sides of me.

"Come in," he breathes, his eyes never leaving mine.

"Oh, sorry to bother you two love birds, but Noah and I want everyone from the party to join us outside on the patio."

Colin kisses my cheek and looks over to Suzy, who is standing by the door. We both nod. Suzy is frozen by the door, still watching us.

"Suzy?" I say.

"*Uh*, yeah, sorry." She nervously laughs, closing the door behind her.

"How'd you know she'd come by?" I say.

Colin stands up and walks over to the bathroom. "I didn't."

CHAPTER 48

"Noah and I are so incredibly grateful for each and every one of you. Thank you for joining us on our magical wedding weekend."

Ah, there's the bar.

"I really hope everyone's having as much fun as Noah and I are already having."

I will...in thirty seconds.

"Jade?"

I turn my head dramatically towards the wedding party on the outside deck. Close, yet so far from that tray of champagne... My sundress flows from the light breeze, and my body freezes as I make eye contact with Suzy.

"Did I do something wrong?" I ask Suzy. Maybe champagne this early in the morning isn't allowed?

I glance at Marni, who lets out an obnoxious laugh before covering her mouth. She then rolls her eyes.

Suzy gives me a strange look but quickly recovers, giving me a smile. "No, silly, didn't you read the schedule?"

"Why would she? She's too busy at the bar." Marni crosses her arms as she gives me a fake smile.

I blink a couple of times and turn my direction back to Suzy. "I'm sorry, Suzy, I haven't. I guess I got a little distracted by Marni."

Suzy looks at Marni then back at me. She gives Noah a kiss on the cheek and slowly walks over to me. All I can hear is Suzy's heels tapping the wooden pavement.

"Do you remember when I called you a couple of weeks ago, and you agreed to teach the girls how to sew? Marni—well, actually—I thought it would be fun to make our own scarves today and wear them at lunch. You know how much I adore the '50s."

"Of course! How could I forget?" I fake a laugh as she reaches for a big hug.

Oh, I definitely forgot...

⁓

Suzy hooks her arm with mine as we make our way inside, the rest of the girls following behind. Up the stairs to the left is Suzy's grandmother's sewing room. It's surprising how many rooms this home has. There are two long tables in the middle of the red-painted room with medium-sized sewing machines and every fabric I can think of. Suzy gives me a little shove and claps her hands as she sits in front of a sewing machine; the rest follow suit. I dive right into the basics. My teaching skills are not up to par, but I show Suzy and the rest of the bridesmaids the best I can. After everyone is settled in and sewing their scarf, I eye the empty machine next to a tall window facing the large backyard. It's full of oak trees, a beautiful gazebo, and I can't help but notice the groomsmen in their athletic attire.

"Football, it's in the schedule." Helen winks beside me. It was as if she read my mind. I notice Noah talking to a couple of his friends, and his dad stretching to the side. I play with my blue and green fabric, trying to spot a tall, blonde guy who happens to be my fake boyfriend for the weekend.

"I think you forgot this."

I jump in my seat as I tear my eyes away from the window. Colin is standing in front of me, giving me a half-smile, exposing his right dimple. His dirty blonde hair is slightly messy, and his face is sweaty as he holds my sweater in his hands.

"I thought you might be cold," he kindly says to me. I look down, kind of embarrassed as I feel the girls stare at us. I stand up and walk around the table so I'm facing him.

"You're all sweaty," I say as he hands me my sweater.

"Snuck in a run," he says. His blues are still glued to mine, never leaving contact as if we are the only two people in this dusty room.

"You two are the cutest," Suzy says in awe. She leans her chin against her soft palm as if she's watching some sappy romance movie. "Colin, the boys are probably waiting for you. You know, the football game and all," Suzy tells him.

Colin runs his hand through his hair and nods. "I should probably—"

"Yeah." I look down at my feet, hugging my sweater.

Suddenly, I feel a large hand pressing on my lower back, pulling me forward. I feel my heart beat faster and faster as the heat rises from my stomach to my chest. Colin's lips are getting closer and closer. Time stands still as I close my eyes, parting my lips slightly. My body is making me feel all sorts of ways. These are feelings I've never felt before. I feel a blissful tingle of surprise as Colin's lips touch mine. I melt when his hands touch my cheek as his tongue touches mine. My knees buckle as Colin releases from our kiss, his eyes bleeding into mine. Colin turns away from me, making eye contact with the girls in the room. All their jaws are on the floor.

"Ladies." Colin grins, leaving me alone with my thoughts and wet panties.

⁓

The 1950s-themed picnic consisted of three things for me: a loud trumpet playing in one ear, conversation and laughter in my other ear, and my mind replaying that kiss with Colin. Why did Colin kiss me? What was going on in his mind? I'm so damn confused as I move my garlic-crusted shrimp around on my plate, glancing at Colin, who is smiling at something Helen says to him.

⁓

After towel folding and dance class, Colin and I lazily head upstairs. I watch his long, muscular arm open the door to our room. There's only silence between us.

"I'm exhausted," I finally say, falling onto the soft bed.

Colin falls beside me, letting out a tiny yawn. "Agreed."

I let out a laugh, turning my head, so I'm facing him. His eyes are glued to the white painted ceiling, one hand placed against his chest and the other only a couple of inches from mine. We make eye contact, and I quickly turn away, mentally slapping myself for feeling so awkward and nervous around Colin. Colin lets out a little chuckle, and I turn my head slightly just to see his dimpled smile.

"What's so funny?"

"Cute." He says flirtatiously, tugging on the scarf I've tied around my neck. I sit up, groaning. I unravel it, take it off in seconds, and throw it across the room.

"Someone's aggressive." He laughs, looking up at me. "It looked good on you."

"I forgot I still had it on. It's definitely not my best work," I say with a sigh.

"Hey, sorry about earlier," he says.

"Earlier?"

"You know, that kiss. I got caught up in the moment. Everyone was watching us." He sits up. "Thought I'd win you some brownie points, roomie." He gives me a little shove and gets off the bed, walking towards the bathroom. He takes off his shirt in one motion, throwing it at me. "Sorry for breaking one of your rules. It won't happen again," he says in a serious tone but quickly recovers, letting out a loud laugh. "Fuck, I can't believe I just apologized."

"Yeah, I can't believe it either," I say.

"I call first shower." He winks, closing the bathroom door behind him. I hear the shower turn on as I sit still, staring intensely at the old wooden floor. I feel pathetic. Heck, I feel crazy for ever thinking Colin might have felt what I was feeling—the feeling of electricity throughout my body just from that one kiss.

CHAPTER 49

E very little girl dreams of this day. The feeling of excitement and joy as she walks down the rose petal aisle with her long, pearly white dress following behind as those unexplained butterflies enter the pit of her stomach. The man of her dreams is waiting patiently for her at the altar, trying his hardest not to shed a tear from the pure beauty he sees in front of him as she walks in sync with the sound of the cello playing gracefully.

And the bridesmaids, feeling relieved and pleased as they watch the bride smile behind her veil. This. Exactly this. All of this is Suzy's dream. She's the little girl. The little girl with red pigtails, sitting on her leather couch and looking through every wedding magazine her mother had collected.

At this very moment, I'm the bridesmaid that feels pleased as I watch one of my best friends kiss her father on the cheek. Noah and Mr. Lodge shake hands, and a tear escapes as I watch Noah lift Suzy's veil away from her perfect face. As I stand in my silky turquoise dress, watching Suzy get married, I glance at Colin. He's sitting a few rows back, hands in his lap, and his eyes are focused on Suzy and Noah. I can't help but wonder what his thoughts are at this very moment. The sound of love and bliss moves everyone in the room as we listen to the bride and groom's vows.

This morning was a total blur. Getting ready and making sure Suzy had everything she needed made me forget about yesterday and the kiss I shared with Colin. The kiss I needed to shove to the back of my mind. The kiss that distracts me from seeing how the navy-blue suit he is wearing hugs him perfectly in all the right places.

Everyone claps and stands as Suzy and Noah have their first passionate kiss as a married couple. Tears fall down my cheek as I watch them walk hand in hand down the aisle. Colin and I make eye contact, and a sharp sting hits me when he looks away.

A glass of champagne is immediately placed in my hands at the beginning of the reception. Suzy and Noah are officially announced as Mr. and Mrs. Jadeson.

"Jade Jadeson. That would be one for the books," Colin playfully mocks.

"Is that what you do? Sneak up on someone and say something unoriginal?" I shake my head.

"Hey, I think it was quite amusing." Colin chuckles, taking a sip of his drink.

"I just can't believe it took you this long to figure out his last name," I say, walking away from him, hoping he'll follow.

"In my defense, I never cared enough to ever learn the guy's full name."

"And to think, if you took some time to learn my friend's name, you could have been mocking me all weekend." I give him a cute pout.

Colin smiles. "You mean ex-boyfriend, not friend, roomie."

I cross my arms. "Noah's my friend."

"You can't be friends with someone you've had sex with."

"Says who?"

"Says me." Colin stares into my eyes, giving my forehead a light tap. "If you'll excuse me, a sassy brunette is dying for me to dance with her."

I tilt my head to the side as I imagine Colin's eyes set on someone else. Colin walks past me, brushing his skin against mine. Then he grabs my wrist, leading me to the dance floor. I let out a laugh as I wrap my arms around his neck. Feeling those hands touch my bareback gives me tiny goosebumps all over my body.

"Smooth, Chase." I grin, leaning my chin against his shoulder.

"And to think, if you took the time in the last year or so to actually learn my last name, you could have…." He pauses. "Called me by my last name."

I laugh. "So original."

"I try."

We stop talking as we sway to the soft music playing, and at *this* exact moment, I never want it to end. Helen ends up nonchalantly taking Colin from me, and I laugh as he moves her gracefully around the dance floor. A light chill in the air sends shivers down my spine as I make my way towards the house. The back door creaks open, and the lovely scent of lavender sweeps over me as I make my way to my room.

"Oh, hey."

I stop in my tracks as I spot Noah sitting on the third step of the staircase.

"Hey," is all I can muster. Silence fills the room, and I'm not sure what else to say. I don't think I remember the last time I was in a room alone with Noah. "Is-is everything okay?"

Noah gives me a nod and a smile. I'm relieved yet still confused about why he's sitting all alone on the stairs.

"Would you like to join me?" His eyes meet mine. I don't say a word as I nod, sitting beside him. We sit silently for another couple of minutes. It should feel awkward, but it doesn't. I guess after knowing each other for so long, we somehow fall right back to the way it used to be, comfortably silent moments.

"I just needed a little bit of a breather. You know how my family is." He laughs nervously. "I just feel bad for Suzy."

"Oh yeah, you got yourself a real trooper there. She must really love you," I joke.

Noah lets out a little laugh, gently knocking his shoulder with mine. "Your date isn't so bad. I was expecting the worst, I guess."

I turn my head over to Noah and give him a smile. "Thanks."

"I think it's really great how far we've come." Noah smiles without showing any teeth.

"Yeah, I know. It's so crazy how life has a way of turning out differently than you think it will."

Noah shrugs. "Yeah, I always thought it would be you walking down the aisle."

I laugh. "Me too."

"Crazy, huh?"

"Completely, but I think we always knew that I could never be a Jade Jadeson."

Noah lets out a loud laugh, hitting his knee. "Yeah, that would be tragic."

"I've missed you." I laugh with him. I wipe a tear away from his eye, and I hear him let out a tiny sigh. "You were always my person...until you weren't." I pause. "I hope you know that I'm truly happy for you and Suzy. I honestly wouldn't want Suzy with anyone else. She deserves someone as wonderful as you."

Noah turns his head so that our eyes are level. His smile quickly turns to a sulk, and I notice that he suddenly looks very sad. "Jade, I'm not sure if this is the right time to tell you this. Heck, it's probably never the right time, but I can't live with this lie anymore." He pauses. "Especially after what you just said. I-I think you deserve to know the truth."

"Noah, what are you talking about?"

The look on Noah's face tells me that I'm not going to like what he's about to say.

"I hope this doesn't change anything regarding this weekend," he says, "but the truth is…I was cheating on you with Suzy a year before we broke up."

I was cheating on you with Suzy.
I was cheating on you with Suzy.
I was cheating on you with Suzy.

That horrible, dreadful sentence replays in my ear as I watch his lips form words I can't hear anymore. I stand up, and I feel his hand grab mine, but I quickly pull it away.

"There you guys are!" I hear in the distance as Suzy walks towards us. Her rosy cheeks turn pale as she takes in the serious expression on my face.

"Jade…" she says quietly.

Without saying a word, I run. I want to be as far away as I can be from those liars I called my friends. I swing the back doors open, making a loud thump. I head back to the wedding party, trying to catch my breath. Suzy and Noah are behind me seconds later, looking like scared puppies.

"Jade," Suzy cries.

"How could you? How could you?!? Suzy! You are my best friend! He was my boyfriend!"

Tears fall down Suzy's cheeks, and she nods, her eyes falling to the ground in shame. Marni stands beside Suzy, wrapping her arms around her. "It's okay, Suzy; she was going to find out eventually."

I tilt my head to the side. This large backyard filled with tons of people seems to be closing in on me. I look around as every eye is glued to me, knowing exactly what happened—everyone but me.

"Really? Everyone is in on the truth but me?"

"It's not like that, Jade." Suzy cries even harder. "We never wanted to hurt you."

"You never wanted to hurt me? So, lying all these years? Going behind my back?" I shake my head. "You're disgusting!" I yell at her. I turn around, and it feels like every single person there is staring at me.

"The show's over," I say, running away as fast as I can.

I catch my breath by a large oak tree a couple of houses away. I hear footsteps behind me. "Jade?"

I turn around to find Colin walking up to me. "Colin, please. Just leave."

"No."

"No?" I say, wiping the tears away from my tear-stained cheeks. "I'm the laughingstock of this whole wedding, Colin. Everyone seems to know but me."

"I didn't."

I shake my head. "I don't need your pity. You did me a favor and pretended to be my boyfriend so I wouldn't look pathetic. I guess the lesson of this story is that I've always been Noah's pathetic ex-girlfriend." I laugh. "Can you please do me a favor and leave? The party's over. You did your job. We can go back to being roommates, and I can go back to my pitiful life."

"We're not leaving yet."

"What?"

"Come with me." He reaches his hand out for me to grab, but I shake my head. "Oh, c'mon. Can you trust me?"

⁓

Colin asks me to wait for him by the oak tree. I watch him run back to the house to grab our car. He picks me up on the side of the street without saying a word, and we sit in silence as he drives. I lean my head against the window and close my eyes, replaying everything that just happened. I'm trying my hardest not to cry as Colin pulls into some sketchy parking lot.

"If you're going to kill me, just tell me now," I say, realizing how depressed I sound.

"Always the one with a joke." He shakes his head, amused.

I follow Colin across the parking lot and into a bar named Bar. I really didn't have to ask him where we were; the title gave it away. Cheap tequila is served, and cigarette smoke surrounds the place. Colin takes my hand as we make our way to the bar. Colin orders us two shots as we sit down on the dirty stools. I lean my arms on the paint-chipped bar and sulk, too exhausted and sad to even acknowledge the people currently around us—dirty, old, and already drunk bikers.

"Why are we here?" I turn to Colin. The bartender slides two yellow-colored shots towards us, and Colin holds his up, motioning for me to do the same. I sigh, holding mine up as well.

"To leaving those prissy yet dreadful people behind us—" But before Colin can finish his terrible speech, I take the shot. I already ordered two more before Colin even takes his. Colin matches my disgusted face but is ready for round two as the bartender refills our glasses.

"To all the liars out there. This one's for you." I laugh, taking my second shot. The bartender refills mine again, and I once again, take it seconds before Colin even takes his.

"Slow down, partner." Colin laughs. The alcohol feels amazing as it runs through my body. The loud music playing makes my body sway.

"Let's dance!" But before Colin can answer, I'm dancing with some man with a gray beard. I feel Colin's hand wrap around my waist, pulling me back to the barstool.

"Don't you just hate people? Why trust them to begin with, ya know? You live your life, and you love people, but what's the point? Right, Earl?" I laugh, pointing to Earl, who has fallen asleep beside me.

"These dirty biker dudes are more sincere than Suzy has ever been. And Noah?" I let out an obnoxious laugh. "Don't get me started on that fucker. And to think, the year he was banging Suzy behind my back, I was so depressed because he never wanted me. Who knew he was getting it from someone else—someone I thought was my best friend? So pathetic." I shrug. "Makes sense, I guess."

"What makes sense?" Colin asks.

"Every guy that's ever been with me gets tired of me."

"Oh, please." Colin shakes his head.

I nod. "It's true. They like me in the beginning, but then something changes, and they want to break up. It's my personality, or maybe I'm awful in bed."

"I highly doubt that," Colin says over the music.

"How would you know? You were repulsed the second you saw me."

Colin shakes his head.

"Yes! I had to lie that I owned a bird just to get away from the way you were looking at me," I say, playing with the stem on my cherry.

"You reminded me of someone I knew, and it scared me."

I laugh. "Oh please, that's a load of crap."

"It's true, Jade." Colin's playfulness leaves and his seriousness comes out.

"Okay, then who did I remind you of?"

"Someone I used to love deeply."

I look down at my empty shot glass. "I don't know what to say to that."

"Because you're drunk." He laughs.

I shake my head. "If I reminded you of someone you loved, then why didn't you like me?"

"Oh, so you wanted something to happen between us?"

"I'm not answering that."

Colin chuckles. "You want the truth?"

I look at him. "I think I deserve that, considering what happened an hour ago."

Colin nods. "The truth is, if you must know, the person I love or loved isn't too fond of me. She hates my guts. I really hurt her, and I knew I'd never get her back. When I met you, you reminded me so much of her. You're this beautiful, free-spirited, know-it-all, and I wanted to always have you in my life, and I knew if I just slept with you that night, there would be a chance I'd never see you again."

"So, you were an asshole just so I would stay in your life?"

"I probably should have just said that. It would have been easier, so yes."

I nod. "What did you do to her?"

"I left without saying goodbye. And I broke up with her over a text message."

I lean my head against his shoulder. "Oh, gosh. No."

"I know. Terrible."

"And for your information, I am not a know-it-all. I just know a lot of things."

"Hence, know-it-all."

⌇

Colin and I decided to take a cab back to the house. Well, Colin decided. I'm busy singing that Bon Jovi song from earlier at the bar. I cling onto Colin's muscular body, and I sing in his ear as the yellow cab pulls over to the curb. I've completely forgotten that we took our car to the bar. I'm so in my head that I'm trusting Colin to bring me somewhere that has a bed. Even if it happens to be in the house of liars. It's three a.m. so there's no way anyone is still awake.

"Colin?" I ask him loudly. "I only took two shots! Two! So why do I feel so drunk?"

Colin laughs besides me. "I'm honestly kind of surprised as well. Did you eat anything the entire night? Every time I saw you, you were running around like a chicken with its head cut off."

"I think I had some bread...ah, I don't remember! I was too busy performing bridesmaid's duties for my backstabbing friend." I laugh bitterly at the thought.

⌇

Colin shushes me as we enter the quiet and dimly lit house. The house still smells like lavender. I cover my mouth, trying my hardest not to giggle as he practically carries me up the stairs.

"Trust me, Collie. I can call you that, right?" I laugh, leaning against the door to our room. Colin gives me a look as he takes off his already loosened tie.

I look down at my blue, silky dress that was once clean. The bottom is filthy from cigarette ash. My face is puffy from crying, and somehow, I'm wearing Colin's suit jacket.

"We look like who did it and ran, but the wedding edition."

Colin shakes his head with a chuckle and motions for me to come over to sit down next to him. I plop on the bed, and my eyes do a quick scan of his torso as he takes off his white buttoned shirt.

"I overheard a couple of people asking if we came from prom."

I hit my forehead and let out a loud laugh. "Prom! I wish we went to prom." I continue to laugh. "I bet you were prom king."

Colin looks at me funny and shakes his head. I let out a loud laugh but quickly cover my mouth.

"Why do you look so surprised that I would think that?"

"Because I am not prom king material."

"Oh please, yes you are. You are tall, extremely good-looking. Check and check. Dirty blonde hair and killer blue eyes." I shrug, pointing my finger and touching his hard stomach. Colin's smile turns quickly intense as he stares into my eyes. "I'm sorry. I-I just thought—"

But before I can come up with some lame apology, both of Colin's hands grasp my makeup-stained cheeks. Colin hunches over, so we're eye-level. My breath is still as I wait for what's coming next. My body is on fire. Those familiar tingles engulf me; I didn't realize how much I wanted and craved them. To feel them again. His lips are soft against mine as I follow his lead.

"Colin..."

"Don't think," he breathes into my mouth, untying my dress. He grabs the pillow and tucks it under my head. I can't help but shut my eyes as I roll to my side, nuzzling my face into the soft pillow. I feel

Colin's hand caress my cheek as he leans in and gives my temple a gentle kiss.

"Goodnight, beautiful."

~

I peel my eyes open, trying to figure out where I am. I'm quickly reminded by the large curtainless window's reflection shining on my face. I slowly ease off the bed, feeling thirsty and restless. I gulp down a tall glass of water and stare at my tired eyes through the mirror's reflection in the bathroom. I touch my saddened face and glance down at my dirty dress. I pull the blue straps off my shoulders and watch as the dress falls to the floor. I step out of it and throw on the t-shirt I luckily left in the bathroom. The floor slightly creaks as I tip-toe back to the bed where Colin is lightly snoring. I stop in my tracks, admiring him as he sleeps on his back. He's shirtless, and the blanket lays just below the band of his boxer briefs. I move closer, standing along his side of the bed, lost in thought. My mind is going in a million directions, and I can't think straight as his chest moves in a rhythmic motion. My body stands still, and my feet are frozen against the hardwood floor. I imagine myself climbing on top of him and feeling his lips against mine. I never would have thought I'd feel this way about Colin. His thoughtfulness and kindness surprised me this weekend, and—

As if Colin read my mind, I feel his hand gently grasp my wrist, pulling me closer. He stares into my eyes and gives me a small smile, sending heat waves through my body as he moves a strand of hair away from my face. I wonder how long he was staring at me while I was imagining myself with him. Suddenly, I feel his hands around my waist, and I silently moan as he places me on top of him. I straddle his torso and trace my fingers along the outline of his jaw, leading up to his lips. He lifts his face closer to mine and places his hand against my cheek, his fingers threading through my hair. I feel his lips kiss my chin and the sides of my jaw.

I close my eyes from his touch, and my head falls back. His tongue swirls against my extended neck, and the anticipation of feeling his tongue everywhere sends electricity through my whole body. My mind shuts off for the first time, and I never want this moment with Colin to end. Colin moves his hands to my hips and gently shifts me onto my back. I wait for Colin's lead as my chest moves up and down; my heart is beating a mile a minute. Colin hovers over me, but doesn't do a single thing. He licks his lips as he listens to my every moan as if it's music to his ears and wants that sound to last forever.

Colin leans in and kisses me deeply. I can't help but moan as I feel his tongue exploring my mouth. He pulls on the bottom of my white t-shirt, and my hands move to the sides of my cheeks, silently telling him to take my shirt off. Colin gives me a grin, but I close my eyes from the feel of his hands against my bare skin.

"You're so beautiful," Colin breathes, taking in my naked body. I bite the tip of my finger as I smile at his kind words. Colin kisses my lips but moves to my neck, then to my breasts, giving them soft nibbles. I let out a moan and his body tenses from arousal.

The moment we become one transcends me to a place I've never been before.

～

Later, I lay still under the silk blanket and graze my fingers along the outline of Colin's tattooed bicep as he snores lightly. I close my eyes as I replay the events that just occurred. Every touch, caress, and feeling all over my naked body.

I study Colin's relaxed face, and I admire how his lips are slightly parted as he sleeps. I lean in and give his temple a soft kiss.

"*Hmm*," he breathes, opening his eyes slightly.

"I didn't mean to wake you," I whisper.

"No, I like it. Keep doing it," he says, his voice a tad raspy.

I smile to myself as I move my index fingers all the way down to his forearm, where a forest of trees is tattooed.

"I never really noticed all of your tattoos," I say, turning to my side. "Do they have any personal meaning to you?"

"No." He laughs, turning himself over onto his back. "Each song I've ever written is based on each tattoo I have," he says.

I gradually sit up, still covering my naked body.

"Hey, don't leave." I feel Colin's hand wrap around my wrist. I lean my chin against my shoulder as I stare into Colin's blue eyes. His chest moves up and down as he lays shirtless with his head resting against the headboard.

Colin's mouth opens, and I wait for him to speak as I lay back down, leaning my head against his tattooed chest. He runs his fingers through my hair, and I close my eyes from his touch.

"Do you remember when you and I went shopping for Reese's birthday present?"

I nod, waiting for him to continue.

"I purposely took my time."

I turn my head so my eyes meet his. "Why? Just to get under my skin?"

"Yes." He pauses, a small smile starting to form on his face. "Also, I just wanted to spend more time with you."

"Why didn't you ever tell me that?"

Colin shrugs. "I guess I've always felt like you kept me at arm's length."

Colin's thumb grazes my bottom lip and a small smile forms on my face. I give his thumb a gentle bite as I move my face up over his chest to nuzzle his neck.

CHAPTER 50

The sun shines brightly through the room as I stretch my body. I turn around to find that I'm alone. I brush my fingers along the wrinkled sheets and smile, thinking about the few hours I've just spent with Colin. I gradually sit up, casually glancing at the clock that reads ten-thirty. Suzy's face pops into my head, and I climb out of bed in seconds. A sharp pang hits my head, but I have no time to acknowledge it—I need to leave this house as soon as possible, even though I have no idea where Colin is. He wouldn't leave me, right? I shake these thoughts out of my throbbing head and throw every piece of clothing I can find in mine and Colin's bags. Heck, these bags are going back to the same apartment anyway. I quickly change into a pair of jeans and a tank top, and I haul our bags down the long winding stairs. Suzy, wearing a long sundress, is standing at the bottom of the stairs. Worry is plastered on her tired face as she perches her hands on the railing. I purposely look away from her distressed eyes.

"Excuse me," I say under my breath.

"Jade, please," Suzy says, sounding frightened. The front door seems so close but yet so far as I'm carrying my heavy bags.

"Jade?"

"What, Suzy?" I say loudly.

She rubs the back of her neck and exhales. "I know you want to leave, but can you at least let me explain myself?"

"Why should I? All you're going to do is lie again."

She shakes her head. "It's not like that—"

"But it is, Suzy. There isn't anything you can say that will justify what you did. The sneaking around my back. The cheating."

Suzy nods, her eyes glued to her flip-flops. "I messed up, I know. If I could take back everything I did to you, I would." She finally looks into my eyes. "I-I don't want this to end our friendship. You-you mean more to me than anyone. I need you in my life, Jade."

One of the bags slides off my shoulder, and I sigh seeing Suzy look so broken.

"What hurts me the most is the year before Noah and I broke up, I came to you and shared my sadness with you. We sat for hours trying to figure out what was going on with our relationship."

Suzy nods but doesn't say anything. She just sulks, waiting for me to continue.

"And to think, that whole time, you both were going behind my back. You watched me cry, and you still continued the affair. That's what hurts me the most—the lying. You didn't care about my feelings. You only cared about yourself."

She nods. "I know. I'm selfish."

The jingle of keys distracts us from our intense conversation, and I turn my head to see Colin standing by the door. I can't help but feel relieved when I see him and the car keys in his hand.

"I took a walk over to the bar and got the car," he says to me. I nod as I watch him grab our bags from the floor. "I'll be in the car."

"Jade, I know we can never go back and undo this, but I hope this doesn't end us forever."

"Suzy, I love you more than anything, I do, but you hurt me. I need time," I say, walking over to the front door. I hold onto the doorknob and turn my head so that I am facing her. "You and Noah deserve each other." And with that, I leave without saying goodbye.

~

"You said that to her?" Colin smiles as he merges onto the highway.

I sigh. "Yeah, I figured it was better than just saying bye."

"So, is this the end for you two?"

I look at Colin's profile and shrug. "I don't know, honestly. I don't even want to think about it, frankly."

Colin nods and turns the music up. I feel relieved as the wind blows my hair all around. I close my eyes underneath my sunglasses, making wave motions with my hand outside the window as the sun shines and the music is blaring.

An hour into the drive, Colin reaches over to the radio and lowers it. I glance over at him.

"Anything wrong?" I ask him.

"Oh nothing," he says, then clears his throat. "It's just my sister keeps texting me. I sort of agreed that we'd have lunch with her today."

I reposition myself. "Today? Your sister in New Jersey?"

"Yeah, I figured it'd be okay since her place is technically on our way back home. But I get it if you're not feeling up for it."

I look forward, watching the other cars drive past us, and nod. "I guess it's fine."

"Okay, great because we're ten minutes away."

~

"Remember, roomie, you're still my girlfriend." Colin grins as we get out of the car.

"*Ah*, yes." I chuckle, but it quickly fades as soon as he takes my hand in his. Colin's hand is rough yet soft at the same time, and I never want him to let go. We walk down the long concrete driveway and up the two-stepped porch. As Colin knocks on the tall, white door, I glance at the perfectly cut green grass and the cookie-cutter, suburban-style homes beside Colin's sister's identical two-story house.

The front door swings open in seconds, and we're immediately welcomed by Addison. I automatically feel underdressed as I take in the woman in front of me. She's the definition of stunning—long, straight blonde hair, rose-red lips, hourglass frame, and legs as long as skyscrapers. I feel like a shrimp compared to her. Addison rests her hand against her hip, giving her brother a grin from ear to ear. Colin lets go of my hand to hug his sister, and a ping of sadness hits me. I like the way his hand feels against mine. Addison releases from her hug with Colin and moves straight to me. The smell of lemons fills the air as I hug Addison.

"So, who's hungry?"

We follow Addison down a hallway full of pictures of her and the family, including a photo of Colin. He's laughing next to Addison as they sit on a bench. It looks like a beautiful day with trees and flowers blooming right beside them. The sound of laughter is heard as we enter the kitchen. A man with silky brown hair sits at the kitchen table. His legs are crossed under the table, and he's holding a glass of wine as he plays with a pen in his other hand. He's wearing thick glasses as he studies his computer screen.

"Harry, put that away." Addison laughs nervously as she hands us a couple of empty wine glasses.

Harry pulls himself away from pure concentration, taking off his glasses. "Pardon me." He smiles. "Just catching up on some work on this fine Sunday."

"Well, work can wait, hun. Colin and his lovely girlfriend Jade are here."

Harry stands up and smooths his wrinkled slacks. Addison and Harry seem well-dressed just for a day at home.

Harry and Colin shake hands, and I shake his hand as well. Addison pours Colin and me a glass of red wine and begins talking my ear off. I nod and smile, and I notice ten minutes into Addison's monologue that Colin has disappeared.

"I have to show you our garden," Addison beams, checking her watch. "Lunch should be ready any minute."

"It smells amazing." I smile.

"Garlic. It's always garlic," she says.

I nod, taking a sip of my wine.

The sound of laughter and tiny voices boom through the hallway. I turn my head and watch Colin carrying two little kids on his shoulders. They're kicking and laughing as he brings them into the kitchen.

"Addi, you got some kids on the loose," he says, tickling them.

Addison laughs, turning to me. "He's so great with them." She touches my arm, giving me a grin. I bite the inside of my cheek and laugh as I watch Colin play with his niece and nephew in the kitchen.

"Emma, do you remember Jade?"

Emma runs over to her mother's leg and nods shyly, putting her thumb in her mouth.

I kneel, giving her a smile. "Hi, Emma, you look beautiful today. Just like your mommy."

Emma smiles, handing me the pink teddy bear she's holding in one hand.

"Thank you." I laugh, looking up at Colin. He crosses his arms, watching us with a pleased smile.

"Jade, my other little one is Ethan. Ethan, this is Jade. Can you say hi?"

"Hi, Jade," Ethan smiles. "Want to see our playroom?" He's not quite as shy as his sister.

"After lunch. Go wash your hands," Addison orders. I hand Emma her teddy bear and watch Ethan grab Emma's hand, leading her to the bathroom upstairs.

"They are adorable." I smile at Addison and Harry.

"Very much appreciated. Thank goodness they have their mother's good looks," Harry jokes, giving Addison a kiss on the cheek.

I glance at Colin, who is leaning against the kitchen counter. He's watching his sister with joy, and tiny butterflies enter my stomach.

We help Addison bring all the delicious plates of food to the long dining room table. Addison went all out. Tons of food fill the table, it's as if she cooked for an army. There's pasta with a creamy pesto sauce, breaded chicken, and homemade bread. Everything looks terrific, and the smell of the food reminds my stomach how hungry it is. Addison is the last to sit down. She places a peanut butter and jelly sandwich in front of Emma.

"Please, dig in," she says, leaning her chin against the front of her palm.

Everyone fills their plates high as we devour the delicious food in minutes.

"Good, isn't it?" Harry asks. "We're pretty spoiled here."

"Oh, Harry, stop." Addison chuckles, taking a sip of her wine.

"I could definitely get used to it so I completely understand." I smile at Harry.

"You see, dear. You're a great cook."

"Besides being a doctor in psychology, cooking has always been my favorite thing to do."

"It's good, Addi," Colin says, taking a big bite of chicken.

After lunch, dessert is served; it's blueberry and lemon pie. I feel like I should be rolled out of this room with how much food I've consumed.

"Colin, what do you say? I have a couple of cigars…."

"Yeah, man, sounds good." Colin nods.

"Outside only!" Addison orders, finishing the last of her coffee.

Before I can feel sad about Colin leaving me, Addison enthusiastically says, "I can show you my garden if you want."

I nod. The sun is already setting, and I wonder how long we've been here. Didn't seem so long so I guess lunch was dinner as well.

"Took me a long time to get exactly what I wanted. My gardener and I became very close." She laughs to herself, opening a gate. I follow her down a pebble-filled path, leading us to a little pond and a bench surrounded by vines. We sit down simultaneously, and she points and explains all the herbs and vegetables she's growing.

"There's nothing like going into your home-grown garden, picking the basil you're growing, and using it in your food."

"It's gorgeous." I smile, watching the fountain spit water out.

"You have no idea, Jade, how thankful I am for you."

I turn, and we make eye contact. I don't say anything because I'm not sure what to say.

"I see the way my brother looks at you. He really loves you."

My mouth falls opens, but I stop myself from saying anything.

Frankly, I'm not one hundred percent sure what to say in response either.

"He hardly visits, especially with a girl." She laughs. "We've really missed him. The kids miss him. Even Harry. So, thank you."

I smile, "You don't have to thank me—"

"I do, though."

I give her a small smile.

"Colin's happy. I haven't seen that twinkle in his eye in a long time. I'm not sure if Colin has opened up to you about our family feuds."

"He has," I say quietly. Addison looks shocked. Stunned. I immediately regret lying. I'm not sure why I lied in the first place. Tears fall down her eyes, and she smiles, reaching in and giving me a tight hug. "He really does love you. I haven't seen him love someone this much since Ariel."

~

The sun has completely set, and Colin and I decide to get going. We give our last hugs, and I watch Colin give sweet bear hugs to his niece and nephew. I give Addison one last hug, and a feeling of happiness runs through me as we walk to the car.

"What?" Colin asks as we get in.

"I like your family."

Colin smiles to himself but doesn't say anything back. The music is playing softly, and we sit in silence as we head home.

"Colin?" I turn to look at the side of his face as I hug my legs in the passenger seat.

"Jade?" He gives me his dimple.

I look away and stare down at my bent knees. "Who's Ariel?"

Silence fills the car, and I immediately regret bringing her up.

"What did my sister say to you?"

"N-Nothing. She just casually brought her up when she showed me her garden."

"You don't just casually bring up Ariel." And with that, the conversation about Ariel ends.

"But she asked me if you've told me about what happened between you and your family."

He pulls his eyes away from the road to look at me. "And what did you say?"

"I-I said you have." I pause. "I'm not really sure why I said that."

Colin sighs. "That's why she brought up Ariel."

"What does that mean?" I ask.

Colin exhales and I look at him.

"You don't have to tell me, I get it."

"Shit went down between my family and me before I left California," he explains. "I never talk about it because it's the past, and it infuriates me to no end."

"You don't—"

"It's fine. Considering what happened to you this weekend, you might as well hear my sob story." He laughs to himself.

Silence fills the car yet again. All I can hear is the sound of cars passing as Colin clears his throat. "My whole family consists of doctors. Which you already know."

I nod.

"A few months before I practically fled California, my grandfather passed away. He was eighty-four. Rigid, stern, rich, and a retired neurologist," he says. "My grandfather was angry that I was slacking off. I didn't go to my classes, was partying all the time, and for damn sure, I knew I was never becoming a doctor like my father, my brother, and my sister. In my grandfather's eyes, I was a disgrace. He thought I was some drug addict who played in a stupid band." He glances at me. "His words, not mine. He couldn't have been more wrong about me."

"So, your grandfather was angry because you didn't choose the same path as your siblings?"

"Yeah, pretty much." He shrugs. "So right before he died, he drew up a will, and in that will, he gave all the money to my brother, and my brother split it with my sister and not me. My brother made it clear that he based his decision to not share it with me because I was a loser and wasn't in medical school like my sister was."

"Your brother didn't leave you anything?"

"No. The fucker didn't leave me a penny. When I sat my brother and sister down, Addi agreed to split her portion with me, which made me feel terrible because Addi has a family to raise. My brother Kirk, the asshole, just sat there so smug, believing he made the right decision."

"But what about your parents? Why do you hate them so much?"

"I don't hate them, Jade. I resent them. I resent them because when I went to them for help, they were so lax about all of it. They got mad at Kirk, but it only lasted a minute. They knew I wasn't at all what my grandfather painted me to be, and when I needed them the most, they weren't there for me. They slapped Kirk's hand for being bad but then had dinner with him the next day."

I nod, feeling so sad as I listen to Colin's pain.

"Honestly, it's the past. I gave up my relationship with Kirk completely, and Addi, well, I see her. However, it's hard knowing that she still has a relationship with Kirk and my parents. That's all I see."

"So how does Ariel come into all of this?"

"She doesn't. She's just the girl I loved. Well, the first girl I've ever really loved. I left her and my whole life in Pasadena."

"She's the one who I remind you of?"

Colin looks at me but then quickly looks away. His eyes answered my question.

I would never have guessed that a weekend like this could open my eyes to all the sides of Colin I didn't know existed.

～

We pull into Wes' parking spot and share a cab back to our apartment. Colin seems different...happy, like a weight has been lifted off his shoulders. Colin grabs our bags, and we walk up the stairs leading to the apartment, relieved to be back home. Colin and I kid around with each other. He makes me laugh like a little schoolgirl. We turn the corner, and my heart skips a beat and then falls out when I see him. His hair is a lot shorter than the last time I saw him. His slumped body is sitting outside the front door with arms hanging on both bent knees. He looks up from his lap, looking hopeful yet afraid when we make eye contact.

"Eric," I say without thinking. The walls seem to close in on me as I watch him stand to his feet. He's wearing a long-sleeved striped shirt and vintage slacks. I find myself just standing so still as if I'm a statue.

"Hey, man." Eric half-smiles, holding his hand out for Colin to shake. This sudden surprise makes me forget Colin is even behind me. Colin looks at me then back to Eric. He seems angry, and I'm not sure why. They shake hands, and Colin enters the apartment, slamming the door behind him.

"Surprise," Eric jokes.

I look into his brown eyes. "What are you doing here?"

"I see you're returning from the wedding. How was it?"

I shake my head. "Eric, what are you doing here?"

Eric sighs, looking down at his dirty converse. "I didn't realize how much I'd miss you when we broke up. I was a total wreck. I was eating lunch with a friend I met at the gallery, and he asked me what I loved most in this world." He pauses. "And I said you. I look at tons of paintings every day, and I'd pick you to look at every time, Jade."

"This is too much right now." I rest my hand against my cheek, feeling a sudden brick on my chest. I'm torn. As I listen to the words that are coming out of Eric's lips, I am also picturing Colin's smile when we were lying in bed only a few hours ago.

He looks confused. "I thought you'd be happy to see me. When I realized how much I messed up and how much I missed and loved you, I got on the first flight here. Don't you love me anymore?" he sulks.

"I-I do," I say.

Eric's sulk quickly becomes a smile. He walks slowly over to me, and all I want to do is hide.

"Eric, I really can't do this right now."

"I get it. I'm sorry for just showing up here like this. I'm here until Thursday, so if you want to see me, you have my number," he says, leaning in and giving my cheek a gentle kiss. My eyes close from his familiar touch, and when I finally open them, he's gone. I stand still for a couple more seconds until I can gather my thoughts.

Colin's sitting on the couch, obviously angry.

"Hey," I say to him, walking over and plopping on his chair. He's drinking a beer, eyes glued to a program on the television. "So what? You're not talking?"

He looks away from the television. "There's nothing to say, Jade."

"I sent him home."

"And I care?" he bites.

"Well, I thought you would, you know, with what happened this weekend between us."

"Leave me out of your sappy fantasy, Jade. If you're talking about me fucking you, it happens. People have sex. All we are is friends, that's it."

I sit up, trying my hardest not to cry. "I thought you said friends can't have sex."

He ignores me, and I can't help it, a tear falls down my cheek, and I don't bother to wipe it away. "I knew this weekend was too good to be true. So, what, you're back to your old self? Douchebag? Eric came back for me, and I was considering..." I stop myself.

"You were considering what?"

"Oh, so now you want to hear what I have to say?" I say, walking past him. "I guess I thought you felt the same as me. But I'm just being stupid Jade, right?"

He sets his beer down and stands up.

I walk over to my room and open my door.

"Jade—"

But before I can hear what he has to say, I slam my door behind me.

CHAPTER 51

I watch Reese's face show every emotion as I tell her every detail from the weekend. From Suzy and Noah's lie to exploring feelings with Colin that we didn't know were there and finally, to Eric coming back for me. I take a sip of my latte as Reese goes from being angry to feeling happy and finally to feeling sad. She shakes her head, playing with the mixer in her hot chocolate.

"I have no words. I'm sorry about Suzy. She really is disgusting."

I nod.

"But I'm happy for you and Colin. I always knew you two were made for each other. Now you understand why I set you guys up to begin with."

I groan. "You have no idea how little sleep I got last night. I always thought deep down inside that I'd end up with Eric, and if he had shown up a few days earlier, we wouldn't be having this conversation right now."

Reese nods, waiting for me to continue.

"But I felt something I never knew I could feel with Colin. He makes me feel alive and well…Eric makes me feel safe."

"What do you mean?"

I look down at my latte and shrug. "I've learned so much about Colin this weekend. He's sweet and caring but, Reese, he's a bartender. I'm afraid I'm just another notch on his belt."

"He's also a musician," Reese reminds me.

I nod. "It doesn't change the way I feel about him, but—"

"You have it all wrong, Jade."

"What?"

"Colin's so much more than that. He never told you?"

"Told me what?"

Reese rolls her eyes and sighs. "I don't get why he's so secretive, but Colin owns a furniture business that does really well. Where do you think he goes all the time?"

I tilt my head. "I don't know."

"He started his furniture business when he moved to New York. He's so talented. I have no idea why he never shares his success with anyone. The only reason Wes and I know about it is because Colin has been making furniture since they were kids."

"Why haven't you ever told me?"

"I just figured he'd eventually tell you when he brought home the kitchen table that he made," she says with a smile.

My eyes widen. "I always thought he bought the table at some second-hand store. That's where we get most of our stuff." I laugh. "Even though our table is so above a second-hand store. It's beautiful."

Reese nods. "It really is."

"I'm just so torn," I sigh.

"The heart wants what it wants, and that shouldn't change how you feel about him or Eric. You have to pick. You can't have both."

"I know Eric loves me. He told me so last night. There's a chance

Colin doesn't feel the same way as I do, though."

"I wonder the same thing too." She tilts her head and looks up at the ceiling, almost as if she is experiencing an *ah-ha* moment. Her eyes meet mine. "I just remember when Colin was crashing on Wes' couch, he was looking for his own apartment. When I decided to move in with Wes, we suggested he'd move in with you—"

"I know this, Reese."

"Let me finish." She rolls her eyes with a small smile. "Colin's plan was to only live with you for a couple of months while he searched for his own place."

"Reese, what are you trying to say here?"

"What I'm trying to figure out is why Colin chose to live with you for as long as he has."

"Maybe his lazy ass just got comfortable." I shrug, leaning my back against the chair.

Reese rests her chin on her palm and says, "Well, when Wes came to Colin with possible apartments that were available, Colin wasn't even interested in looking at them."

"Reese, are you trying to tell me that Colin rejected those apartments just so he could still live with me?"

Reese looks into my eyes. She gives me a slight grin as she nods. "Yes, I truly believe that."

I nod, replaying our conversation as I watch Reese grab her jacket and sigh. "I'm sorry to do this, but I have a test in an hour."

"Go." I smile. "I'm fine. I'm going to finish my coffee then leave."

Reese smiles, getting up and giving the side of my head a tiny kiss. The air conditioning is pumping in the cafe, and my hands are frozen as I hold my coffee mug. I place my hands in the pocket of my jacket, and I feel something strange. I grab what feels like a crumpled piece of paper, and confusion is plastered on my face as I unravel it. I read the first sentence, and my mind goes back to when I snuck into Colin's room.

Woke up this morning,

I read the first sentence a couple of times, touching Colin's handwriting with my finger.

Was feeling okay
I let out a contented lover's sigh
And rubbed the sleep from my eye
It's your sweet taste on my lips
The familiar shape of your hips
Assuring me it's always been you

I'd strum my guitar
Watching you from afar
I couldn't see you over the walls I'd built
But it was you that slowly knocked them down
I never knew if I should laugh or cry
It's always easier to play the tough guy
But for you, it wasn't just about playing a part
Not when it came to my heart
Your loving ways, sexy gaze
Setting my body ablaze

It's you, my love, the words to my song
With you by my side, nothing can go wrong
Stay with me, stay by my side
Together let's take this crazy ride

I'm just a cocky guy in a band
But not if you're beside me holding my hand
I want you babe, your heart, body, and soul
I need your lips against mine
Together we shine

It's you, my love, the words to my song
With you by my side, nothing can go wrong
Stay with me, stay by my side
Together let's take this crazy ride

A tear crawls down my cheek as I read the poem for the tenth time. I fold the paper and hold it against my chest, knowing exactly what I have to do.

I rush out of the cafe. The sidewalk is full of people going in all directions. My feet can't move fast enough. Of course, construction is being done precisely where I need to walk to get back home. I wait impatiently for a cab and my phone's dead. I finally decided to cross the street. Might as well. As I hold Colin's poem in my hand, I'm replaying all the words he wrote on that paper. The words he doesn't know how to say out loud. I rush past people until my feet finally stop going a mile a minute.

Flower guy.

He's waiting in line for his famous bouquet. As the crowd of impatient New Yorkers rushes past me, I'm stuck standing in the middle of the sidewalk watching him pay for the white flowers. My feet move towards him. At this point, I'm not even thinking. My fingers lightly tap his shoulder as he grabs the flowers from the lady behind the cart. He turns immediately, and I'm suddenly at a loss for words.

"Can I help you?" the flower guy asks me.

"*Uh*, yeah, well no. I'm sorry to bother you, but for years I've been sitting at that cafe across the street, and my friends and I watch you."

"You watch me?"

I would think he'd be weirded out, yet he seems amused by my words.

"I guess you can say we are hopeless romantics. We see you buying those flowers every day, and we always come up with different scenarios that involve epic love stories." I half-smile. "I know, so cheesy."

"I feel so honored that you and your friends actually noticed me." Has this man never looked in the mirror?

"I have to ask you, who is the lucky woman receiving these flowers?"

The flower guy glances at the flowers he's holding and then looks back at me. "I wish I was in one of those cheesy scenarios," he sighs. "These are actually for my daughter who passed away a few years ago. I bring her white daffodils, which were her favorite. I replace the flowers every day by her grave. My ex-wife and my daughter were in a car accident. My wife survived, but my nine-year-old baby didn't."

I touch my forehead and shake my head. "I'm so sorry."

"Please no, you have no idea how much you made my day. I buy daffodils every day from the same woman for years, and not once has she ever asked me why. So, thank you...."

"Jade, my name is Jade," I cry with happiness.

"Jasper. It's nice to meet you, Jade."

"Yes, it really is."

Jasper gives me a kind smile and continues down the sidewalk until he disappears in the crowd.

∽

It feels like years until I finally get back to my apartment. I run up the stairs as fast as I can and swing open the front door. Without even closing the door behind me, I scurry around the whole apartment, calling for Colin. The apartment is empty, but I'm full of worry and excitement. I quickly plug my phone in, and as soon as it turns on, I immediately call Colin. Of course, there's no answer. I call him again but still no answer. I even call Wes, but he doesn't answer either. What is up with people not answering their phones? I catch my breath as I click on the next contact to call, even though everything in me doesn't want to.

"Jade! What up! Didn't expect you to ever reach out, but I'm glad you did—"

"Randy! Please stop talking. Do you know where Colin is?"

"I'm going to pretend you didn't just say Randy, but no, why?"

I groan. "I need to get in touch with him."

"Well, I'm on my way to band practice, but I'm not sure if he's going to show. He seemed pretty mad this morning."

"Where's the practice?"

~

I get out of the cab the second the driver pulls over to the side of the street. I follow the instructions Randy gave me, even though they seem a little shady, and I open the door to some old building. A sense of relief flushes through me when I hear music playing upstairs. A man and a pregnant woman walk down the stairs as I walk up. I knock a couple of times on the old paint-chipped door. Randy opens the door seconds later with a dirty grin on his face.

"Well, hello."

"Is Colin inside?"

"What a surprise," he says smugly.

I roll my eyes. "Randy, you knew I was coming. Is Colin inside?" I raise my voice.

He nods, and I rush past him. I follow the guitar sounds coming from the other room, and my eyes meet Colin's almost immediately. His fingers strum the chords on his guitar, but his face is motionless.

"Colin—"

"I'm practicing, Jade. Not now."

"Can you please take a break? I need to talk to you."

"No."

I sigh. "Colin, please."

"Shouldn't you be off with Eric by now?"

"That wouldn't be fair to him now, would it? Running away with him while I'm in love with someone else."

Colin's eyes meet mine. "What are you saying?"

"Well, if you stopped playing for a second, I can explain myself."

"Aren't you still mad about what I said last night?"

I shake my head. "No, because I know what you said to me wasn't true."

Colin stops playing, and the apartment, full of his other bandmates, becomes quiet.

"Can we go somewhere private and talk?" I ask, nervously playing with my fingers.

Colin puts his guitar down and nods. I follow him out of the room and out of Randy's apartment. We stand in silence in the dirty hallway.

"So, talk," he says, a hint of anger in his voice.

"I never thought in a million years we'd ever be in this position. You were always this narcissistic ass that purposely got under my skin. Still, this past weekend that we spent together..." I pause, looking into his saddened eyes. "I saw the real Colin. The Colin who is sweet and generous and who can love and be loved."

"So, what? You love me?"

I study his arms that are crossed on his perfect body, the way his Yankees cap is covering his messy hair, and his beautiful, structured face looking down at me.

"Yes. I love you, Colin Chase."

He takes a step back. Did the impact of my words make him lose his footing?

"What if I don't love you back?"

"But you do. I know you do. Stop running away from how you truly feel."

"I have to get back," he says quietly.

I tilt my head, scared that I was wrong all along. "Just say it, if you say you don't…." I pause. "I'll leave you alone and never bring it up again."

Colin looks past me before opening the door and leaving me alone in the hallway, heartbroken and pathetic.

$\sim$

As I make my way back home, I feel sad. I feel sad because I put myself out there, took a chance, and it completely backfired on me. I throw my bag and keys on my floor and make myself a cup of tea to ease my thoughts and embarrassment. I want to crawl into a hole and never come out.

"Jade!" I hear as the front door opens. Reese and Wes are strolling inside, and they look concerned when they see me drinking tea. My eyes are still red from crying.

"What happened?" Reese asks, putting her arm around me.

"I told him how I felt, and he doesn't feel the same."

"That's how Colin is. He's afraid to show any emotion."

"Yeah, well, he had the chance, so that's it. I called Eric on my way here, and I told him I need to be alone. He's so understanding," I sigh. "The funny thing is, I know Eric is the right guy for me, but all I want is Colin. Stupid." I let out a fake laugh.

Reese rests her head on my shoulder and nods. "I'm so sorry, Jade."

"Me too," I sigh.

After Reese and Wes leave, I decide to watch some television before going to bed. I feel so numb as I watch some stupid lifetime movie. A gentle knock disrupts this terrible movie, and I groan, walking over to the door.

"Hey, I'm sorry to bother you."

"You like to just show up unexpectedly." I half-smile.

Eric runs his hand through his hair and nods. "I can't help it."

"So why—"

"Before you ask me why I'm here even though you broke up with me...again a couple of hours ago, can you at least come with me? I want to show you something. As friends."

"Eric, it's late."

"When did that ever stop you?" He grins.

～

Eric and I share a cab to this unknown destination. He takes my hand into his and leads me to an abandoned building. I share my location with Reese, just in case. Even though I know Eric would never hurt me.

Eric gives me a grin as he pulls out a pair of keys. He jingles them and unlocks the door in seconds.

"Where are we?" I ask as I watch him turn all the lights on in this empty room.

"My gallery," he says, beaming.

"Wait, what?"

"My whole life has been about painting, and I feel like I haven't lived my dream. I always run other people's galleries and even sold some paintings in other galleries, but this one is mine. Only my work."

"Wow, Eric. That's incredible." I smile, giving him a tight hug. "I'm so proud of you, but what about California?"

"I was never a palm tree type of guy anyway." He shrugs.

I nod. "Why did you bring me here?"

"Despite us not being a couple—and I'll give you as much time as you need—I have always enjoyed your company. Dating you or not dating you, I love you, Jade."

See? It's not that hard to say...

"Thank you, Eric. For showing me this. I can't wait—" Before I can finish my sentence, a loud bang rattles the front window of this empty gallery. I turn and spot a breathless Colin hitting the window.

"Colin?" I say, walking past Eric to open the locked door.

"Because I didn't tell you right then and there, you ran back to Eric?" he says, out of breath.

"It's not like that."

"It sure looks like it."

"What are you doing here?"

"And by the way! I was looking everywhere for you! You have no idea."

"Colin," I say, walking out of the gallery. I shut the door behind me, knowing very well that I am also shutting the door on my relationship with Eric.

Colin runs his hand through his hair and exhales. "I shouldn't have left you today."

"What?"

He rolls his eyes. "You heard me."

"You know what, Colin? I don't have time for all this back and forth." But before I can turn away, he grabs my wrist, pulling me back.

"A wise person once said to stop running away from how I truly feel. I should've listened to her when I had the chance. I should've stopped her from leaving, but I was a coward. And I never want to see you leave me like that again."

Colin's hand moves from my wrist to my hip as we stand in silence, staring into each other's eyes.

"I should have told you this a long time ago, but I guess that weekend reminded me of those feelings I've always pushed aside. I love you, Jade. I really love you."

I bite my bottom lip gently, and I can't help but smile. I push his messy hair aside, and I move my fingers all the way down to his hairy chin.

"I love you too, roomie." I grin.

Colin lets out a laugh before pulling me into a kiss.

This whole time, I've been *chasing* something I thought I knew and needed. I wanted so badly what I thought the flower guy had. I craved my own flower type of love, but sometimes, love is found where you least expect it.

The End.

ACKNOWLEDGMENT

I'm sitting down to write the acknowledgment page for my novel… I'll say that again… *my novel*. Wow! It is absolutely surreal. To me, it's quite reminiscent of watching home movies. A trip down memory lane of sorts. Flooding of emotions, good and bad, exhilarating and draining to name a few. Writing *Chasing Daffodils* has contributed to my maturity in so many ways. I've grown first and foremost as a writer. I've learned to be persistent and not give up. I've learned to set goals and to stick to them. I've learned to listen and observe more and finally, I've learned and gained self-confidence. For me, *Chasing Daffodils* consists of all the elements I personally look for in a book. I guess you can say that I've taken the advice to write the book I'd want to read. I *love love love* books set in New York City. I enjoy the banter between good friends, the innuendo of sexual tension, and above all, I love when a character grows and comes to certain realizations by the end of the book.

My main goal with my stories is to hopefully have my readers feel warmly embraced by my characters. To feel connected to them and entertained. I want my readers to flip through the pages of my book and feel a balance of happiness and sadness, humor, and hope. A lighthearted escape from life's struggles.

I'm lucky to have a bunch of friends who have offered their support and feedback when needed. They believe in me and their excitement to read my published novel has been an invaluable confidence booster.

I don't know where I'd be without my family. Writing a book is harder than I could ever have imagined. I must begin by thanking my mom. Thank you for always being the person I can turn to for support, inspiration, direction, and understanding. You've single-handedly pulled me out of very deep moments of doubt. You've believed in me and encouraged me. I'm grateful that we share a similar sense of humor. I can always count on you to appreciate the humorous side of my stories. For this, I am eternally grateful.

As writers, we feel immensely satisfied when we can finally write *The End* on the last page of our story. But only too soon do we realize that it really is only the beginning of the publishing process. For this reason, I would like to thank my dad immensely. His determination to hire proofreaders, a book cover designer, multiple beta readers, book formatting professionals, and copywriting experts is a huge business undertaking. Thankfully he learned the ins and outs of the business side of book publishing and marketing. Continually keeping me to deadlines and focused is very appreciated. Most importantly, his unwavering belief in me is why I am where I am today.

Lastly, I would like to thank my brother Brian for unknowingly being an inspiration for *Colin*. Quietly observing Brian's sense of humor and mannerisms helped build a multi-faceted main character who keeps us guessing and is full of delightful surprises.

To my readers… I thank you from the bottom of my heart!

ABOUT THE AUTHOR

Emily was born in 1998 in South Jersey. When she was 13, Emily and her family relocated to Florida. Her parents were born and raised in Brooklyn, New York and Emily spent a lot of time visiting family there. It was during one of these visits that inspired Emily to write. Her adoration for New York mixed with her personal experiences and love for writing helped shape *Chasing Daffodils*. She has a deep-rooted love for cities and hopes to settle down in one someday.

When Emily isn't writing she divides her time between working towards a college degree and spending time with family and friends. A favorite pastime is taking long walks or drives with her dog Lily while listening to decades-old classic rock music. It is usually during these long walks that much of her character development for her stories take place.

Emily enjoys reading your typical romance novel. Her favorite is romantic comedies. She also enjoys relaxing while watching her favorite television shows *Sex and the City, Girls,* and *The Office.*

Emily is so appreciative of her readers and looks forward to hearing from you. If you have questions about her book, promotional material, book signings, or other general questions, feel free to reach out through social media, email, or website.

www.instagram.com/emilysam_author

www.facebook.com/emilysam.author

inquiry@chasingdaffodilsbook.com

www.chasingdaffodilsbook.com

Made in the USA
Middletown, DE
24 November 2021